Praise for

SANDRA HILL AND HER NOVELS

"Sandra Hill writes contemporary romance with flair, and she has certainly captured the essence of the Cajun culture."
—*EyeOnRomance.com* on *Tall, Dark, and Cajun*

"Some like it hot and hilarious, and Sandra Hill delivers both in this intoxicating addition to her Cajun bad boy series."
—*Publishers Weekly* on *The Cajun Cowboy*

"Hill, who has made readers chuckle, guffaw, and giggle with her hilarious Viking series, will tickle their funny bones yet again as she writes in her trademark sexy style, the perfect accompaniment to a hot Cajun setting. A real crowd pleaser, guar-an-teed."   —*Booklist* on *The Cajun Cowboy*

"I'm surprised Ms. Hill was able to get this book to her publisher without the pages burning up. Rene. Oh, Rene! Lots of deep sighs and there really are no good words for this Cajun hunk...A must read! It's just too fun and steamy to miss."
—*Fresh Fiction* on *The Red-Hot Cajun*

"4 ½ stars! Top Pick! Hill's books always contain an impeccable mix of humor and romance, this one is no exception."
—*RT Book Reviews* on *Snow on the Bayou*

Other Titles by Sandra Hill

TALL, DARK, and CAJUN

SANDRA HILL

GRAND CENTRAL
PUBLISHING

NEW YORK   BOSTON

Copyright © 2003 by Sandra Hill
Excerpt from *The Cajun Cowboy* copyright © 2004 by Sandra Hill

Forever
Hachette Book Group
1290 Avenue of the Americas, New York, NY 10104
forever-romance.com
twitter.com/foreverromance

Originally published by Forever in July 2003
Reissued: May 2007, May 2018

Forever is an imprint of Grand Central Publishing. The Forever name and logo are trademarks of Hachette Book Group, Inc.

The publisher is not responsible for websites (or their content) that are not owned by the publisher.

The Hachette Speakers Bureau provides a wide range of authors for speaking events. To find out more, go to www.hachettespeakersbureau.com or call (866) 376-6591.

Printed in the United States of America

OPM

10 9 8 7 6 5 4 3 2 1

This book is dedicated respectfully—in a most non-religious, ecumenical manner—to St. Jude, the patron saint of hopeless causes. St. Jude has played a role in a number of my books, including *Tall, Dark, and Cajun*, as has God, or whatever celestial being(s) there might be, all of whom surely share a wonderful sense of humor.

For instance, can you imagine God's laughter when he placed Adam and Eve in the Garden of Eden with the snake? Or Noah's Bill Cosby–like reaction when God asked him to build an ark? Or Moses saying the archaic version of "Whoo-ee!" when he saw the Red Sea parting?

Don't you think God smiles on occasion at the predicaments we humans get into? Can you imagine how many times good ol' Jude must have rolled his eyes at the myriad hopeless prayers he was asked to answer?

Surely, laughter is a gift of the gods, no matter what your belief. And that's what I celebrate in this book—the sheer joy of humor.

TALL,
DARK,
and
CAJUN

Chapter 1

When the thunder bolt hits, duck, baby, duck

"Happy birthday to you . . ."

Remy LeDeux's head shot up from the mug of "burnt roast," the thick Cajun coffee he'd been nursing at his galley table. Who came out to Bayou Black to visit him on his houseboat?

"Happy birthday to you . . ."

Oh, no! Oh, no, no, no! Please, God, not today!

Steps were approaching his door.

It better not be Luc and René. I am not in the mood for their games. Unbidden, a memory flashed through his mind of a birthday twelve years ago when his brothers Lucien and René had shown up at the VA burn hospital following one of his numerous operations. They had brought with them Ronald McDonald, but what a Ronald McDonald! Underneath the clown outfit had been a half-naked, six-foot-tall, Bourbon Street female impersonator with a body that could rival Marilyn Monroe's, appropriately singing, "Happy, Happy Birthday, Baby!" There had been a lot of military vet patients cheered up that day when she . . . he . . . whatever . . . had passed out Happy Meal cartons as favors, all containing talking condoms, red vibrator lips and edible thongs.

"Happy birthday, dear Remy . . ."

Remy peered through the dust-moted dimness toward his open door. It was definitely not Ronald McDonald, or a sexy stripper, not even his teasing brothers. Much worse. It was his seventy-nine-year-old great-aunt Lulu, who was all of five feet tall, and she was carrying a cake the size of a bayou barge with a pigload of candles on top.

"Happy birthday to you," she concluded and used her non-existent butt to ease the wooden screen door open and sidle inside. Today his aunt wore a Madonna T-shirt with cone cups painted in the vicinity of her non-existent breasts, and a flame red spandex miniskirt. Who knew they made them in midget sizes? On her feet were what could only be described as white hooker boots. Her hair today was short and curly and pink—no doubt due to the efforts of his half-sister Charmaine who ran a hoity-toity beauty spa over in Houma, Looks to Kill, as well as a regular hair salon, Kuts & Kurls, in Lafayette. Uncertain whether the pink color was in honor of his birthday or an accident, he decided not to ask.

Despite her age and always outrageous appearance, his aunt's services as a noted *traiteur* or healer were still needed up and down the swamp lands. Unfortunately, of late she believed that he was the one most in need of her care.

If he could have, he would have fled, but where could a six-foot-two ex–Air Force officer hide in a houseboat? Besides, he couldn't ever be rude to his aunt, who was dear to him.

"Tante Lulu! Welcome, *chère*, welcome."

He stood and emptied his mug into the sink, then took the cake from her, placing it on the table. On its white iced top, mixed in with the thirty-three candles, was the message, "Happy Birthday, Remy," in bright blue letters. Typical sentiment. But in the corners stood four tiny plastic statues of St. Jude, the patron saint of hopeless cases. St. Jude was a favorite of Tante Lulu. He almost asked her what his birthday and hopeless cases had in common, but he caught himself just in time.

She kissed him on the cheek then, which involved her standing on tiptoes and his leaning down. And wasn't it just like his aunt to kiss his bad cheek, the one so disfigured by that 'copter crash in Desert Storm twelve years ago? Most people would at least flinch. She didn't even blink.

"Didja think I'd let you stay here alone like a hermit on your special day? Bad bizness, that—being alone so much. Lost your *joie de vivre*, you have. Never fear, I have a feelin' this is gonna be your year for love. Whass that smell? *Poo-ey!* Stinks like burnt okra."

He plopped back down to the bench seat and watched his aunt sniff the coffee in his pot, wrinkle her nose, then dump the contents down his sink. Within seconds, a fresh pot perked on the stove.

"Tante Lulu, this is not my year for love. Don't you be starting on me. I am not interested in love."

"Hanky-panky, thass all you menfolks are interested in. I may be seventy, but I ain't blind."

"More like eighty, sweet pea," he reminded her. "And don't for one minute think I'm gonna discuss *hanky-panky* with you."

"Not to worry, though, sweetie," his aunt rambled on. "I got time to concentrate on you now. I'm gonna find you a wife. Guar-an-teed! Love doan ask you if you're ready; it jist comes like a thunder bolt."

Over my dead body, he vowed silently. "That's nice." He decided to change the subject. "How did you get here?"

"Tee-John drove me in his daddy's pick-up truck." His aunt was bent over now—and, yes, he'd been right about her having no behind anymore. She was trying to shove off to the side the saddle he'd left in the middle of the room— a reminder of his ranching days.

But then his aunt's words hit him belatedly, like a sledgehammer. "Tee-John? *Mon Dieu,* Tante Lulu! He's only fourteen years old. He doesn't have a license." Tee-John was his half-brother, the youngest of many children, legitimate and otherwise, born to Valcour LeDeux, their common father.

His aunt shrugged. "My T-bird's in the shop. This place, she needs some light. Mebbe you oughta install a skylight. It's so dark and dreary. No wonder you're always so grumpy."

A skylight in a houseboat that's as old as I am? "About your car?" he asked grumpily.

Now she was checking out the mail on his desk. "Someone stole the spark plugs. Can you imagine that?"

Yeah, he could imagine that. It was probably one of his brothers, trying to keep their aunt off the highways.

"Where *is* the brat?"

"Outside playin' with that pet alligator of yours, I reckon. You oughta get yerself a wife. A man your age should be pettin' his woman, not some slimy bayou animal. If I dint know you better, I'd think you were into those pee-verse-uns I read about in one of Charmaine's *Cosmo* magazines. You got any heavy cream for *café au lait?*"

He decided to ignore the wife remark, and the perversion remark, and, no, he didn't keep heavy cream in the house. "Useless? I do not pet Useless." He'd named the old alligator who lived in his bayou neighborhood Useless because he was, well, useless. "I toss him scraps occasionally. Tee-John better not be feedin' him Moon Pies and RC Cola again. Last time he did that, Useless was so jazzed up he practically swam a marathon up and down the bayou. A sugar high, no doubt."

Tante Lulu was nosing around in his cupboards now. Most likely, searching for evidence of perversions.

"Dad's gonna be furious at Tee-John for driving without a license—and taking his vehicle."

"It doan take much to make that Valcour red in the face . . . which he use'ly is from booze anyways," Tante Lulu said icily. His great-aunt hated their father with a passion, with good reason. "He's already spittin' mad at Tee-John. The boy is grounded for two weeks."

Remy was about to point out that driving her to his remote bayou home didn't count as grounded, but figured logic was not a part of any conversation with his aunt. "Why is he grounded?"

"Went to a underwear option party up in Natchitoches. That boy, he is some kind of wild." She shook her pink spirals from side to side and clucked her tongue to show her disgust.

"Huh?" *A lingerie party? A teenage boy at a lingerie party? That doesn't sound right.* Then, understanding dawned. "Oh. Do you mean underwear *optional*?"

"Thass what I said, dint I? There was a hundred boys and girls running around with bare butts wavin' in the wind when the police got there. Lordy, Lordy!"

He started to grin.

But not for long.

She was standing before his open freezer, empty except for two ice-cube trays. The way she was gawking you would have thought he had a dead body in there—a very small dead body, considering the minuscule size of the compartment. "You ain't got nothin' in your freeze box," she announced, as if he didn't already know that. "Where's the ice cream? We sure-God gotta have ice cream with a birthday cake."

"Tante Lulu, I don't need ice cream." Really, the old lady only meant good. At least, that's what he told himself.

"The youngens do."

His neck prickled with apprehension. "What youngens?"

"Luc and Sylvie's chillen, thass who. You dint think we'd have a party for you without the rest of the fam'ly, didja?"

Of course not. What was I thinking? He would have put his head on the table if the cake didn't take up all the space.

"René couldn't come 'cause he's in Washington on that fish lobby bizness, but he said to wish you 'Happy, Happy Birthday' and to expect a Happy Meal in the mail. Do you know what he's talkin' 'bout?"

"Don't have a clue," he lied.

In walked Tee-John. What a misnomer! Tee-John was definitely no Little-John. At almost fifteen, he was not done growing, not by a Louisiana long shot, but already he was close to six feet tall. And full of himself, as only a born-to-be-bad, good-looking, bayou rascal could be. He was soaked from the neckline of his black "Ragin' Cajun" T-shirt to the bottoms of his baggy cargo shorts. He grinned from ear to ear.

"Hey, Remy."

"Hey, Tee-John."

"Happy birthday, bro."

"Thanks, *bro*."

"Can I go check out your 'copter up there on the hill?"

Nice try, kiddo. "NO!" The boy would probably decide
to take the half-million-dollar piece of equipment for a
spin. Never mind that it was the backbone of Remy's em-
ployment or that he was in hock to the bank up to his eyeballs. Never mind that Tee-John didn't know a propeller
from a weed whacker.

Tee-John waggled his eyebrows at him, as if to say he
had just been razzing and Remy had risen to the bait.

"You jump in that pick-up, boy, and go buy us some ice
cream at Boudreaux's General Store," Tante Lulu ordered
Tee-John. "How come you wearin' those baggy ol' shorts?
Yer Daddy lose all his money and can't afford to buy you
new pants?"

"That's the style, auntie." He chucked her playfully
under the chin.

"What style? Thass no style, a'tall." She swatted his
teasing fingers away. "And don't you be flirtin' with that
Boudreaux girl, neither. Her Daddy said he's gonna shoot
yer backside with buckshot next time you come sniffin'
around."

"Me?" Tee-John said, putting a hand over his heart with
wounded innocence.

Outside, a car door slammed, followed by the pounding
of little feet on the wooden wharf. The shrieking of three
little girls could only be three-year-old Blanche Marie, two-
year-old Camille, and one-year-old Jeanette. The admoni-

tion of Luc and Sylvie echoed: "Do not dare to touch that alligator."

Remy heard a loud roar of animal outrage, which pretty much translated to, "Enough is enough!" Then a loud splashing noise. Useless was no fool; he was out of here.

Tee-John headed out the door to buy ice cream, or to escape the inevitable chaos that accompanied Luc's family. "Guess what Luc is considerin'?" He threw over his shoulder.

"Putting you in a dimwit protection program till you're, oh, let's say twenty-one?" he offered. Luc was a lawyer, and a good one, too. If anyone could tame Tee-John down, it was Luc. Look what he'd accomplished with him and René.

Tee-John ignored Remy's sarcasm. "Luc is thinkin' about gettin' neutered."

"The hell you say!" was Remy's immediate reaction.

"Well, kiss my grits and call me brunch," Tante Lulu said. "Where did you hear such a thing?"

"Sylvie told her friend Blanche who told Charmaine who told everyone in Houma that Luc went to see a doctor about one of those vas-ec-to-mies. Luc and Sylvie got a scare last month when Sylvie thought she might be knocked up again. She wasn't but, whoo-boy, they were sweatin' it. Guess those little squigglies of his are too potent." He grinned as he relayed the gossip.

Really, keeping a secret in the bayou was like trying to hold "no-see-ems" in a fish net. The little gnats were impossible to contain.

On second thought, Remy could see Luc taking such drastic action. After having "Irish triplets"—a baby born every nine months—he and Sylvie were both ready to shut down the baby assembly line. But a vasectomy? He cringed at the thought. And wasn't it ironic that Luc was determined to stop having kids when Remy would never have any of his own?

Just before Tee-John went out the door, his aunt added, "Tee-John, when you come back, remember to bring in Remy's birthday present from the truck." She smiled broadly at Remy. "Your very own hope chest."

"A hope chest? A hope chest for a man?" Remy winced. "No friggin' way!" he exclaimed, then immediately chastised himself. He didn't speak that way in front of women, especially Tante Lulu. "Sorry, ma'am."

"You'll be feeling lots better, once I get your hope chest filled, and we find you a good Cajun wife. I made a list." She waved a piece of paper that had at least twenty names on it.

Remy groaned.

"Plus, I'm gonna say a novena to St. Jude to jump start the bride search."

Remy groaned again.

"I'm thinkin' we should launch this all off with a big *fais do do*, a party down on the bayou."

"Launch what?" Remy choked out.

"Your bride search. Ain't you listenin', boy? With all the women there, you would have a chance to cull down the list."

"Bad idea, auntie."

"Mebbe we could have it at Luc and Sylvie's place. They have a big yard where we can set up tents for food and a wooden platform for the musicians and dancing. René might even come play with his old band."

She talked over him as if he wasn't even there.

He shouldn't be surprised. It was *se fini pas*, a thing without end, the way his family interfered in each other's lives.

Forget about the government contract he was about to undertake. If he had any sense, Remy would run off to some faraway country, like California, where no one could find him, especially his interfering family. But first, he'd set fire to everything here: the houseboat, the 'copter, all his belongings, the hope chest.

He was only half kidding while playing out this tempting fantasy in his head.

It would be the biggest bonfire in bayou history, though.

Then, he would be free.

Yeah, right, some inner voice said.

It was probably St. Jude.

Chapter 2

Come on, baby, light my . . . whatever . . .

"This is gonna be the best damn bonfire anyone has ever seen in the parking lot of The Summit, or I'm gonna die trying," Rachel Fortier said as she tossed another wooden chair onto the blaze, then whisked her hands up and down briskly.

The fact that there were tears in Rachel's eyes as she headed back toward the open door of her townhouse in the D.C. suburbs could be attributed to the smoke. She hoped.

"At least since a certain female senator, who shall remain nameless, set her philandering husband's Lexus ablaze five years ago," her neighbor Laura Jones stated just before she added a chair to the fiery pile. Laura must have caught sight of her tears because she looped an arm over Rachel's shoulder and gave an encouraging hug as they headed up the sidewalk together. In some ways, Laura was more outraged on Rachel's behalf than Rachel was herself—but not by much.

Halfway up they met Jill Sinclair. She was carrying the last of the wooden chairs for the bonfire.

Rachel had purchased the oak kitchen table and chairs at

a fleamarket for a song and wasn't all that upset about their loss. However, what the fire represented had her on the verge of bawling—something she'd done a lot of the past two days.

Jill gave them the a-okay sign. Thanks to Jill, the fire department hadn't arrived yet, and probably wouldn't, in no small part because Jill was married to Hank Sinclair, the chief. Besides, there were several gardening hoses at the ready. "I just got off the phone with Hank. You owe me big-time for this favor," she said with a laugh. "I had to promise lots of *stuff* to get Hank to wait an hour or two to check this out." Jill, the mother of three adolescent boys, loved her husband passionately. She was always regaling them with stories of her colorful sex life. *Who knew a couple could do that with a fireman's pole?*

"What kind of stuff?" Laura wanted to know.

"Never mind," Jill said with an impish grin. "It would probably end up on the six o'clock news. 'Firemen Have Big Hoses,' or 'Firemen Can Light Your Fire, As Well As Put It Out,' or some such thing."

They all laughed.

"Do you think the bonfire's hot enough yet?" Laura asked.

"The fire is perfect," Rachel said, swiping at her eyes with the back of one hand. "Now for the good stuff!"

Over the next fifteen minutes, working together, they carried out all the exercise equipment in the apartment, and there was a lot of it.

"You know, I'm five-feet-ten and weigh a hundred and thirty-five pounds . . . okay, a hundred and forty," Rachel declared. "I'm in good shape for my height. Really, I am. I could be the poster girl for body tone. Why should I be made to feel like a blimp?" She threw her hands out in question to her friends.

"Men! They claim to want Miss Bountiful, but what they really want is Miss Anorexia." It was Jill speaking, and she really had no reason for concern in that regard. She was a perfect size eight, and always had been.

Shoving a Stairmaster into the blazing fire, Rachel recalled, "This was my Christmas present two years ago. God, how I hate this thing!"

"I sold mine in a yard sale last summer," Laura said. "They claim you can read or watch TV while exercising on it, but it gave me motion sickness."

"I gained five pounds after using mine for a month," Jill added. "Do you think they're designed by women-hating men?"

"For sure," Rachel agreed.

"Stairmasters make a great clothes rack," Jill offered.

They agreed about that, too.

"Valentine's Day, last year," Rachel said and pushed forward her infamous Butt Buster machine. She gave it a particularly hard shove into the inferno. "Is there anything more romantic than a guy inferring that his lover's butt is too big?"

"Yeah, it would be comparable to a woman giving a man a Weinie Widener . . . you know, something to build up the little hot dog." Laura waggled her perfectly arched eyebrows as she imparted that particular observation.

"I had a friend once whose husband wanted her to get a boob job. When she countered by buying him one of those penis enlarger thingees you see advertised on the Internet, he divorced her. No second chances." Jill looked as if she was still affronted on her friend's behalf.

"You guys are sooo bad," Rachel said. But what she thought was, *Thank God you are here, good friends. I need your support for this final ending.*

Next came the Body by Jake machine, engagement gift, a year ago; Bow-Flex, another Valentine's day gift; treadmill, a thirty-second birthday gift last year; and two exercise cycles—his and hers—from the previous Christmas.

They all stood staring at the fire for a long moment, almost as if it were a funeral pyre—which it was in a way. Rachel didn't expect all the metal parts to melt or anything, but they would be scorched beyond use.

"Is that everything?" Jill asked.

Rachel tapped her chin pensively with a forefinger, then smiled. "Not quite." Within seconds, she had gone into the apartment, then returned with a few more items for the fire. An unbelievable twenty-seven different kinds of vitamins, plus various sets of running shoes (male and female), three jock straps (male only), and two bottles of Rogaine.

"Here's to new beginnings!" Rachel said. She and her friends sat on three of the five pieces of matched Louis Vuitton luggage stacked outside her front door. They sipped at fluted glasses of champagne which Jill had had the foresight to bring with her.

Tenants of the posh development still stood on their postage stamp–sized lawns and peeked out designer window shades. Most of them were grinning. A few gave her a tight-fisted punch in the air for encouragement.

"I'm going to miss you," Laura blurted out.

Tears rose collectively in all their eyes.

"Me, too," Rachel said on a sob.

"You will come back, won't you, Rach?" Jill took one of Rachel's hands in hers and squeezed hard.

"Definitely." Rachel's employer at Serenity Designs, Daphne Fields, had graciously given her a three-month leave of absence, but Rachel expected to be back in the city in a month, or six weeks at the most.

"You need this time away from here," Jill concluded, as if they hadn't discussed the subject to death in the last few days. "And, personally, I think it was synchronicity that you got that letter from your grandmother inviting you to come for a visit right when everything started to hit the fan here."

Gizelle Fortier's letter had, indeed, come at the perfect time; a lifeline, in a way. Rachel had never met the woman, or even heard of her, until she'd received the terse invitation following her birth mother's death last month. Apparently, Gizelle was the mother of Rachel's father, who had died before Rachel's birth.

Her grandmother lived in a quaint place called Bayou Black in Terrebonne Parish, Louisiana. Rachel pictured a kindly, white-haired lady in a modest plantation house with a sweeping lawn leading down to the meandering stream. A miniature *Tara*. Rachel needed this kind of quiet setting to make some life-changing decisions. Out with the old, in with the new.

The noise of squealing tires jarred her out of her reverie, causing her half-filled glass to slosh over onto her jeans. She rubbed her palm over the spot, then shrugged with unconcern. Even before she glanced up, she knew what she would see. A silver gray BMW sedan entered the parking lot at a fast rate of speed, barely making the corner. It came to an abrupt stop in its designated parking space out front, its occupant practically flying out the door before the engine had barely turned off.

Rachel stood, bracing herself.

It was David Lloyd, her fiancé. Well, *former* fiancé, she reminded herself as she pictured the two-carat solitaire diamond ring sitting on the dining room table beside her good-bye note.

"Okay, kiddo, time to go," Laura advised Jill. Then she addressed Rachel. "Jill and I will go pick up your rental car, Rach." Rachel had sold the VW convertible she'd had since college two years ago when she got the use of a company vehicle.

"Are you sure you don't want us to stick around?" Jill asked, standing, too. They gazed at her with concern.

Rachel shook her head.

"We'll be nearby, at Laura's. Just call if you need us," Jill said as they left.

Time for Rachel to face the music. Actually, it was time for the man of the hour to face the music. The man to whom the bonfire was dedicated.

David must have gotten her message on his answering machine. As one of D.C.'s most renowned plastic surgeons, he'd been out of the country the past five days at a medical conference in Switzerland. He must have come straight from Dulles, if his business suit and loosened tie were any indication. David had specific suits for specific purposes; travel, office, social, conferences—all of them Armani or Boss. Ditto for overly expensive designer shoes.

David stopped in the middle of the parking lot and was staring, practically bug-eyed, at her bonfire. His face began to redden and his fists were clenched at his sides. Then he turned to look at her across the lawn. A twitch at the side of his mouth was the only sign of just how angry he was.

Coming up the sidewalk, he waited until he stood in

front of her. David had long ago mastered the art of cool-
ness and civility and masking true feelings. So it wasn't
surprising that he addressed her in an even tone of voice,
"Are you nuts, Rachel? Have you lost your freakin' mind?"

*Does he realize how weird it sounds for him to ask those
questions in such a calm manner?* "No," she answered with
equal composure. "I haven't lost my mind. I've finally
found it."

"Bullshit!" He waved a hand toward the pile and pointed
out, "There must be ten thousand dollars' worth of exercise
equipment out there going up in flames." He glanced briefly
with disgust at the fire, then did a double take. "And another
thousand dollars' worth of vitamins and health supplements."

"How like you to equate everything to the almighty dollar! Why do men always measure everything in terms of
money?"

"Men? *Men?*" The fact that he sputtered was an indication of just how much fury he held in check. "Is that some
kind of femi-Nazi, Sex-and-the-City, I-hate-men statement?"

"Yeah."

"Why? This all started with those loony-bird friends of
yours, didn't it? All of a sudden you're on this female
equality kick." He passed a hand back and forth in front of
his face in an erasure board fashion, as if none of that was
important now, which it wasn't. He stared at her for a long
moment, the kind of telling silence he often used to manip-
ulate his staff and patients—and, yes, her—into complying
with his wishes.

But she didn't bend now.

"All right, I get it now. You're going off the deep end
just because I wouldn't set a date for the wedding, right? I

told you before I left that we'd discuss this when I got back."

"That's what you always say."

"Don't pressure me, sweetheart. It is not attractive, and I will not allow it."

She laughed. The man was clueless. "David, we've been together for five years, three of those years living together, and one year of that engaged. If I were going to *go off the deep end* over your marriage phobia, or your electronic organizer timetable for life, I would have done so long ago."

Just then, he seemed to notice, with horror, that they had an audience, watching and listening. "Holy hell!" he muttered and steered her forcibly inside the open front door. Then he repeated, much louder, "Holy hell!" as he got his first look at the half-empty townhouse.

Rachel was a Feng Shui interior decorator. She had loved this townhouse and had decorated it with extra care, creating a home with harmony and balance of space, utilizing color, mirrors, crystals and plants to their optimum effect. She had made sure that the dwelling's life force or *chi* flowed freely, unobstructed by clutter. It had been her best work. Even David—never a Feng Shui advocate—had admitted her expertise when it came to their distinctive abode. Many of his friends and colleagues, after visiting, had sought out her decorating services.

"Where's my furniture?" he demanded to know.

"*Your* furniture is still here. *My* furniture is in storage where it will remain until I decide where I want to live. I left the drapes and all the plants."

Because of the missing objects, a negative aura was seeping into the townhouse already. The rooms felt out of balance, which they were, of course. She felt out of balance. Hearing some wind chimes outside, she remembered that she'd left them to dispel negative forces. Still, she shivered.

Meanwhile, David's eyes scanned the rooms as he walked briskly through the living room with its Persian carpets, gas-fired log fireplace, and floor-to-ceiling arched windows filling one wall, then into the step-down den with its U-shaped, soft Moroccan leather sofa of a buttery yellow color. The whole time he seemed more concerned about taking inventory of his precious antique Roseville pottery collection that filled built-in bookcases lining most of the walls in every room. One hundred and fifty-three of the vivid colored pieces at last count . . . or, rather, one hundred and fifty-two. David was obsessive about his collection.

Roseville pottery was first produced in the 1890s in Zanesville, Ohio, where David's parents grew up and introduced him to the art of collecting. The finely crafted pottery included everything from umbrella stands to spittoons to vases and was known for its vivid colors. At one point, the pieces could be purchased in a five-and-dime store for almost nothing. Today, even the cheapest pieces cost more than a hundred dollars and the rare ones, ten thousand dollars and more, especially since the company stopped production more than fifty years ago.

When he got to the dining room with its ornate French doors leading out onto a tiny, but colorful patio—the biggest selling point for Rachel when David had bought the place—his attention snagged on the ring sitting on the table next to her note. He cocked his head in question. And, to give him credit, there was hurt in his eyes and in the shrug of his shoulders. He picked up the paper and read her note quickly, then tossed it onto the table as if repulsed. "You really are serious about leaving, aren't you?"

Well, golly, I guess so. Wouldn't you think the bonfire, the missing furniture and the ring would be message enough? She just nodded.

"I thought you loved me." From David, that was as close to pleading as he would ever get.

"I did."

The word *did* stood out in the glaring silence like a foghorn.

"And you don't anymore?"

Surely . . . *surely* that wasn't a crack in David's hard-as-nails exterior? She felt her determination falter, but only for a second. "I don't think so."

"Five years, Rachel! We've been together five years, and you're just going to throw it away?" He was back to being angry; it showed in the way he carefully folded his suit jacket over the back of a chair, then walked slowly back into the living room, with her following. He opened the armoire with the built-in bar and poured himself a cut-glass tumbler of Chivas over ice, tossing it back neatly. She would have been more impressed if he'd drunk it straight from the bottle.

"I'm not throwing it away, David. You are."

"Huh?"

"You said that it's been five years and asked if I was just going to toss it all away. Well, you're the one that did that."

"By failing to set a wedding date fast enough to suit you?" There was venom in his voice now, and not an ounce of the emotion she'd seen moments ago.

"Not entirely. Something more important than that."

"And that would be?"

"Your vasectomy." *How's that for blunt, baby?*

David looked as if he'd had the air knocked out of him. In truth, Rachel felt the same way—and she'd known about it for two days now. "How . . . how did you find out?" he asked finally.

"Dr. Sylvester's office called to reschedule your follow-up appointment. He's got a golf date the same afternoon."

Raking his fingers through his hair—something he rarely did because of his fear of a receding hairline—he muttered something under his breath that sounded liked, "Sonofafuckingbitch!"

"How could you, David? How could you make such an important decision that affects us both without discussing it first?"

"I intended to tell you—"

"When?"

"It's my body. Isn't that what you women always say?" He was trying to joke, but he saw immediately that the humor was lost on her. "What's the big deal? You never indicated any particular desire to breed. Have you developed some sudden maternal instinct? The ol' baby time clock starting to tick?"

"You bastard!" She punched him in the stomach. Hard. Rubbing a hand over the sore knuckles, she turned away from him, not even trying to stem the tears which welled over in her eyes. "I don't know if I want to have kids. That's not the issue. I should have been given a choice."

The punch didn't seem to have done him any harm, but David stared at her as if she'd grown two heads. "What the hell is wrong with you? Yeah, I had a vasectomy. Yeah, I should have discussed it with you first. But I did it for you, for chrissake! Some women would be grateful."

"For . . . for me?"

"Honey, you know how long it's taken us to get your body in shape. Two years."

Yeah, two years of agony. Do you have any idea how much I hate exercise, thanks to you? And what's this "us" business? I was the one huffing and puffing.

"Finally, we've got you almost perfect."

"We" again. I do not want to hear about "almost" perfect.

"A few more pounds, a little body sculpting with the weights, perhaps some plastic surgery on your butt."

Mention plastic surgery and my behind in the same breath one more time, and I might just sock you again, buster.

"Six more months, a year at most, and you'll be thanking me, sweetheart."

I—don't—think—so. She glared at him, but did he notice? No! He was on a roll, or thought he was.

"But if you got pregnant . . . man, your hips would balloon and your ass cheeks would probably swell like giant marshmallows. And I know better than anyone else that once females pack on the cellulite, it's impossible to get rid of it."

The dimwit jerk just likened my butt to marshmallows. I think I am going to kill him. She folded her arms over her chest to restrain herself.

"So, see, I was just being considerate of you. We can always get a dog—a *small* dog—if the maternal hormones start humming again. That is, if you *really* want one." David was not fond of animals; this was a big concession for him. Smiling broadly at her, he opened his arms and extended them to her as if he actually expected her to step into his embrace.

Meanwhile, Rachel was frozen in place with disbelief.

"As for the bonfire, I even forgive you for that. Let's say we're even."

"Let's not," she said, regaining her voice. "Listen, David, you and I have too much history together for me not to feel some sadness about leaving. It's been a long time coming, though. The vasectomy was just the last straw."

He threw up his hands in surrender, but the small smile that tugged at his lips meant that he thought she would be back. "Where are you going, then?"

"I don't know," she lied. "A road trip for now."

He frowned with confusion. "A vacation?"

Just then, a horn blasted outside. A bright red pickup truck was out in the parking lot. Huge, impish smiles were plastered on the faces of Laura and Jill, who leaned against the front bumper. They were supposed to go pick up her rental car, a comfortable sedan; this last-minute change was obviously their idea of a jumpstart for Rachel's *new* life. The truck stereo blared some rowdy, though appropriate, he-done-her-wrong, country music song.

A pickup truck? Is it . . . yes, I recognize that truck. It's Hank's . . . a classic he restored last year. Good Lord, what did Jill promise him to get him to lend me his precious baby? Oh, my God! Am I going to make a thousand-mile road trip in a pickup truck, with my Louis Vuitton luggage in the back like sacks of meal, and he-done-me-wrong songs blowing out my eardrums?

"Don't tell me. You're leaving me in a pickup truck?" He smirked in a most unbecoming way.

Okay, so she'd had the same reaction, but she wasn't

about to let him look down his surgically sculpted nose at her. "Yes."

"You really have lost your mind."

Maybe. Rachel grabbed her vintage denim jacket from the hall tree, leaned up and gave David a quick kiss on the lips—and thanked God that she felt nothing—and waved back to him over her shoulder.

"So long, honey," she called out.

But David didn't catch the sarcasm. He still thought she'd be back. "Have a nice time."

"I plan to."

Chapter 3

Truckin' her life away

She'd driven only eighty miles or so on I-95 South before Rachel began to have second thoughts.

It wasn't the hokey Elvis wobble figure her friends had placed on the dashboard. *If he shakes his tushie at me one more time, though, I think I might puke.*

It wasn't the Dixie Chicks ad nauseam on the tape player—a gift from Jill who shared her enthusiasm for country music. *If they don't kill Earl soon, though, I will.* She saved them the trouble by switching from tape deck to radio station—a country station, naturally.

It wasn't the way people—men especially—gave her second looks as she tooled down the highway—a redhead in a lipstick-colored truck. In case the bozos didn't get the visual message, the vanity plate her friends had dug up somewhere proclaimed, REDHOT. *If one more man calls me "Red," though, I'm going to do something I've never done before with my middle finger.*

It wasn't even the bumper sticker, also a "gift" from her friends, which read, DECORATORS DO IT WITH STYLE. *I hope*

*no one I know sees me, though. That non-too-subtle mes-
sage is way too graphic for my tastes.*

Nope, what had Rachel wondering if she did the right
thing were the tears making wet paths down her cheeks.
She harbored no serious misgivings, but she *was* sad that a
five-year relationship had come to this. She'd had doubts
about herself and David from the beginning, but it had been
flattering to have a good-looking, successful man in love
with her. Plus, he'd offered a stability she'd never had,
being in foster care all those years before being adopted.
She kept telling herself that she was better off with a sure
thing—which she hadn't been, of course. And turns out he
hadn't been a sure thing, either.

Oh, well, maybe she would find someone in Loo-zee-
ann-ah. Some long, tall, Southern boy with a sexy Southern
accent. She thought a moment and laughed. "On the other
hand, maybe not," she said aloud.

Really, the last thing she wanted or needed was a man in
her life anytime soon. Just a couple of months to settle back
and relax. No complications. Just *me* time for a change.

The disc jockey broke in then, "And now, how about a
little Toby Keith from his 'Pull My Chain' album?" Immediately, a deep male voice crooned, 'I Wanna Talk About
Me.'"

"Criminey, do country singers have a song about *everything*?" she murmured.

"Yep," she answered herself.

Rachel wasn't a die-hard country music fan, but she did
like some of it: Garth Brooks, Alan Jackson, Bonnie Raitt,
K.D. Lang. Mostly, she liked the way country music made
her smile. However, by the time she pulled into the "Knock,
Knock" motel outside Knoxville four hours later, Rachel

was definitely not smiling. Who knew there were that many corny country music songs? Driving through Tennessee, hardly anything else played on the radio. Oh, the standard Garth and Reba–type recordings got their fair share, but there were also such mind-boggling, ear-numbing songs as:

"Bubba Shot the Jukebox."

"I Changed Her Oil, She Changed My Life."

"Don't Come Home A-Drinkin' with Lovin' on Your Mind."

"It Ain't Easy Being Easy."

"She Offered Her Honor, He Honored Her Offer, and All Through the Night It Was on Her and off Her."

If that wasn't bad enough, once she settled in the motel room decorated in Elvis chic—velvet bedspreads, velvet paintings and lava lamps—Rachel checked her cell phone, which she realized had been turned off. Three messages waited for her.

The first was barely intelligible because of the heavy Southern accent. "Hullo! It's one o' them goddam answer machines, Granny. Hey, what'd ya slap me fer? Anyhow, is that you there, Rachel? This here is yer cuzzin Beauregard Fortier. Jist call me Beau. Granny sez to tell ya she got yer letter and she's expectin' ya tomorrow or next day. She even washed the bed sheets. Gater gumbo's on the stove, awaitin'. Watch out fer snakes. Ha, ha, ha! Stop slappin' me, Granny. Thass all."

The next call was from Beau, again. He whispered, "Granny sez to pick up a bottle of Wild Turkey on yer way."

Yeah, right. We know who wants the booze, big boy.

The third call came from David. Despite everything, Rachel's heart skipped a beat. Was he calling to beg her to return? To apologize profusely? To say that he loved her?

Nope.

"Rachel, where the hell's my Della Robbia? You know that vase is one of the rarest pieces in my Roseville collection . . . worth ten thousand dollars. I want it back, and I want it back now. If you haven't returned it by tomorrow, I'm calling the cops. Where are you anyway? Never mind. The police will be able to trace you through your cell phone." The line went dead then.

So much for apologies or warm sentiments. Rachel should have known. David cared more for his stupid pottery than he did for her. The clues had been there all along. Still, it hurt.

Rachel glanced pointedly at her largest suitcase where the infamous piece was wrapped in a bath towel. She had taken the valuable vase because she could . . . and because she deserved it, in her opinion. Mainly, it represented a symbol to her—of what, she wasn't quite sure yet.

However, it was one thing to be confident about her rights personally and another to flaunt the law—not that she was sure that cops could actually trace cell phone calls. But she took no chances. As she headed down the street to a diner where she planned to have a solo dinner in a local diner, Rachel made a quick call, cancelling her service, then dropped her cell phone in the parking-lot Dumpster.

"Trace that, David," she murmured under her breath.

Meanwhile, down on the bayou

"This is the stupidest, most half-assed, lamebrained idea you have ever talked me into," his brother Luc complained. For about the fiftieth time.

"I'm telling ya, Luc, we gotta look like we mean business."

Remy wore a cowboy hat, vest, jeans and boots, with a gun belt strapped onto his hips—just for effect. He wanted to appear formidable. Luc carried a rifle and wore a bulletproof vest under his denim shirt. The only saving grace to their dignity was that they hadn't ridden in on horses. Instead, they'd pulled a "Go Devil" out of Remy's storage shed and used the small boat to skim over the bayou water to his neighbor Gizelle Fortier's place where he hoped to negotiate a land deal.

The woman they intended to talk with was sometimes referred to as "The Wicked Witch of Bayou Black." The last time Remy had approached her, she'd told him to drop dead.

"We look like Dumb and Dumber," Luc continued to grouse.

Yep, Hopalong Tweedle-Dee and his sidekick, Tweedle-Dum. But he wasn't about to say that to his brother. "Packing heat is a good idea, no matter what you say."

"*Packing heat?* What the hell cop show have you been watching on TV? I'm carrying a hunting rifle, which I wouldn't use to kill a deer if my life depended on it. And those pistols in your hip holsters probably haven't been fired since nineteen fifty-two. Geesh! Talk about!"

"We have to look as if we can defend ourselves. Ol' Lady Fortier is a loose cannon. You never know what she's going to do. Shoot you in the ass with buckshot, or cast a voodoo spell on your private parts."

"Uh-oh! Hold the reins, cowboy. You didn't say anything about voodoo. All I promised was to intercede on your behalf in a land purchase. I'm a lawyer, for chrissake, not Wyatt Earp."

"Luc, I need the land. The DEA will give me the contract for aerial drug surveillance if I can expand my helicopter pad. I don't have enough land myself to do that. Unless we can talk Gizelle into selling, I'm out on my butt. Frankly, if this falls through, I'm off to Alaska and a charter business." That last was a low blow thrown in guiltlessly. He knew how much his brother wanted him to stay here.

And, actually, Remy had other reasons for wanting this government contract. He had been running in place for years, like one of those gerbils on a wheel. There was no real purpose to his life; he had taken whatever jobs came along. Removing a few scummy drug lords from the face of the earth would restore some of his much-needed self respect.

Now that Luc appeared not quite so anxious to skedaddle, Remy suggested, "Let's roll this rock and see what crawls out."

They both started walking up the grassy incline toward Gizelle's home.

"Yer trespassin', fellas," Gizelle screeched in a high-pitched voice. She had just stepped out onto her porch, and she carried a weapon which looked from here as if it might be an Uzi, but was probably just a souped-up shotgun.

Gizelle Fortier and her home were a stepback to another era. *Better Homes 'N Slums*, it was not, but then *Architectural Digest* wouldn't be knocking on her door anytime soon, either. It could be a hundred and fifty years ago, and this log cabin on stilts would have fit right in. Built in the dogtrot style of the Cajun pioneers, there would be a central hallway leading front to back for ventilation, rooms on either side, with a loft on top for sleeping, and the requisite wide front porch.

On one side of the house, a clothesline stretched, filled with newly laundered clothing. Most everywhere else there were wood frames on which were stretched the skins of muskrats, possum, beaver and mink. Chickens wandered around the yard at will, pecking at the dried earth for feed. A pig oinked from a pen out back. And a vicious-looking hunting dog tied to a tree on the side barked wildly as it strained at its chain.

As for Gizelle's clothing, "witch-chic" came to mind. Her ankle-length skirt and hip-length blouse, belted at the waist, were made of some homespun Acadian cotton that was colorless after so many washings. Her long hair hung gray and straggly. On her feet were men's hiking boots. She had a bulge in her cheek—probably long-cut tobacco—and a matronly mustache. In essence, she looked mean as a coot. A witch, for sure.

"How are you today, Ms. Fortier?" Remy tried to be polite.

She fired a bullet in the dirt near the tip of his boot.

Holy shit! So much for politeness.

"Now, Ms. Fortier, you don't want to be breaking the law," Luc advised.

Her next bullet winged the barrel of the rifle Luc had braced over his shoulder. He jumped and muttered, "Jesus, Mary and Joseph!"

"This is my prop'ty. Yer the ones trespassing. So, I ain't breakin' nothin', 'ceptin' maybe that zipper on yer overalls."

Luc glanced down at his private parts, then glared at

Remy. It was one thing to voluntarily get a vasectomy. Quite another to have a witch take care of the business.

"Ms. Fortier, my name is Remy LeDeux, and this is my brother, Lucien LeDeux. He's an attorney down in Houma. We . . . I . . . just want to talk to you about a little land purchase," Remy tried again.

She narrowed her eyes at him. "I know who you are. Valcour LeDeux's whelps. What? You wanna drill fer some oil on my land? Ruin some more of the bayou?"

"No, ma'am," Remy said with as much sincerity as he could put in his voice.

"That Valcour! As crooked as a barrel of snakes!" She spit out a stream of tobacco over the porch rail, her gesture bespeaking contempt for their father—or maybe for them. "I knew him from the time he was a youngen. Randier than a three-pronged goat, he allus was. You the same, boy?"

Oh, yeah. Absolutely. All the time. "Hardly."

Luc stifled a snort of laughter. "He can barely handle one . . . uh, prong."

"Think I'm funny, do ya, ambulance chaser?" She aimed her weapon in the vicinity of Luc's . . . prong. He stopped laughing.

Just then, Gizelle's grandson Beau came ambling around the corner of the house. He carried a long-bladed skinning knife in one hand and a machete in the other . . . well, okay, a hay scythe. Beau was about twenty years old and not too bad looking if, number one, you disregarded the trailer park hairdo—short on the top and sides and long in the back . . . a "Mullet," some people called it, or an "Ape Drape" . . . and, number two, if you disregarded the blood stains on his jeans and bare chest.

"What's goin' on, Granny?" Beau inquired lazily.

"These no-account LeDeuxs wanna buy a piece of my land." She still had her weapon raised.

"Now, be reasonable, Ms. Fortier," Luc said. "You haven't even heard my brother's offer yet."

"Reasonable? I'll give you reasonable, you young full-a-yerself shyster." To Remy, she added, "Keep flying that whirly bird over my prop'ty and I'm gonna haul that Civil War cannon from the town square back here and blast you outta the sky."

"Violence is not the answer," Remy said.

"You come one step closer and I'm gonna prettify up the other side of yer ugly face. *Mon Dieu*, you look as if you fell sideways in a cement mixer."

"That is totally uncalled for," Luc yelled, coming to his defense like a raging bull. "My brother got injured fighting for this country, fighting for ignorant witches like you." Red-faced, he began charging toward the house, hell-bent on beating up on the old woman.

Meanwhile, she yelled back, "Don't you be having' a hissy fit on me, you . . . you . . . you LeDeux, you." Then she shrieked something about blowing the gizzards out of them all.

And Beau jumped into the melee by giving an old Rebel war cry and rushing forward with his raised knife.

They were all stopped dead in their tracks by a commanding voice coming from the back side of the house. A female voice, which demanded, "Stop this nonsense, all of you!"

To everyone's utter amazement a big ol' farm horse came cantering around the house, carrying what had to be the world's oldest version of Dale Evans. It was Tante Lulu, wearing a fringed cowgirl skirt and blouse and tooled leather boots. A wide-brimmed Stetson, kid sized, topped her still-curly hair, which was white today.

"A horse, auntie? A *horse*?" Remy choked out.

"My T-bird's still in the shop. Get me down off this beast before I fall on my face. I kin walk faster'n he trots."

"What the hell are you doing here, Tante Lulu?" That was Luc, full of tact.

"Holy Sac-au-lait! Come to save your sorry behinds, thass what I'm doing here."

"How did you know we were here?" Luc wanted to know.

"Sylvie tol' me you two were engaged in some bizness." Then she turned on Remy and wagged a bony finger up into his face, "What for you ask Luc to help you with Gizelle? You gettin' dumb or sumpin'? I'm a better go-between than Luc with bayou folks, and don't you forget it."

"Are you saying I can't handle a simple business deal on my own?" Sometimes Remy didn't know when to shut his mouth.

"Sometimes you don't know when to shut your mouth," his brother whispered to him.

Sure enough, his aunt shut it for him. "I'm saying you have as much chance with Gizelle, on your own, as a one-legged man at a hiney-kicking contest." Then his aunt turned on Gizelle, who still stood on the porch, thankfully with her weapon lowered by now. "Ellie, *chère*, how you bin?"

Ellie? Gizelle is Ellie? A witch named "Ellie"?

"Come sit your pretty self down here, Lulu," Gizelle said with a wide smile, waving a hand toward a glider on her porch. "You so little the crows gonna carry you off, girl. I get you a bowl of gumbo, yes?"

He looked at Luc and Luc looked at him. Was this the same Gizelle Fortier? Smiling? With a hospitable attitude?

"It's hot, hot, hot today. You got any of that sweet tea you make so good?" their aunt asked Gizelle.

"For sure, darlin'."

"I'm thinking about throwing up," Remy said.

"Ditto," Luc agreed.

A horn honked and a candy apple red pickup pulled into the crushed clamshell driveway. Bonnie Raitt was belting out "Something to Talk About" on the truck stereo.

The redheaded woman in the driver's seat maneuvered the truck in a circle so that she could park off to the side. She opened the truck door and stood on the running board, stretching, as if she'd just completed a long drive, which she must have since the vehicle sported a D.C. license, in addition to a vanity plate up front that said, REDHOT, and a bumper sticker which read, DECORATORS DO IT WITH STYLE. Remy couldn't begin to ponder the tempting implications of both of those messages because he was too intrigued by the thick swath of her fiery hair, which she pulled back off her face into a high ponytail. Only then did she jump down off the running board.

Remy found himself, involuntarily, taking a step forward. The fine hairs stood out all over his body and the air left his lungs. Time seemed to halt, then restart in slow motion as the woman took a step toward them. Toward *him*. It was as if only two people existed in the world . . . him and Redhot.

She was tall . . . about five-ten. And built fine—very fine. A wide Julia Roberts mouth. Big, brown eyes. Breasts that jutted out, high and round. A rump that filled her jeans very nicely.

The only intelligent thing Remy could think to say was, *"Mon Dieu!"*

But she was in no better shape. Her intelligent eyes gave him an equally thorough once-over, from head to toe and back again. He really feared, for the first time in twelve years, that a woman—she, in particular—would be repulsed by his disfigured face, but he had to know up front; so, he turned to give her a better view of himself, in all his non-glory. He saw the fact of his mangled face register with her, but she did not care. Instead, she stared at him hungrily, as if he were a Whitman's Sampler and she was a chocoholic. Some inner, crude part of his testosterone-ridden body wanted to say, "Eat, baby, eat!" But, of course, he said nothing because his tongue was frozen to the roof of his mouth.

"Holy Smoke!" she whispered.

He understood completely. He felt as if he'd been sucker-punched, then given a blast of blessed oxygen.

She asked the oddest thing then. "Do you own any exercise equipment?"

He shook his head slowly from side to side. *I'll go buy some if you want, though.*

But, no, she just smiled her approval at him.

And he smiled back at her, the slowest, sexiest smile he could conjure up. There was a time, before the accident, when he could turn the heat on at will with a mere smile. It had been a dubious talent he'd perfected.

She whimpered.

He guessed his smile still generated some heat.

Something really strange was happening here. He wasn't sure what this chemistry swirling about them was. He didn't care. His life was changing before his very eyes, and he didn't give a freakin' damn. *Who knew? Who knew?*

In the background, he heard Luc laughing, and Gizelle muttering, and Beau sharpening his knife, and Bonnie Raitt still wailing, but the only thing that really made it through his fuzzy brain was Tante Lulu's loudly expressed prayer: "Thank you, St. Jude."

Chapter 4

And then her hormones began to polka

He looks good enough to eat.

Well, okay, that was crude and poorly expressed, Rachel chided herself. But, really, this guy standing before her in an honest-to-God cowboy outfit had to be the world's best-kept secret—that they made male specimens like this below the Mason-Dixon line. Southern belles throughout the past century and a half had to have been chuckling at their Northern counterparts, knowing full well what they had tucked away back home on the plantation—or down on the bayou.

He was probably dumb as a doodad—a rodeo rider, or something equally brain-nonrequisite which required him to wear such attire. Maybe even one of those Angola Prison Death Row rodeo riders. Otherwise, he was still dumb as a door nail if he dressed like this for the fun of it.

Although, I've got to admit, he does look fine.

A further "although": he said he doesn't own any exercise equipment. A definite plus, that.

One last "although": he is the first man to jump-start my motor, so to speak, in a long, long time. And that in-

cludes David. A jump-started "motor" is a very definite plus.

Bottom line: Yee-haw!

The right side of Rachel's brain told her to slow down, that up until two days ago she had been engaged, that the last thing she needed right now was another man in her life.

But the left side of her brain—the side with a mind of its own—said, *Whoo-ee! Off to the races!* Rachel mentally fanned herself, especially when the man smiled at her— slow and easy and so damn sexy that she swore her toes began to curl. At the least, her engine was revving. *Va-room!*

She was no longer aware of the people around them, whether they were talking or moving. There was only this man and her.

He stood tall and muscular, but not pumped-up muscular—*Thank you, God!* His dark brown, almost black hair was not overly long, but he'd slicked it back off his face. That face was a sculptured work of art: chiseled, high cheekbones, a straight nose, lips so firm and full and sensual that they kept drawing her eyes back again and again.

One side of his face had been damaged badly, probably from a burn—which probably meant an accident, not birth. The skin itself was puckered and without pigment in places; even so, his eyes on that side and his mouth were untouched, with no apparent nerve damage. For some reason, the mangled skin did not repulse her. Instead, it complemented his beauty. Without it, he would have been godly handsome, too pretty to be masculine. And he was definitely masculine.

Despite the total package of attractiveness—the long, lean, meant-to-be-touched body and the glorious face—it was his dark, surely Cajun eyes that made her catch her breath. Such pain! If eyes were the windows to the soul, as the old cliché went, his soul had been to hell and cried for help to return to life.

She turned to look about the rural setting, and wondered why no one rushed to his aid. Why couldn't anyone else see his distress? The answer soon became clear to her. His eyes spoke to her, and only her. What a glorious, frightening prospect!

"Hello, I'm Remy LeDeux," he said, extending a hand to her. "I'd be pleased to make your acquaintance, ma'am." His voice was low, and intelligent, and exceedingly polite.

She gave a silent prayer of gratitude for the intelligence. She might just have died if he'd said something dumb and dorky, like, "Yo, baby! What's shakin'?" And, yes, she'd been addressed in that way on first meeting guys in the past.

"Rachel Fortier," she responded, though how she managed to speak above a whimper was a miracle.

His fingertips, then his calloused palm, touched hers. An electric current, or something equal to an erotic shock wave, traveled up her arms, out to the tips of her breasts, down to her toes, then lodged somewhere important between her legs.

She reminded herself of an old jalopy that hadn't been driven in ages. You could put a key in the ignition—*and didn't that conjure up some carnal images?*—but that didn't guarantee an immediate response. Nope, the engine had to chug and chug and vibrate and vibrate until it finally turned on. She'd stalled in the chugging-vibrating stage, but the *turn-on* was sure to come.

He blinked. Then blinked again several times in rapid

succession, the whole time looking down with amazement at the place where their hands were still joined.

"Who are you?" they both asked at the same time.

Their reverie broke before they had a chance to respond because a female voice cried out, "Rachel!" Actually it sounded more like a cackle than a cry—a *Southern* cackle. A bizarre apparition in neck-to-toe, bleached linen fabric came flying down the steps of a raised log cabin.

Please God, don't let this be my grandmother.

Out of her peripheral vision, she saw dozens of skinned animals, and a few that looked as if they'd been stuffed. A raunchy odor permeated the air, no doubt due to all the animals that had to have bitten the dust to produce all those skins. And, oh, no! Could that possibly be an outhouse over there?

This couldn't possibly be the family plantation. Couldn't, couldn't, couldn't.

But, deep inside, she knew. She'd followed the directions exactly as explained by the Houma gas station attendant. Her first clue should have been when he'd laughed at her question if it was a sugar plantation, and said, "More like a muskrat plantation."

Yep, this is it. The Fortier version of Tara. *I think I'm going to be sick.*

"Grandmother? Gizelle?" she finally choked out to the woman in long, stringy gray hair who approached her.

"Thass me, but you kin call me Granny. Granny Gizelle. Ever'one does," the elderly woman declared. She put her hands on Rachel's shoulders and studied her closely. "Look jist like yer Daddy, you do, 'ceptin' fer that red hair. The spittin' image, I vow. He was the bestest chile till he met . . . well, never mind." With a little sniff, presumably at the memory of her long-dead son, the woman pulled Rachel into a warm hug. She was tall and bony but strong as an ox; there was no escape. The lady smelled faintly of lavender and tobacco, and Rachel soon discovered from whence the tobacco odor emanated; it was the plug in her cheek. *My grandmother . . . "Granny" . . . chews tobacco. Can life get any worse than this?*

Her grandmother, who matched her in height, wrapped an arm around her shoulders and began to draw her toward the house when the old lady noticed the man in cowboy gear still standing nearby. "Don't you be gettin' all hot and bothered by any of them LeDeuxs," she warned Rachel.

"Hot and bothered? Me?" *Was I so transparent? He must think I'm some kind of slut. I feel like a slut. A Feng Shui slut. Ha, ha, ha! Aaaarrgh! My brain is melting here. Must be the humidity. Or my engine's overheating.*

"Them LeDeuxs are all a bunch of horny toads. Ain't fit-tin' to roll with pigs. Besides, that one," she pointed directly at Remy, "wants to steal my land. What kinda man tries to bamboozle a senior citizen? Tsk-tsk!" They were out of hearing range, but still Rachel was embarrassed that her grandmother would speak so rudely.

A horny toad? A thief? Rachel glanced back at him over her shoulder as she was being led toward the house. He had his face in his hands. A man stepped up to his side—clearly his brother, or a relative, by his similar appearance—and was laughing so hard he bent over at the waist with his hands on his thighs. If that wasn't bad enough, a tiny old lady in the most ridiculous cowgirl outfit gave Rachel a little wave and a big smile.

If this was *Gone With the Wind*, Rachel was hoping for a big wind.

And then they dined on Gator Gumbo. Yeech!

"Was I pathetic?" Remy asked Luc (which in itself was a sign of how pathetic he was—that he would ask his brother such a wussy question).

Everyone had gone into the cabin, except the three of them. His aunt was sure to hightail it in soon, though, to gather all the gossip, and meddle in his affairs, no doubt.

"Ab-so-lute-ly!" Luc took great pleasure in answering.

"It was the thunderbolt," Tante Lulu diagnosed. "Does that all the time. Makes the menfolks go all tongue-tied and wobble-kneed. All vine and no taters. *Pathetic* about sez it all."

"It was not the thunderbolt," Remy insisted to his aunt. "I was just taken a bit unawares is all. You have to admit, she is the best-looking woman to hit the bayou in a century or so, even if she does have red hair." Remy had never much favored women with red hair. He did now. The vanity plate on the front bumper of that pickup truck parked over there just added to the whole tantalizing image, RED-HOT! *That's for damn sure! Whoo-ee!* Then, there was the bumper sticker, DECORATORS DO IT WITH STYLE. *I'd like to see that—stylish screwing. In fact, I'd like to experience it. For sure!*

Luc and his aunt stared at him, then shook their heads and clucked their tongues.

"What?"

"You've got it bad, bro. And so sudden."

"I better start sewing."

He was afraid to ask, but never fear; Luc asked for him. "Sewing what, auntie?"

"The bride quilt for Remy's hope chest, thass what."

Remy groaned.

Luc grinned.

And Beau came out on the porch to yell, "Hey, Miss Lulu, my cuzzin is pukin' up her guts, jist cause she saw a gator snout in the gumbo. City folks! Sissies, all of 'em! Granny sez to ask if you got any stomach herbs in yer saddle bags."

"Sure thing," their aunt said, already morphing into her *traiteur* mode as she rushed over to the horse, busy munching on carrots from Gizelle's garden. If Gizelle got sight of the animal, they'd probably be serving horse gumbo here tomorrow.

"And some Wild Turkey," Beau added. "Granny needs some Wild Turkey to settle their innards."

"The only turkey you're gonna see, boy, is the ones what nest in Atchafala Swamp," Tante Lulu commented.

"I better come in with you . . . to see if there's anything I can do to help," Remy offered.

Even as she was pulling tiny zip-locked plastic bags of herbs from her saddle bag—the days of hand-sewn burlap plackets being long gone, he supposed—Tante Lulu glared at him. "If you want to help, go home. And pray. I need to talk with this Rachel girl and see if she's suitable for you."

"What do you mean *suitable*? Don't you dare go matchmaking for me. I can handle my own affairs."

"Hmpfh! *Affairs* is right. You been havin' too many affairs. Time for the big time, big boy."

"Big time?" he choked out.

"No more hanky-panky," she explained. "Lust out, love in. Well, lust is okay, as long as there's love first. And weddin' bells."

"No meddling," Remy insisted in as respectful a tone as

he could muster. He did not want to be discourteous to his aunt, but he had to put his foot down. "No matchmaking. I mean it." *Mon Dieu*, that's all he needed in his life. A Cajun yenta.

"Whatever you say," Tante Lulu agreed too readily as she scurried toward the cabin with her stomach herbs.

"Your goose is cooked," Luc commented to him when they were left alone in the yard. The cowboy and the undercover lawyer—them and about seventy stinkin' animal skins and a stuffed cougar and two lifelike alligators from Gizelle's taxidermy days.

"Oh, yeah."

Being blue on Bayou Black

"You're a taxidermist, Granny?" Rachel asked with more than a little alarm.

"Was. Ain't no more," her grandmother said. "The work's too hard, and the pay's too small. Not much call for stuffed critters these days, I reckon."

Rachel had asked the question because the creatures she'd seen about the place looked eerily alive. She would have expected such an occupation from her cousin Beau who trapped animals for a living, selling their pelts to local furriers. When she'd asked him why he trapped animals for a living, he'd replied, "Beats pickin' cotton." She couldn't argue with that. Still, a lady doing taxidermy work surprised Rachel. Not that her grandmother was ladylike. Far from it! Even as her slender fingers gracefully worked the spindles of a loom with soothingly rhythmic sounds— *clunk, clunk, clunk*—she would occasionally spit a stream of tobacco juice over the porch rail into the bougainvillea bushes. And that post-menopausal fuzz above her upper lip would never cut it in city society.

It was early evening of the day of their arrival, and Rachel sat on a glider on the front porch while Granny worked away, making a rag rug, on a large wooden loom situated at the far end of the wide front porch. Rag rugs were traditionally crafted by poor women of many cultures as a practical way of using worn-out clothing or curtains or other fabrics. But Granny's rug was something more than that: fine art at its folksy best. Working on a pattern that must be imbedded in her brain, passed on through generations of Fortier women, the old lady's bony fingers wove yellows with pale blues and deep greens and the occasional reds in a floral pattern that pleased the eye, like a springtime garden. In truth, the colors were as vivid as David's prized Roseville pottery. For sure, Rachel planned to write to Laura, who worked for the folk art museum in Washington. She would be interested in knowing about this craft still being practiced on the bayous with a Cajun twist.

"Tell me about the Fortier family," Rachel invited her aunt.

"Ain't much to tell," her grandmother said, her nimble fingers working as she spoke. "We Fortiers arrived with the first Acadians from Canada back in the seventeen-hundreds. We been workin' the land ever since. Ain't never a one of us been on Relief, I kin say that much. Dint have two pennies to rub together at times, but our fam'ly never took charity. We Cajuns are a prideful bunch, if you ain't noticed yet."

"Were you farmers?"

"Nope. Well, yes, of a sort, I s'pose. I got fifty acres here what we had planted in sugar fer generations up till Justin died fifteen years back when he had a heart attack, right in the middle of cane harvest. Justin was yer gran'pappy."

"Sugar cane? It's hard to picture that. Everything is so overgrown here, except for this spot where your cabin is located."

"Don't take long fer the swamp to take over a cleared field along the bayous. One season, two at most, and the work of a century is gone."

"Weren't there other family members who could have taken over when my grandfather died?"

Her grandmother shook her head. "Yer father, Clovis, died when he were only eighteen. Racin' that motorcycle of his down the highway to Nawleans past midnight. He and yer mother had jist got hitched, her breedin' with you and all, but they weren't livin' together. Don't abide no woods colt in the family, we Fortiers don't, but Clovis weren't in love with yer mother, either. I doan mean to be disrespectful but Fiona O'Brien was a wild one, and she were only fifteen then. Lordy, Lordy! The things that girl did to get attention. They still talkin' 'bout her dancin' buck nekkid on Bourbon Street durin' Mardi Gras, but thass neither here nor there now. When Clovis died, she took the little bitty insurance money he had and hightailed it off to Memphis. We dint hear nothin' about her or you fer many a year. Everyone suspicioned that she had one of them abortions. I never knew Fiona had adopted you out. I swear I dint. Shameful, that. A sinning shame! Wasn't till I saw her obituary in the *Times-Picayune* that I knew where to find you."

Rachel blinked back tears, which surprised her. She would have thought she was long past tears about her childhood and the perpetual wish that someday her "family" would come rescue her. But her grandmother was telling her things about her father and mother—and herself, really—that she'd never known . . . not even when she'd located her birth mother a year ago in Chattanooga. Her mother, only forty-nine, had already been dying of uterine cancer, and she was a bitter woman, not overjoyful to be reunited with the daughter she'd given up thirty years before, or inclined to share details about the O'Brien or Fortier families.

Just then, a loud noise erupted overhead—an airplane or something, flying really low. Her grandmother's face suffused with color as she raised a fist skyward. "Damn LeDeuxs! I oughta buy myself a machine gun and shoot the bugger down."

"Huh?"

"Remy LeDeux is flyin' his whirly bird overhead. Does it a half dozen times a day. My chickens don't lay half as many eggs since he moved next door, and I swear the hogs are losin' so much weight they're downright scrawny."

"A whirly bird?"

"Helicopter. He's a pilot or sumpin'. Thass why he wants to steal some of my land. Soz he kin build a bigger landing space. Hah! He'll have to kill me first."

"Remy LeDeux is a pilot?" Now, this was interesting. "I thought he was a cowboy or rodeo rider or something because of the clothes he was wearing."

"He usta run cattle up on some ranch in northern Loozee-anna, but, no, he wore the cowboy gear today to scare the bejeesus out of me soz I'll sell my land lickedy split. Dint fool me one bit."

"Were you scared?"

"Hell, no." She stopped to spit her wad of tobacco over

the porch rail and wiped her mouth with the back of her hand. "But I'm warnin' ya, girlie, stay away from them LeDeuxs. They could charm the skivvies off a nun and think nothin' of it. Bad blood, they got. Bad, bad blood."

Rachel wanted to change the subject. "Didn't you have any other children to take over your farm, or whatever you called it . . . the sugar fields . . . when your husband died?"

"The babies never did catch well fer me. Lost a few through miscarriages. Only other living chile I had was Merle, Beau's Daddy. He was eight years younger'n Clovis. He and his wife Josette had a little bait shop over in Lafayette, but they got a divorce a few years back, and Beau come live with me. Too difficult, they said. He was ten at the time. Difficult? Pfff! Talk about! He's jist a little different, thass all. Merle died in a boat mishap five years ago."

Rachel didn't know about different, but he had not been happy when his grandmother had insisted, in order not to offend the nasal sensibilities of his newfound cousin, that he move all his drying racks to the back yard, over by an abandoned barn, just next to a—*yeech!*—pigpen.

"There is one thing I need to say, *Granny*." Rachel was having a difficult time calling her grandmother "Granny." She preferred Gizelle, but every time she'd used that name, her grandmother had corrected her.

"Whass that, dearie?" Her grandmother was tying off the ends of her rug, presumably ending her work for the day.

"Just that I am very happy that you wrote to me. And that you've invited me to come visit for a while."

Her grandmother shrugged. "'Twas nothin'. I must admit, it was a bit worrisome at first, inviting a city girl here. I half expected you'd be uppity, but we are what we are here on the bayou. Beau reminded me of that. If people can't accept that, then I guess they're the losers."

"Still," Rachel insisted, "it was generous of you to issue a blanket invitation to a perfect stranger."

Spinning around on her stool so that she faced Rachel directly, her grandmother made a *tsk*ing sound with her tongue. "Stranger? You? Talk about, girl! You're no stranger here. You're . . ." She sighed deeply, as if choked with emotion, which was odd because Gizelle Fortier was a tough old bird.

"I'm what, Granny?" Her voice was soft with emotion, too.

". . . family."

One word. That's all. And the carefully erected defenses of almost thirty years crumbled. The lies she'd told herself. The dreams she'd hidden so well that even she didn't know they lingered. Tears filled her eyes and she put a palm over her mouth to stifle a sob. *Family.* That's all she had ever wanted.

Her grandmother seemed to understand, instinctively, and she did the one thing grandmothers are supposed to do. She stood and walked over to Rachel, pulling her to her feet. She hugged her and patted her back and said soothing nonsensical words into her ear. "Hush now, sweet thing. Doan fret, *chère.* Everythin' gonna be all right. Shhhhh!"

It didn't matter that she was a crazy old coot living in the farthest thing from a Southern plantation. It didn't matter that she smelled faintly of tobacco. It didn't matter that her hair needed a major overhaul and her clothing a visit to Goodwill, if they would accept it. It didn't matter that she was no Waltonesque Grandma.

Her grandmother, Gizelle Fortier, said exactly the right

thing to her. "Welcome home, baby. We been waiting fer you a long, long time."

Feng what?

"She's not the one for you."

It was seven o'clock, and Remy had just come out of the shower in his houseboat. Fortunately, he had a towel wrapped around his middle.

"Auntie, what are you doing here tonight? I thought you went home from the Fortiers. Please don't tell me you rode that glue-factory reject over here."

"I did go home. Cantcha tell?"

Yep, she wore a little pleated skirt with a matching sleeveless blouse, tennis shoes and a headband around her still-curly gray hair. *Pour l'amour de Dieu!* Venus Williams she was not. He glanced out the window and sure enough her baby blue classic T-bird convertible was parked there.

"Beau Fortier put the horse in his barn. He'll take it back to the stable in Houma tomorrow." Under her breath, she muttered, as an afterthought, "If he doesn't skin it first."

Quickly, Remy ducked back in the tiny bathroom and pulled on a pair of running shorts. When he emerged, she had set out two large styrofoam cups of Boudreaux's strong Cajun coffee and a plateful of sugared *beignets*, which looked delicious. After his fiasco of a meeting with Gizelle Fortier, he'd spent the rest of the day meeting with DEA officials, including giving them a 'copter tour of the bayou region from the gulf inward, getting estimates from contractors to install a larger landing pad, in the event he managed to purchase a few more acres from that freakin' bayou version of Elvira, then coming home an hour ago. He was tired and hungry, he realized suddenly. After he'd devoured three of the sweet donuts and his coffee, plus half of his aunt's, he remembered her initial comment when he'd come out of the shower. "Who's not right for me?"

"Gizelle Fortier's granddaughter. Rachel Fortier. Thass who. Forget about her, buddy boy."

Uh-oh! I smell some interference here. Auntie's been meddling again. He should have known better, but still he asked, "Why?"

"Been seeing the same man for five years, she has. Livin' with him for three years, *without marriage.* Talk about! *Tsk-tsk-tsk!* Engaged, they were, but there musta been some hanky-panky, *without marriage.* She's not good enough for you, no, she is not." His aunt gave him a knowing look as if he should share her assessment of this woman's morals.

Remy homed in on one word. "Engaged? She has a fiancé?" It was downright ridiculous the way his heart sank over that news concerning a woman he had just met. Besides, in the past five hours he had convinced himself that the timing was all wrong for him. He'd even made a mental list: 1) If he got the government contract, it could be dangerous to involve someone in his life. 2) If he didn't get the government contract, he was off to Alaska, and it would be unfair to start something, then hightail it out of town. 3) He was not going to turn into a walking penis like his father who jumped the bones of the first female—actually, every female—that lit his flame. In fact, he and his brothers often joked that their Dad must have a perpetual pilot light burning in his groin.

A niggling voice inside Remy's head made a snorting

sound of disbelief at the idea of his No-hit list. Probably St. Jude.

"Not anymore."

"Huh?"

"She's not engaged anymore."

Remy released the breath he hadn't realized he held. *She's not engaged. Praise God and pass the gumbo!* That still didn't mean he was interested . . . much.

"She ended it before she came here. Dumped the man— *a doctor*—then hit the road in that devil red pickup truck. Mus' be she's a tease on top of everything else."

"Tante Lulu, you shouldn't make judgements about women just because they live with a guy before they make it legal. How would you feel if people said I wasn't good enough because I'd engaged in a little bachelor *hanky-panky*?"

"You're good enough fer anyone," she snapped in her usual feisty defense of him and his brothers. "But thass not the only reason I say you gotta look elsewhere. Think about it, boy, she's a Fortier. Bad blood there, and thass all I'll say on the subject . . . 'ceptin', do you really wanna be callin' Gizelle your Grandma?"

He shivered at the prospect. *Morticia the Mother-in-Law.*

"Of course, there's that matter of her fiancé havin' his pecker bobbed. I doan blame the girl for leavin' him over that."

Did Tante Lulu really say the word "pecker"? Does she mean what I think she means? "Rachel—Gizelle's grand-daughter—pulled a Bobbit on some guy?"

His aunt gaped at him for a moment, not understanding. Then she smacked his arm. "When did you turn so thick-headed? No, she didn't whack his too-too off. He had one of those operations—you know, the kind Luc is considerin'—without telling her."

Whew!

"One last thing," his aunt said.

Oh, man, not the "one last thing" thing!

"She's a home decorator." She looked at him pointedly, as if that should have some particular meaning.

"And?" he prodded.

"She practices fungus-way in her bizness." She nodded her head at him vigorously, as if that eliminated this broad from the bride race, without a doubt. "Sounds like voodoo or sumpin' to me. I knew a Damballa once who put fungus in her old lover's house and he died next day, yes, he did. All they found was mildew and rust ever'wheres—and poison mushrooms."

Okay, he decided to bite. "What the hell's fungus-way? I mean, sorry for swearing, auntie, but what is fungus-way?"

"Me, how should I know? But it sounds weird. You do not want a weird woman—especially one who leads men on and lives with them in sin and all that . . . stuff, then drops them."

He had to laugh, especially when he realized that his aunt referred to Feng Shui. "Tante Lulu, it's pronounced *fung-schway*, and it has nothing to do with fungus." He had no idea exactly what it was, just that it wasn't related to dirtying up a house, or killing someone off with mold. "It's some kind of Chinese philosophy crap—I mean, principle—related to how furniture and plants and colors should be used harmoniously in a space." *I think.* That's what a real-estate chick he'd known a while back had told him.

"Hmpfh!" was his aunt's only response to that. As a last-ditch effort, she tried, "She's only half-Cajun."

"That's not important."

"Is so," she insisted.

"Besides, you are not to worry about me or this Rachel person. My attraction to her was only a temporary blip on the remote bride radar screen. I have regained my sanity now."

"Good," his aunt said.

But when she left a short time later, his insanity returned. Why else would he be hopping on his Harley at ten P.M. and driving down a black bayou road with a sudden yearning to learn more about Feng Shui?

Chapter 5

In the still of the night

It was ten o'clock, early by D.C. standards, but already everyone slept soundly at the Fortier house—except Rachel.

Her grandmother and cousin had turned in an hour ago, their bedrooms being on the first level. Rachel had gone upstairs to the loft a short time later, after taking a quick shower in the downstairs bathroom. Turns out that, despite having an outhouse, there was indeed indoor plumbing and electricity furnished by gas and battery-operated pumps and generators. *Thank God!*

Exhausted by the long day, Rachel tried to fall asleep on the feather tick, a fluffy homemade mattress which had been overstuffed with soft goose feathers, all surrounded by swathes of mosquito netting. But her mind kept working with all she'd seen and heard on meeting her "family." So, she had crept downstairs and made herself a Cajun version of Sleepytime tea, with a dollop of honey. At least, that's what she figured was in the Mason jar she'd found in the cupboard bearing the label, "For Sleep." Others of the homemade herbal tea remedies read, "For Cramps," "For

Coughing," "For Loose Bowels," "For Congestion," "For Constipation," "For Hot Flashes," "For Depresssion," "For Tummy Ache," and "For Seduction." Rachel vowed to ask her grandmother about that last one, and she wondered idly if these concoctions came from the senior-citizen cowgirl Lulu who had stormed onto the scene today. She was supposedly a noted folk healer in the area.

Cup in hand, she went out on the porch, then down to the bottom step, to sit and think. She wouldn't be able to stay out long thanks to the numerous mosquitoes and flies that came out at night. The air remained warm and humid, despite a quick shower this evening, followed immediately by drying sunshine, all of which seemed to be the norm here in this region. A soft breeze tonight made it all palatable. The breeze brought with it the not-unpleasant metallic scent of the stream and its fish, the rank odor of dying vegetation, mixed with the pungent odors of evergreen trees and lush flowers: magnolias, bougainvillea, wild roses, verbena. All around the packed dirt yard, lightning bugs darted here and there, like sparkling jewels on black velvet.

A deceptive silence cloaked the bayou at night. At first, it appeared deathly quiet, but then she noticed the soft lapping of the slow current against the banks, the clicking sound of crickets, the mournful cry of a dove for its mate. Harder to detect was the rustling of leaves, whether from the breeze or an animal, she couldn't say for sure. And far in the distance could be heard the crack of Indian summer thunder.

This swampland frightened and repelled her. But at the same time, it tempted her with its outrageous beauty. What would it have been like to grow up here as a child? Would she have run barefoot and uneducated? Would she have developed into an artist of sorts, like her grandmother? Would she have been a happy child, instead of lonely, neglected, never good enough? Had she been better off given up by her young mother, shuffled around from one foster family to another until she was fourteen and finally adopted by a nice older couple . . . too late to ever feel like she had a real family?

"I wish . . . ," she murmured aloud, unsure just what she would wish for.

"You wish . . . ? For what?" a voice asked out of the darkness.

Rachel jumped and set her thankfully empty cup beside her on the wood step. "Who's there? What do you want?" She stood shakily and held onto the porch rail for support.

"It's just Prince Charming, come to grant your wish," he said with a chuckle as he came closer. "Don't get excited, darlin'. Nothing to be jittery about."

"I have a gun." Actually, the only guns she was aware of were Granny's in the kitchen and Beau's over the living room mantle, not that she would know how to use them, but this trespasser didn't know that.

He laughed. Apparently, he did know that. "So do I. Back on my fair steed."

"Steed?" she squeaked out.

"Harley." Even before the stranger walked out of the semi-darkness, Rachel recognized him by his sexy-as-sin, husky voice. Remy LeDeux.

He'd ditched his cowboy gear and instead wore jeans which hugged his mile-long muscular legs and cute ol' butt. A long-sleeved plaid shirt covered him on top, with the two top buttons undone. The smell of some minty fragrance drifted to her . . . probably his bath soap. He'd slicked his dark hair wetly off his face. In this half-light, his disfigurements faded to nothing, and he was beyond handsome.

Her heart, which had already been beating rapidly at the perceived threat, kicked up a notch. *Ker-thump, ker-thump, ker-thump!* She wasn't scared anymore . . . okay, a little bit scared, but for an entirely different reason. Years ago, Rachel had read a book about a female college professor who'd left her seemingly rational life behind for a not-so-rational road trip on which she searched for "love with a warm cowboy." Forget about cowboys. Rachel was beginning to see much more appeal in Cajun men—well, one particular Cajun man. And as for "warm," no way! This Cajun was a scorcher.

"Why are you fanning your face?" he asked.

Good Lord! Did I really do that? "Because of the humidity."

"It's not that bad tonight. There's a breeze. But I guess you're not used to the weather here yet. Hell—I mean, heck—the humidity here usually hovers about eighty to ninety percent and the temperature close to ninety. So, a night like this is downright balmy and actually . . ." His words trailed off as he realized that he'd been rambling. The man was nervous.

Rachel had lost her virginity a long time ago, but she possessed virtually no experience with the flirty games of seduction men and women played. As Remy stared at her hotly, she recognized that she swam way beyond her depth here, dog paddling in the middle of a testosterone ocean.

"My grandmother is asleep." *Well, that was certainly intelligent.*

"I didn't come to see her." His voice was low and raspy.

His stare was direct and unrelenting. His intent was obvious.

She might claim inexperience in sex play, but her body—the traitor—proved to be quite another thing. Her nipples came to immediate attention, and a fiery liquid pooled in her groin.

No, no, no! the sensible part of her brain wailed inwardly. It was unacceptable, that she, a mature woman of thirty-three, should react like a teenager in heat.

But the insensible part of her brain countered with, *Hot cha-cha!* She was turning into a female horny toad.

"How did you get past Beau's hunting dog? I'm surprised Chuck isn't barking up a storm."

"Animals like me."

She arched her eyebrows in disbelief.

"Plus, I brought him a handful of Useless's gingersnaps."

"Useless?"

"My pet alligator."

Aaarrgh! "How did you know I would be awake . . . or outside?"

"I hoped."

"And if I wasn't?"

"Guess I would have thrown pebbles against your window. Like that Romeo guy in the play. Truth is, *chère*, I'm not thinking much tonight."

"I don't think Romeo ever threw pebbles at Juliet's window," she pointed out.

"Maybe he shoulda."

"And what if you had hit Granny's window instead of mine?"

He laughed. "Guess it was a chance I was willing to

take. You know, a man's got to risk some thorny scratches if he wants to pluck the rose."

Pluck? There's not going to be any plucking here, buster. Time for good sense to take over. "Why did you come?" *Another brilliant question! My brain is in lust meltdown.*

"For you."

"I beg your pardon," she choked out and backed up a step and leaned on the wooden rail for support.

He stepped forward, so that the tip of his boots touched the riser of the step. Even with the height she gained by the step, he was eye level with her. "I had to come," he explained, which was no explanation at all.

She said nothing, mainly because she understood without words what he meant.

"I shouldn't have come, especially this late, but I couldn't stop thinking about you. This morning, there was something . . . a strange kind of connection . . ." He shrugged. "I can't explain. Unfinished business, I guess. I couldn't stay away."

Unfinished business? Those words caused Rachel to stiffen with alertness. "The only unfinished business I can think of involves my grandmother, and she swears she's going to blister your be-hind with buckshot the next time you trespass on her property. So, you better go."

He didn't move.

"You're not scared," she stated.

"I'm not scared," he agreed. "And the unfinished business isn't with your grandmother."

Uh-oh! I stepped right into that one.

"Listen, I know I shouldn't have come here tonight. It's the wrong time, baby. Sorry. I shouldn't have called you baby—yet . . . at all . . . I guess. Oh, hell—heck!" He took a deep breath and started again. "No offense, but I don't want—I *can't*—get involved with anyone right now. And yet, here I am." He rolled his shoulders helplessly.

"Wrong timing? Tell me about it! I am definitely not ready for this kind of thing. I just got out of a longtime relationship and—"

"I know."

"You know?" *How could he possibly know?*

"Tante Lulu—my great-aunt—she told me."

"Oh." She thought for a second, recalling how his aunt had blatantly pumped her for information this afternoon. "She doesn't like me. I could tell. Even though we just met. Is it the bonfire?"

"What bonfire?" He reached out a hand and tugged on a strand of her loose hair. "Here in the moonlight, your hair does look like a bonfire . . . threads of liquid fire."

Rachel backed up another step, thus pulling her hair out of his light grip. She hated her hair: the bright red color, the wild, always-needing-to-be-straightened curls. She should tell him that commenting on her hair was no way to get on her good side, but it didn't matter, really. The sexual chemistry ping-ponging back and forth between them was thick enough to slice. *Don't think about that. Think about something that will toss a little ice water on this fire. David. That's right. David is a perfect lust quencher.* "I burned some property that belonged to my ex-fiancé." That should spook Remy, make him entertain a few second thoughts about her.

"What kind of property?" he asked as he casually moved onto the first step. He didn't appear at all spooked. In fact, his eyes just now seemed to take in the fact that she wore only a thigh-high Miss Piggy nightshirt. And she could swear by the sexy grin that nudged at his lips that he was speculating whether she wore anything underneath.

She didn't.

"Exercise equipment. Lots of it. I hate exercise. Do you like exercise?"

"Depends on what kind, *chère*," he drawled.

The hot place between her legs lurched.

"The kind that involves sweat and sore muscles." Before he had a chance to place any double meanings on those words, she added, "Stairmaster, Butt-Buster, Body by Jake, treadmill, stationary bike . . . that kind of stuff."

"You burned all that?" His eyes widened with surprise.

"Yep. In the parking lot of our apartment complex. That, and twenty-seven different kinds of vitamins, and several tubes of Rogaine."

His face showed a quick flash of white as surprise evolved into amusement. He was smiling at her.

Oh, geez, this is a losing battle. Between his drop-dead good looks, the drawl, and now the smile, just call me "Silly Slut Putty."

Just then, a very loud and persistent *brill-brill-brill* sound erupted nearby.

"What is *that*?"

"Just a gray tree frog."

"How do you know—I mean, how do you know it's a particular kind of frog?" *Could I ask a more irrelevant question? As if I care about stinky old frogs. I want to see you smile again. Or hear you smile. Or watch you hitch a hip. Or . . .*

"There are a hundred different frogs here, each with a different song. The deep resonant hum of the bullfrog. The quonk-quonk of a green tree frog. The rattle of a cricket or banjo frog. Living here, you learn to differentiate." At the mention of each kind of frog, he did a probably accurate imitation of their voices.

The shrill *brill-brill-brill* sound broke out again.

"Well, I've never heard one so odd before. I thought frogs were supposed to ribbit." *Dumb, dumb, dumb. Someone please staple my tongue to the roof of my mouth. Next, I'll be talking about the weather. Oh, I already did that.*

"Only the male frogs vocalize, as a way of attracting females. This particular frog is probably calling out to some hard-to-get female frog downstream. Something like, 'Hey, baby, wanna come up and check out my warts?' "

She had to smile at that. And, really, she might as well wave the white flag of surrender. Good looks, the drawl, the smile, *and* a sense of humor. *Yikes! I am done, done, done. Turn me over and prick me with a fork.*

"We were talking about your bonfire. Do you do that kind of thing all the time?"

She shook her head. "Nope, it was a first time for me. But how did we get on the subject of the bonfire?" she asked, frantic with the need to escape from this man's magnetism.

"You were talking about how my great-aunt doesn't like you, but all that doesn't matter. I like you."

"You can't like me. You don't even know me." Even she heard the panic in her own voice.

"There's a surefire way to remedy that, darlin'." As if he'd been given a cue, he pulled her forward, and his head began to lower toward hers with an intent that was impossible to miss, especially when his lips were already parting and his eyes closing ever so slowly.

Oh, man, where's a life buoy when a girl needs one?

"This is not a good idea," she protested, even as she leaned up to meet his kiss. Her soft whimper gave lie to the protest.

"Definitely not a good idea," he said against her mouth. Rachel could have sworn he whimpered, too.

"I need to kiss you," he said.

"No, you don't."

"Okay, I *want* to kiss you."

"Oh, all right."

Remy felt as if he were drowning in quicksand, and it felt so good.

This is wrong, wrong, wrong. I should not be here. I should go home. I shouldn't start something I can't finish. And this is definitely a lousy time for me to start—or finish—anything. If I had a lick of sense, I'd put a zillion miles between me and this goddess in a Frederick's of Sesame Street shirt . . . which probably has nothing underneath. The image that prospect conjured up turned his already hot blood hotter.

She tasted like honey. So sweet. That was Remy's first thought as he put a hand under her swath of silky hair, gripping her by the nape as he settled his lips over hers. Initially, the kiss was merely a soft, soft shaping of his flesh on hers, learning her contours.

No, he immediately corrected himself. *There is nothing "mere" about this kiss, at all. Quicksand, here I come.*

Remy must have kissed a thousand females in his time— well, at least a hundred—but, in truth, he had never really kissed, or been kissed, before this moment, he decided. This was what a kiss was meant to be. A soft exploration. Coaxing. Tasting. Teasing.

And then more.

As his free hand moved to the small of her back and

pulled her flush with his body—*and, yes, she was naked under the flimsy nightshirt*—his kisses grew hungry, harder, more erotic. Pressing. Nipping. Sucking. Plunging.

And Rachel responded to every lead he provided her. They were like old lovers who knew each other's moves on the dance floor—or in bed. When he pressed, she pressed back. When he brushed his lips back and forth across hers to find just the right position, she accommodated him by moving in counterpoint. When the tip of his tongue wet her lips, she parted without question and allowed him entrance . . . no, more than that. She welcomed him with her slick, wet heat.

Remy would have felt embarrassed at his full-fledged erection pressing at her lower belly, but he sensed she was just as aroused as he was. Racing from droopy dick to Blue Steeler in two seconds flat was no record for a guy to be proud of, and Remy certainly wasn't, but hot damn, if he had the nerve to snake a hand under the hem of her shirt, he would bet she was more than ready for him, too. A heady thought, that. No pun intended.

He realized then—his fuzzy mind being two beats behind testosterone overload—that Rachel had wrapped her arms around his neck and was moving her hips against him, all the while kissing his brains out. Before he had a chance to react to that tantalizing exercise, she began to suck lightly on his tongue, which just happened to be planted in her mouth. His rocket about launched, prematurely.

Praying for strength, he pulled away from her slightly and rested his forehead against her forehead. They both panted for breath. He noticed that she hadn't resisted his breaking the kiss, probably because she was as shocked as he was by their lightning response to each other.

"I should have known," he murmured. He withdrew his one hand from her nape and the other from her back, then used both hands to hold her by the upper arms a foot away.

Her lips were kiss-swollen and her eyes misty with passion, but she appeared relieved that he had put a stop to their runaway kiss. "You should have known what?" she asked dreamily.

"I came here tonight to see if the attraction I felt on first meeting you this morning was a passing fancy or . . . something else." Remy was already backing down the step and away from the porch. He desperately needed to put some distance between himself and this witch . . . that's what she must be, to have entranced him so quickly and soundly. Or a sorceress. There was still voodoo practiced in the remote bayous, but did they know about all this woo-woo stuff in the nation's capital?

"And? What did you decide?"

"Something else, baby. Guar-an-teed!"

And then he was gone.

Rachel stared after him for a long time, no longer sure it hadn't all been a dream. One thing was certain, she felt as if her heart would stop beating—that a huge emptiness swelled in her chest—just because of his absence.

And the beat goes on

Unbelievably, Rachel agreed to Feng Shui a beauty shop.

Actually, Looks to Kill over in Houma was more a beauty spa than a beauty shop, but that's not what was so unbelievable. The business was owned by Charmaine LeDeux. *Criminey, was everyone related to each other here in the South?* Charmaine was a half-sister of Remy LeDeux, best known, to her at least, for "The Kiss." That's how she'd come to regard the event that had occurred between them a week ago—well, actually six days, fourteen hours and thirty minutes ago. Not that she was counting. Rachel had done a good job of avoiding the rogue all week. Or maybe he avoided her.

Even if she didn't see him, he was still there, in a manner of speaking. Who knew that the mere touch of a man's lips to hers could change her life? She couldn't stop thinking about him—the way he talked, the way his butt filled a pair of tight jeans, the way he grinned, the way he looked *overall* including his disfigured face, the way he looked *at her.* Most of all, the way he kissed.

But she was determined to forget about him. As he had said so succinctly, "Wrong time, baby." So, she'd decided that work was the answer, especially after her cousin Beau had introduced her to the wacky Charmaine. Beau had come in to the salon—which, surprisingly, had a male clientele, too—to have his mullet hairdo trimmed. The clincher had come when Charmaine had told Rachel, in passing, that she rarely saw her many half-brothers and half-sisters. Apparently, the father, Valcour LeDeux, was a well-known womanizer throughout Louisiana and had bred children all over the place, legitimate and illegitimate, which Charmaine was. At least, Rachel wouldn't run into Remy here. And she probably wouldn't think about "The Kiss" anymore.

Yeah, right!

"So, what do you think, so far?" Charmaine asked.

Rachel had been moving about the various rooms in the huge space that Charmaine rented on a busy street in

Houma. It was Charmaine's second business establishment, the other being located in Lafayette. Hands extended, Rachel tried to get a feel for the energy that traveled through the various spaces. You'd think people would look at her funny, behaving the way she was, but most barely gave her a second glance. Sometimes, Rachel forgot this was the land of voodoo, and mystical stuff didn't faze them at all. Flexing her fingers, she moved to a new area. A true Feng Shui expert could see, hear, smell, taste and sense energy with little effort, then decide what corrections needed to be made to establish harmony in the area. Rachel wasn't that good yet, but she did have the gift to some extent.

Apartments and offices occupied the upper floors of the historic faded brick building, but Looks to Kill had enough square footage on the ground floor to be divided into numerous rooms serving a variety of spa purposes. The usual hair salon. A massage parlor. Nail emporium. Make-up alcove. Exercise room. Hair removal and body waxing room, including the full monty for those so inclined. *Ouch!* And there was even a room specifically designated for the mullet hairdo for men, also known as the "Kentucky," and a bunch of other names, many of them disparaging but proudly claimed by their owners. That's where Beau was now. This short-on-the-sides-and-top, long-in-the-back style, sported by Billy Ray Cyrus, was so popular it even had its own website, which proclaimed it to be as much a lifestyle as a hairstyle. In fact, there were more than a thousand sites on the information highway devoted to this trailer-park hairdo.

"Well, I definitely have some thoughts, even this early," Rachel answered, "but first I'd like to ask you some questions."

Charmaine motioned her to a little lounge area where she served frosted glasses of sweet tea before they both sat down. "Shoot away, darlin'," she said. "By the way, don't be insulted, but you need a good conditioner, and more pouf to your hair."

Pouf? Oh, no! All my life, I've been fighting pouf. Definitely no pouf. "This scorching sun here in Louisiana is baking my hair. I'm just not used to it."

Charmaine shrugged. "Not to worry, hon. We'll fix you up in no time."

That's what Rachel was afraid of. Charmaine was a good-looking woman in her late twenties of medium height. Her high-heeled sandals made her tall. She wore skin-tight white jeans and a sleeveless, V-necked shirt with the sequined logo, HAIRDRESSERS LIKE TO TEASE. Her long, teased brunette hair was the type often referred to as "Texas Hair." About the salon, Rachel saw photos displayed of Charmaine, who had been Miss Louisiana a decade ago, even then sporting her Texas Hairdo. Also displayed were photos taken thirty or more years ago of Charmaine's mother, with matching, presumably bleached blonde Texas Hair, from her infamous stripper days. *Lordy, Lordy!*

This was not the look Rachel saw for herself. Bad enough she had her wild red hair. Stripper chic would turn her into the Decadent Decorator, at least, or the Happy Hooker, at worst.

"What impression do you want to convey with your spa? Sophisticated? Serene? Fun? Sexy? Subdued? Expensive? Inexpensive? Healthy? Successful?" She arched a brow at Charmaine in question.

"All of those," she replied, without hesitation.

"Some of them conflict," Rachel pointed out with a smile.

"So?"

"Let's start with what you have," Rachel suggested. The spa could only be described as a combination of the debauched Roman baths and a bordello, with faux marble floors and walls, intersected by fake columns, and those interspersed with a good amount of purple velvet draperies with gold loop fringes. Water fountains gurgled in practically every corner. "Do you want to gut the place and start from scratch with a whole new concept? Or do you want me to work with what you have and make minor changes?"

Charmaine put a long-tipped, shocking pink fingernail to her shocking pink lips and thought for several long moments. "I'm leaning toward the latter, but give me all your ideas and we'll see." She sighed on a loud exhale. "I feel as if I've been standing still for a long time, both personally and professionally. I need something to jumpstart a change." She shrugged. "Maybe this is it."

Rachel shouldn't ask, but she did. "Personally?"

"I've been married and divorced four times. *Four times.* All of them skunks. The worst part is my first husband, Raoul Lanier—we called him Rusty—has been sniffin' around lately, and I swear he's lookin' mighty good. A world-class stinker, Rusty was, but, *merci*, he could make a woman purr like a cat in heat 'mongst the bed sheets. Plus, he's still got a butt that defies gravity. Whoo-ee!"

Rachel had never expected such a detailed and intimate answer, but one thing stuck out. Her ex-husbands had all been skunks. "I left my ex-fiancé because he was a skunk, too."

"I know," Charmaine said, reaching over to pat her hand in sympathy.

"You know?"

"Sure. Ain't no secrets here. The bayou grapevine picks up everything. Personally, I think you're better off without the skunk. Not that I'm partial to babies or anything like that, but dammit, your man had no right to take that choice away from you."

I can't believe it. This outrageous, garish, totally-different-from-me person has cut right to the quick. She recognizes how I feel. Tears burned Rachel's eyes, which she immediately blinked away. "Thank you."

"No problem." Charmaine seemed to understand perfectly how she'd touched her.

"Color is the first thing, then. My instincts say to get rid of all the purple draperies and fake marble walls, but leave the marble linoleum floors, the columns, and the fountains. I'll bring a color palette with me next time, but I'm thinking red might be good for the walls, and—"

"Red!" Charmaine exclaimed. "Isn't that color sort of low-down and Bourbon Street-y?"

Rachel smiled. People often reacted to the color red that way, especially when it was used in an office or elegant dining room. "Not when it's done right. Red is a vital, energetic color. It can stimulate sexuality and even bring happiness."

"Sexuality? I like that."

"Most important, red can sometimes help to halt dissipating energy in a room, and I have to tell you, there is some serious bad *chi*, or energy, floating around here. I felt it strongly as I walked around, arms extended."

"Really?"

She nodded. "It makes me wonder about the history of this building. Oftentimes the history of events, especially traumatic events, gets imbedded in the walls of a place."

"This building was a market back in the eighteen-hundreds," Charmaine disclosed somewhat reluctantly.

"Hmmm. A farmer's market shouldn't do it."

"No, a different kind of market." She still seemed hesitant in her answer.

"Oh?"

Charmaine blushed, which made her pink lipstick look oddly attractive. "A slave market."

Rachel was shocked. "We have serious work to do here. And definitely not red. We need something to soak up this bad *chi*—maybe green, or blue. Lots of bushy plants, too. Not artificial or silk ones, like you have now. But live ones, which can have a calming effect. No synthetic fibers. Plus, we need to rearrange some of your furniture and work stations; there are too many sharp corners."

"Sharp corners make bad *chi*?" Charmaine asked.

"Definitely."

Just then, the chimes over the front door rang out. Charmaine got up and looked through the archway. "Uh-oh," she said. "Excuse me for a moment."

Rachel followed her as she made her way toward the front of the spa and a most amazing sight. A little old lady in mussed-up white curls, a house coat and slippers stood there. Outside, parked in a no-parking zone, was a blue T-bird convertible.

"Hello, Tante Lulu," Charmaine greeted her new arrival. Apparently, all the LeDeuxs must refer to this woman as aunt, even though she was blood relative through the mother of only three of the males.

"Heard you been doing the hanky-panky with Rusty again? When you gonna learn, girl?"

"I did not!" Charmaine said indignantly. "For the love of Pete, the gossip mill in this town is freakin' incredible."

Tante Lulu rolled her eyes in disbelief at her language.

Charmaine gritted her teeth, inhaled and exhaled visibly, then asked ever so sweetly, "What can I do for you?"

"Woke up this mornin' and decided I need a makeover. I saw Joan Collins on the Regis show yesterday, and she said mature women need to change their make-up and hair ever so often to keep up with the times. So, make me over, Charmaine. I'm expectin' to come outta here today lookin' twenty years younger. Like Joan Collins, 'ceptin' she's prob'ly my age."

"*Mon Dieu!*" Charmaine said under her breath, but aloud, "Whatever you want, *chère.*"

"Are you still here, girlie?" Tante Lulu was looking at Rachel now. "I thought you'd be back in the big city by now."

"Yes, I'm still here, and hello to you, too."

"Doan you be givin' me no lip. How come you're still here?"

"I'm visiting my grandmother for awhile. Plus, I'm about to do some work for Charmaine here at her spa."

Tante Lulu looked disgusted at that news. "Did you put a spell on my nephew?"

"Huh? What nephew?"

"Are you a little slow like that cousin of yers? Remy, thass the only nephew I'd be talkin' 'bout. Caint stop thinkin' 'bout you, the boy caint."

"He told you *that*?"

"Of course not." In an aside to Charmaine with a hand

cupped to her mouth, she remarked, "Slow, for sure." Then she addressed Rachel again. "No, he didn't tell me *that*. I jist know. My boys cain't hide nothin' from their auntie."

Rachel felt as if she'd fallen into Alice in Wonderland's hole and hadn't a clue what was going on. One thing was clear, though, she liked the idea of Remy thinking about her. A grin began tugging at her lips.

Tante Lulu heaved a deep, dramatic sigh and said, "Well, I guess there's nothin' to be done but hire you."

"What?" Rachel practically shrieked.

The old lady narrowed her eyes at her. "You'll work for Charmaine, but you're too good to work for me?"

"No, it's not that at all. What would you like me to do?"

"Fungus-way Remy."

"Tante Lulu!" Charmaine chastened. "Did you even mention this to Remy?"

"It's a surprise. A birthday present." The old lady looked guilty as sin.

"I thought his birthday was several weeks ago."

"It's one of them belated gifts."

"I sense a Tante Lulu bombshell coming," Charmaine said.

"Bomb this," Tante Lulu said, and stuck her tongue out at Charmaine. It was a ludicrous gesture from the self-proclaimed senior-citizen diva.

Charmaine laughed. "You want I should pierce that baby while you're here, auntie? You askin' me for a tongue ring?"

Tante Lulu actually seemed to ponder the question.

"What's fungus-way?" Rachel asked.

"I think she means Feng Shui," Charmaine explained.

"I think I doan need you to do my interpretin'," Tante

Lulu snapped. "If I want her to fungus up Remy, I can speak fer myself. So, how about it, girlie?"

"Oh, I couldn't. Really. Besides, I thought you didn't like me."

"It's not that I don't like you, but you're a Yankee. And you carry all those suitcases with you."

"Huh? What suitcases?" Rachel asked. Had someone told her about the expensive Louis Vuitton luggage she'd brought with her?

"I think she means baggage. Like, you carry a lot of baggage with you."

"Goldurn it, Charmaine. I kin speak for myself. Suitcase, baggage, whass the difference? As to you, Missie, when the thunderbolt hits, a person's just gotta go with the flow."

"Don't ask," Charmaine cautioned.

But she was too late. "What thunderbolt?"

"The love thunderbolt."

"Leave her alone," Charmaine told Tante Lulu in a mortified whisper.

"Shut up, Charmaine, and go buy yerself a chastity belt. Yer gonna need one if that Rusty is after you again."

Charmaine was doing this open-mouthed gasping thing at Tante Lulu's nerve.

Rachel hadn't a clue what Tante Lulu talked about with love thunderbolts, *unless* she inferred that she and Remy had been hit by such a thing. That was preposterous. Ridiculous. Totally out of the question. Time to be assertive. "I'm here on vacation," Rachel protested. "I only agreed to redecorate the spa because it's such a challenge. I usually only do private residences, or offices."

"Remy would be a challenge, guar-an-teed."

Does this woman never give up? "No."

"Think about it."

"No." *No, no, no! The last thing I need is to put myself in close proximity to that walking sex magnet.*

"Remy's place is kind of small," Charmaine pointed out.

Tante Lulu glared at her. "Who asked you?" She turned back to Rachel. "Do you only do big places?"

"Noooo," she answered tentatively. "I've done all sizes."

"See," Tante Lulu boasted to Charmaine. "She can so do Remy."

Do Remy? Now, that brought up ideas that Rachel was not about to contemplate—at least not willingly. "I cannot take on another job. I will not be *doing* Remy. And that's final."

"We'll see," Tante Lulu said.

Rachel was pretty sure she'd landed in bedlam—Cajun bedlam.

Chapter 6

Jambalaya, crawfish pie, filé gumbo

Remy had invited Luc to lunch at a downtown Houma restaurant, following a morning of meetings with the DEA folks and an extensive 'copter tour of the bayou. He was halfway through his oyster po'boy and Luc was almost done with his Jambalaya topped with warm beaten biscuits, and they still hadn't gotten down to talking yet.

Good eating: there was nothing like it! Especially for a Cajun. An oft-told legend in Louisiana claimed that a man who died and went to heaven decided to come back when St. Peter told him there was no gumbo on the other side.

"So, you're really going to do it?" Luc asked as he motioned the waitress for a coffee refill.

The thick Cajun brew would keep his adrenaline going for another hour, or five. "*Mais, oui.* I made the commitment days ago, but we got down to the nitty-gritty today. You wouldn't believe the operation these Colombian fellows have established already. And their target is teenagers, and even younger. Hook 'em young."

"Scum of the earth," Luc commented.

"Yep."

"But the bayous hardly seem like a haven for drug lords."

"It makes a lot of sense when you think about it. There are a thousand different bayou streams, many of them unnamed. Some appear, some disappear with every storm. Even the oldtimers get lost sometimes. What better place to bring in barges with heavy lead boxes filled with cocaine or heroin, drop them down in the murky depths for future retrieval? Hell, the bayous have been a haven for the bad guys for ages—way back to that pirate, Jean Lafitte. And the Rebs hid gold there during the Civil War."

Luc nodded. "Wait till René gets a whiff of this. That's all he needs, one more thing polluting his precious bayou environment, besides the oil industry and sport fishermen."

Remy nodded now.

"What exactly will be your role?"

"Surveillance, especially night watching. Locating suspicious activity. Flying in the SWAT teams. The job description is a work in progress."

"Did they cave on the use of your small pad? I assume you've had no luck with old lady Fortier."

"You would be right. I didn't even try again with the witch yet. And the government regulations are a bitch. More red tape than a Hallmark store at Christmastime."

"And so?"

"I've got to use the airport landing strip for now. A damn nuisance. Of course, I'll continue my charter business from home, just to maintain a cover, and to annoy the hell out of Gizelle baby with my low flyovers."

"Be careful she doesn't trim your tail feathers, bro, and I don't mean your *metal* equipment."

"Speaking of having your tail feathers trimmed, have you decided yet whether you'll go under the knife?"

"Nope. I'm in favor of it, but Sylvie is resisting."

"Really?" That news surprised Remy. Most guys would be crossing their legs at the hint of such an operation.

"She wants to give me a boy. I keep telling her that I'm happy enough with my three girls, but she has it in her head that every man wants a son."

Do I want a son? Remy asked himself.

No! he answered.

Yes! another voice in his head countered. Probably that plaguey St. Jude. He was being a real pain lately.

Actually, Remy hadn't thought about kids much at all, whether they be girl or boy babies—mostly because he'd resigned himself to never having a family. He'd told himself over the years that he had no real drive to produce a mini-me, but, bottom line, he'd been rendered sterile by all his operations—some of them way too close to his genitals. Still . . .

The image of a little girl with curly red hair flashed into Remy's brain, and he almost choked on his coffee. *Where did that notion come from? And why red hair?*

As if you don't know! that bothersome voice in his head said.

Ironic, isn't it, that Rachel left a man because he fixed himself so they couldn't have children, that Luc is fixin' to fix himself because he doesn't want any additional children, and here I am high and dry, unable to produce children? And, dammit, Rachel must really want a family to have left a five-year relationship because of a little snipping.

Nothing in life is really hopeless, the voice inside his brain countered.

He almost told St. Jude to do something that would be sacrilegious.

"You're daydreaming," Luc pointed out with a hoot of laughter. "Sylvie's been reading lots of magazines about new methods to predetermine the sex of a child. Most of it is bullshit, but, hell, I'm willing to try." He jiggled his eyebrows at him in emphasis.

"*Laissez les bon temps rouler*," Remy quipped the famous Cajun saying.

"Oh, yeah, I'm gonna let the good times roll, for sure."

"While you're having all those good times, keep a few hours open for Saturday. René is flying in to Naw'lins that morning. One of his old band members is getting married on Saturday afternoon, and he's in the wedding party. Guess they're all gonna play a few sets at Swampy's that night, for old times' sake. Even the groom."

René, their middle brother, was an environmental activist in D.C., lobbying hard to protect the bayou ecosystem. At one time, he'd worked as a shrimp fisherman and he'd played a mean accordion in a rowdy band called The Swamp Rats. It should prove to be a fun evening, and it was always good to see his brother.

They walked out the doors of the restaurant into the steamy Louisiana sun. It had rained a half hour ago, hard and fast, but was now mostly dry. "How's your love life, bro?" Luc asked.

"Non-existent."

"As bad as that?"

"Worse." Once again, there was a flashing image of red hair in his head, but this time it was not a little girl, but an all-grown-up one.

"No prospects?"

"None."

Liar, that nagging inner voice said.

Go away, St. Jude. I'm not interested in her. It's the wrong time. Remember? I'm not getting involved with anyone. Anyone. Do you hear me?

Now, there was laughter in his head. Then silence.

Yo, Jude! Has God ever mentioned that you have a talent for developing a deaf ear at the oddest times?

"Did you say something?" Luc had already turned toward his law office, down the street, where he was taking a deposition today. Remy had parked his vehicle in the back parking lot. But both of them stopped in their tracks when they saw a blue T-bird parked in front of Charmaine's beauty spa.

Not today. Please, God, not today.

That odd laughter erupted in his head again. Maybe he was having a delayed reaction after all these years to the traumatic events in his life. Maybe he was going crazy. Maybe he would turn into one of those drooling nut cases in a mental hospital who stumbled around talking to the voices in his head. Nice thought, that.

"Tante Lulu!" Remy announced unnecessarily.

"Oh, shit!" Luc contributed.

Remy hadn't seen his aunt this past week, and he sure as hell wasn't up for her usual interrogations now. She probably had a boxload of crocheted linens in her back seat for his hope chest. *Gawd!* Maybe he could sic her on René, or start her on a hope chest for his brother, to divert attention away from himself. *Nah! That wouldn't be fair.*

Despite their misgivings about running into their aunt, neither of them had the heart to turn back. Luc entered the door first, tossing an "Uh-oh" over his shoulder.

"Uh-oh" about said it all, Remy concluded, as he entered the spa and took in not only his aunt in of all things a house coat and house slippers, but his always-outlandish half-sister Charmaine who had a mouth that could out-blue a sailor when it suited her. But there stood the splinter that had been stuck in his brain for the past week—an erotic splinter, to be precise. He'd been trying for six days, fifteen hours and who knew how many minutes to forget about the impact of "The Kiss." And, yeah, hokey as it sounded, that's how he'd come to think of that mind-blowing lip exercise they'd participated in—the one that had sucked the good sense out of his good intentions and turned his mind on one track only. Could a man die from thinking about sex too much? If so, he was dead as a swamp stump.

Rachel Fortier stood staring at him. Her red hair was upswept today into some kind of little knot atop her head, leaving her long neck exposed and oddly vulnerable. She wore a halter sundress in a green and white floral pattern which barely reached her knees. All that skin! Remy fanned himself mentally. On her bare feet coral-tipped toenails peeped out of white sandals. She was the sexiest thing he'd ever seen.

Am I going nuts, or what? Getting turned on by toes, for chrissake! No matter. There was one thing that became clear to Remy in an instant. Rachel Fortier looked good enough to eat. And he meant that in the worst—rather, best—way possible.

"You're gaping," Luc cautioned him in a whispered aside.

Remy pulled himself together, and noticed that everyone was staring at him staring at Rachel. He pressed his lips together, just to make sure his tongue wasn't hanging out. *Jesus, Mary, and Joseph! What is happening to me?*

I know, I know, that pesky voice in his head said.

"What are you doing here?" he and Rachel asked each other at the same time.

"I'm going to redecorate Looks to Kill," Rachel said.

"Why?"

"Why not? Do you think I'm not good enough?"

"Hell, no—I mean, heck, no. I just thought you were going to be here for a short time, and you'd want to spend that time with your grandmother. Besides, I thought you only redecorated high-class places." *I sound like a moron.*

"Hey, hey, hey!" Charmaine interrupted. "Are you calling my spa low-class? Where do you get off, you full-of-yourself Cajun jackass? You don't know shit from shinola when it comes to beauty spas or decorating."

Remy cringed at Charmaine's foul language and her right-on assessment of his knowledge of those areas. He felt like slinking out the door, if he could do so unobtrusively. But he was saved by Tante Lulu. Or not saved, depending on one's perspective. "Guess what? I'm giving you a birthday present," Tante Lulu announced.

"You already gave me a birthday present. Don't you remember?" *Mon Dieu! Who put a motor on my tongue? I know exactly what she's going to say next.*

"A hope chest. 'Course I remember."

"You have a hope chest?" Rachel's lips fought a smile.

"Yeah," he said defensively. "Haven't you ever heard of a hope chest before?"

"Not for a man."

"Well, we started a new trend in our family. Luc was the

first, now me." He couldn't believe he was defending his aunt's inane practice of giving her nephews hope chests.

"I never got a hope chest," Charmaine complained.

"That's because you've been married four times," Luc remarked with a grin.

Charmaine jabbed Luc with an elbow, hard.

"Ouch," Luc yelled. "I didn't say you were hope-less, Charmaine. You've got more hope than most women I know."

"Keep it up, Luc. You won't need that vasectomy everyone's talkin' about."

"I like the idea," Rachel said, putting a fingertip to her lips in speculation. "A hope chest for men, I mean." She would probably be adding it to her decorating repertoire. Martha Stewart would be featuring it in her magazine. *Good Morning America* would do a special segment on unisex Cajun customs. In essence, he would become the laughingstock of the world.

But that was neither here nor there. That fingertip to her lips only reminded him of "The Kiss." He would embarrass himself in front of all these people if he wasn't careful. Hell, he'd probably already embarrassed himself.

"Dontcha want to know what my second birthday gift to you is?" Tante Lulu looked pointedly at Rachel and did everything but say, "Ta-da!"

Huh? "You're giving me Rachel for a birthday gift?" *And I thought a hope chest was an amazing gift!*

"Not herself, you dimwit. She's just going to do you."

"*Do* me?" Remy gurgled with shock. *Yep!* Amazing *about said it all.*

"No, I'm not," Rachel said, her face a bright red. Everyone else was laughing hysterically. "I already told you I don't have time."

"It won't take that much time to do Remy, believe me," Tante Lulu said.

This was absolutely the most insane conversation Remy had ever been engaged in. Even for Tante Lulu, it was over the top.

"She wants me to Feng Shui your place, and I'm *not* going to do it."

"Thass what I said. Fer a birthday present, I want her to fungus-way you up real good."

Oh. Now he understood. Sort of. But, man, oh, man, the last thing he needed was this hot redhead within a bayou mile of him and the incessant, royal, pain-in-the-ass hard-on that had her name on it. Knowing that, he astonished himself at his utter derangement when he asked Rachel, "Why won't you do me? I mean, why won't you work for me?"

Just then, a group of teenage girls passed by them in the large vestibule. They'd been chattering and giggling as young girls do, before they spotted him. As one, they went quiet. One of them gawked at his disfigured face. Another one pretended to retch by sticking a finger in her mouth. The third muttered something about, "Freaks."

He was used to this type of reaction to his mangled skin, especially from those who didn't know enough to hide their responses. His family was accustomed to it, too. But not Rachel. Too late, he saw her tight fists and her bloodless face bespeaking outrage. *On my behalf. Oh, geez, that's what I need—a pit bull female rushing to my defense.*

She shot out the door and stormed after the teenagers, intent on doing what, he had no idea. Either beating them up or giving them a tongue lashing. The latter, he expected. Grabbing her by the nape, he pulled her up short.

"Let me go," she snarled. "Those kids deserve a reprimand."

"Why? They're only being honest."

"They are not!" She slapped his hand away, but luckily just stood in place, glowering at the retreating girls.

"Look at me, Rachel. Look at me real close here in the bright sunlight. I *am* a freak."

"What a crock!" she exclaimed. "You're beautiful, and you know it."

"I beg your pardon." She deluded herself if she really believed that, but he couldn't help but smile.

"I think you're the best-looking man I've ever met," she whispered. Tears misted her dark eyes. Tears, for God's sake! "Even with your burned skin." She reached up and lightly touched the damaged side of his face.

That was it. He was sinking fast with no life buoy in sight. Remy did the only thing he could think of. He asked, "So, are you going to do me?"

You want me to do WHAT?

"A houseboat?" Rachel exclaimed two days later. Her voice echoed two decibels above a shriek. "You want me to Feng Shui a houseboat?"

"It wasn't my idea. It was my aunt's." Remy shifted from foot to foot, nervously. He ought to be nervous. The louse! Having her come over here for nothing. Not to mention having to defy her grandmother who practically foamed at the mouth at the prospect of her doing *anything* with a male LeDeux.

Not that she was overly concerned about his nervousness. Nope, what concerned her more was his appearance. Remy wore only cut-off jeans, a plain white T-shirt and a Saints baseball cap. No shoes. No shave. He looked so good, he made her breathless.

He wore the baseball cap because the wind blew strongly outside. A storm was predicted for this afternoon. He'd been feeding cheese doodles to a *pet* alligator, of all things, when she arrived. A man who loved animals—was there anything more touching? Even if it was a carnivorous reptile as old as Noah and not a cute little doggie.

"Well, this is impossible," she declared.

"Because it's a houseboat?"

"Not exactly."

"I would think this would be a challenge—an even bigger challenge than Charmaine's spa."

"Are you daring me?"

A slow, sexy grin crept over his lips. It was exactly that grin of his that turned her insides to butter, all hot and liquidy. Was he aware of the effect it had on her? Did he do it deliberately?

He wiped the grin off his face. "Nah. I never thought this was a good idea to begin with, but I got caught up in the emotion of you pit bulling in my defense against a couple of teenagers."

"Why? Why didn't you think it was a good idea?" *Am I demented? Time to get out of Dodge while the getting is good.*

"Are you serious? Honey, I want you so bad my teeth

hurt. Being in a room with you for more than ten minutes . . . well, I can't predict what I might do."

Rachel sank down onto a bench at the galley table and stared at him in disbelief. "Do you say that kind of thing to lots of women?"

He shook his head from side to side. "No. Actually never." In a low murmur, not intended for her ears, he added, "And that's what scares the stuffing out of me."

Every hair on Rachel's body stood at attention. If her nipples got any harder, she would need a really thick bra to hide her instant arousal. Forget that. Much more of this and she would need flame-proof panties.

"You certainly know how to make a girl feel good."

"You feel it, too? This crazy attraction?"

She nodded, reluctantly.

"Maybe we should just shuck our clothes and make love a dozen or so times 'til we get this out of our systems."

Marathon sex? A dozen or so times? Yikes! He probably wasn't serious, but she took the suggestion seriously and shook her head vigorously. "No way! I just ended one disastrous relationship, and I'm not about to start another. Besides, my grandmother would have a fit if I were involved with you, even for a brief fling. I can't do that to her, not after just meeting her after all these years. No way!"

To her chagrin, he didn't even argue. But he did joke, "And here I was, all set to lick the polish off your toes."

He was kidding, of course.

She hoped.

No, she didn't. She liked the idea of him sucking on her toes. And, yep, once again she was assailed by torpedo nipples and liquid fire. *Sluts 'R Us should be my new slogan.*

"I'll just tell Tante Lulu that we changed our minds, and you were unable to do the job here."

"Hey, how come you're blaming it on me? Why not say that *you* decided you like your houseboat the way it is?"

"She'd never believe me."

"And there's another complication. Your aunt already gave me a thousand-dollar retainer."

"*Mon Dieu!* That's it, then. We'll have to do it. She'll never take the money back once she's paid it out. My aunt is tighter than Scrooge with her money. If she gave up that much, it means she is *really* determined to have this done."

"It sounds as if you're scared of your aunt. A teeny little thing like her?"

"Damn straight I am. There's no stopping my aunt when she's determined about something. Just ask Luc. He's married with three kids, even though he was cruising along, happy as a bachelor. She may be small, but she's a bulldozer."

Rachel's shoulders slumped. She wasn't entirely disappointed, to tell the truth. There was something to be said for tempting the fire—and she meant that literally. "You would have to agree to stay away while I'm working here, to avoid any contact, whenever possible."

"I can do that. I'm starting a new job that will require me to be gone long hours. Sometimes, I'll be gone overnight."

"Maybe we can make it work," she said. "Let's talk about what you want to do, what kind of budget you're thinking about. I assume you don't want your aunt to pay for the redecorating."

"Is it going to be that expensive?"

"It can be."

"Give me some suggestions, and I'll tell you what I like and don't like."

"Do you like mirrors?"

"On the ceiling?"

"No, not on the ceiling, you lech." She laughed, despite herself. "On the walls, though you don't really have much wall space." Rich cypress paneling covered most of the walls and floors, even the ceiling. It was lovely, but overpowering. "The problem is, it's so dark in here, even with the windows. What would you think of a skylight?"

He brightened. "My aunt suggested the same thing."

The idea that she and his wacko aunt had something in common was mind-boggling.

"Normally, skylights are not a good idea, according to Feng Shui, because they allow too much positive energy to leak out, but in your case, the strong water influence could balance that out. But never a skylight in the bedroom." She talked aloud, not really waiting for replies, as she pulled a notebook out of her purse and began to walk about the houseboat, making drawings and taking notes as quickly as the ideas came to her.

Remy's houseboat was fairly large. The great room combined a salon, galley kitchen, and desk/office alcove. There was also a small bathroom and a separate bedroom. More important, top-quality materials had been used to build the craft several dozen years ago. The wood paneling was made of cypress to withstand dampness, with triple-pane windows all around, fine brass trim and lamps. The houseboat had probably been quite an expensive item for its time, a luxury craft, for sure. Feng Shui-ing a houseboat would be a challenge she would enjoy, Rachel had to admit.

"This boat doesn't move, does it? I mean, you aren't planning to drive it around to different places, are you?"

He laughed. "Nah, it's anchored permanently. If you knew what a job we had getting this thing moved from Houma to here, you'd understand why I'm laughing. I bought it from a friend of my brother René, in a fit of madness, I suppose. Or else, I was drunk. Either way, I've grown attached to the old boat."

"How much money do you want to spend? Do you see this as a lifelong residence, or something temporary?"

"I have no idea what I'm going to be doing tomorrow, let alone lifelong. But since I'm living here now, I'm ready to give up some cash. You come up with the ideas and the amounts, and I'll decide from there."

"First things first. You've got to get rid of the clutter."

"Clutter? What clutter?"

Really, men were clueless sometimes. "Like that paperwork overflowing the desk and window sills and the kitchen table. Like the fishing gear all over the outside deck. Like the clothing scattered here and there. Like the saddle in the middle of the room. Like that motor beside your bed, which I assume is a boat motor. Like the collection of wine bottles on the window sills. The hope chest beside the refrigerator."

"That's not clutter. It's organized chaos."

"Clutter," she repeated emphatically. "You have a lot of negative chi in this place, and I suspect most of that bad energy is coming from the clutter. You know what they say about clutter, don't you?"

"Can't say I've conversed about clutter before."

She flashed him a glare for his sarcasm, then went on,

"Clutter is nothing more than a postponed decision. And you have lots of postponed decisions laying about."

"Spare me, Lord. I am with a beautiful woman, and we are talking about clutter." He rolled his eyes hopelessly.

She ignored his remark, put her notebook down and began to walk once again through the rooms, arms extended, like a blind person. Sometimes she closed her eyes to get the full effect.

"Oh, shit! I mean, oh, darn! You're not into that woo-woo stuff, are you? I don't think I want you bringing any voodoo nonsense into my place."

Her eyes shot open. "No, I'm not into woo-woo. But I'm surprised at you. A big ol' boy like you afraid of voodoo."

"Darlin', anyone with a lick of sense is afraid of voodoo. Best you learn that if you're gonna be in the South for long."

Since she didn't intend to be here that long, she didn't give his warning much weight. "Okay, I think we should get some estimates on a skylight. That's what will make the biggest difference. Then, we need to have a woodworker come in and deep-clean all this cypress. It has a wonderful patina on it. Still, it will look much better when it's clean. The kitchen could use a little remodeling. I like the vintage appliances, but if we replace the table with a built-in booth in the corner, it would give you lots more room. Finally, I think some red fabric on the bench seats and about the windows would do wonders, in addition to a moisture-resistant Oriental carpet. Originally, I told Charmaine that red would be good for her spa, but I think you need it much more. Next to black, red is one of the most powerful colors."

"Red? Red?" he sputtered. "Are you going to turn this into an Austin Powers bachelor pad?"

"No. I'm going to give you a comfortable, classy home. Now, about the bathroom. It's pitiful." There was only a shower stall, sink and toilet in the ten-by-ten space.

"You know, if we're going to be spending some big bucks here, I'd like one of those super-duper, high-tech shower stalls. You know, the ones where you have water jets hitting you from every angle. And cool lighting."

"In other words, sexy," she remarked dryly.

"Yeah." He waggled his eyebrows at her.

"Do you have enough water pressure for something like that?"

"I should have. There's a humongous gas-operated generator and a cistern up the hill. You can't see them because they're screened by tall magnolia bushes."

She nodded, then moved on to the bedroom. "Are you satisfied with this bed?"

"Have I been satisfied in this bed?" He deliberately misheard her, a lazy grin quirking his lips.

And, no, no, no, I am not going to think about those lips. And, yes, it does bother me that he has a bed here in which he might have slept with some other women. Not that I'll ever sleep here. Not that I'm even thinking what it would be like. Not that my brain isn't in major hormone meltdown.

"What I meant was . . . this is a queen-sized bed. You're a big man. Wouldn't you prefer a king-sized?"

"Would it fit?"

"Well, it would be a tight squeeze, but it could be done if we removed the two dressers and replaced them with more built-ins. And if we removed the *clutter.*"

He winced, as if he got her point. "Whatever you think."

"Another thing to consider. The placement of the bed can be important. You always want to have a clear view of the doorway, but aside from that, if the headboard points north, it promotes sound sleeping. If it points west, it promotes lethargy or laziness. If it points south, it promotes irritability."

"Which way does it point to promote bone-melting sex?"

She shook her head at his teasing. "Actually, there are some things, but we can discuss those later."

"Oh, boy!"

"And, now that I think about it, a queen-sized bed might be best, placed catty corner with the footboard facing the door. It's usually recommended that some type of wardrobe be placed at the bottom of the bed to slow the energy, but I'm thinking that your hope chest would look lovely there."

"Lovely." He grimaced. "Whose bright idea was it to slow energy in bed, by the way? Not a healthy, full-blooded male, I'd be willing to bet."

"Are you going to argue about everything I suggest?"

"Probably."

"In terms of enhancing your love life, we could create a romance corner in that southwest corner over there. Include some figurines of lovebirds or heart-shaped stones. Perhaps some crystals, as well."

"You can't be serious. That sounds way too girly-girly for me. Besides, you set up some love shrine in the corner and my aunt is going to hot-tail it over here and insert some St. Jude statues as well."

"Isn't St. Jude the patron saint of hopeless causes?"

"Yeah," he admitted. Then, "No romance corners."

They walked back to the salon area. Remy poured cold soda into two glasses and motioned for her to sit at the galley table across from him.

"Tell me about this Feng Shui business and how it works."

She took a sip of the cold beverage, which was refreshing, although the houseboat wasn't hot, what with the breeze off the bayou stream and the overhead fan. The lapping of water against the boat, birdsong everywhere, a serenity that defied description . . . really, Rachel would be a fool not to recognize the charm in this place. In fact, one of the strongest assets Remy's abode held was its placement on moving water, which almost always brought fresh *chi*. Hopefully, she would only build on the assets already here, not weaken them.

But as to his question. "When I first studied decorating in college, I was only interested in traditional methods. But I interned with Daphne Fields, an interesting woman in D.C. who practiced Feng Shui. I work with her now. Daphne taught me that Feng Shui is an ancient art with modern implications. It's a way to redesign your home to redirect energy, the goal being harmony or balance. Does that make sense?"

"Not yet. Keep going."

"It's all about the yin and the yang, two opposite ends of the energy spectrum and how to bring them together. Light and dark, active and passive, hard and soft, male and female—it's all a balancing act."

"Hey, I've heard of yin and yang. They're sexual, aren't they?"

She had to smile at his one-track mind.

Remy smiled back at her, and Rachel felt her world tilt on its axis. She feared that she was falling in love with this rascally Cajun.

Was this what was known as love at first sight?

Or love at first lust?

Or had his wily aunt put a spell on her?

Whatever.

Rachel was tempting the devil here, and instead of running for her life, she gave him a mental high-five.

Chapter 7

But then he discussed her butt

Remy stared at Rachel sitting across from him, and had to smile at the way her mind worked. He loved teasing her. He loved the way she turned bristly as a hedgehog at the least affront. He loved how she spoke so enthusiastically about her work. He loved the way her pink tank top with the butterflies on it hugged her body and displayed just the rise of erect nipples. He really, really loved the curve of her butt in those white calf-length pants. And, of course, he still loved those coral-tipped toenails.

Truth be told, he loved too many things about her.

"Stop looking at me like that," she ordered.

"How's that?" *Uh-oh! Betcha I look like I'd enjoy jumping her bones, which I would.*

"Like I'm a nine-course meal and you're honing your knife and fork."

She got that right. "That would be an apt description," he said with a laugh. "As long as I'm not drooling."

She exhaled with a whooshy sound of disgust. "You know, I don't understand why you say things like that. I am not anything special, physically. Believe me, I've had that drummed into me for some time now."

"Huh? Who's been beating that drum?"

A light shade of red bloomed on her cheeks. "My ex-fiancé, David. He's a plastic surgeon, and therefore an expert on perfection in the human form."

More like an expert in dumbness. "I think you're perfect."

"Oh, puh-leeze. You just want to get laid."

He winced at her crudity. "Sure I do," he admitted, "but that doesn't mean I'm lying about how perfect you are."

"First of all, I have red hair. Curly red hair, when it's not straightened chemically. That is a definite disadvantage in the beauty department. By my book, anyhow. I've been fighting it my entire life. Little Orphan Annie jokes, redhead jokes, you name it, I've heard it."

"You have a point there," he teased, "although I'm coming to admire red hair more and more."

"Bull!" she responded.

More crudity. Did he bring that out in her?

"If you must know, my biggest flaw is . . . oh, God, I can't believe I'm about to reveal this." Her face turned redder.

"What?"

"I have a big butt."

He stretched his neck as if trying to see around the table. "Stand up so I can check it out."

"Not in a million years."

He started to laugh then. He could tell she'd like to reach across the table and swat him a good one. But he couldn't stop himself.

"It's not funny. David bought me a Butt Buster machine

just for that purpose. Not to mention all the other exercise equipment. God, I hate exercise. Do you like exercise?"

"Depends on what kind," he managed to get out through his continuing laughter. Her ex must be one helluva guy. Even he knew enough not to buy a woman a Butt Buster, even if she had an ass the size of a Mardi Gras float.

"David gave me a different piece of exercise equipment for every holiday—Christmas, birthday, Valentine's Day. And he had a schedule taped to the refrigerator detailing what routines to do, *every day*. It was for my own good, he said."

He swiped at his eyes and tried to stop laughing. Why he should be so joyful at another man's cluelessness defied explanation. Then again, no, it didn't. He was happy that Rachel had been so unhappy with this fellow. He didn't like the idea that she might be having regrets, might be considering going back to him. Man, oh, man, he headed down a dangerous road, and he knew it. Finally, he calmed himself and said as straight-faced as he could, "Seriously, Rachel, you have a very nice derriere. I noticed that the first time I met you."

"You did not. What a liar!"

"Did so. Ask Luc."

"You discussed my behind with someone else? Another man?"

"He's my brother; so, that doesn't count."

"What kind of insane male illogic is that?"

He shrugged. "Bottom line: you have a bodacious butt. Flaunt it, baby." Hey, if she could be crude, so could he.

She practically gurgled with indignation.

"Shouldn't we be getting back to this Feng Shui business?"

"Absolutely," she said, obviously glad to change the subject. Really glad. What was it with women and their fixations on the size of their asses. Men didn't worry about things like that. Now the size of what hung loose on the other side—that was another thing altogether.

What he should do is cut this conversation short and send her on her way. Then he should either 1) go get drunk, 2) go get laid, 3) go get drunk and laid. All in an effort to cut short this progressively increasing obsession he was developing for this woman. So, what did he do? He told her, "Tell me more about Feng Shui." As if he cared a rat's ass how she decorated his houseboat! He just wanted to keep her here a little bit longer, to hear the sound of her voice, to look at her nipples.

But she bought it, and immediately launched into her Feng Shui 101 spiel. "There are so many beneficial things Feng Shui can do for a person. Improved health. Better sleep. Revving up a business. Relaxation. More control of one's life. Starting a new career. Selling a home. Getting a job. Romance."

"Romance? How can Feng Shui help a person with romance?"

"Well, suppose you have a woman sitting in the wrong position at a cocktail party, let's say, facing away from the door, and she's facing east with the guy she's trying to attract facing north. This means she is in the most aggressive position, and he's in the quiet position, which would be intimidating to most men. She should face north, and the man should face west."

Huh? What a load of you-know-what! What the woman should do is wear sheer stockings, high heels and a short skirt. Then, sit her fanny down facing wherever and cross her legs. Or spread her legs, a la Sharon Stone, if she has the nerve. That would get the guy's attention, guar-an-teed. But what Remy said was, "How interesting!" He was no dummy.

Just then, his cell phone rang. A quick check of the Caller I.D. disclosed it was his DEA contact, Larry Ellis.

"Excuse me for a minute. I have to take this call."

"Sure, I need to take some measurements anyhow."

He went outside on the deck for privacy. "What's up, Ellis?"

"A deal is going down tonight. A barge will enter the gulf about midnight, then unload into smaller barges or river rafts that'll travel down one or several bayous for unloading—we're not sure which. Is the night vision equipment installed?"

"Yep."

"You understand the way we're going to run this operation. You'll stay in the 'copter at all times. You are *not* to get involved in any action."

"Yep."

"You'll be at the airport by ten hundred hours?"

"Yep."

"One last thing: this is dangerous business, Remy. Don't be fooled into thinking you're safe inside your 'copter, or anywhere else if they discover your identity. Whatever else you do, keep a low profile. Be safety conscious at all times."

"Yep."

Another reason not to get involved with Rachel—or any woman—at this time. Not just his safety, but hers, could be in jeopardy.

But then he entered the houseboat again and got a good

look at what Rachel was doing. Using a collapsible yardstick to measure his office alcove, she was on her hands and knees with her butt in the air.

If that's a big butt, then, whoo-ee, baby!

His safety-conscious brain just blew a fuse.

Snakes, and gaters, and mudbugs, oh my

Three days later, Granny awakened Rachel and Beau at dawn for an early, multi-purpose expedition into the swamps. To gather duck eggs. Dig up wild endive. Pick blackberries. And in Beau's case, to shoot a rabbit or two for a special adaptation of a traditional Cajun dish, which they'd named "Hoppin' Jampalaya." *Yeech!* It was Beau's favorite, and today was his twenty-first birthday.

Peeping out the window, Rachel gasped over what must be a routine ritual for those living here, but a spectacular sight for a newcomer like her. The dark predawn skies began to pale slowly to a grayish-blue, then suddenly burst forth with bright blue as the new day came on fast, like the flash of a camera's bulb. All the wading birds—egrets, ibises, herons, and many others—came up out of their roosts in whooshy clouds, searching for places to feed. The morning sounds of the bayou, especially the myriad of birdsongs, filled the air.

Rachel showered and got her eyes open with a mug of *café au lait*, Granny style, which involved a cup of hot milk, half of which was heavy cream, topped with a good amount of strong chicory coffee. If she wasn't careful, she was going to have to invest in an exercise machine.

Not!

Something would have to be done, though, because here came Granny with plates of that popular Cajun sausage, *boudin*, poached eggs, toasted and buttered homemade bread, and reconstituted orange juice. In the background, "*Jolé Blon*" played on a local radio station. Rachel recognized the song, in this case sung by the popular group Beau Soleil, because her cousin had been teaching her about the sometimes-rowdy, sometimes-poignant Cajun music which was particular to this region. Granny put one plate in front of Beau and another in front of Rachel, but made sure she patted her on the shoulder as had become her custom, as if Rachel needed reassurance of her grandmother's continued presence in her life.

"So, what are you doing for your birthday?" Rachel asked Beau when she was halfway through her delicious meal. Granny had sat down at the table with them, with smaller portions of everything.

"You mean *after* he comes out with us this mornin', and *after* he eats his birthday dinner this evenin'?" Granny interjected before Beau had a chance to answer.

"I wanna go to The Swamp Shack t'night. Listen to some good Cajun music." He gave Rachel a pointed look at that last. "Do a little dancin'. Have my first legal drink, now that I'm twenty-one."

"Swampy's? That honky-tonk over in Houma?" Granny exclaimed indignantly. "You ain't gonna *chank-a-chank*. No, you ain't."

"Now, Granny, I dint say nothin' 'bout no bar hopping. Jist one place, and it ain't a bad place, either."

"You doan go diggin' for gold in an outhouse."

"Who's lookin' for gold? Not me. And I ain't lookin' for no wife, either, if thass what yer hintin' at."

"Nothin' but trouble in those booze clubs."

"Rachel's goin' with me."

"I am?"

"Yep, sorta a birthday present to me," he replied with a wink at her. If he only knew how ridiculous he looked. His mullet hairdo in the morning resembled a haystack that had been caught in a windstorm.

"Well, I don't know," Rachel said. "I have to go over to Remy LeDeux's houseboat this afternoon and meet with the contractor about the skylight. Plus, Charmaine and I need to pick out some upholstery fabrics for her spa."

"We wouldn't go 'til about nine o'clock. You have plenty of time," Beau pleaded.

"I don't like you associatin' with them LeDeuxs, no, I don't. Bad company, for sure. Especially that Remy. He's trouble, girl. I can feel it in my bones."

"I'm *working* for them. That's all it is. Work," Rachel said, even if it felt like a lie. "Besides, I like Charmaine."

"Her mother was a stripper," Granny pointed out.

"So? My mother wasn't any better."

Granny made a harrumphing sound, not a concession, but not agreement, either.

"Granny, I haven't even seen Remy since I originally signed on to do the work three days ago. He's out of town, I think."

Just then, his 'copter flew over, real low, as if announcing his return, almost as if he said, up close and personal, "Here I am, ready or not."

Rachel groaned.

Her grandmother arched her eyebrows in a gloating fashion.

Beau let out a hoot of laughter.

Rachel probably should have surrendered to her grandmother's wishes regarding the LeDeuxs, as irrational as her prejudices against them seemed to be. But, dammit, all her life she'd tried to be good, to live up to other people's expectations—potential adoptive parents, David, everyone, really. Time for her to live by her own standards. To thine own self be true, for a change.

By seven A.M., the temperature and humidity already soared. Rachel's long-sleeved blouse stuck to her back and rivulets of sweat ran down behind her thighs in her hot jeans as she and Beau followed her grandmother down a path. Rachel was too much of a coward to wear shorts in an area where mosquitoes the size of golf balls loved nothing more than performing kamikaze maneuvers on virgin flesh. Granny claimed the Avon Skin So Soft soap in the bathroom was a good-enough bug repellent for anyone. Maybe so. Rachel recalled hearing years ago that Skin So Soft, originally just bath oil, became better known by word-of-mouth as an insecticide than a beauty product; even hunters and fishermen applied it liberally. Instead of being appalled, Avon jumped on the bandwagon, and began to market that asset, too.

Rachel's attire was intended as protection from bugs, but she also harbored a healthy fear of snakes popping out of nowhere, taking one look at her bare skin, and announcing loudly in reptile language, "Party!"

Her grandmother carried a big basket over one arm, Rachel carried a blue-and-white enamel bucket, and Beau carried a rifle. The path they walked on was pretty wide and clear, but occasionally a bush or tree branch had to be brushed aside. Steam rose off the lush vegetation as a new day began.

It really was another world here—an everchanging other world. Overhead the clouds swirled and writhed incessantly from the high humidity, a beautiful phenomenon distinctive to the region. Here, the colors, the smells, the tastes, the feel—everything was to the nth degree. Never just red, but bright red. Not blue, but vivid blue, or crystal blue, or dark as midnight blue. A Garden of Eden in many ways.

Oddly, without effort, Granny's property fell into perfect compliance with Feng Shui principles, mainly because no one had interfered with the natural flora and fauna. Nature provided its own balance of contrasting elements. Even inside her rustic home, earthy browns, beiges and tans provided a harmony that decorators worked hard to achieve.

They reached their destination.

The Mommy and Daddy ducks swam in the middle of the stream, nibbling on watermeal—tiny green dots floating atop the water—when they snuck up on the nest. Granny quickly filched five of the eggs, leaving one "for luck," and placed them carefully in her endive-lined basket. She'd dug up the bunches of endive with a special pronged tool. Beau kept guard the whole time. Snakes and other animals apparently craved eggs.

"Duck eggs make the bestest vinegar cake," Granny proclaimed, smacking her lips.

Next, they picked blackberries 'til their tummies were full, their hands stained, and the bucket overflowing. Then they sat down on several big boulders by the stream at Granny's insistence because she was short of breath. Nearby a possum dug in the moist soil of the bank, searching for grubs, Rachel supposed.

"Will you make a pie with these?" Rachel asked, glancing down at the bucket of berries.

"Nope. Gonna make preserves this time. Gotta replenish my supply. Nothin' like blackberry jam on warm bread on a blustery, cold winter day."

Rachel couldn't imagine any day in Louisiana, even wintertime, being cold. As to her grandmother's supplies, well, holy cow! She'd shown Rachel her root cellar several days ago which had floor-to-low-ceiling shelves filled with jars of everything from preserved fruit to chow-chow to pickled pigs' feet to okra—lots of okra. Besides that, a battery-operated box freezer down there was half-full with white paper–wrapped native fish, wild game, pork in every variety—chops, roasts, hams, bacon, scrapple, souse— turkey, chickens, even alligator and snake. Yes, snake, which Granny said tasted just like chicken when sautéed with butter, to which Rachel had replied, "I'll never know."

A sudden question occurred to her. "Granny, are you and Beau able to get by on your own garden and animals, supplemented by hunting and fishing and egg hunting and berry picking?"

Granny shrugged. "Pretty much. I get a small Social Security check from Uncle Sam since Justin and me usta sell our sugar to the coop, and they took out the taxes. Thass enuf fer us to get by, 'long with Beau's fur sales. Plus, he sells the meat to them hoity-toity restaurants in Naw'lins where peoples pay big money to eat such lowdown meats as possum and squirrel."

"I haven't noticed you off trapping lately," Rachel said to Beau.

"Trappin's best in the winter when the pelts are thicker,"

he answered. "Won't be startin' up again fer another two months or so."

Thank God! I'll be long gone by then.

At first, Rachel had pitied her grandmother and Beau, to be living in such a primitive way, at what appeared mere subsistence level to her, but she realized now that she'd been wrong. They met their own needs by working hard. They took from the land but treated it with respect. Except for a few extravagances—like the television and satellite dish so that Granny could watch her soaps and *Emeril Live*, and Beau could watch the Nascar races—a must here in the South—they had everything to make them happy, or at least content. It was not a bad life. Really.

And that made Rachel wonder about her own life. She'd worked so hard since she graduated from college a decade ago. For what? Money? Success? Self-satisfaction?

Was she happy?

Well, yes, to some extent. She did enjoy decorating, especially the Feng Shui aspects of it. And she took pride in her work. As to success? If money was any indicator, she was fairly successful.

Bottom line, *Am I really happy?*

Not totally, was her immediate answer.

She was only now beginning to realize why. It was family, pure and simple. Oh, not family as defined by babies and all that. Her leaving David was about his autocratic decision-making, not the baby issue itself. But she missed being part of a family, her adoptive parents having died six months apart when she was a senior in college. She'd never experienced family life as a child. That made her wonder if she really did yearn to have a family of her own, including babies. Hmmm. Something to think about.

The oddest thing happened then. Into her head flashed an image of a little boy with black hair and dark Cajun eyes, playing with, of all things, a pet alligator.

Quickly, Rachel shook her head from side to side to rid herself of the ridiculous, outrageous, out-of-the-question notion. Because there was no doubt in her mind at all. The little boy she'd just seen belonged to Remy LeDeux.

"Whass a matter? Got a bug in yer ear?" Beau asked.

Rachel realized she was still shaking her head. "No, just daydreaming."

"'Bout that Remy LeDeux, no doubt," Granny griped.

"I was picturing fabric samples in my head," Rachel lied.

She couldn't fool Granny. "Whass the world comin' to when a Fortier goes all knock-kneed and wooly-headed over a LeDeux?"

Me? Knock-kneed and wooly-headed? That is just swell.

"Time to go shoot us some dinner," Beau said, standing up and reaching for his rifle.

Oh, God, am I really going to watch someone kill a little bunny rabbit? Hah! Not if I can help it! "Just a minute, Beau. I was wondering, uh, let's make a bargain here. If you'll forego the rabbit hunting today, I'll make you the best five-cheese macaroni and cheese you've ever tasted in all your life, topped off with a *crème caramel* for dessert."

Beau looked interested, but he hesitated. "Don't suppose you'd agree to go to The Swamp Shack with me tonight, as a little added *lagniappe*." Rachel knew even before coming to Louisiana that *lagniappe* was the old French custom of merchants tossing in a little something extra for a customer. Like a baker giving a patron thirteen donuts, instead of a dozen.

"How many cheeses did you say was in that dish?" Granny asked. "I ever was partial to cheese. And caramel."

Rachel looked at Beau, who practically gloated.

"Swampy's, it is," she agreed.

Rachel could swear she heard laughter in her head.

Honky-tonk angel, or whatever

Remy was in the mood for a good time tonight.

He sat at a round ringside table with Luc, Sylvie, Charmaine and one of his newfound friends from the DEA, Larry Ellis, who couldn't stop gawking at Charmaine's chest in a low-cut, glow-in-the dark, sparkly T-shirt which quoted a suggestive hairdresser logo, FLIP THAT! You'd think Larry had never witnessed the effects of a push-up bra before.

Remy had worked hard all week, and he needed a little R&R. The beer went down smooth and cold, the company warmed his soul, and the music . . . well, who couldn't be happy when good Cajun music played on the jukebox?

René would be here soon with his group to provide some live entertainment. He couldn't wait. The Swamp Rats were a local legend. The place was especially crowded tonight, anticipating an encore of The Swamp Rats' renowned low-down Cajun music, mixed in with a little zydeco. René should have been here hours ago, but the wedding party had been held up by rain at the photo shoot. His brother had asked Remy to go over to his apartment and grab a change of clothes and his accordion.

A slow rendition of "Cajun Born" was playing now, and Luc stood, holding out a hand for Sylvie. They'd been married four years now, but you'd never know it the way they looked at each other. Sylvie looped her arms around Luc's neck. Luc looped his hands around her waist, then tugged hard so they were flush against each other. Their dancing amounted to little more than swaying from side to side, but, man oh man, it was the best dancing Remy had ever seen. The whole time they just stared into each other's eyes, little smiles on their lips.

Remy's chest walls tightened with a fierce yearning.

If only I . . .

What if . . .

Are soulmates fated or . . .

These half-thoughts drifted through Remy's mind as he struggled to understand his emotions. It had taken him three full days to wipe one redheaded witch from his mind, and he'd succeeded, dammit. Enough! It was Saturday night. No time to be sappy.

Just then, someone pulled the plug on the jukebox. In the stunned silence, everyone turned toward the front door where a man in a tuxedo, Clarence Dubois, let out a wild Rebel yell, then pulled his bride through the door with him; he carried a guitar in the other hand. His ushers, who also happened to be former band members, followed, dancing in a snakelike fashion up to the small stage, already singing and playing their instruments—fiddles, accordions, trumpets, *frottoirs*, which were over-the-shoulder washboards. A loud, rowdy rendition of "Sugar Bee" filled the air. René, still in a tux, like the rest of the party, played a mean accordion. He waved as he snaked by.

Once on the stage, one of the band members sank down to a piano stool. They immediately segued into "Colinda," which the groom sang to his bride, whom he'd brought up onto the stage with him. It was an old song, and just a coincidence that the bride's name happened to be Colinda, too. When he crooned, "My Colinda," it was as if he'd written the song himself for his very own sweetheart.

The crowd sang along with the band, clapping to the beat of the music. Remy tipped back his chair, took a swig from his frosty long-neck bottle of Dixie beer, and scanned the large room. It was always a good idea to keep an eye out for strangers, suspicious characters who might be in the area selling drugs, looking for connections, that kind of thing. The bayou had an extensive grapevine and its inhabitants were aware of any newcomers to the area. Still, best that he be on his toes, considering his job.

As he quickly scrutinized the room, his visual search snagged on a woman in a red dress, standing near the bar. Then shot right back in a double take of enormous magnitude.

It was Rachel Fortier, with her cousin Beau, who was hitting on some chick in tight jeans and a push-up bra, the attire du jour tonight, it would seem. But the push-up bra ladies had nothing on Rachel, who wore a short, skintight dress of hotter-than-sin red with only thin spaghetti straps holding it up. Her red hair billowed out around her, down her back and over her bare shoulders, held off her face slightly by barrettes on each side. Her high-heeled sandals made her taller than usual. She was overdressed for this crowd by a Yankee mile, but who the hell cared. She looked like pure temptation—the quintessential Eve in the Garden of Eden. He was no Adam, but he hot damn suspected he was about to bite the apple.

Remy stood abruptly, almost knocking over his chair.

"Where are you going?" Luc asked. "The band's just starting."

"Are you sick?" Sylvie inquired. "You look a little odd."

"I know that look, and it ain't odd," Charmaine commented and took a long swig of her highball.

Ellis was still on another planet over Charmaine's boobs.

As he walked back toward the bar, the band ended one song and immediately broke into "Lady in Red." As far from Cajun music as any band could get. Obviously, they saw where he headed. René—*blast his hide*—sang and laughed at the same time.

All the people in the bar craned their necks to see where such a lady in red could be. They quickly found her. Sure as sunshine, Rachel was going to be deluged within moments by hordes of men, asking her to dance—and other things.

Rachel looked as if she'd like to sink into the floor with embarrassment over all the attention she garnered. In fact, she turned on her heels and was about to flee when he grabbed her upper arm and pulled her to a halt.

"Whoa, *chère*, where are you off to in such a hurry?"

"I've got to get out of here."

If he was a smart man, he would escort her to her car and say, "So long, sugar." If he was a smart man, he would stop ogling all that bare skin. If he was a smart man, his heart would slow down to a mild roar. If he was a smart man, he wouldn't be so freakin' happy to see this woman, who was either a witch sent by Satan to bedevil him, or an angel sent by God or St. Jude as reward for some long-ago good deed.

Remy—obviously not a smart man—said in a voice so husky he barely recognized himself, "Don't go, angel."

Chapter 8

What was I thinking?

Rachel stood frozen in place, mortified, as the band played "Lady in Red," and everyone looked at her. Even Remy seemed to be in total shock.

The dress, which clung to her body like static electricity, didn't even belong to her. It was one of Jill's castoffs; Jill must have slipped it in her suitcase as a practical joke, to go along with her husband's REDHOT loaner truck. Rachel never wore red, not with her red hair—too much of an attention grabber. And she never, ever wore such revealing clothing—not with the body issues she harbored under David's exercise regimen. Her only excuse was that she'd been feeling more independent of late, breaking away from her old please-everyone-but-me mode. Wearing the dress had been an act of rebellion, in a way. Or stupidity.

Remy finally shook himself out of his stupor and tugged on her arm, steering her into a quieter corridor, which led to a billiard room. Meanwhile, the band continued to play that horrible song.

"Aliens must have invaded my brain," she said on a moan of disgust. She sagged against the wall and Remy leaned over her with an arm braced above her head, placing his face far too close to hers in an attempt to hear her words.

"Why is that?"

"This dress." She waved a hand downward to illustrate.

"Honey, you look hot in that dress."

She didn't even pretend to misread his words. "I hope you don't think that's a compliment."

He ran a forefinger under one spaghetti strap, from shoulder to bodice and said, "Definitely a compliment."

She shouldn't have been pleased. She shouldn't find the mere brush of the back of his fingertip erotic. She shouldn't be standing here, plastered to the wall like a swooning twit, but she seemed unable to move.

"The dress is great, but it's what's inside that blows my mind."

Oh, my! "It doesn't belong to me—the dress, I mean." *That was a sparkling bit of irrelevancy, Ms. Twit.*

"You smell like heaven."

It's Granny's 'Skin So Soft' soap. It repels insects." *Where did my brain go? Twit, twit, twit.*

He grinned. "It's doing a lousy job of repelling me." Then he immediately turned serious. "What are we going to do, babe?"

"About what?" *Like I don't know.*

"Us."

Oh, my! Again. "There is no 'us,' Remy."

"I thought I was over you."

Me, too. "There was nothing to get over."

"Three days away, total cure, then one gander at you in that kiss-me-quick red dress, and I'm a goner. What are you doing to me?"

"What am I doing to you? That's a good one! What are you doing to me?"

He smiled that slow, sexy grin of his to show his masculine satisfaction that he did something to her. She ought to smack that grin right off. Or kiss it off.

Their conversation halted momentarily with the passage of three women in their mid-twenties who headed toward the pool room. They were big haired, big breasted and poured into their jeans. Each of them gave Remy a very interested once-over, but their faces went immediately blank when he turned slightly and they saw the other side of his face.

"Don't you dare go pitying me. Don't you dare," Remy practically hissed once they had passed.

"They're blind. Why can't they see what I see?"

"Maybe you're the one who's blind." Remy's voice was husky as he wiped the tears about to overflow her eyes.

Just then, the band abruptly ended "Lady in Red" and someone in the band began to sing loud and clear, "Reeeeemmmmy! Oh, Remy!" In the background, the band played a soft instrumental version of that old Hank Williams' song, "Jambalaya."

"Huh?" Rachel frowned. Who would be calling for Remy, from the band, no less? They couldn't even see him back here.

"Ooooh, Remy. Come here, cowboy. And bring the lady in red with you. Time for a first dance—'Lady in Red' meets 'Loo-zee-anna Man.' Time for a good ol' Cajun boy to show the city girl how it's done. What do you think, folks?"

"It's my brother René," Remy said on a moan.

"He has a warped sense of humor."

"For sure."

The crowd clapped and cheered, "Remy, Remy, Remy!" along with the man who started it all, alternating with, "Lady in Red, Louisiana Man... Remy, Lady, Remy, Lady..."

"I'm going to kill him," Remy said.

"Can I help?"

"We better go out there, or he'll keep it up." Remy stepped back from her, and already she missed his body heat.

"Can't we just sneak out?"

"Not without being seen."

He took her hand and pulled her toward the end of the corridor that opened into the tavern itself.

She walked in front of Remy, but she glanced back over her shoulder at one point to make sure he wasn't looking at her butt in the tight dress.

Yep, he was looking at her butt in the tight dress.

When she turned back around, a huge bald guy with a mustache and one gold loop earring blocked their way. He held out a tray of shot glasses. Some of them held raw oysters, one per glass, the others some type of liquor.

"Hey, Gator, what's up?" Remy asked, looked pointedly at the big guy with the tray of drinks—presumably the bartender.

"Luc sent them for you. Said you'll probably need them since René is in rare form tonight."

"Oyster shooters?"

"Yep, said they worked for him and Sylvie. I know for a fact they did. I was here that night." He rolled his eyes at Rachel to illustrate his point, which she missed.

"Do you like raw oysters?" Remy asked her.

"They're okay."

"These have Cajun lightning on them. Tabasco sauce. They're so hot you need a wet chaser—in this case one hundred–proof pure bourbon." He illustrated by tilting his head back, downing the oyster, then immediately following it with the shot of bourbon. "Whoo!" he said, shaking his head briskly from side to side.

Tentatively, Rachel did the same thing, and, holy smoke, she should have listened to Remy's warning. It felt like liquid fire going down her throat, to her stomach, and out to all her extremities—both the tabasco and the bourbon. She said, "Whoo!" as well, and had to hold onto Remy's arm because she suddenly felt woozy.

"There they are," René yelled out to the crowd, which began clapping. "Come on, you two. You can't hide from us."

She hadn't realized they were visible to the stage from here. "I think I need more fortification." Rachel reached for another set of shot glasses.

Remy did the same.

"Oh, my God," she choked out. If one oyster shooter had her insides boiling, this second one had every hair on her body standing on end. She could swear all the muscles in her legs had turned to jelly, as well.

"Hot damn!" was Remy's response to the second set of drinks. Then he said, "Let's get this over with."

"Okay, but you go first. No more ogling my butt."

"Oh, heck!" He grinned from ear to ear.

By the time they reached the small dance floor, the band was well into "Louisiana Man." René didn't skip a beat when he said into the microphone, "Hi, Remy."

Rachel could swear Remy told his brother to do something very vulgar to himself with his accordion, which was unlike Remy. He usually exuded excessive politeness around women. He probably thought she couldn't hear under the strain of the booze buzz that assailed her.

Remy turned toward her, opening his arms in invitation. Most men in her experience either couldn't dance or didn't do it well, and definitely didn't like dancing, considering it a useless exercise.

"Can you dance?" she asked.

"Darlin', I'm Cajun," he said, as if that was answer enough.

She put her hands on his shoulders. He put his hands on her waist. And Remy soon proved that Cajun and dancing went hand in hand. Oh, he wasn't flamboyant or anything. Just smooth. So smooth that she wasn't even self-conscious anymore about how she looked or people staring at them or hooting encouragement to Remy or whether her butt resembled a caboose in the slut dress. All she was aware of was the soft movement of their hips, the warm heat which suffused her body—which had almost nothing at all to do with liquor—and the absolute rightness of her being in his embrace. She hadn't even noticed when the bride and groom, Luc and his wife, Charmaine and some man who kept gawking at Charmaine's chest and a whole lot of other people joined them on the dance floor.

"You weren't lying. You *are* a good dancer," she said, tilting her head back to see him better.

Remy laughed. "We haven't started dancing yet, *chère*."

"What do you call this?"

He thought for a long moment, as if unsure whether to say what he really thought. Then he pulled out one of those slow, sexy grins of his. "Foreplay."

She tripped on her feet. Probably the alcohol buzz. Or the Remy buzz.

"So, you plied me with liquor to seduce me."

"Oh, no! You're not laying that one on me. *You* are the one seducing me."

Her mouth dropped open with indignation, but she never had a chance to sputter out a reply because the rogue yanked her closer, took her right hand in his left one, and spun her around, emerging into a lively Cajun two-step with other couples in the room.

Remy was a big man, at least six-foot-two, but he was light on his feet. And he had rhythm. Why that should arouse her was a puzzle. But she was.

When "Louisiana Man" ended and the band segued smoothly into "*Cochon de Lait*," Remy smiled at her, as if asking if she wanted to continue. She smiled back. When he leaned down to place his cheek against hers, she turned her face at the last moment so that his disfigured side pressed against her cheek.

He gasped softly at her action, stiffened, then relaxed. "Have you ever heard of St. Jude?" he murmured against her ear. "I swear, you two are conspiring against me."

After that, they danced several more sets in a row. "Big Mamou." "Zydeco Gris Gris." "Louisiana Saturday Night." "*Je Veux Me Marier.*" Sometimes they danced without their bodies touching, but mostly Remy held her pressed against him shoulders to groin. Rachel felt his heart beating against hers and relished the sweetness of life. She was alive and in this time and place with this man—this *healthy* man if his rapid heartbeat was any indication.

"Do you go dancing often?" she asked breathlessly.

"No."

Well, that was blunt. "When was the last time?"

"I can't remember."

"Seriously?"

"I don't go out much, Rachel. I'm only here tonight because my brother René is back in town for the weekend. He's an environmental lobbyist in Washington."

Well, that was interesting, and surprising, that the extremely handsome man on the stage with the wild sense of humor worked in such a sober profession. But that was beside the point. "C'mon, Remy, I can't picture you staying home, celibate and lonely. I imagine you go out with lots of women. And the way you dance, you must have lots of practice."

"I never said anything about being celibate," he said, lifting his chin in defense. "But I haven't had a date in months, and that's the truth."

Rachel snuggled up against him then, pleased for some odd reason that he didn't date much. Remy reciprocated by running the flats of both his hands up and down her back before settling them on her hips.

She loved that he was taller than she was, even in high heels. She loved the way they fit so well together. She loved the way his dark hair curled on the back of his neck, in need of a haircut. She loved the smell of his skin, a male scent unique to Remy, discernible even through his soap and aftershave. She loved the way he was so polite when he bumped into another couple. She loved the way his dark eyes were alternately somber and twinkling as he gazed at her. She loved the way his long fingers held hers firmly and possessively. She loved his disfigured face . . . and the pain he tried to hide. She loved how he was scared to death by what was happening between them.

In fact, she was beginning to love way too much about this man. And, truth be told, she was scared, too.

The band took a break then, and Remy led her, fingers intertwined, to a round table at the edge of the dance floor. Luc and his half-sister Charmaine greeted her warmly. Remy introduced Rachel to Luc's wife Sylvie, who was dark haired, lovely, and clearly besotted with her husband—who wouldn't be with those teasing eyes?—and to a man named Larry Ellis from D.C., a client of Remy's charter helicopter business, or something like that. Then, too, his other brother René came up, looped an arm around hers and Remy's shoulders, and said, "Aren't you going to introduce me to this lady, bro?"

"This rat is my brother, René," Remy said with mock reluctance. "And this is my, uh, friend, Rachel Fortier."

"Rachel is 'doing' Remy," Charmaine announced. "And me, too."

"I wouldn't mind her doing us, too," Luc interjected, and winced in an exaggerated fashion when Sylvie elbowed him.

"I beg your pardon," René choked out. "Are you a . . . hooker?"

Hah! No wonder he thinks that, with me in this hooker dress!

"Charmaine is being deliberately crude," Remy explained. "Rachel is a decorator. She's going to Feng Shui my houseboat and Charmaine's spa. So, watch your mouth, René."

René gave Rachel a closer look, his dark eyes dancing with mischief. "My apologies for jumping to conclusions," René said. Then he turned his attention to Remy. "Feng

Shui? A houseboat? Isn't Feng Shui that weirdo decorating crap? *Mon Dieu,* I have been gone much too long."

Rachel bristled at René's coarse description of her profession, but then decided a bar wasn't the place for arguing.

Remy shoved a change of clothing into the hands of René who still wore his suspendered tuxedo pants and cummerbund. René left for the men's room and soon came back wearing a plaid shirt, leather vest, jeans, a jaunty, low-crowned palmetto hat and cowboy boots. He looked devastatingly handsome in both outfits, Rachel had to admit, but not as good as Remy, of course.

They all sat about the table chatting then. Rachel listened, sipping the whole while at a cool glass of white wine which someone had placed in front of her. The men drank from long-necked bottles of beer.

At their table and all around them, Rachel relished the unique Cajun patois dialect which peppered much of the conversation. It was archaic French mixed in with Spanish, English, German, African and Native American, all combined to give a musical lilt to the speech. Rachel had read that at one time the Cajun people had been forbidden to speak their language in public schools. Thank goodness they hadn't lost their heritage totally.

At first, Rachel remained quiet as the three brothers and Charmaine caught up on all the news. Apparently, René hadn't been back in town for several months. He brought them up to date on his environmental concerns and what was being done about it. "Your mother is being surprisingly helpful," René said to Sylvie. "No doubt due to your help, darlin'." Inez Breaux-Fontaine, Sylvie's mother, was a U.S. Congresswoman from Louisiana who usually befriended big oil interests, not the "tree huggers." Remy spoke circumspectly about a new, exciting contract he'd just signed, though for the life of her Rachel couldn't figure out exactly what it entailed. Luc talked about some interesting cases he'd represented in court recently, including the fact that he'd filed a class-action suit on behalf of some alligators against an industrial waste authority—and won. Sylvie, who appeared a bit shy, volunteered that her work as a chemist still involved continued studies of a love potion, of all things. And Charmaine regaled them with stories of her four ex-husbands and about a man who came to her health spa this week, requesting a colon cleansing. "As if!" in her words.

What an interesting group of people! Rachel thought. A pilot, a lawyer, an environmentalist/musician, a spa owner, and a chemist all in one family.

And that's what intrigued her most of all. The *family.* Even as they talked over one another, teased, sniped, and argued, it was clear that they had deep love for each other, especially the three brothers. Rachel envied that experience fiercely.

Their attention turned to Rachel. Remy's hand still held hers, and he squeezed slightly. "Don't be intimidated by my family. I'll protect you," he whispered in her ear.

His breath in her ear caused slingshots of erotic darts to ricochet throughout her body, and Rachel wondered who was going to protect her from Remy. When her eyes connected with his, he winked at her, and Rachel felt the wink all the way down to her toes. He knew exactly what effect he had on her, and he liked it. Well, she liked it, too. A lot.

She looked up to see everyone grinning at her and Remy, except for the D.C. guy who was gazing at Charmaine's chest.

Luc said, "Tante Lulu gave Remy a hope chest," as if that had anything to do with them.

Everyone nodded.

"Dum-dum-dee-dum," René hummed.

That made Rachel sit up straighter. *Dum-dum-dee-dum* she did understand. These people couldn't possibly think she and Remy had marriage on the horizon. Talk about premature! They hadn't even done . . . well, *anything*. Yet. And maybe they never would. But, hot damn, the prospect of doing *anything* with Remy sent shivers down her spine, and other places, too.

"Are you cold?" Remy drew her closer to his body heat.

"Huh?"

"You were shivering."

"Not from the cold."

He grinned at that. The louse.

Beau walked up then with a giggling blonde Barbie attached to his hip, their arms over each other's shoulders. "Mary Sue and I wanna go to a club the other side of town. Any chance you could give my cousin a ride home in her truck?" Beau asked Remy, the whole time batting his eyelashes at Rachel imploringly. "Rachel drove me over here, but I'm not sure she knows the way home in the dark."

"Sure thing," Remy answered too quickly before Rachel could even get out her, "Oh, I don't think that's a good idea."

"Thanks, Remy, I owe you, bud," Beau said and rushed off before she could grab him by his mullet and wring his neck. "You're the best, cuz," he called back to Rachel.

Mary Sue just giggled as a departing goodbye.

Rachel groaned inwardly. It was one thing to shiver around Remy in the safety of a crowded room, quite another to shiver alone with him in a cozy private car—uh, truck.

As if on cue, René once again hummed, "Dum-dum-dee-dum!"

Sweet temptation

Remy drove the long way home.

Surprise, surprise!

He was going to relish the sight, the sound, the smell of Rachel Fortier sitting next to him for as long as he could. Forget about the fact that she sat stiff as a board as far away as possible on the bench seat of her truck.

"Relax, Rachel, I'm not going to jump your bones." *Not yet, anyhow.* In truth, he was the one feeling as REDHOT as her vanity license plate.

She turned slowly to look at him. "What if I wanted you to?" Immediately, she clapped a hand over her mouth in horror. "I must be drunker than I thought."

Okay, maybe she's a little REDHOT, too. If I'm lucky. "You're not drunk, baby. Just a little tipsy. Here, breathe in some of this fresh air," he said, lowering the electric windows. What he thought was, *Laissez les bon temps rouler. Let the good times roll.*

She did just that, closing her eyes and leaning her head back against the seat rest, which in turn caused her breasts to arch outward while she breathed deeply, in and out.

He felt as if he'd been given an electric shock to his groin—a delicious electric shock. That in-and-out business was giving him ideas. In and out. In and out. *God, I'm turning into a lech with these hair-trigger hard-ons.*

"What's hard?" she murmured, with her eyes still closed.

For the love of St. Jude! I must have been thinking aloud. "Nothing, honey. Not a thing."

For a while they were quiet, enjoying the cool breeze through the open windows and the silence of the night. The back roads of Louisiana were like a trip back in time. They passed roadside diners and old vintage gas stations. Weathered barns still had painted signs advertising soda pop. Some of them were even in French.

"You have a nice family, Remy," Rachel remarked all of a sudden. "You should be thankful."

"I don't know about nice. Most times they're royal pains in the patoot."

"It's obvious how much you all care about each other."

"I suppose. But then, we had to be close, growing up with the father we did. Our mother died when we were pretty young, and Luc, being the oldest, pretty much raised me and René."

She opened her eyes and turned toward him, her face against the head rest. "Why didn't your father take on that role?"

"Because he was an alcoholic, greedy, whoring, abusive, mean bastard." For once, he didn't take back his coarse words.

Rachel homed in on one word. "Abusive?"

"Mostly toward Luc. Our big brother kept us hidden away and took the beatings whenever Dad caught up with him."

"Granny said Valcour LeDeux was an oil man."

Remy nodded. "Yeah, later he was, when oil was discovered on some family property. Before that, we lived in one rusted-out trailer after another. But that's enough about me. Have you talked with your ex since you've been here?"

Remy hadn't intended to ask Rachel about her former lover. He'd wondered, but wouldn't have actually asked the question unless he was a little bit tipsy, too. He slowed down the truck, just in case.

"Actually, I did talk to David. Today, in fact. He's been bugging two of my best friends back home. So, I called to tell him to lay off."

That's all she said. Nothing more. Like that was any kind of an answer. "So?" he prodded.

"So?" she responded.

"So, what did you say, and what did he say?"

She smiled in a way that said it really wasn't any of his business. It wasn't. On the other hand, hell, yes, it was. He half expected her not to respond, but she did. "He said he was sorry, please come back, and make sure I bring back that, um, an object that I mistakenly took with me."

"That's all?"

"Yep."

"He didn't even tell you he loved you?"

Her eyes widened with surprise. He could see that even in the darkened car, the only light coming from the full moon and his headlights. "No, Remy, he didn't, now that you mention it."

"Dumbass." Remy didn't apologize for that word, either.

"The contractor is going to install your skylight next week," she informed him, clearly wanting to change the subject. That was okay. He'd learned what he needed to know.

"That's good. I'll be gone most of the week, but I expect that won't matter."

"No. At some point, I need to show you some fabric samples for the drapes and seat cushions and bedspread, but we can wait to see how the skylight looks first. I left the samples on your bedroom dresser if you want to look them over sometime."

"On the other hand, would you like to check out the houseboat *now*?" he asked, holding his breath.

She sat up, giving him her full attention.

He thought she would never answer. He prepared himself for the disappointment of her answer. He prayed as hard as a lapsed Catholic could pray in three seconds flat.

"Yes."

The voice in his head said, *You owe me bigtime, big boy.*

Chapter 9

Rock the boat, baby.

Remy stopped the truck along the road and kissed her right after she said "Yes." Lightly.

And he kissed her when he stopped the truck by his houseboat. Not so lightly.

He kissed her some more on the deck before he unlocked his door. Harder.

And he kissed her lots more once they entered the houseboat, before he even turned on the lights. Ravenously.

He probably pressed his advantage, thinking she might change her mind. No way, baby! This was the new Rachel Fortier, the one who made decisions based on what *she* wanted. The one who valued her own opinion of herself over everyone else's, the one who no longer strived to be everybody's "good girl." In fact, she was going to try damn hard tonight to be a bad girl.

Without preamble, he led her to his bedroom. All the dressers and loose furniture had been removed, except the bed, leaving extra space there now.

"Are you sure?" he asked tenderly.

How like this overly sensitive man to give her a second

chance to change her mind, even when he obviously wanted her to stay!

"I'm sure."

He nodded.

"How about you? Are you sure?"

He grinned, that slow, sexy grin that she'd come to love. "Guar-an-teed!"

She reached behind her to pull down her zipper when he put up a halting hand. "Let me," he urged huskily.

Was there anything more exciting to a woman than her being able to turn a man's voice husky like that? Maybe it was a learned talent some males cultivated. She didn't think so in Remy's case, but if so, God bless an experienced man.

"Just stand still and let me," he said, drawing the spaghetti straps of her dress down so that they lay loose over her upper arms. He used his fingertips then to trace the line of her shoulders, from her ears, down the sides of her neck and over her collarbones. Then he traced the line across her bodice, just above the swell of her breasts.

She could have swooned at the sweet sensations.

"You have beautiful skin. Like satin."

That was a stretch, but who was she to argue?

"Put your hands behind your neck. Please."

Oh, boy! What a vulnerable, completely erotic position to place myself in.

I think I like it.

He shifted a bit so their faces were level, and slowly placed his lips against hers—softly exploring at first, then more bold as his tongue glided into her parted lips. He tasted of bourbon and beer and hot searing arousal. While he kissed her, he reached around and unzipped her dress, undoing her strapless, lace bra.

When he drew back to look at her, her dress dropped to her waist, and he pulled her bra the rest of the way off, flipping it over his shoulder. Then he gasped.

She still held her hands clasped behind her neck. She had to hold onto something, for goodness sake! Rachel wasn't surprised by the gasp. While she had lots of issues about her body, her breasts had never been a concern. They were larger than average, and surprisingly uplifted and firm, considering their weight. Probably due, in part, to years of physical exercise, and good genes.

"I think I've died and gone to heaven," Remy murmured as he cupped them from underneath and lifted them even higher. Still holding them in his palms, he thumbed the nipples to sharp peaks.

She moaned softly at the instant streaks of pleasure that ricocheted out from them to all the important erotic zones in her body. There were lots of them, she discovered.

"Do you like that, *chère*?" he whispered as he continued to stroke the erect buds, now pinching and pulling on them as well.

She opened her eyes drowsily, unaware that she'd even closed them. Instead of answering his question, she said, "Take off your shirt. I want to see you, too."

He shook his head. "Not yet." He leaned forward and took one nipple in his mouth, sucking hard.

Hot liquid pooled between her legs, and she feared she might come. Luckily, he gave her breasts a temporary reprieve and shimmied her dress over her hips 'til it slid to the floor. She wore only lace bikinis and the high-heeled sandals.

"You look like one of those old Vargas pinups that used to run in Playboy magazine. Almost too perfect."

"Remy, I am not perfect. My hips are too wide, and my—"

"I know, your butt is too big," he finished for her, grinning the whole time.

"Exactly."

"Women don't see their bodies the way men do," he said, tugging her panties down to join her dress at her feet. "Believe me, from my view, your body is perfection." His voice couldn't get any huskier if he tried.

"David didn't think—"

He put the fingertips of one hand on her lips. "David was a blind schmuck."

She would have responded to the remark, except that Remy had sunk down to his knees in front of her and was examining the tight curls between her legs, with just the tips of his fingers.

"Red, too," he murmured.

"Yes, and I hate it," she said fiercely.

He laughed, and she felt his breath *there*.

Oh—my—God!

"You have no idea how much I am beginning to appreciate red hair." Then, he said the most outrageously titillating thing. "Spread, darlin'. Let's see how much fuel there is in this fire."

And she did. Where she got the nerve, she had no idea, but she spread her legs enough to give him access. When his fingers discovered the slickness of her desire for him, he made a grunting, male sound of satisfaction.

Remy inserted one long finger inside her, and she yelped with surprise, backing up a step. The backs of her knees hit the bed and she fell back abruptly onto the mattress. Remy's finger was no longer inside her, but he remained on his knees, planted firmly between her legs which he proceeded to spread even wider.

For the next hour—or what seemed like an hour, but was probably only minutes, Remy used his fingers and tongue and teeth to bring her to the brink of orgasm. Each time, he stopped and whispered soothing phrases to her, promising satisfaction if she could just let him do one more thing. Meanwhile, she keened with need and writhed from side to side.

Finally he used his thumb to vibrate rapidly over that engorged flesh where she craved his touch most. Over and over and over and over. Back and forth and back and forth and back and forth until her body was rigid with tension, her hips raised off the bed. Remy whispered, "Shhhh. Relax. Let it come." She wanted to hit him, or jump on him, or something. But then the tension broke, and she rode the cascading waves of pleasure that rose higher and higher before breaking, then lower and lower.

She lay on the mattress like a rag doll, legs spread, body sated. When she managed to open her eyes a crack, she saw that he stood over her, just watching her.

Yikes! I must look like a wanton. And there he stands, fully dressed. "You better have those clothes off in two seconds flat, buster, or I'm out of here."

He began to unbutton his shirt, slowly, while she watched. "Darlin', you're not leaving now, come hell or high water. You're mine till dawn."

Till dawn? Oh, my! "Is that a fact?"

"That's a fact."

Tit for tat

How could a man who'd fought in a war, suffered through seventeen operations, lived dangerously every time he hopped into his helicopter be so freakin' scared?

Remy was unbuttoning his shirt slowly. Very slowly. He wanted so badly to turn off the lights, but he knew Rachel wouldn't accept that after the way she'd exposed her body, with all her misplaced insecurities.

Insecurities. Yep, that's exactly what he had, too, but far more than she had and with better reason. Rachel had accepted his disfigured face, that was true, but half his chest, hip, belly, buttocks and thigh looked like raw meat. Repulsive, that's what he was. It's not that he'd never shown his naked body to other women in the past twelve years. Of course, he had. But Remy hadn't cared spit about any of them, much less their opinions. They could take him or leave him, and vice versa, as far as he was concerned. Rachel was different. He didn't want to blow it with her. Not this early in the game.

With a long sigh, he pulled his opened shirt out of his pants and shrugged it off.

Rachel had been leaning back on her elbows, watching him with a little Mona Lisa smile on her face. At first sight of the scars and twisted flesh on his chest, she sat up straighter. The smile disappeared.

"I don't suppose you'd let me dim the lights."

She shook her head slowly from side to side.

He toed off his boots, leaned down to pull off his socks, then straightened, undid his belt and slid open the zipper. "It's really bad, Rachel. *Really* bad."

"Do it," she demanded softly.

"Hey, babe, gotta warn you. This sideshow is definitely not one of *Playboy*'s seventeen all-time best turn-ons," he tried to joke. "In fact, you might say this will be an erotic buzz kill."

She looked angry all of a sudden and came smoothly off the bed to stand before him. "If I can subject my less-than-perfect body to your scrutiny, you can do the same for me. Was my big butt an *erotic buzz kill* for you?"

"No, but—"

With a soft growl of impatience, she reached for his waistband and began to tug both jeans and boxers down over his hips so they puddled at his feet. Luckily—or not so luckily—his penis, which had been at half-mast, was deflated at the moment. No shocks for her there.

Remy was no coward. He folded his arms over his chest and allowed her to examine his body in detail, walking all around, touching. On the outside, he probably appeared calm, even aloof, but inside he churned with apprehension.

He hoped she wouldn't throw up. A woman had actually done that one time. She had probably been drunk, too, but that was beside the point. His body had been the last straw to cause her to hurl.

Rachel completed her examination and stood directly in front of him, waiting 'til he made eye contact with her. Only then did she say, "Big fat deal, Remy."

Tears immediately misted his eyes, which he blinked away. Rachel saw his badly mangled body—she hadn't tried to hide that fact, thank God. But she *chose* to give the grotesque flesh little or no importance. How could that be? "It *is* a big deal, Rachel. To most people."

"I'm not most people, and it's about time you understood that. You have a few scars and discoloration. So what?" Before he could respond to that ridiculous statement, she looked pointedly down at his penis. Stroking it slightly with a forefinger from head to base, she asked, "Any damage here?"

His penis flexed and immediately started to grow. He shook his head. "None at all."

She arched her eyebrows at him. "Then, what are you waiting for, sailor? Let's rock this boat."

Ship of dreams

Rachel couldn't believe her nerve.

She'd never been brazen before. Never teased in the bedroom. Never used suggestive language. Never exposed her naked body for any length of time. Never taken the initiative in sex. In essence, she had always been a bit of a prude.

Not anymore.

Remy had been the catalyst that forced her to lose her inhibitions. My God, the pain he must have gone through to have sustained all that mangled flesh! It had taken everything she had to keep her face blank and her hands from shaking as she'd examined the scars in detail. She knew he watched her for signs of pity, something he seemed to deplore. Silly man! Caring about him and his suffering was not pity.

At her teasing challenge that they rock the boat—*How could I say such a crude thing?*—Remy just stared at her open mouthed for several seconds, stunned. Then that slow, sexy grin spread across his lips and he said, "Hold onto the oars, baby. Here comes a wave."

Before she could say "Man the lifeboats," Remy lunged for her, taking her by the waist, lifting her high off the floor, then throwing her back onto the mattress. He followed, landing on top of her.

"Your surfboard's caught in a sandbar," she teased. There was, in fact, a hard object pressed against her cleft.

"Not for long, honey," he said, jiggling his hips from side to side so that his "surfboard" fit better between her legs. He turned serious. "Thank you, Rachel."

"For what? I haven't done anything yet."

He chucked her playfully under the chin. "For not throwing up."

"Huh?" *Please, God, don't tell me some dingbat woman vomited when she looked at his body. No wonder he was so reticent about taking his clothes off.*

"Never mind." He braced his upper body on his elbows, bracketed her face with his hands, then placed his lips over hers gently, testing and adjusting to get the perfect fit. Obviously, the man took his kissing seriously.

"You're a really good kisser," she said against his mouth, when he had drawn back a mere hairsbreadth.

"How would you know? We've hardly kissed at all." He ran his mouth up her jawline to her ear and back again.

"All it took was 'The Kiss' for me to know how good of a kisser you are." She arched her neck to the side to give him better access.

"You think of it as 'The Kiss,' too?" he asked with surprise. "That first kiss of ours, I mean?" He resumed brushing his lips lightly over hers.

She nodded. "Whoo-ee, yes!"

He just smiled against her lips.

A smiley-kiss. Then she stopped thinking at all.

He kissed her and kissed her and kissed her . . . every way imaginable and some Rachel had never imagined. Men just didn't understand how much women enjoyed prolonged bouts of kissing. At least, most men didn't. They'd rather skip to the good stuff. To Rachel and a gazillion females through the ages, kissing was the good stuff, too.

When Remy finally began to move his attention down her body, Rachel said, "No!" She pressed hard against his chest to emphasize that she meant what she said.

"No?" His lips were slack and his eyes glazed with passion.

"Roll over on your back. I want to make love to you this time."

He exhaled visibly with relief. Apparently, he had thought she'd changed her mind about making love. No way! "Let me. Just this time, *chère.* I need to ease into somebody—*you*—touching my body."

He's still worried about me being repulsed by his body. Foolish man! "Okay, but I'm not leaving here tonight without touching you—all over."

He smiled. "You're not leaving tonight, period."

Now that is a tantalizing prospect.

"You have beautiful breasts," Remy murmured as he shifted to his side and rose to one elbow. Almost reverently, he traced their contours, observing how they grew firmer under his scrutiny and the nipples distended at the slightest touch. When he leaned forward to suckle her, she moaned and put a hand to his nape, holding him in place. With every rhythmic pull of his lips, she felt an answering tug between her legs. His right hand was lying flat over her tummy, and she sensed that he could feel the pulsing he had set up inside her. Then he moved to the other breast, which he suckled as well, alternating the sucking with flicks of his tongue.

When he began to go down on her again, Rachel slid her hips under his, taking him by surprise. Before he could grasp her intent, she had grasped his penis and was guiding him toward her.

"Enough, Remy. I want *you*. Now."

Rebelling, Remy sat back on his heels between her legs. "I hoped to prolong the foreplay, to make this first time special for you."

"Oh, Remy. It *will* be special . . . because it's you."

She led his hand to her moist cleft to show him she was ready for him. He ran a finger several times over the hard nub of flesh, which caused Rachel to about shoot off the bed with the almost too-intense pleasure.

Chuckling, he took her fingers off his blue-veined erection and began to guide himself into her body. Rachel would have liked to watch his face, or touch his chest, or wonder about the incredible ecstasy that seemed to be sweeping over her, but she did none of that. All her concentration was centered on this one thing: Remy about to fill her body.

He stopped suddenly and jerked his head in various directions around the bedroom, as if searching for something.

Now what?

"Where'd you put my bedside table? I need a condom. Quick."

She laughed, or as close to a laugh as she could come up with considering the pulsing he had ignited between her legs. "Don't worry. I'm on the pill."

"Well, some women worry about diseases and stuff. I'm okay, though. Not to worry."

"Remy, I'm not worried," she said, obviously amused by his nervous rambling. "Really."

"Thank God!" He plunged inside her effortlessly. For one long moment, complete silence filled the room, except for their soft breathing, the whir of the overhead fan, and the rhythmic lapping of the current against the houseboat outside. Life stood still, but for the movement of her inner muscles as they conformed in quick spasms to Remy's size, allowing him to inch in even further. She savored the feeling of fullness, of being filled almost beyond what was comfortable. She more than savored the sense of completeness their joining brought her, as if they were the only two people in the world who could fit together this well—as if they were meant to be.

Remy sensed her mood. "This is not just about sex, Rachel."

"I know," she said. "I know."

Then he moved.

And, God above! She'd heard people talk before about the world moving when they had sex, but she'd never really believed it. She did now.

When he pulled back, then ever-so-slowly filled her again, she felt waves of intoxication. Something important was happening here, her body told her. She bent her knees and spread her legs wider to accept him more deeply.

He grunted his approval.

Rachel leaned back on her elbows, wanting to see everything. *Everything.* The way he supported himself on straight arms on either side of her shoulders, arms highlighted by corded veins of tension. The way his mouth pressed together in concentration. The way his eyes held hers. The way he moved his hips against her expertly in a rhythm that was growing progressively faster.

She raised her buttocks up off the mattress and entered in the dance, matching him point for counterpoint. Already her inner muscles convulsed around him in preparation for the final cataclysm—to Remy's pleasure, she was sure, as indicated by his sharpened breathing.

"Oh, oh, oh . . . ," she moaned.

"Uh, uh, uh . . . ," he moaned.

Then he stopped and sat back on his heels between her legs, his penis only partially inside her.

"Nooooo," she wailed, trying to force him to resume the pace by bucking her hips against him.

"Shhhhh," he said. Before she had a chance to protest, he lifted her legs over his shoulders and began to pound her in earnest—the hard in-and-out strokes that caused her to cry out in bliss. She was losing control. In truth, this position had taken away her control totally, if she'd ever had it. Lying thus exposed, she had to allow Remy to do all the work.

When he placed his thumb over her clitoris and began to strum, at the same time pumping rapidly into her body, she lost it. Moaning, crying, yelling, she rode the crest of the most incredible orgasm of her life. Who knew—*who knew*—that the female body could feel so many agonizing, wonderful sensations at the same time? Who knew the pleasure exploding in her female parts could ripple out with such intensity to every other part of her body? Even her hair and toenails felt erotically charged.

And then she crashed.

Her breathing settled down a bit and her eyes unglazed. Only then did she look up to see Remy watching her closely. He hadn't yet come himself. When he saw that she was finally sated, he thrust into her body one last time, so hard that he moved her up the mattress a good foot. And sweet, sweet, sweet was the look of pure male satisfaction on his face as he reared back his head and shoulders and said through gritted teeth, "Yeeeesssss!"

It seemed like hours later that Remy rolled off Rachel to his back, tucking her under his arm. He kissed the top of her head gently. "I think I love you."

"You're probably just saying that because I didn't vomit."

He laughed and pinched her butt for teasing at such a serious time. Heck, she was being playful because she was scared to death. Scared of the intensity of her feelings, scared to be entering another relationship so soon after her previous disaster, scared that she might be falling under the influence of a lust bonanza, scared that he just gave her a line . . . scared that everything was happening too darn fast.

Most of all, she was scared to tell him what her true feelings were. But then, she did.

"I think I love you, too."

She could swear she heard a voice in her head say, *Whew!*

I love the way you love me, baby

Remy had never said those three words to a woman before. "I love you" just wasn't in his vocabulary.

So why did I say them to Rachel?
Damned if I know!

Well, duh! Because you meant them, you fool, St. Jude offered, or whoever it was talking inside his head.

Truth to tell, the words had just slipped out. Not that he regretted saying them, exactly, especially since Rachel had reciprocated. But what if he'd confused lust with love? And now had he bound himself in some way? Had he made a commitment of sorts? Was this the beginning of something? And did it matter?

No, he decided almost immediately, it didn't matter. He had been honest in expressing that sentiment.

But, man oh man, was he shaking in his boots!

Then he recalled that he wasn't wearing any boots.

"What's so funny?" Rachel asked, raising her head off his heaving chest.

"Nothing, honey, nothing at all." He kissed the top of her head.

Of course, that started her engine all over again. He could tell by the way she was eyeing his body and running a palm over his nipples and watching with interest as they stood up like good little soldiers. Okay, to be truthful, his motor began to hum again, too, which was amazing, really, considering what they'd just done.

Outside, he thought he heard Useless thump his tail against the houseboat a few times, as if to say, "Way to go, big boy!" Maybe tomorrow he would try to find Useless a girlfriend . . . to share the sexual joy.

Then, Remy stopped thinking altogether as Rachel began a slow, wonderfully torturous worship of his body, deformed flesh and all. If he hadn't thought he loved her before, he did now.

Chapter 10

After the party's over

Rachel tiptoed into her grandmother's home before dawn. She felt like a teenager sneaking in the house after curfew, not a thirty-three-year-old woman out on her own.

Luckily, Granny and Beau were still asleep, and Remy had performed some special talents with the guard dog, Chuck—who obviously wasn't much of a guard dog—preventing him from barking. It probably involved large numbers of gingersnaps, his pet alligator's favorite treat, second only to cheese doodles, though Remy claimed the dog's silence was due to his "special talents." And, whoo-ee, she knew better than anyone just how many "special talents" the wily Cajun had.

As she crept up the staircase to the loft, her knees wobbled, and a wonderful abrasion between her legs reminded her of the unbelievable four times they'd made love. The last time had occurred in Remy's minuscule shower where he'd attempted to show her the famous Cajun C-spot, which was reputedly much better than the traditional G-spot. They'd been laughing so hard, and loving so hard, that they broke the shower door and almost broke their necks on the slick tiles. They'd finished on the galley table, which was fortunately bolted to the floor. Afterward, they'd eaten chocolate ice cream from the carton. It was just about the only food in Remy's refrigerator. He'd explained that it was his leftover birthday ice cream. She'd asked if he wanted her to sing "Happy Birthday" to him, and he'd replied, "Only if you're naked and wearing Ronald McDonald's costume." Whatever that meant!

And talk! All night long, they had talked in between bouts of making love. She'd wanted to know everything about him: what he'd done in the past, his work, his hobbies, his dreams, everything that would help her know this stranger she had come to love. And vice versa. "Remy, I've been hurt terribly by a man I was with for five years, and obviously didn't know at all. He kept secrets from me—well, one big secret that I know of. You and I haven't known each other long, but I feel as if we've known each other forever. Can I trust you?"

His answer had been a mind-melting kiss.

Now, exhausted beyond belief, Rachel sank down to the feather-tick mattress. Within minutes, she drifted off to sleep with a smile on her face. She didn't want to think about the three ominous words that had hung between her and Remy like a blinking neon sign, never repeated after that one time. She was happier than she'd been in a long, long time. And that had to count for something.

Hours later, she awakened to the sound of her grandmother calling up to her. "Rachel, you got company. Come on down here, sleepyhead."

Rachel jackknifed into a sitting position. Was it Remy? No, he'd told her he had to fly somewhere today. Maybe he'd changed his mind. Oh, God, she better hurry. Granny would be serving him poison oak oatmeal, if she got the chance.

It took her ten minutes to get herself presentable in a pair of jeans and T-shirt, with athletic shoes. She pulled her hair back into a ponytail. When she entered the kitchen, she got the shock of her life. It definitely wasn't Remy. It was his great-aunt, Tante Lulu, chatting amiably over coffee and *les oreilles de cochran*, or "pigs' ears" with her grandmother. The Cajun confection was nothing more than fried twists of dough, doused with cane sugar and sprinkled with chopped nuts. Well, there was one saving grace in this situation: if Granny was up to making sweet stuff, she must not know Rachel had stayed out with Remy all night, or she wouldn't be in such a pleasant mood.

"I met up with Lulu at mass this mornin'. She came to see you," her grandmother announced.

"Me?" Rachel squeaked out, reaching for the cup of black coffee her grandmother poured for her.

"Yep. Gonna take you into the swamps with her. Show you how to pick healing herbs and such. Take you along on her rounds of patients."

Into the swamps? With her? Oh, geesh, maybe she wants to kill me, or something. Feed me to the alligators or shove me in quicksand. Well, at least I know why she's dressed so . . . weird. For a jungle trek. Today, Tante Lulu wore a safari-style shirt and pants with a pith helmet. Her hair was normal today, curly gray. No, Rachel was wrong about that. It was curly gray with purple streaks. *Lordy, Lordy!*

"Dr. Livingstone, I presume," Rachel quipped.

"Huh?" Tante Lulu replied. Then, "Me, I figured you being into that there fungus-way stuff, you oughta learn how us bayou folks find balance in our lives. The old-fashioned way. We doan need no fungus mumbo jumbo."

"I can't come with you," Rachel said, thinking quick. "I have an appointment with Charmaine to look over paint samples."

"It's Sunday, girl. A day of rest. The spa, she is closed. Charmaine won't be comin' in to meet you, anyways. Nosirree. That girl, she's hidin' out from Rusty."

"Her ex-husband?" Rachel asked.

"Yep. She's been married four times, but he was the first, and I imagine he's hopin' to be the fifth."

"I thought Rusty was in jail," Granny said.

"Got out last week," Tante Lulu informed her. "And he's as lustsome as a jackrabbit where Charmaine's concerned."

"Why can't Charmaine just tell him to get lost?"

"Huh?" Tante Lulu and Granny said at the same time.

"He's a Cajun," Granny explained, as if that said it all.

"Hard for any woman to resist a Cajun man when he lays on the charm," Tante Lulu agreed.

Tell me about it.

All of her excuses proved fruitless, and soon she was going outside with Tante Lulu, about to embark on her swamp trek with the *traiteur*. Granny had one last comment for her, though, thus disproving Rachel's theory that her grandmother hadn't been aware of her nocturnal activities. "Doan be thinkin' that I'm gonna throw a weddin' fer you and that LeDeux boy. You're on yer own, iffen you doan wanna take my advice 'bout that brood."

"Be careful what you say 'bout my kin, Gizelle," Tante Lulu cautioned. "We're proud folk same as you."

Rachel gasped. "Who said anything about a wedding?

There definitely is no wedding in the works. Forget about it. Geesh!"

"Doan worry," Tante Lulu said, patting her on the arm. "I'll take care of the weddin'. Gotta work on the bride quilt first, though, and crochet some more doilies for Remy's hope chest. Who you gonna have fer yer bridesmaids? I know a seamstress in Houma what can whip up taffeta gowns in no time. No offense intended, dearie, but do you plan to wear white?"

Granny just snorted with disgust and spit a stream of tobacco juice over the porch railing.

"There is not going to be a wedding," Rachel insisted.

No one was listening.

"There better not be any hanky-panky, though. Caint be rushin' a good weddin' and have it ruined, which is 'zackly what will happen iffen we have a big belly at the church services."

"Hah!" Granny called after them as they walked down the path. "There's already been a mess of hanky-panky, iffen I'm guessin' right."

"Really?" Tante Lulu gave Rachel a brisk *tsk-tsk!* before changing gears. "Well, I reckon I best get my quiltin' needles out. Mebbe I kin ask the ladies' auxiliary from Our Lady of the Bayou Church to help out. Hmmm."

"There is not going to be a wedding, and don't you dare make me a bride quilt." Rachel heaved a huge sigh of distress. "I thought you didn't even like me."

"Like has nothin' to do with it. I jist thought you weren't right for Remy, him being a sensitive county boy and all that. But, when the thunderbolt hits, there ain't no stoppin' love." She gave Rachel a sideways glance of examination. "That red hair of yers is off-putting at first. Not that there's nothin' bad about being a carrot top, no. It jist doan seem fitten fer a Cajun girl to have red hair."

"I'm only half-Cajun."

"See."

"And you would have preferred a full-blooded Cajun bride for Remy, right?"

Tante Lulu shrugged. "Woulda, coulda, shoulda doan make the gumbo boil."

Carrying on a conversation with Tante Lulu was like speaking a foreign language. You needed an interpreter.

They got into Tante Lulu's blue T-bird, with the top down. Thank God Rachel had the foresight to snap on her seat belt, because the old lady took off like a bat out of hell, gravel shooting up in her wake.

"Good thing you put your hair in a horse's tail. Otherwise, we'd have red hair whippin' all over the place. Thass why I wear this here helmet."

Of course, why didn't I think of that? A pith helmet in a convertible to hold down the hair.

"Do you have to drive so fast?" Rachel shouted over the roar of the engine and the back wind. It was only a narrow one-lane road.

"You betcha. We got things to do and places to go, girl."

That's what Rachel was afraid of.

First, they stopped at Tante Lulu's cottage to pick up some supplies. It was only ten minutes away from her grandmother's place, but Rachel wasn't sure if that was due to the short distance or Ms. Nascar-maniac.

Like many Cajun homes, Tante Lulu's had an exterior finish made of *bousillage*, a fuzzy mud mixed with Spanish moss and crushed clam shells to produce a cement-like finish. In her case, though, the stucco had been covered in a charming fashion with logs accented by whitewashed chinking. The house was situated up on a rise of neatly trimmed grass leading down to a much narrower stream than the one at her grandmother's. Unlike her grandmother's home, there were no stilts, but it did have the requisite wide front porch with several wooden rockers and a lifesize plastic statue of St. Jude. In the center of the lawn was a spreading fig tree laden with fruit. Rock-edged flower beds surrounded the house on all sides, providing a myriad of colors and fragrances. A rooster crowed from the small chicken coop in the rear. Neat rows of vegetables were arrayed in a patch surrounded by wire mesh fencing to keep out hungry animals.

They entered and Tante Lulu checked the answering machine of the cell phone attached to her belt. After listening to the half dozen messages, all from patients describing symptoms or wanting to set appointments, the *traiteur* began to answer her calls. In between, she told Rachel to rest a spell while she finished with the telephone business and then gathered her materials.

Rachel chose to nose around instead. The rooms were small and the ceilings low—in deference to the diminutive lady, she supposed. The living room had comfortable stuffed furniture, with doilies on all the arms and backs.

There were framed photographs of family members everywhere. One of an attractive young woman with three young boys caught her eye. It must be Lulu's niece and the mother of the three LeDeux boys. Rachel smiled as she picked out Remy, about four years old at the time, his two front baby teeth missing. Nowhere visible was Valcour LeDeux, the miscreant father she'd heard so much about. A lovely wedding picture of Luc and Sylvie held prominence. Charmaine looked pretty in a ball gown, big hair and tiera in a photo taken about ten years ago when she was Miss Louisiana. There were also school photos of Luc and Remy and René. And one of Remy looking stunningly gorgeous in an Air Force uniform, before his accident.

Behind the living room was the kitchen with its cypress cabinets and white porcelain sink. Red-and-white-checked curtains matched the cloth on the 1940s-style enamel table. Two bedrooms opened off the hall which ran front to back. One contained an old four-poster bed covered with a hand-woven Cajun spread and unbleached curtains. A small alcove with a shrine to the Blessed Virgin Mary and St. Jude was in the hallway, and throughout the home hung crucifixes and holy pictures, indicative of the Catholic faith.

Down the hall was a bedroom with a set of bunkbeds and a cot, undoubtedly the landing pad for the three boys when they came to visit. On the walls were New Orleans Saints and Tulane University pennants, along with some rock posters, a blow-up of Richard Petty at a Nascar race, and a pin-up of Heather Locklear. On a bookcase rested three framed photographs side by side of the boys on their respective First Communion days, wearing cute three-piece suits, rosaries around their necks, and their hands folded in prayer. Each had a twinkle in his eye, even then. Little rascal saints!

Rachel found the home meticulously clean and cozy. Why she should be surprised by that, she did not know. Probably because the old lady was so eccentric in her physical appearance and outrageous in her actions. She'd halfway expected to find newspapers and magazines piled everywhere and dirty dishes in the sink with some voodoo paraphernalia hanging from the ceiling.

Rachel discovered Tante Lulu in a large pantry behind the kitchen where she was filling zipper plastic bags with herbs from the labeled bottles which filled the shelves from floor to ceiling. Dozens of containers held the usual herbs, whose pungent odors filled the room, but bizarre things, too, like alligator grease, pigeon hearts, dried rabbit blood, snake rattles, chicken dung, lamb placentas and pig anuses.

"Alligator grease!" Rachel exclaimed. She couldn't imagine how one would actually obtain such a thing.

"Oh, yeah," Tante Lulu said, without looking up. "Bestest thing for the asthma and shortness of breath. Mix it with honey and add a bit of orange juice. Very tasty."

I—don't—think—so.

A well-worn butcher block table stood in the middle of the pantry. On it were various knives, wooden bowls and pestles, and an ancient book with handwritten notes on healing remedies, its leaves brown with age. Several decanters of oil and holy water sat off to the side.

"You have a very nice home."

"Thank you. It belonged to my parents. Me and my older sister Clarice grew up here. Clarice was Luc and Remy and René's grandmommy."

"Did you ever marry?"

She shook her head. "My parents and Clarice drowned in a boat crash off Grand Isle when I was only sixteen, bless their souls. I had to raise Adèle, who was only ten. Then, after she married, I had to care for her youngens every time they run away from their Daddy's belt. Lordy, Lordy, he was a mean ol' bastard. Still is."

Rachel began to get a clear—and not pleasant—picture of what Remy's childhood must have been like.

"Then Adèle died, too, and my boys needed me." She shrugged as if to say she had had no choice.

Well, Rachel knew a lot of older, career-minded women who would have put their own interests first. "They were lucky to have you."

Instead of pretending false modesty, Tante Lulu said, "*Mais, oui!*" But of course.

Tante Lulu scribbled notes on a little pad, explaining that she was low on some herbs. Before she made some stops to treat patients, they would go into the bayou and gather the plants. "Do you mind?" the old lady asked.

"I'm enjoying myself." And that was the truth.

Out of habit, Rachel grabbed for her leather shoulder bag and followed Tante Lulu out the door, down the steps, then off to the stream where a small boat with an outboard motor sat. Heat shimmied over the water, and the clouds swirled overhead. Tante Lulu motioned for Rachel to get in first.

"Whoa! You didn't say anything about us going by water."

"Get in, you, and stop bein' a scaredy cat."

That was certainly blunt. Rachel eased her way into the boat, put her purse on the bottom, and then immediately grasped the sides in white-knuckled grips. Tante Lulu chuckled and got in behind her, rocking the boat deliberately to tease her.

"You swim, dontcha?"

"Yes, but I've never swum in a swamp."

"First time for everythin'." Tante Lulu chuckled some more. "Make sure you hold onto that oar in the bottom.

Iffen we flip over, it's the bestest thing for beatin' off gators. Hee, hee, hee!" With a sharp pull on the outboard motor, they were off.

"That's not funny." Maybe Tante Lulu didn't like her after all. Maybe she'd lured her out to the swamps so Rachel would disappear forever.

"You got whisker burns up one side of your neck and down the other, didja know that?" Tante Lulu commented out of the blue, as she steered the small craft down the narrow steam which soon branched off into a much wider one. "On your arms, too. If I know that Remy, you prob'ly got a hickey on your butt, too."

Rachel gasped at the old lady's words. Not that they weren't true. In fact, she had Remy's marks in some other places, too—places too intimate to mention. And she'd marked him, as well.

Before she could tell Tante Lulu to mind her own business, she spouted off again. "Not to worry. I got some ointment that'll cure abrasions, cuts, itches, snake bites, jock itch, crabs and hickeys, lickety-split."

That's just what I need, a multi-purpose crab/hickey cream. Oil of Ol-bayou-ay. Yeech!

"Pig slobber mixed with cow poop."

Rachel's jaw dropped with astonishment. Did people actually allow her to put such a concoction on their skin?

"Just kidding. You sure are gullible, aren't you."

"Did I say earlier that I was enjoying myself? I lied."

A loud roar, followed by a hissing noise caused Rachel to jump in her seat, which caused the boat to sway.

"Relax, lessen you want to join those gators over there."

Rachel stared, google-eyed. In the shallow water near the opposite bank sat a seven-foot-wide platform which rose up about four feet, comprised of a soggy mess of mud and vegetation. A couple dozen eggs held center court—eggs which were about the circumference of regular chicken eggs but much longer. About to plop down on this nest was a mama alligator the size of a minivan, at least eight feet long. She chewed noisily on some reeds and mud that she carried in her mouth, then spit the masticated glob onto the eggs and soon spread it about by squirming her heavy body over the whole slew of eggs. It was Ms. Luggage-To-Be who was doing all the hissing.

Even worse was her hubby, Mr. Luggage-To-Be, a good fifty percent bigger and uglier, who stood guard in the water, roaring his outrage at them. He probably told his wife, in gator talk, "Hey, hon, take a look at these idiots. Do you have a hankering for people steak for dinner tonight? Yum-yum."

"I want to go back. Right now," Rachel demanded.

"Those gators are harmless, long as you doan go disturbin' their babies, or decide to go skinny dippin' in their backyard. Besides, alligators are king of the bayou, and you best get used to 'em iffen you're gonna be livin' here after the weddin'."

Rachel gritted her teeth, counted to ten silently, then said in as even a tone as she could manage, "*There is not going to be a wedding.*"

By then, Tante Lulu had already maneuvered their boat some distance past the alligators' nest; so, her insistence about going back was a moot point, she supposed.

Of course, now she had other things to worry about. In South Louisiana, the bayou system presented an intricate web of intersecting waterways—splitting, turning onto themselves, disappearing one day, reappearing another.

Sometimes they were wide as a river, other times they were so narrow as to be unnavigable. Right now Tante Lulu went up, down, around, left, right—to the point where Rachel would never be able to find her way back if the old lady should have a heart attack or something. Finally, she took them into a remote, gloomy area where the trees formed a canopy overhead, like praying hands, and light came through only in occasional shafts where there was a break in the leaves. You'd never know it was still morning. The water, which at first appeared to be black, was really dark brown on closer examination, stained by the tannin in centuries of sunken trees. In some places, the current swirled and eddied; in others, it didn't appear to move at all. Vampires and werewolves would be at home in this eerie atmosphere.

"We're here," Tante Lulu announced cheerily.

Rachel felt like walloping her over the head with an oar. "Here" amounted to Tante Lulu running her little boat up onto a muddy bank and tying it to a nearby bush, which probably contained a gazillion snakes or giant spiders.

Tante Lulu stepped out of the boat and proceeded to plod off, oblivious to the fact that Rachel still sat in the boat. At first, Rachel was determined to stay put, but she soon changed her mind after hearing an odd crying noise like a wildcat—or more likely a big bird—and after taking a good look around at the ancient cypress tree with its out-flaring base and roots that pushed themselves up out of the water some distance from the base like trolls, seeking precious air for survival . . . or people food. It was a fanciful thought, but in this dreary atmosphere, with spooky Spanish moss hanging in clumps from the trees like monster cobwebs, well, anything seemed possible.

She grabbed for her purse and slung it over her shoulders, then jumped out of the boat, immediately sinking down in the pudding-like mud up to her ankles. Emitting some swear words she hadn't used in ages, Rachel stomped after Tante Lulu. "Wait for me, you bloody witch. Take me in the swamps and abandon me, will you? Hah! Call me a scaredy cat! Hah! We'll see who cries wolf first. Hah! You're gonna buy me a new pair of shoes, that's for sure, Ms. Indiana Imbecile," she muttered. Along the way, her arms kept brushing against the numerous jewelweed plants, which immediately burst forth with bright orangish flowers when touched. Jewelweed was also known as "Touch-Me-Nots" for obvious reasons.

Tante Lulu was bent over a bush, picking up clumps of small green berries from a tree she identified as prickly ash, or "The Toothache Tree." Rachel was too angry to ask for an explanation. And, frankly, she could have cared less, even when Tante Lulu informed her that these berries could be used to alleviate toothache pain.

She tossed Rachel another canvas bag and ordered, "Yer taller'n me. Pick off some of that Spanish moss."

"What for?" she asked in a surly fashion, even as she shifted her shoulder purse, then reached up and gingerly stuffed some of the gray swathes in the canvas bag. The moss was probably loaded with bugs.

"The Indians usta clothe their infants in it, or cover a sick man with it during the sweating exercise. Some folks still use it to stuff mattresses. I likes to boil it up fer fever."

"Look at that unusual tree over there," Rachel said, pointing to the large-leaved tree, which stood out from some of the others here in the swamp.

"Thass a Sacrifice Tree. Good for colds, but you gotta gather the leaves at the first full moon."

As Tante Lulu continued to pick and choose among the various plants, even pulling out a knife to cut some mamou roots which would be used for pneumonia, Rachel asked her questions about her *traiteur* work. Folk healing was the popular name for it today, or alternative medicine. "Who taught you all this stuff?"

"My auntie was a *traiteur.* Later, I learned from watchin' other healers in the area. But you gots to have the gift to begin with, or you can't never be taught the ways."

Rachel noticed that the old woman made the sign of the cross often when picking her herbs. When she asked why she did that, Tante Lulu said, "Healing is a gift from the Lord. Can't never forget that, or the gift will go away."

"How many people do you treat?"

"'Bout two hundred, give or take. Oh, not all at once. Mebbe a dozen a week these days. Lots more when I was younger."

They suddenly heard the sound of men's voices a short distance away. Rachel went rigid with attention, and Tante Lulu put a forefinger to her lips, calling for silence. Spinning silently on her feet, Tante Lulu put down her canvas bag and began creeping toward the men's voices, which Rachel could now hear were gruff and mixed with Spanish. Rachel carefully placed her purse and canvas bag on the ground, too. Then, she followed. What else could she do?

Are we nuts? We should be hightailing it out of here. Unless Tante Lulu thinks it's someone she knows. But, no, she wouldn't be taking such care to be quiet if that were the case. God, I feel like this is a bad Lucy and Ethel routine.

When they got to the point where they were ten or fifteen feet away and hidden by bushes, they stopped. Peering through the foliage, they saw four men who were cursing in both English and Spanish as they tried to maneuver a large raft with a metal box on the top by working long poles in the stream bottom. Industrial-strength belts were wrapped around it, with one of the lengths connected to an oak tree on the bank.

"Is it a coffin?" she whispered to Tante Lulu.

"Ain't like no coffin I ever seen," Tante Lulu whispered back. "Too big."

"Maybe it holds two bodies."

"Mebbe."

"Guns!" Rachel murmured, as she noticed the weapons that all four of them carried. Rifles, and pistols in shoulder and hip holsters.

"There it comes again, Carlos. The helicopter," one of the men said.

Yes, in the distance, there was the whir of a helicopter which got louder as it came closer. It appeared to be low riding and slow moving. Was it Remy? It could be anyone, she supposed, Louisiana being such a touristy state.

"For chrissake, Juan, you're too goddam nervous. Jumpin' at every little thing."

"I'm telling ya, Carlos, everywhere we go lately, I keep hearing a helicopter. I think it's followin' us."

"I think you're full of shit. Let's get this job done and get out of here. Sonnier, do you have the map, so we can get out of this hellhole? I don't know how we ever would have found this place without you for a guide."

Sonnier, who was unshaven like the rest and the youngest at about twenty-five, nodded as he folded a paper into his pocket.

"Valdez, get over here and help us shove this box over the side. It's heavy as hell." Standing knee deep in the muddy water, the four men huffed and swore as they pushed the metal box over the side. Because of its weight, it immediately sank to the bottom. Then, they did the same to the raft itself. The only thing visible, but only if you were looking for it, was the cloth belt leading from the base of the tree into the stream. The four men prepared to board a boat that resembled Tante Lulu's, except bigger.

That's when Tante Lulu's cell phone chose the perfect time to ring—a loud *brrrr-iiing, brrrr-iiing, brrrr-iiing!*

"What was that?" Carlos said.

"Jesus H. Christ! Someone's watchin' us," Sonnier exclaimed.

"I tol' you that 'copter was suspicious," Carlos put in.

"Let's get 'em," Valdez shouted, drawing his pistol.

Rachel looked at Tante Lulu and Tante Lulu looked at her, both horrified. Then, Tante Lulu turned quickly and ran back in the direction from which they'd come. Rachel ran right after her. There was no path; so, they just shoved branches and bushes aside in their path. Forget-Me-Nots were blooming all over the bloody place. God bless the old lady for being in such good shape. She was no sooner in the boat, revving the motor, than Rachel slip-slided down the bank behind her. They were twenty feet away before the men arrived at the stream edge and began shooting at them.

"Duck," Tante Lulu yelled with misguided glee.

As if Rachel wasn't already burrowing as close to the bottom of the boat as she could get! When they passed the alligator nest on the way back, Rachel wasn't even afraid.

"Do you think they were burying a body, or bodies?"

Rachel asked once she could speak over the loud thudding of her heart.

"Mus' be."

"But why?"

"Bad guys would be my guess."

"Do they have the Mafia in Louisiana? Maybe it was a Mafia hit."

"Like *The Godfather,* you mean? Like, 'swimmin' with the fishes'? They dint look much like Marlon Brando, iffen you ask me, but I s'pose so. *Mon Dieu*! Can't wait to tell the church ladies about this. Ain't had this much excitement since the oil men tried to kill Luc and Sylvie, or the time I went to the voodoo lady and—"

"The oil men tried . . . ? Voodoo . . . ? Never mind. We should probably go to the police. Let's call nine-one-one, or something."

Tante Lulu shook her head. "No police. Not yet. I'll talk to Luc about it. He's a lawyer. He'll know what to do. Mebbe it was jist some trappers tryin' to hide their illegal catches."

"You don't really think that, do you?"

"Nope. Ain't many Cajuns speak Spanish like that. Plus, trappers wouldn't go to that much trouble to hide their furs from the law. Mostly, they just flip the bird to the game warden when he comes snoopin' around."

Flip the bird? This old lady continually surprises me. "Oh, my God! I left my pocketbook back there. We left the canvas bags, too. Do you know how to get back to that spot?"

They'd arrived safely back at Tante Lulu's house by now, and the old lady was tying the boat to a small dock.

When she finished, she gave Rachel a disbelieving scowl. "You wanna risk going back there?"

"I guess not. You don't seem worried about all this, now that we escaped the danger."

"Of course, I'm worried. We Cajuns doan like strangers coming into the bayou, messin' around."

"Burying caskets with dead people," Rachel added sarcastically.

Tante Lulu missed the sarcasm totally. "That, too. But you gotta know, Rachel, that we Cajuns have our secrets, too. Nope. I ain't goin' to the po-lice till I talks to Luc first."

"And how about Remy? Are you going to talk to him, too?"

"Hell, no! He's too upright, by half. He'd go straight to the po-lice."

"Aaarrgh!"

As if to satisfy Rachel, Tante Lulu punched Luc's office number into her cell phone. "He ain't in. I got his answer machine," she told Rachel. Then she spoke into her phone, "Luc, call me," was all she said. Noticing Rachel's glower, she added, "It's important."

Rachel grabbed the phone out of Tante Lulu's hands and punched in Remy's number. She, too, got an answering machine. Her message repeated Tante Lulu's. "Remy, call me. It's important."

She and Tante Lulu glared at each other. The stubborn old biddy broke eye contact first. She said, "Well, let's get a move on it, girlie. I gots works to do."

"Take me home first," Rachel ordered, already walking beside her towards the car.

Never one to take orders, Tante Lulu buckled herself

into the T-bird's driver seat, adjusted her pith helmet, waited for Rachel to get in, and again took off like a bat out of hell.

"Did you hear me? I want to go home!"

"I heard you, I heard you, but I gotta go smoke a baby first."

How could Rachel resist such a tantalizing prospect?

Chapter 11

Here comes trouble.

Remy was in a meeting with the DEA folks in a hidden office behind a warehouse in Lafayette.

Already, they had the names of *some* of the low-level culprits involved, including a Louisiana fellow named George "Sonny" Sonnier, along with some other scumbag locals, who probably gave the Romero cartel all the geography lessons they needed to stash the drugs. All morning, they'd scanned from the air the various suspected bayou hiding spots being contemplated by the Colombian drug kingpins. Now they were making corrections and additions to the maps spread out before them and pinned to the four walls. Alarmingly, he'd discovered that one of those hiding spots was in his own Bayou Black region.

Up to this point, it had been an investigative, studying and waiting game. They didn't want to go in for the kill, so to speak, until they'd identified all the individuals involved, as well as the hiding spots. But they couldn't wait too long.

In the midst of all this serious business, Remy kept thinking about Rachel.

How sweet she'd smelled.

How silky her skin had been.

How she'd shed her inhibitions and clothing, just for him.

How her innocent expertise at lovemaking touched his soul.

How she'd allowed him to do whatever he wanted, no matter how shocking.

How the memory of her soft moans aroused him, even now.

How she'd touched his deformed skin, without flinching.

How his otherwise physically fit body ached in certain places from too much lovemaking, if there was such a thing.

How he'd said those three scary words to her.

How she'd said them back to him.

"Earth to LeDeux. Earth to LeDeux," Larry Ellis said.

Remy came back to the present with a mental thud. *Mon Dieu*, he was letting Rachel, and an important part of his anatomy, rule his life. He had to straighten up and fly right.

"What were you saying?"

"Just that timing is everything," the head of the operation, Shelton Peters, or "Pete" as he was known, explained. "Yes, we can't rush things by making the arrests too early, but, on the other hand, if we wait too long in hopes of catching the big apples, we may end up with no apples at all."

"So, what's the answer?"

"I say we set a deadline," Ellis offered.

The others nodded in agreement.

"Monday, a week from tomorrow, will be D-Day," Pete said.

More nods.

"We'll bring in more field agents and make all the arrests that day," Pete said. "Plus, we'll need to confiscate all the submerged drugs, simultaneously."

"We're talking a lot of freakin' manpower," Ellis noted.

"Yep, and a lot of synchronization. Timing is everything," Pete concluded.

Another man named Frank Porter looked at Remy. "Will you be briefing our pilots this week?"

"Yes, six of them will be flying in on Wednesday," Remy replied. "We'll spend at least two days in the air, checking out all the sites in question. On D-Day, one of us will be assigned to each of the hiding spots. We'll use 'copters for surveillance but hydroplanes to land in the bayou and unload the divers who will bring up the metal boxes."

"Boats will come in as well, after the air power; boats small enough to maneuver these streams but big enough to handle the weight when carrying the lead coffins out," Pete elaborated.

"You know, this operation is only the beginning," Ellis pointed out. "The tip of the iceberg."

Everyone agreed that the drug problem was more pervasive than this one operation.

"You've got to get a larger landing pad if you're going to continue working with us," Pete said to Remy. "I've bent all the rules in the book so far, but it can't go on forever."

"Why should the size of my pad matter so much? It's illogical," Remy argued.

Some of the men rolled their eyes.

"You don't know Uncle Sam, boy," Pete said with a laugh. "Logic is not a word recognized by the U.S. government, especially when it comes to rule making. I swear, there are some assholes in this nation's capitol who must have Ph.D.s in busywork. If something can be said in five words, they use five hundred. Common sense is not part of their vocabulary."

"Remember the time they made Baldwin fly from D.C. to Baltimore because his SUV didn't have clearance?" Pete recalled.

"And how about Louis and the five thousand-dollar road map," another guy, Matt Landeau, pointed out.

"Then there was the time some yahoo with his head up his ass decided it would be just swell if agents carried Mace, instead of pistols. That went over real big," Pete said. "It took the threat of a thousand resignations before that effin' rule was dumped."

Remy threw his hands up in surrender. "I hear you, I hear you. I'll do my best to expand the pad within the next month. I promise." *That means another encounter with the Wicked Witch of the South. On the other hand, it also means another encounter with the Wicked Witch's yummy grand-daughter.*

"I'd love to know what that grin of yours means," Ellis whispered to him.

"Never mind," Remy said.

The meeting broke up after an hour. Pete called out, "Good luck, everyone."

As Remy left, he checked his cell phone. There was only one call, and it was from Rachel. *Yum-yum*, he thought to himself.

Her message said, "Remy, call me. It's important."

She probably missed him. That was important, wasn't it?

Or her grandmother had locked her in her gingerbread house and was firing up the ovens. That was important, too.

Giving himself a silent scold for standing in the middle of the parking lot daydreaming, Remy punched in the number for Gizelle's place, praying that Rachel would be the one to answer.

No such luck.

"Hello!" the old witch squawked.

"Is Rachel there?"

"Who's this?"

He hesitated for a long moment. "Remy LeDeux."

"She's not here."

"She's not there *to me*, or she's not there *in general*?"

"Dumb cluck," she said, not even bothering to say it under her breath. "That girl, she's not here any which way. She went off with your great-aunt a long time ago."

Uh-oh! "How long ago?"

"They left here 'bout ten o'clock, I reckon."

"That was five hours ago." What could his aunt have been doing with Rachel for five bloody hours? It boggled the mind and scared the hell out of him.

"Iffen you mus' know, Beau took a change of clothes fer her over to Lulu's house a bit ago. But, yeah, she's been gone since ten o'clock."

"Five hours ago!" he practically yelled.

"You doan hafta yell at me," Gizelle said, and slammed down the receiver of the phone.

"The old bat hung up on me," he said to himself, not really that surprised. Next, he tried his aunt, who told him that she had dropped Rachel off at Charmaine's an hour ago. "Lordy, Lordy, that girl is a Nervous Nellie."

"Uh, Tante Lulu, what were you doing that Rachel would have been nervous?"

"*Me?* Why does everyone blame me? Wasn't me. Was all them bad guys down in the swamp. *Cou!* Beatinest thing I ever did see! Did you know Rachel has a hickey? *Tsk-tsk.* Best you brush off yer go-to-weddin' suit real quick, boy. Dum-dum-dee-dum! Oops! Can't talk now. Here comes Luc, and he's mad as a bull with his hiney caught in barbed wire, jist 'cause I got another speeding ticket. 'Bye."

Remy stared blankly at his cell phone. Another old lady had just hung up on him.

Then some other worries assailed him.

Bad guys? What bad guys?

Another speeding ticket! They're gonna take her license for sure this time.

I wonder if Tante Lulu has talked about weddings to Rachel.

Hah! I know Tante Lulu has been talking to Rachel about weddings. She wouldn't miss an opportunity like this if her life depended on it.

Bad guys? What could she have meant by that?

Remy exhaled with disgust. *Can my day get any worse?*

Yep, you-know-who said in his head.

Once is not enough. For sure, baby

Rachel literally shook as she entered Charmaine's spa in mid-afternoon.

She would kill Tante Lulu if she spent one more minute in her company, and she'd told her so, too. She would walk all the way to Bayou Black before she'd get in a car with that dingbat again. Even the cop who stopped the T-bird for speeding had looked at Rachel and said, "Do you have a death wish, lady, getting in a moving vehicle with Louise Rivard?" That was Tante Lulu's full name. "She's a living legend with the highway patrol." The trooper had been laughing as he spoke. Rachel had not.

The front door of the spa displayed a CLOSED sign, but Rachel found Charmaine in a back office, doing payroll. Charmaine's gee-whiz hairdo stood out as bouffanty as usual today, even on a day of rest. The big hair went perfect with her black capri pants and a cropped T-shirt that said, I DO BANGS. The ultimate bimbo! She took one look at Rachel and said, "You've been with Tante Lulu. Come sit down, *chère*, and let me pour you a cup of chamomile tea. If you want, I can give you a Prozac, too."

After Rachel told Charmaine about her harrowing experiences of the day, Charmaine regaled her with her own stories about the outrageous Tante Lulu, including the time when she was seventy-five and Charmaine was twenty-eight, right after her last divorce, and the daffy bird entered both of them in a belly-dancing contest in Opoulousa—and Tante Lulu won.

"In her defense, I will say that Tante Lulu was very impressive today in dealing with her patients." On the first patient visit, Rachel had learned what it meant to "smoke the baby." There had been a little baby outside Houma who was suffering from a severe case of colic. Tante Lulu had cut up some scraps of the mother's pregnancy clothing and a piece of the baby's cloth diaper. She'd placed those on a foil plate, along with several snips of the mother and child's hair. After they'd been set afire and started smoking, Tante Lulu kept passing the smoky concoction over and around the baby's head, forcing him to breathe in some smoke. To Rachel's amazement, the baby immediately calmed and fell asleep, the colic presumably cured.

Then, too, Tante Lulu had given out herbal remedies in a very professional manner to other patients for fever, nausea and diarrhea. She'd even used a remedy Rachel had heard of as a young girl for curing warts. The little Cajun boy had shown them warts all over his one hand. Tante Lulu had rubbed a raw potato over all of them, then told the mother to bury it in the yard where the water spout ran off the roof. When the potato finally rotted, the warts would be gone, Tante Lulu promised. In every case, Tante Lulu had made the sign of the cross and said a short prayer before she started.

When Rachel had expressed astonishment at some of her work, Tante Lulu had told her, "Sometimes the old ways are still best."

Now, after drinking two cups of tea and passing on the Prozac, Rachel prepared to discuss the spa remodeling project. Charmaine pulled out some of the wallpaper books that Rachel had left with her. They spent the next hour deciding on paint and floor colors, and some wallpaper. Rachel was excited about the cloud paper they would be putting on the massage-room ceiling with murals of a bayou stream on all four of the walls.

When they finished, Charmaine whisked her hands together, gave Rachel an assessing look, then announced, "Now, let's concentrate on you, girl."

"Oh, no! You are not going to pouf my hair."

Charmaine laughed. "No. But, after the day you've had, a little tender loving care is in order."

And Charmaine was right. A half hour later, after a hot

conditioning of her hair, a warm waxing of her hands and feet for relaxation, and a honey facial peel, Rachel was loose as a goose. She was lying on her stomach, clad only in a thick towel, on one of the planks in the spa's sauna to "cleanse the pores." Another towel was wrapped turban style around her damp hair. Afterward, Charmaine was going to give her a full-body massage.

"I don't think I'm going to need the massage, after all, Charmaine," she said, on hearing the door click open. "I'm so relaxed now my bones are about to melt."

"Oh, you definitely need a massage," a husky voice said.

Definitely not Charmaine.

Rachel's eyes flew open to see Remy standing inside the now-closed door. And he wasn't wearing a towel.

Oooh, boy! He gives new meaning to "Tall, Dark, and Cajun." More like, "Ragin' Cajun."

Remy watched with amusement as Rachel assessed his body and his already raging erection, then sat up, tugging the towel tighter around her breasts. How could she be so modest after her behavior last night? But that's how women tended to be, in his experience. Madonna at night, Mother Teresa in the daylight.

He took her hand and pulled her up to a standing position, making sure both towels dropped in the process. It was about two hundred degrees inside this sweat box, and towels were an un-necessity. "I missed you," he said, just before he kissed her deeply. If she wasn't already boneless, as she'd mentioned, he planned to make her that way—or die trying.

Remy ran his palms down her perspiration-slick back, from shoulders to buttocks, which he cupped in his hands. He pulled her close up against his body. She stood on tiptoe to align them just right. *Accommodating woman, Rachel is. I like that in a woman.*

"I'm sweaty," she said.

"I will be, too, in a minute . . . but not from the sauna."

She laughed against his mouth.

He liked that, too.

"Did you really miss me?" she asked, teasingly.

"How can you ask, darlin'?" he teased right back as he sat down smoothly on one of the benches, forcing her to sit on his lap, astraddle. He could be smooth when he wanted to be.

"That much, huh?" She wiggled her hips against that part of his anatomy which was showing her just how much he'd missed her.

He about saw stars, so intense was the pleasure of her brushing over his penis. And, hot damn, she knew the effect she had on him . . . because the witch did it again, and smiled.

He laid back and stretched out his legs on the long bench with her still straddling his middle.

"Aren't you afraid Charmaine will walk in?"

He shook his head. "I told her to get lost."

"And she listened to you? That doesn't sound like Charmaine." She arched her eyebrows at him, disbelieving.

"Well, I did tell her I saw Rusty headed this way, and he was wearing a cowboy hat, boots and tight jeans. Charmaine never could resist a cowboy, no way. She was out of here faster'n a hog on market day."

Propped on straightened arms, she smiled down at him. "I like cowboys, too, *cowboy*. And cowgirls, too. I've never ridden a horse before, though. Could you give me a lesson?"

"Guar-an-teed!" He lifted her hips, up, then down, so that she impaled herself on him. Her eyes went wide as saucers as she rippled around him. And he grew to about ten inches long and six inches around, give or take an inch or two . . . male exaggeration being a God-given right at a time like this.

"Oh!"

"Is that all you can say, darlin'?" He was pretty damned impressed with himself. She better be, too. He was impressed with her, as well, of course. All that rippling and flexing—he'd have to be a freakin' saint not to appreciate that.

But then, she really, really impressed him with her perfect answer. "Giddyup!"

And he did.

And so did she.

Define perverted, please

Rachel lay flat out on the spa massage table, buck naked, with a gel mask over her eyes, and, no doubt, a pair of dark Cajun eyes perusing her from head to toe.

When had she stopped being inhibited about her body's imperfections? When had she decided to give wanton behavior a try? When had she turned into a sexpot? She'd never been this way with David, or any of the other few men with whom she'd been involved. It was probably the mask which gave her courage, she decided. Or a mutant gene that suddenly came to the forefront—a slut gene.

"Is this the most perverted thing you've ever done?" she asked, not sure exactly where Remy stood. How she'd let him talk her into this, she had no idea. Well, yes, she did. He'd smooth-talked her into this "experiment" when she'd been in the afterglow of a mindless orgasm.

"Define perverted," he replied with a chuckle. He was standing at her side. "Man, you have the most beautiful breasts in the world."

"You've said that before."

"It bears repeating, sweetheart. Believe me, it bears repeating."

"I don't know about this, Remy. It feels really odd."

"Good odd or bad odd?"

"I don't know. Tingly in the bottom of my tummy odd."

"That's good odd," he concluded.

"How about you being the one lying here, vision-impaired, while I'm the Dr. Feel-Good character?"

"Later, babe. Later." His voice came from another direction now.

"What are you doing?"

"Checking out Charmaine's stash of body oils. Geesh, who would want to slather themselves in snake oil?"

"Whaaaat?"

"Just teasing. Which scent do you prefer, lavender, rose or lemon? Oooh, oooh, oooh, hold the train. I just spied something better. Edible oils."

She had to laugh at that. "Who gets to pick the flavor? Me or you?"

"Definitely me. At first. You get dibs second time around. Hmmm. I think I like banana. No, I changed my mind. Coconut."

"That's not fair."

"Yes, it is. The licker gets to pick what he or she is going to lick."

Lick? Oh, my goodness, I can feel my nipples getting harder. I hope he doesn't notice.

"Have I told you how much I like your breasts?"

Yep, he noticed.

"I thought this was going to be a massage, not a . . . licking thing."

He chuckled. "Honey, we Cajuns do things our way. There's nothing wrong with mixing the two. A licking massage sounds mighty good to me."

It did to her, too.

She jerked suddenly as she felt a cool liquid drizzling on her pubic hair.

"It looks like dew melting on flames there, Rachel. Did you know that?"

"Of course, I don't know that. Do you think I put edible oil on myself and look in a mirror?"

"Some women might," he replied. "Which gives me an idea. I don't suppose . . ."

"What?" she prodded when he never finished.

"Would you be willing to do something for me that is a little, um . . ."

"Perverted?"

"Different."

"Like what?" *As if this isn't perverted or different enough!*

He drizzled the oil all over her breasts. "Lift them, and touch them. Yourself."

"Remy, I can't."

"Please."

"This is far beyond the pale of anything I've ever done."

"Me, too."

"Liar."

"Honest."

She inhaled and exhaled deeply, then asked, "What do you want me to do?"

"Touch them the way you would want me to. Make love to yourself, but pretend it's me."

And Rachel did. God help her, but she did. And not just her breasts either. At the end of fifteen minutes, which seemed like fifteen hours, Rachel was completely sated, by her own hand and Remy's husky, wicked words of encouragement. And she smelled like a piña colada.

Bringing herself to orgasm while a drop-dead sexy man watched was a mind-blowing experience for Rachel, one that a mere two weeks ago she never would have expected she would agree to. Now, she would never smell coconuts again without remembering—and probably blushing.

Then it was Remy's turn—buck naked, masked, and on the massage table, at her insistence.

"You can do anything you want, babe," he offered with typical male magnanimousness.

"A massage," she decided, opting for the more tame of all the possibilities that *anything* encompassed. She wasn't sure she could watch Remy touch himself without bursting aflame with embarrassment, or just bursting aflame, period.

"Coward," Remy hooted. "Go for it, darlin'."

She gave him a massage, every blessed inch of him, with chocolate oil. The chocolate "fudgesicle" she saved for the final entree. She massaged, she licked, she caused Remy to moan one long, "Ooooooooooohhh!" When she finished, and he was sated, too, she said, laughing, "The two of us smell like a Mounds bar, chocolate and coconut. The only thing missing is the nuts. Then, we would be an Almond Joy."

"Hey, I have nuts," he pointed out, chucking her playfully under the chin.

"Don't I know it!" She laughed again.

They sat side by side, naked, on the massage table with Remy's arm around her shoulders and Rachel tucked under his arm, her cheek resting on his oily chest.

"What we need is a shower, babe. I assume this spa has a shower."

"I'm not getting into a shower with you. I know where that would lead."

"Where?" he inquired with mock innocence, the whole time ogling her breasts.

"I'm turning into a slut," she said on a groan, as she realized just how much she liked the fact that he liked her breasts.

"I like sluts."

"Aaarrgh!"

"Well, it's your choice as to the shower, Ms. Slut, but I told Luc and Sylvie we would come to the crawfish boil at her mother's place tonight, if you agreed. Her mother is a big-shot politician, and she's having some kind of fundraiser at the Breaux family digs. Do you want to go smelling like sex and candy bars?"

"No."

"Well, then?"

"I'll get the soap. You get the towels," she said, sliding off the massage table and heading toward the showers.

"That's what I like, an easy woman." Remy slapped her on the butt as he caught up with her.

Yep, Rachel was feeling very easy.

And she liked it.

As they opened the shower door, she told him, "No touching."

He just grinned, slow and sexy.

Rachel wondered where she might find a twelve-step program for slutism.

Blowing the afterglow

An hour later, as they were driving to the outskirts of Houma for Inez Breaux-Fontaine's party—*and, yes, they spent an hour in the shower*—Remy remembered something.

He looked over at Rachel on the bench seat of his Jeep, real close. She still smelled slightly of coconut, and he probably still reeked of chocolate, despite their having scrubbed each other raw . . . and screwed each other raw, as well.

She wore a knee-high denim skirt with a little slit up the middle and a stretchy, white T-shirt which—*she would no doubt die if she knew*—showed off her nipples, much distended, thanks to his enthusiastic attentions of the past two hours. Skimpy sandals covered her mostly bare feet. She sat demurely with her hands folded in her lap, but he thought she looked sexy as sin.

But that was beside the point. He'd totally forgotten the call Rachel had made to his cell phone today. Could a man die of too much testosterone? He doubted it, but, man, what a way to go! "You never told me why you called me this afternoon. What was the *important* thing you needed to discuss?" he asked.

"Oh! I can't believe I forgot. You really do scramble my brains, Remy. I've got to stop letting you do that to me."

Remy kind of liked the idea of being able to scramble Rachel's brains.

"Your aunt took me into the swamps to pick some herbs and we came across some guys sinking a big coffin into the stream. Her cell phone went off, which alerted them that we were there, and that's when they shot at us. We escaped just in time. Whew! Who would have thought your aunt could run so fast? Who would have thought I could run so fast? I wasn't even afraid of the alligators after that."

Remy slammed on the brakes and pulled over to the side of the road. Car horns beeped behind him, and one redneck in a rusted-out pickup, which flew by, gave him the finger while yelling obscenities about his mother and his driving skills. But Remy couldn't be concerned about all that. *Swamp? A coffin? Shooting? Alligators?* He shouldn't be surprised. Everywhere his aunt went, trouble seemed to follow. But now, she'd involved Rachel, and he couldn't allow that.

"Start from the beginning," he ordered. "Why were you with my aunt, to begin with?"

"Darned if I know! She came to my grandmother's house and insisted I accompany her on her rounds, but first she had to go get some herbs in the swamp."

"Why did she want *you* to go with her?"

"Beats me! I think she was casing me out. She has this outrageous idea about you and me getting married."

What's so outrageous about that? Not that I'm interested in getting married. But why is marriage to me so outrageous? "Just ignore her marriage chatter. She does that with everyone. What I can't understand is why you'd go with her."

"I had this notion that maybe I could incorporate some of her herbal expertise into my Feng Shui decorating. Don't look at me like that. It's possible."

He couldn't imagine Rachel and his aunt working together, but he supposed stranger things happened. "So, you went into the swamps with her, and . . . ? Please don't tell me you went by boat."

"Yep, a little outboard motorboat. Geesh, it was so small we could've been eaten, boat and all, by those alligators who were guarding their nest. They were big as SUVs, honest to God."

Remy put his face between his hands. Gators were not often aggressive, except when they were threatened by someone entering *their* territory. A gator nest was definitely *their* territory. As for them being as big as SUVs, well, alligators lived thirty or more years and could easily reach twelve to fifteen feet. She might not be exaggerating.

"Go on," he said when his blood pressure went down a notch.

"We went to this really out-of-the-way bayou. Well, it seemed out-of-the-way to me. Your aunt was picking herbs and moss and stuff, and I was avoiding snakes and spiders and stuff, when we heard men's voices. Some of them spoke Spanish, but at least one guy appeared to be Cajun, according to your aunt, especially since he was called by the name Sonnier. That's a Cajun name, isn't it? Anyway, we crept up close and saw them lower this big metal box down into the bayou stream with a strap still attached to a tree on the bank. It looked like a giant coffin, twice the size as usual."

Pour l'amour de Dieu! Her rambling sounds just like Tante Lulu. Is my aunt's ditziness wearing off on Rachel?

But then, Remy's body went cold and his hands literally shook as the full impact of her words hit him. *A metal coffin? Sonnier?* It appeared that his aunt and his lover had accidentally caught employees of the cartel in the act of hiding drugs on U.S. soil. And Rachel had referred to a *big* metal coffin. That was the first clue they'd had as to size. These hidden caches might be worth several million each, which meant they would kill anyone who dared to interfere with their plans, including two dingbat women picking posies.

"What did the police say when you reported this?"

"Well, we didn't exactly report it, yet."

"*What?*"

Rachel looked everywhere but at him.

Well, hell's bells, she ought to feel guilty. Remy exhaled with a mixture of exasperation and relief. Exasperation, because they'd placed themselves in danger and hadn't sought help. Relief, because this was a matter better handled by the DEA. He would have to call Pete the first chance he got for privacy.

"Why didn't you report it, *yet*?"

"Your aunt thought it would be better to tell your brother Luc first, and let him decide what course of action to take—him being a lawyer and all, and presumably having police contacts."

He nodded. *Good idea. Keep it quiet as much as possible. Although Tante Lulu has probably already told half the congregation of Our Lady of the Bayou Church. Hopefully, they'll discount it as the rantings of a fuzzy-headed senior citizen.* "I'll talk to Luc about it tonight." *And my aunt, too.*

"Of course, that was before your aunt got a speeding ticket. Luc was *really* angry about that. Good Lord, Remy, do you and your brothers realize what a maniac she is behind the wheel?"

I will definitely be talking to Tante Lulu. She is getting totally out of hand.

He put his hands on each side of her face and kissed her gently. "You could have been hurt."

"I know. I will never get in a boat or a car with her again, and I told her so, too."

I meant danger from the cartel. Yep, my aunt's flakiness must be wearing off on you.

"A raving lunatic, that's what she is. And she had the nerve to tell me she never *raved* in her life. Talk about homing in on the most irrelevant word! I swear, I had to restrain myself from doing her bodily harm, and I'm not a violent person."

He smiled at the vehemence of her response. He would have liked to be there when she'd been telling his aunt off.

"And do you know what your goofy aunt said when I was done with my tirade against her?"

Don't ask. "What?"

"She asked what colors I wanted in my bride quilt!"

It wasn't funny. Really. Still, Remy had to press his lips together to keep from laughing.

"Do you know, she was wearing a pith helmet today?"

His jaw dropped open, then clicked shut.

"Why does your aunt keep changing outfits and hair colors?"

Beats me. "I think she's trying to find herself."

"Do you think those men were Mafia?"

That knocked the laughter impulse right out of him.

"Mafia?" he choked out. Where did she get such an outlandish idea? Hah! Probably from his aunt.

"Yeah. You know, hit men getting rid of their hits."

"Maybe." *Babe, you've been watching too much of the* Sopranos. *Best to let her think that, though. Divert her attention away from the real culprits.*

"Remy, it was a harrowing experience today, but I'm confident that Luc, or you, or the police will take care of it. I'm more concerned about some personal issues bothering me right now, things we need to discuss."

Uh-oh!

Rachel turned on the bench seat so she was facing him directly. Her sober expression portended what would probably be an unwelcome subject for him.

"Do we have to talk about this now?"

"Yes. Yes, we do."

He sighed, recognizing that there would be no stopping her. When women got a bit between their teeth, they never let go.

"We've got to slow down this relationship, Remy."

I can't argue with that, but how do you stop a runaway train? That's just how I feel, out of control and headed for a collision. "I agree, babe, but holy hell, how are we going to do that? It's like a hooker deciding she's going to become a virgin again. There are some things you can't undo."

"I'm not sure I like your analogy."

"You know what I meant."

"I'm not asking to undo what's happened with us so far, even though it's too much too soon. It's been beautiful, Remy, to me anyhow and I wouldn't erase the memory of any of it."

"But . . . ?"

"But you make me breathless every time I look at you," she admitted.

Hot damn! He smiled. "And that's bad?"

"Yes, it's bad. I mean, it's good, but I can't think when you're around. My brain turns to pudding with hormone overload. I don't know if I'm making logical decisions or not. And stop smiling at me like that."

You should not be telling me this stuff, honey. I will use it against you, sure as summer lightning. Whoo-ee, I see more "perversions" on my male radar screen. I'll show you breathless, baby. Breathless in Loo-zee-anna. "Maybe it's just the heat. Some people react strangely to the high humidity." *Dieu, I can barely keep a straight face.*

She gave him a look that pretty much put him in the same class with the brain deficient. "For sure, I'm turning into a slut," she concluded with a big sigh.

What's wrong with sluts? "You are not a slut."

"I am where you're concerned. Where are my morals? Where is my good sense? Remy, I've known you little more than a week, and I've hopped in the sack with you any number of times."

"Seven to be exact, not that I'm counting. That's assuming that you count oral sex as sex, which I do—Bill Clinton notwithstanding." He grinned at her, hoping to break the mood.

But she plodded on somberly. "I have trust issues, Remy. Hard to hide that fact. They probably started long before David. A lot of people have let me down, starting with my mother."

"Why look for trouble, sweetheart? You should be happy that you found me," he teased.

"It's just so out of character for me, and I'm scared that I'm making decisions for all the wrong reasons."

He was afraid, too, that they were rushing at warp speed into a relationship—a *committed* relationship, for the love of St. Jude! But he was more afraid that she was going to end the relationship, committed or otherwise, before it even began. Quickly, he took both of her hands in his and tried his damnedest to state his case. "Men don't analyze things the way women do. If we're lucky enough to get laid—I mean, have good sex, we thank the gods for it, even if that good sex occurred on the first night. Hell, especially if it occurred on the first night—which it didn't with us," he was quick to add. "Love at first sight is something that happens in books or women's magazines, not in real life. At least, that's what I thought before I met you."

Rachel cocked her head and studied his face. "What are you trying to say?"

"We've been handed a gift, Rachel, like a special flower. I don't just mean the sex. You and I both know this is way more than sex. I think we should handle this gift with care, stop questioning why it happened and whether we should give the gift back, and just see whether it blooms or withers on the vine."

She pondered his words for what seemed an eternity. "So, you don't think we should step back for a breather. Stop seeing each other for a while."

"Definitely not."

"How about we see each other, but no sex. Get to know each other without all that extraneous matter clouding our brains."

Extraneous matter? That's a new way of referring to

good ol' hot sweaty rolling in the hay. "You've got to be kidding. I want you too much, babe."

"Same here."

Whew! Then why are we discussing this to death? "What do you want, Rachel?"

"Trust," she said, then immediately amended it to, "Love *and* trust."

"Bottom line, it's up to you. I can't make any promises about tomorrow or next week, not yet. *Maybe never.* But I'm willing to take a risk. Are you?"

Without hesitation, she nodded.

Thank God! He gave her a gentle kiss on the lips, then smiled at her. "Well, then, lady, let's go party. If there's one thing we Cajuns know how to do, it's party. *Laissez les bon temps rouler.* Let the good times roll."

"I can think of other things you Cajuns do well."

He just smiled at her.

Chapter 12

And then the you-know-what hit the fan

Rachel was stunned by the opulence of Inez Breaux-Fontaine's "family digs," as Remy had called it, on the out-skirts of Houma.

Sylvie's mother stemmed from an old Louisiana Creole family, the Breauxs, and she was, after all, a U.S. Congresswoman. Still, except for the hundred or so cars lined up in the vast semi-circular driveway and on the street below, it was like stepping back in time. Although it didn't have the huge grounds that would have gone with a Tara, this monument to excess was nonetheless a grand plantation house, complete with columns and sumptuous landscaping.

Hard to believe that a woman as down to earth as Sylvie had grown up in a place like this. And she was a working woman, too—a chemist—or so Rachel had been told, not a pampered Southern Belle.

"It's something else, isn't it?" Remy commented as he looped his arm in hers and they began the trek up the driveway.

"I'll say."

"I wouldn't be invited within a mile of this place if it wasn't for Sylvie. My brothers, neither."

Rachel raised an eyebrow at him in question. "You three are professional men, nothing to be looked down upon."

"We're not high-born. Nor do we have the money or influence that matters to Inez, which might counter our low social status. You'll see what I mean. I swear, that lady could freeze a person with just one look down her condescending nose. That's why they call the women in her family the 'Ice Breaux.'"

"Why are we here if she treats you all so rudely?"

"Family," he answered in one word. "We're here to bolster my brother and his wife."

Luc and Sylvie must have been watching for them because they emerged onto the front veranda and were coming down the marble steps to greet them. Luc appeared to be walking gingerly. Their three little girls in matching pinafores with Mary Jane shoes were playing tag around the wicker furniture, a nanny standing in the background supervising their play. Actually, the littlest one, only a year old, was just holding on to a wicker chair arm, squealing with delight at her sisters' antics.

Luc wore jeans and a soft plaid shirt. With his black hair and dancing eyes, he was almost too good looking for a man. And Sylvie was no slouch, either. She wore a sleeveless, gauzy sundress over a nicely rounded figure. Her dark Creole features provided a wonderful complement to her husband's appearance.

But the only thing that mattered to Rachel was relief that she wasn't underdressed. Remy had assured her that she wasn't, that even the famed Inez knew how to throw a lowdown, casual affair, but what did men know about such things? Once, David had invited her to a garden party, which turned out to be a White House garden party, posh to the *n*th degree.

"I'm so glad you came," Sylvie said, giving Rachel a quick hug and kiss on the cheek. Luc did the same.

"Where the hell have you been all this time?" Luc asked Remy. "I talked to you two hours ago, and you said you were on your way to pick up . . ." Luc stopped mid-sentence and grinned. Then, he sniffed in an exaggerated fashion. "I smell chocolate."

"No, it's coconut," Sylvie disagreed.

"Hah! It smells like S-E-X," Luc spelled out in deference to his children, still grinning at his brother.

"Luc," Remy said in a warning tone.

"Luc," Sylvie said in a chastising tone.

Rachel felt like sinking down into the clamshell driveway and disappearing.

"Mind your own business," Remy said, putting his brother in a headlock as they began walking up the steps. Over his shoulder, he cast Rachel an apologetic look. At one point, Luc's headlock appeared more like leaning on his brother for support. She saw Remy look funny at Luc and ask a question.

"What can I say? My husband has a crude streak," Sylvie said to Rachel, not all that bothered. "He doesn't mean any harm."

As they followed the two men up the steps, Rachel said, "I'm becoming used to the bluntness of people here. After all, I spent the morning with Tante Lulu. Nothing can shock me now."

"You poor girl!" Sylvie laughed companionably with her. "Has she started the bride quilt stuff with you yet?"

"God, yes!"

"She did the same thing with me, and wouldn't let up 'til Luc and I were married."

"Remy and I have just met," Rachel quickly pointed out. No way did she want to give the impression that she and Remy were about to become engaged, or anything close to it.

"Really?"

"Really. There are no marriage plans. We don't even know each other very well. In fact, I'm . . ." Rachel let her words trail off as she realized that she protested too much, and Sylvie wasn't buying a bit of it.

"You've got it that bad?" Sylvie asked with sympathy.

"Worse," Rachel admitted on a groan of dismay. "And I hardly know him."

"Hey, I knew Luc all my life, but it felt like love at first sight once he came back into my life."

"You seem very happy."

"We are. We've been married four years, and I love him more every day." Sylvie's face glowed as she spoke of her husband, and Rachel couldn't help but envy her that kind of relationship.

Through her peripheral vision she saw Remy down at the end of the veranda in a serious conversation on his cell phone. Luc was sitting on one of the chairs with the youngest girl on his lap and the other two girls on either side of him. He seemed to be telling them a funny story if their giggling was any indication. The older ones kept saying, "Oh, Daddy," but the littlest one could only manage, "DaDa."

While they waited for Remy to finish his call, the two women leaned against the balustrade. Rachel remarked to Sylvie, "You have a beautiful family."

"Yes, but this is the end of it. Three is enough for us to handle. Luc had a vasectomy this morning."

Well, that explained his strained walk up the steps. "On a Sunday?"

Sylvie nodded. "He has a doctor friend who did the outpatient work in his office for him. You know men and hospitals. And, really, it's only a minor procedure."

Rachel felt rather uncomfortable discussing this with a relative stranger. She'd only met Sylvie once before.

"Don't be shocked by my telling you such an intimate thing. Luc will be telling everyone himself tonight, trolling for pity."

"You're rather young to be taking such a drastic step."

"Not really. We're both thirty-seven. And, frankly, I want to share more time with my husband than I would be able to if we kept having more children. Luc offered, which saved me having to have my tubes tied. I love him for being willing to do that for me. Criminey, I can't believe I'm confiding all this stuff in you. I used to be so shy."

Rachel smiled. She couldn't imagine this warm, lovely woman ever being shy. Perhaps being married to a rogue like Luc had brought her out of her shell.

"I hear you left a man for having a vasectomy," Sylvie said hesitantly.

Rachel rolled her eyes. "Are there any secrets here in the bayou?"

"No." Sylvie patted her arm. "I hope I didn't offend you by bringing up a painful subject."

Rachel shook her head. "It's all over now. And I didn't leave David because he had a vasectomy. I left because he had the operation without telling me first. There's a difference."

"Of course there is."

"It's a matter of trust."

"Geesh! Some men are just born clueless, and then they get dumber as they get older. When it comes to understanding women, anyhow."

"We're quite a pair, aren't we?" Rachel said with a rueful smile. "A woman who dumps a man for having the Big V, and a woman who loves a man for the same reason."

Sylvie reached over and hugged Rachel. "I'm glad you came to Louisiana. I think we're going to be good friends."

"Hey, y'all, the crawfish are ready," Luc called out. "Get 'em before they're all gone."

Two of the little girls were already running into the house ahead of their nanny, who carried the toddler. All three of them were shrieking joyfully.

Remy came up beside Rachel, having finished his call. He put his arm around her shoulder, tugged her against his side, and pressed his lips against the top of her head. Rachel noticed that Luc and Sylvie were watching his gesture closely, seeming to give it some importance.

"Is everything okay?" she asked Remy, referring to his phone call.

"It is now. Sorry to leave you for business."

"It's all right. Sylvie and I had a nice talk."

As the four of them walked through the wide central corridor of the house and out to the back patio, which pretty much amounted to a stroll through a museum, Luc announced without warning, "I got snipped today."

Sylvie rolled her eyes at Rachel as if to say, "I told you so."

"I thought you looked different," Remy teased.

"I do?" Luc asked with sudden alarm and pretended to

cross his legs in an effeminate manner. "Well, no wonder! Did you ever take a needle in your family jewels? Ouch!"

"Should you be out and about?" Remy patted his brother on the shoulder.

"I've had an ice pack on the family jewels all day. Lots of fun, that. And I'm wearing a scrotal supporter." Luc glanced at Rachel sheepishly, as if he knew he pushed the bounds of polite conversation in her company.

"He's supposed to avoid excessive walking and lifting heavy objects," Sylvie told them with a disapproving glower at her husband. "And, yes, he should have stayed home."

"He was probably afraid you might run off with some handsome devil if he left you out of his sight," Remy commented.

"Bite me!" Luc said to Remy with a huge smile.

Remy just shook his head at his brother's coarseness.

"Stop it, you two," Sylvie warned. "Here comes my mother. And the rest of the Breaux warrior women." She pushed Luc down into a wooden deck chair on the patio and plopped herself on the arm, the mother hen protecting her injured rooster. Remy and Rachel stood on either side of the chair, watching the group approach.

In the forefront was an elegant woman who had to be almost sixty but could pass for fifty or less, no doubt due to numerous plastic surgeries, collagen injections, and expert make-up. She wore her dark hair in a short bob, and her trim body was covered with understated chic in a jade green silk jumpsuit, belted at the waist. The emerald posts in her ears probably cost more than Rachel's annual salary last year.

"Sylvie, darling, I didn't see you arrive," her mother

said, giving her an air kiss and a hug which involved no touching. Then she did the same to Luc, who winked at them over her shoulder, right at the moment when she said, "Luc! How nice to see you again."

"Mother, you remember Luc's brother, Remy."

The two of them nodded at each other, barely civil. Inez's perfectly tilted nose turned up slightly with distaste as she avoided looking at the disfigured side of Remy's face.

Rachel reflexively made a low growling sound deep in her throat and Remy moved to her side and grabbed onto her upper arm as if to restrain her. Rachel saw that Luc and Sylvie had noticed the whole exchange between her and Remy; they looked from Remy to her, then at each other, before smiling.

"And this is his friend, Rachel Fortier from Washington, D.C. She's a decorator."

Inez extended a limp hand toward Rachel in a half-hearted shake. "I use a N'awlins decorator exclusively," she said, as if Rachel were going to solicit her for business on the spot. "I have a townhouse in Georgetown when Congress is in session. Have you done the homes of any Representatives or Senators?"

"No, not yet," Rachel said.

"*Anyone* I might know?"

"Probably not." She could feel her face flaming.

Inez immediately turned away, as if Rachel obviously couldn't be that good if she hadn't done any of the important people in the nation's capital.

It was Remy who made a low growling sound deep in his throat now and Rachel who grabbed onto his forearm to restrain him from doing something hasty, like slap the rude, condescending woman.

The three other ladies were promptly introduced as well. First, there were Sylvie's aunts Margo and Madeline, who owned a mail-order herbal-tea company and apparently disliked Luc even more than Inez did, if their hostile glares were any indication. Next came Sylvie's ancient grandmother, Dixie Breaux, with her impeccably coiffed white hair. She must visit the same plastic surgeon as Inez because her face was unlined and not a liver spot dared peek into sight. Even at her advanced age, Dixie still worked as a lobbyist for the local oil companies.

The four ladies prepared to leave them after making polite small talk, and not so polite when Inez scolded Sylvie for not keeping a better eye on her children, who were nearby scarfing up avocado dip like it was going out of style, with the nanny looking on indulgently.

Luc did the growl thing now, and Sylvie restrained him from belting his mother-in-law by putting a forceful hand on his nape. But Luc got back at the disapproving ladies in his own way. "Did I tell you all I had a vasectomy today?" he inquired with an innocent smile on his handsome face. "Would you like to hear about the operation? It was very interesting."

Four senior citizens made gurgling noises of shock, and turned on their designer shoes, to leave Luc's presence ASAP.

"Your family is very . . . interesting," Rachel said into the silence the followed.

Sylvie, Luc and Remy all turned to gape at her, then burst out laughing.

"You don't have to be polite," Luc said. "They're a

bunch of snobbish prigs. And I was about to drop my pants and show them my scar, too."

"Do you have a scar, honey?" Sylvie asked Luc.

"Only a teeny tiny one, and it will fade in two or three weeks, but they wouldn't know that." He grinned impishly at his wife. "Wanna see?"

"I think we could all use a watermelon margarita," Sylvie said, waving for one of the floating bartenders who circulated through the crowd of two hundred of Inez's closest friends—in other words, people who could help her career.

"With all due respect, darlin', I think Remy and I would prefer a cold beer."

"With all due respect, darlin'," Sylvie said back at her husband, "you aren't having anything alcoholic with those painkillers still in your system."

Luc made a face at his wife, then reached up for one longneck from the tray for Remy and a lemonade for himself. Sylvie and Rachel took stemmed glasses encrusted with salt around their rims.

"Cheers!" they all said.

"Here's to a lifetime of sex without condoms." Luc raised high his glass.

"You are so crude," Sylvie said.

"And you love it," Luc countered, waggling his eyebrows lasciviously at his wife.

Rachel and Remy just watched the interplay with amusement, while Remy took a long swallow of beer and Rachel sipped at the delicious drink.

Just then, they had more unwelcome visitors to their little circle. The infamous Valcour LeDeux and his nymphet wife, Jolie, who was a good twenty-five years younger than he was, entered.

"First the mother-in-law from hell, then the aunts and grandma from hell. Finally, the father from hell. Can life get any worse than this?" Luc grumbled, downing the rest of his lemonade.

"Only if Satan decides to drop by," Remy added, also emptying his long neck.

He and Luc reached for second beverages from a passing waiter as their father approached. "It's always best to keep one's hands occupied when my Dad's around—to avoid hitting him," Remy explained to Rachel.

Papa LeDeux was on the back nine of his fifties, while Jolie, in her mid-twenties, was barely up to the tee. Being the mother of fourteen-year-old Tee-John, she must have been a mere fifteen years old when she first got involved with Valcour. Jailbait, for sure.

Dressed in Boss slacks, an Armani golf shirt, designer alligator shoes, and a Rolex watch, Valcour was clearly a wealthy man. He must be one of the many people invited who could help Inez with her political ambitions, if not through influence, then through money contributions. Silver threads were visible in his black hair and his middle wasn't quite as buff as it probably had been at one time, but he was still a handsome man, like his sons. The biggest imperfection was his flushed face, which bespoke years of excess booze.

"How are you, boys?" Valcour said, raising a martini glass toward each of his sons in turn.

"Just super," Remy said.

"Super duper," Luc added.

"I love your dress," Jolie said to Sylvie.

"Thank you," Sylvie responded. "You look lovely, too." And she did, Rachel conceded, and why not? She was young, slim and attractively dressed in a Donna Karan outfit that probably cost a bundle. She would have appeared almost gamine-like, except for her long blonde Texas big hair that seemed to be popular with the beauty-pageant circuit. Not that Rachel knew that Jolie was in such a mindset.

Valcour asked Remy, "Who's your friend?"

Remy jolted to attention. The dolt must have forgotten about her. "This is Rachel Fortier, from Washington, D.C. She's a decorator. And Rachel, this is my father, Valcour LeDeux, and his wife, Jolie."

Everyone shook hands all around.

"A decorator? We're going to redo our den. Maybe I could call you," Jolie said.

"Rachel is a Feng Shui expert," Remy bragged, to Rachel's surprise.

"What the hell's fung sway?" Valcour asked with a smirk.

Instead of answering Valcour, Rachel addressed Jolie. "Feng Shui is a type of decorating. I'd be glad to look at your den, but I'm afraid I won't have time. I'm only visiting Louisiana, and I'm already doing Charmaine's beauty spa and Remy's houseboat."

"You," Valcour said, waving a drunken finger at his wife, completely disregarding Rachel's words. "You spend too goddamn much money as it is. We don't need no fancy-pantsy decorator to tell us we need a ten thousand–dollar couch."

Jolie ducked her head with embarrassment. Then, to give her credit, she shot right back, "Don't talk to me like one of your workers over at the oil plant."

"For, chrissake, Remy . . ." Valcour's attention drifted from one to the other of them without logic. He must be drunker than he appeared. "What do you need an interior decorator for in a houseboat?" He gave Rachel a slow lecherous once-over from head to toe and back up to her breasts. He snickered.

What an unpleasant man!

Rachel dug her fingernails into Remy's forearm to keep him from jumping his father. He and Luc were chugging down their drinks like wanderers in the desert, probably for fortification.

"I heard Tee-John drove Lulu out to your place last week," Valcour said to Remy. "You better keep that bitch away from my boy. She's a bad influence."

"Bad influence," Luc sputtered, still in his seat. "The only bad influence in Tee-John's life is you. Why don't you hop on the wagon and straighten yourself out? After all these years, you'd be doing the world, and your family, a favor."

"You'd like me to hand you some favors, wouldn't you, boy? Beef up that ragtag law practice of yours. Make you something more than 'The Swamp Solicitor'."

Luc's face turned red with fury. Now Sylvie dug her fingernails into Luc's forearm to restrain him from doing bodily harm.

"Once a bastard, always a bastard," Remy snarled.

"Speaking of bastards, tell that brother of yours, René, that if I hear one more word from another legislator about oil pollution in the friggin' bayou, he's gonna find his ass in a sling, and I'll be tyin' the knot. Don't think I don't remember how to beat the crap out of any one of you boys."

With that, Valcour turned on his heels and staggered off, pulling Jolie with him.

"Well, that was certainly enjoyable," Sylvie said with a shaky laugh.

"No blood was spilled. That's a relief," Rachel added.

They all looked at her, then burst out laughing.

"You're right, darlin'. You're ab-so-lute-ly freakin' right. No blood and my Dad is an accomplishment," Remy said, giving her a one-armed hug.

Luc stood then, shrugging off Sylvie's help. "Stop coddling me, Sylv. I'm not an invalid."

"Has anyone seen Charmaine?"

They all turned around to see a tall man standing right behind them with a glower on his face. He was a cowboy, by the looks of him, complete with straight-leg jeans, boots, denim shirt, and a Stetson. A camel-colored corduroy blazer had been added for dress-up. He was about six-foot-three, dark haired, lean, and absolutely gorgeous. Plus, he was very angry.

"Where's Charmaine?" he demanded of Remy. "I've been looking for her for three days."

"Well, hello to you, too, Rusty," Remy said.

"Howdy," Luc added. Then he winced when Sylvie prodded him with a sharp elbow in the side.

Rusty made a grunting noise that was probably intended to be hello to all of them.

"Why do you want to find Charmaine?" Remy asked.

"I have a proposition to discuss with her."

Remy laughed. "I don't think she's interested in getting married again, Rusty."

"Married? Are you nuts? Is that what everyone thinks?

Is that what Charmaine thinks? Holy bloody hell, I've been in jail, not the loony bin."

Oh, my goodness! This must be Raoul Lanier, the ex-husband. Somehow, Rachel had imagined some redneck trailer-park type, possibly with a mullet and a wad of tobacco in his cheek, not this delicious specimen of manhood who could actually put words together in an intelligent manner.

"I don't know where Charmaine is," Remy said. "Try leaving a message on her answering machine, telling her what you want. Or make an appointment for a massage. That works for me."

Rachel elbowed Remy in the ribs, following Sylvie's suit.

"God, she is a flake," Rusty said, referring to Charmaine, of course. "Why can't she just talk to me?"

"I think she's afraid you'll wink at her and she'll land on her back in the sack," Luc informed him drolly.

"Or on a massage table," Remy added in an undertone.

Rachel elbowed him again, and he pretended to be hurt.

"Yeah, right," Rusty said, but he grinned just the same. Then he turned on his booted heels and stomped away, muttering something about wringing her pretty little neck.

"Why is he dressed like a cowboy?" Rachel asked Sylvie, still a little stunned by the appeal of Charmaine's ex-husband.

"Because he *is* a cowboy. His father owned a ranch in Loo-zee-anna, which he inherited last year."

"I thought he was in jail."

"He was, but—" Luc never got to finish his explanation because the shrill sound of triple giggles from the vicinity of the pool jerked both him and Sylvie to attention. Sylvie ran off to round up their children with Luc following at a slower pace. It appeared as if their three little ones might be a little too much for just one nanny.

"What do you say to eating some mudbugs, darlin'?" Remy nuzzled her ear as he spoke.

"Muddy bugs? I don't think so. I'll stick to chips and dip, thank you very much." Actually, there were tables all around the property laden with a vast array of finger foods, everything from caviar on toast points to chips and dip.

"Mudbugs are crawfish, silly," Remy informed her with a chuckle. "They get their name because they burrow down into the muddy stream beds, but, believe me, they are triple washed and spanking clean before they're thrown into the pot. C'mon, sweetie. You'll like 'em. They're like miniature lobsters."

A short time later, they were seated, side by side, at long tables lined with white butcher paper at the end of the back lawn, along with about a hundred other people who were eating the tiny creatures with gusto. Off to the side, huge cauldrons were boiling over open fires into which burlap sacks of crawfish, peeled potatoes and corn on the cobs were being tossed, along with a bunch of spices.

"There's an art to eating crawfish," Remy told her as he dumped large mounds in front of each of them. "First you break off the head from the tail and suck the juice from the head. Like so," he explained, demonstrating. "Then you dig out the fat from the head with your finger, or a paring knife if you're particular, and eat that, too, if you want. Some people don't like the fat. On the other hand, there are some who say it's what makes Cajun men so smooth and virile. Helps us charm the pants off the ladies." He winked at her.

"How about Cajun women? What happens when they eat the crawfish fat?"

"Turns them into regular hotties."

"I'm hot enough, thank you very much."

"Anyhow, then you peel the first couple segments of shell off the tail, grab that little piece of meat between your teeth, and pinch the tail. It should slide right out. Yum!" He demonstrated with several more crawfish, at one point having her taste a morsel, which was indeed yummy. Then he said, "Okay, your turn, *chère*."

Rachel stumbled through the first couple crawfish, getting virtually no juice or meat, but eventually she got the knack. She was sucking and pinching and biting like the best of them 'til she suddenly noticed that Remy had been silent next to her for some time. When she turned, she saw that he had stopped eating and was staring at her.

"What?" she asked as she finished off her margarita and licked the salt off her lips.

"Jesus, Mary and Joseph!" he prayed. "Do that again and we may just have sex under the table."

"Do what again?"

"Sucking and licking. Sucking and licking. You've got a tongue that could turn a monk to sin, babe."

"I like to watch you eat, too," she confessed and licked some more salt off her mouth.

"Do you now?" He placed one elbow on the table and propped his chin on his fist. "I am falling fast and hard for you, Rachel, you know that, don't you?"

"Because of my sucking and licking?" she teased.

He used a forefinger to wipe some salt off her upper lip, then put the finger in his own mouth to taste. Finally, he shook his head. "No. Because of you."

"Maybe that mudbug fat does work after all?"

"You thinkin' about takin' off your pants?"

"Maybe."

He stood and helped her to stand beside him. "Time to dance, sweetheart, before you seduce the hell out of me." The Paul Trebel jazz band was playing up by the patio where couples had just begun to dance.

"What makes you think that I can't seduce you while we're dancing?" she asked flirtatiously.

"I know you can. But, hey, I'm willing if you are."

They danced several sets to the soft jazz. Maybe it was the setting—the gorgeous plantation house, the pool which resembled a lagoon, the scent of hundreds of different varieties of irises which filled the formal gardens—but Rachel felt dreamy as she lay her head against Remy's shoulder and slow-danced, matching his rhythm perfectly. "I love you," she whispered in Remy's ear.

His only response was to hug her tighter, almost desperately.

She understood perfectly. She wanted to hug him tight, too, and never let go.

"Hey, bro, how about watching the kids for a few minutes so Sylvie and I can dance?" Luc said, tapping Remy on the shoulder.

"Sure," he said. Remy and Rachel walked over to the pool area and sank down onto the grass where the three girls were rolling and giggling beside their mother.

Luc and Sylvie strolled arm in arm toward the patio dance floor. Sylvie could be heard saying, "Are you sure you can dance with your *wound*?"

"I'm relyin' on you to hold me up, babe," Luc answered as he pinched his wife's behind and she yelped. Then Luc swung around behind her, and did a little shimmying, dirty dance against her backside as they continued toward the dance floor. He was wincing the whole time in exaggerated pain. Sylvie just laughed at his antics.

Nearby, Inez Breaux stood with a hand clapped over her chest in shock, watching the whole scene. The aunts' mouths hung open. But Grandma Dixie smiled.

"Uncle Remy's gonna play with us," the oldest girl said to her sisters.

"Yippee!" the other two cheered.

Remy was already surrounded by the children who obviously adored him. "Okay, what'll it be, munchkins?"

"Hide-and-seek!"

"Racing!"

"Patty-cake," the youngest offered in garbled baby talk, and the other two groaned.

"Girls, I want you to meet my friend, Rachel. Rachel, this big girl is Blanche Marie; she's three years old." The little girl beamed with adoration at Remy for referring to her as "big."

"How do you do?" Rachel reached out a hand to the girl's tiny one and shook. Blanche appeared impressed that anyone would want to shake her hand.

Remy turned to the next girl and said, "This beauty with the runny nose is Camille; Cammie is two, going on thirty; she wants to be on Sesame Street when she grows up." The black-haired mop-top looked as if she might be hurt over his mentioning her runny nose, which Remy was wiping with a napkin, but flashed him an adorable smile when he commented on her muppet aspirations.

Rachel shook hands with her, as well.

"Then, there is the baby of the family, little Jeanette;

Jeanie Beanie likes to give her Uncle Remy sloppy kisses, and he likes to give her raspberries." With that he tossed the little one onto her back, lifted her shirt and blew raspberries onto the bare skin of her abdomen.

"Me, too. Me, too," the other girls squealed.

They launched into a game of "I See" then as Remy mentioned objects about the grounds, and they had to guess what it was. "I see something big and green." "I see a tiny red animal." "I see something blue and wet." "I see something hot and sexy." He winked at Rachel. "Oops, I meant hot and spicy."

After that, they took turns riding on the "horsie," which was of course Remy. Then, he danced with each of the girls in turn, ending with a dance involving all three girls in his arms at once.

When Luc and Sylvie finally returned, Remy pretended to be exhausted from all the hard work of babysitting. Luc, who looked a little white about the gills, and his tribe went off to find a bathroom for the little bladders which were no doubt overflowing, including the one in training pants. He was probably going to put an ice pack on his groin, as well.

Remy and Rachel leaned back on their elbows, enjoying the ambience.

"You are really good with children," Rachel commented. "Do you plan to have lots of them someday?"

It had been an idle question, but Remy's silence alerted her that something was wrong. When she turned, she saw that he was staring straight ahead, stone-faced.

"Remy?" A chill of foreboding shook her.

He turned to her with a bleak expression on his face. Instead of answering her, he asked his own question, "Having children . . . it's really important to you, isn't it?"

"Yes . . . no . . . actually, I don't know. I never thought about it much before, but lately I've been thinking that, yes, I would like to have children—well, at least one child." In her mind came the sudden picture of a dark-haired Cajun boy, the same image she'd seen once before.

He looked stricken at her words, which was really odd.

Numb with apprehension, she asked, "How about you?"

At first, he just shook his head. Finally, he regarded her gravely and confessed, "Rachel, I can't have children."

"Can't?" She frowned with confusion. "Or don't want?" A suffocating sensation tightened her throat.

"Can't. I was damaged there by the fire," he elaborated, pointing to his groin. "Oh, the equipment is in working order, as you well know, but I'm shooting blanks."

Rachel jackknifed to a sitting position. Remy sat up, too.

"Let me get this straight. You knew that I just ended a relationship because a man failed to tell me that he took measures to prevent his having children, and you started a relationship with me, but didn't consider it important to tell me that you can't have children?"

"I suspected it might be important, but I hoped . . ." He shrugged. "I guess I just hoped."

"Let me see if I understand this. You suspected it would be a problem, but you expected it to just go away if it was never mentioned?"

"Something like that. Dammit, Rachel, I didn't know that children were that important to you." His eyes were dark pools of appeal.

She grabbed her own hair with both hands and pulled with frustration. "God, you men are clueless! It's not about the children, you lunkhead. It's about the failure to inform me ahead of time, to give me the choice."

"Rachel! We've only known each other two weeks."

"Don't you dare . . . Don't you dare . . ." She had to stop for a moment to calm herself. "You and I knew from the moment we first met that something was happening."

"Did you expect me to blurt it out that first afternoon in Gizelle's yard?"

"Don't be snide with me. These two weeks have gone like warp speed in terms of regular relationships. And you had plenty of opportunities for telling me."

"Like when?"

"Like last night, when we talked all through the night. I thought I was getting to know you. Then today, in the truck, when we were coming here, I told you—*I told you*—how important trust was to me. That was your perfect opening. Why . . ." Tears choked her, and she was unable to continue.

"Rachel, let me explain."

"Explain? Were you ever going to tell me?"

"Maybe."

"Maybe?" she practically shrieked.

"If our relationship had progressed, yeah, I would have told you."

"Our relationship had already progressed, in case you hadn't noticed. Sex, I-love-you's, more sex, more I-love-you's. Call me a fool, but I thought we were a couple—a new couple, maybe—but a couple just the same."

"Don't you think you're being oversensitive?"

Wrong word! "You are a real piece of work, LeDeux."

He tried to take her in his arms, but she slapped him away.

"Maybe I am oversensitive, but you knew trust was an issue with me. This is just like David all over again, except it took five years for him to pull the zinger on me. It only took you two weeks."

"That's unfair. I am nothing like that jerk."

"If it looks like a jerk, and feels like a jerk . . ."

"I love you, Rachel. You said you loved me."

"Too bad love isn't enough."

"I'm sorry. I'm sorry that I can't have kids."

"Good Lord! Have you heard a word I've said? It's not about making babies. It's about trust."

"Hell, Rachel, I told you now. Why isn't that good enough?"

"You never volunteered the information. I practically forced you into it by asking a point-blank question. To tell the truth, I probably wouldn't have cared if you'd told me last night, or earlier today. But now . . . !"

"Now?"

She stood shakily and stared down at Remy. She almost felt sorry for him as he stared hopelessly up at her—almost, but not quite. "Now, it's over."

With that, she stomped off, tears streaming down her face. *Betrayed again! When will I ever learn? I knew this was too good to be true. I knew I was headed for disaster. Oh, God! Betrayed again!*

Chapter **13**

Men and the clueless hall of fame

Rachel stayed burrowed in her loft bed-cocoon until noon, trying to sleep, or not think. Neither worked.

All she could think was, *It's over.*

Finally, her grandmother launched into a campaign to shame her into coming downstairs. After climbing the steps on her arthritic knees, huffing and puffing loud enough to wake the dead, Granny leaned over her and asked, "You sick, girl?"

"No."

"Then get your be-hind out of that bed and stop feelin' sorry fer yerself."

"I'm not feeling sorry for myself."

"Oh, yes, you are, and it's gonna stop now. Yer a Fortier. We Fortier women are strong. We doan let our men tromp all over us, nosirree."

It's over. "No man—*nobody*—tromped all over me."

"Hah! That Remy LeDeux did, I'll wager. Beau sez you were a sorry case when he picked you up last night in Houma. Cryin' and a-shakin' like it was the end of the world. I tol' you not to mess with them LeDeuxs. Man trouble, sure as shootin'."

It's over. "What makes you think I have man trouble?"

Granny gave her a look that pretty much said she was a brainless twit if she tried to convince her otherwise. "So, what did the varmint do? He dint hit you, did he? Iffen he did, I'll cut his worthless heart out with my paring knife, I will."

"No, he didn't hit me. For heaven's sake!"

"What did he do then?"

"It's not what he did, it's what he said."

"What?"

"I can't tell you."

Her grandmother threw her hands up in the air with exasperation. "How come you smell like coconut?"

Oh, geesh! Still?

"It must be sunscreen."

"In bed?"

Holy moly! Talk about persistence! "Granny, leave me alone. I'll be down in a minute."

"Get out of bed."

"Oh, all right," she grumbled.

As she slid out of bed, her silk nighty rode up practically to her crotch and the straps slipped down to her breasts.

Her grandmother exclaimed, "For the love of Mary! What have you been doing with that man? 'Pears as if you been wrestlin' with a bear."

Rachel looked down, afraid of what she would see. Then, she wished she could sink back under the feather tick.

There were whisker burns all over her chest.

A bite mark stood out on her inner thigh.

The nail polish had been sucked off of three of her toes.

Fingerprints marked Rachel's outer thighs where Remy had grabbed her legs and lifted them high. Good thing her grandmother didn't know that.

"*Tsk-tsk-tsk,*" Granny said, staring at those very prints.

Yep, she knew.

"This is worser'n I thought," Granny said. "Me, I never took you fer that kind of girl."

"I love him, Granny—or I thought I did." *But, damn, damn, damn! It's over.*

"Love doan make the chitlins fry, and it sure doan justify sinnin'."

Rachel opened her mouth to argue that times were different and it was not immoral to engage in sex with a man to whom a woman was committed. But then she stopped herself. There had never been any commitment between her and Remy, even if she had thought they were leading up to that. What kind of commitment could there ever be without trust? And apparently he hadn't trusted her enough with his secret. Now she could never trust him again because of his huge lie of omission.

It's over.

"You look like yer gonna cry again. You want I should put a *gris* on him?" With a sympathetic sigh, Granny sank down to the mattress and took one of Rachel's hands in her gnarled one. "I'm the fool, I reckon, but iffen you wants him that bad, mebbe things can be straightened out. Mebbe I could hold my nose every time he's around, pretend he ain't a stinkin' LeDeux. Mebbe I could take my shotgun and go round him up fer you."

A shotgun wedding? Oh, God! Rachel smiled despite her

dreary mood. "There's no fixing this, Granny, but bless you for being willing to set aside your biases."

"Biases? Biases? I got every right to my opinions."

"Why? What is it about the LeDeuxs that you find so repugnant?"

"I'll tell you what it is. It's that Valcour LeDeux and his father before him. Was a time when Valcour diddled around with Josette, Beau's Mama, before the divorce. Not that he cared about her. She was jist one of a litter of girls he was fornicatin' with at the time, and Lord knows, Josette allus was a flighty one. Broke up a marriage, Valcour did, and left Beau with neither a father or mother worth a plug nickel. All they did was drink and fight after that. Thass when Beau come to live with me."

So that was the reason for all her hostility.

"They're tomcats, them LeDeuxs are, allus looking fer new alleycats to poke."

"Granny!" Rachel exclaimed. "You can't condemn all the LeDeux because of one bad apple."

"I can and I do!" Her grandmother squeezed her hand. "Does this mean yer gonna skedaddle back to Washington, cut our visit short?"

"No. No, I won't do that," Rachel said, taking her grandmother's hand in both of hers and squeezing back. "The whole point of my coming here was to get to know you, my only family. I just got sidetracked a bit."

Granny nodded. "Just one more thing, girlie, yer gonna end up with a big belly lessen you stop this hanky-panky with that Remy. Thass all I'll say on the subject."

"No, I won't," Rachel wailed and burst out bawling, *because Remy can't have children.* Rachel hurt so bad, and she didn't know how to make the hurt stop. *It's over.*

Her grandmother reached over and took her in her arms, patting her back as only a mother or grandmother could do. "Now, now! Hush you, honey. It cain't be as bad as all that."

The problem was, it *was* as bad as all that.

It's over.

More advice than Dear Abby

Rachel managed to reduce the puffiness in her eyes with some cold cloths and finally emerged downstairs a half-hour later, only to be confronted with thick black coffee and a plate full of fried bacon fresh from the slab, scrambled eggs and grits with two slices of buttered toast. Comfort food, her grandmother probably thought. But to Rachel it just looked like a monumental amount of food to get past the lump in her throat.

While she nibbled and gulped, Granny told her, "I forgot to tell you, Remy called for you five times this mornin'."

"You forgot?" Rachel arched her brows in disbelief.

Her grandmother didn't even look at her. She was busy at the sink, stirring beans which had been simmering slowly on the stove all morning.

"What are you making, Granny?"

"Black beans and rice. Same as allus on a Monday."

"Every Monday?"

Granny nodded. "Black beans and rice is a traditional Cajun meal. The reason it's served every Monday is 'cause Monday is laundry day. The hard beans gotta cook a long time, but they doan need no tending. So, the housewife kin do the weekly laundry without fussin' over dinner."

Peering out the window, Rachel saw fresh laundry on the clothesline in the side yard.

"Gonna cook up some collard greens with this leftover bacon grease, too. And bake some cornbread. Beau likes to sop up the drippings with his cornbread."

"It sounds delicious."

"Back to that Remy LeSkunk," Granny said, resuming her earlier conversation, "I tol' him you was 'indisposed.' That means too busy to come to the phone, in case you doan know. I learnt that word from my soaps. Riva on *The Guiding Light* is indisposed all the time."

Granny and her soaps! The homemaker's thesaurus! "Continue to say I'm 'indisposed' if he calls again," Rachel advised. It was as good a word as any for heartbroken.

Granny also informed her that her two friends from Washington, Laura and Jill, had called at different times the night before while Rachel had been out. "I tol' 'em you went honky-tonkin' with Beau. They was really surprised by that. Guess you doan do much honky-tonkin' back in the city, huh?"

Rachel groaned. "Did you have to tell them *that*? Couldn't you just say I was out?"

"Or indisposed?" Her grandmother grinned at her shyly, then ruined the pretty effect by spitting a stream of tobacco into the sink drain.

Now her friends would be grilling her for information, thinking she was having a wild good time here in the bayou. She wasn't up to returning the calls if she would have to appear perky and happy when every breath she took reminded her, *It's over.*

"Least I dint tell 'em you was off boinking with a lusty LeDeux."

Practically choking on her coffee, Rachel responded, "Yes. Thank God for that."

Deciding that work was the best antidote for depression, she called Charmaine to discuss a schedule for the wallpaper and painting contractors. They chatted about other ideas Rachel had for the spa. When she mentioned having seen Rusty the night before and his having been looking for his ex-wife, Charmaine asked hesitantly, "What did you think of him?"

"Gorgeous."

"Yes, he is, isn't he?" Her long sigh could be heard over the phone. "When I started going with him, he was a college boy, and I just won the Miss Loo-zee-ana competition. We were so young."

"Sounds like you still have feelings for him."

"Oh, I have feelins all right. The no-good lizard! Dumped me when I dropped outta college. Said that next thing, I'd be strippin' like my Mama. Said I was a dimwitted floozie to think I could get by on my looks alone. Well, I showed him. I own two successful businesses and my own home. How dimwitted is that? And I *never* stripped for money in all my life, I swear."

"I can see why you wouldn't start something up with him again." Charmaine's vehemence was daunting.

"He is one handsome devil, though, I gotta admit that. But that's water over the dam. How're things with you and Remy?"

"They're not."

"Oh? What did he do?"

"He didn't do anything. He just told me something . . . something personal, which changed everything."

"Isn't that just like a man? They're like ticking bombs,

men are. At the most perfect moment, when women are swoonin' with love, they'll say or do somethin' to ruin the magic. Happens every time."

Yep. "I don't want to talk about it anymore. Just suffice it to say that it's over, before it began."

After she hung up with Charmaine, Rachel called the contractor who was to install Remy's skylight, the craftsman who was to construct some of the built-in dressers and storage areas, the plumber who would install the bathroom fixtures, the tile man doing the bathroom walls and floor, and the seamstress who was working on the drapes. Once she knew their schedules, she took a deep breath and called Remy's number, hoping against hope that he wouldn't be home.

He wasn't.

She left a coldly voiced message on his machine informing him when the people would be there to work and insisting that he be nowhere in sight when she arrived to check over the end results. If he showed up, she swore she would ditch the project altogether.

Tears welled in Rachel's eyes when she hung up the phone. She hadn't actually talked to Remy, nothing new had happened, but it felt as if she'd pounded one more nail into the coffin that represented their relationship—or non-relationship.

When she went out on the porch, dabbing at her eyes with a tissue, she noticed Granny and Beau working in the vegetable garden. Their hoes and rakes were loosening up the soil which had been moistened by a cloudburst of hard rain an hour earlier. A clod buster, as Granny referred to the hard rains which came suddenly in this humid climate, then dried up just as fast.

"Could you use some help?" Rachel asked as she walked up to the penned area.

Granny leaned against the handle of a rake and wheezed from her exertions. "Can you lift a hoe?"

A wave of guilt rippled over Rachel that she hadn't noticed how hard her grandmother worked, not just today with the cooking, laundry and gardening, but every day. Nor had Rachel offered to help before. She felt especially guilty when she noticed the liver spots that marked the skin on her hands and bare arms in her short-sleeved house dress— "Flowers of Death," some people called them. When had she forgotten that the primary purpose of her trip to Louisiana had been to bond with her grandmother? What better way to bond than help lift her load of work?

"I can learn," Rachel said determinedly.

"You'll be sorry," Beau grumbled. "Pretty soon Granny'll be ropin' you into other jobs. Like butcherin' hogs and pluckin' dead chickens."

"Oh, shush yerself, boy," Granny said, spitting into the dirt. "You ain't as overworked as you think you are."

"I jist wish Rachel would stay here for awhile longer, 'til Christmas at least soze I could go to Florida and do my thing for a bit. Cain't leave you here alone, Granny."

"I doan need no babysitter," Granny snarled at Beau, just before she warned Rachel, "Doan ask."

"Florida?" Rachel asked, ignoring the warning.

"Yep, thass where some of the best professional wrestling schools is. The Funkin' Conservatory. Bone Breakers. Mad Dog's Palace. Skull Krushers. Me, my dream is to get involved with that there WWE, the World Wrestling Entertainment, and, damn, I know I would be good." Beau wore a wife-beater T-shirt tucked into tight jeans today. Not a hair was out of place in his mullet. His arms and shoulders rippled with muscles from all the hard physical labor he engaged in. To some people, he might be considered an attractive man. She supposed those were some of the qualifications for a professional wrestler.

Rachel frowned, thinking over what he had said. "I thought it was called WWF."

"Hah! Those tree-huggers in the World Wildlife Federation took 'em to court and won. Said they owned the letters first. Doan that beat all?"

"But wrestling. Of all careers to pursue, why wrestling?"

Beau lifted his chin haughtily. "Ain't it jist like a city-slicker Yankee to look down her nose at us common folks. Football is fine and dandy, but wrestling is low class. I remember this lady—a Yankee fer shur—who come into a diner over in Houma one day. When the waiter asked her if she wanted butter on her cross-ant, she lifted her nose jist like this." Beau demonstrated by tilting his face up to the sun. "She said, no, she'd rather have honey. Well, you know what that waiter tol' her, dontcha? He said, 'Bee shit, coming right up.' "

Holy cow! What did I say to bring on this sermon? "Beau, all I did was ask you why wrestling? I never said anything about looking down on you. Lighten up."

He ducked his head sheepishly, realizing he'd over-reacted.

"Tell me about the wrestling," she encouraged.

"I love it, pure and simple. My hero is The Rock, of course. I already got my persona picked out."

"Doan ask," Granny warned again.

But Rachel couldn't resist. "What persona?"

"The Swamp Monster. Or mebbe even The Croc Rock,

but I guess that would be too much like the real Rock. I'll wear a crocodile skin over my shoulders and Cajun music will be my theme song. I'll keep my mullet hairdo, of course, but mebbe I'll wear a Daniel Boone–type hat. Not sure 'bout that yet. Ain't that the most hellacious thing you ever heard of?"

"Sure is," Granny and Rachel agreed at the same time.

"I already took some courses at the Louisiana wrestling schools. Now, I'm ready for the big time."

"And you approve of this?" Rachel asked Granny.

"Hell, no!"

"It's better than trappin'." Beau raised his chin defiantly.

"You've got a point there," Rachel said.

"No, it ain't." Granny shook her head decisively at Beau. "You get a steady income from trappin'. That wrestling business is too risky. Besides, you'd probably get dropped on yer head and be even screwier than you are now."

"I ain't screwy," Beau argued.

"Beau, honey, last year you wanted to be a whittler. Now, you wanna be a wrestler. What'll it be next year, a yodeler?"

"A whistler? What kind of work can a whistler get?" Rachel was having trouble following this conversation.

"A whittler, not a whistler," Beau answered with disgust. "Geesh almighty! What you must think of me to imagine I'd wanna work as a whistler! Do you think I'm gay or sumpin'?"

Right. Wrestling is okay, whistling is not okay. And what does homosexuality have to do with whistling? I think I've landed in a bayou version of One Flew Over the Cuckoo's Nest.

The whole time they talked, they also worked, and it was backbreaking work, at that. The garden plot must be at least twenty by twenty, and the neat rows overflowed with lush staked tomatoes, climbing string beans and peas, collard greens, various squashes, onions, garlic, broccoli, cucumbers, asparagus, and more okra than any one person had a right to grow.

"Why are you growing so much okra?" Rachel asked.

"Why, sweetie, you cain't live in Louisiana and not use okra in every other dish. It adds taste and acts as a thickener. Why, we'd no sooner give up okra than our rouxs or *filés*." Rachel already knew that the Cajuns were famous for their rouxs, brown sauces, which were added to just about anything cooked in liquid. *Filé* or ground sassafras was also used as a thickener; it was an ingredient passed down from the Native Americans who'd lived here at one time. But okra? No way! It must be an acquired taste.

As if reading her mind, Beau glanced over and winked at her. "You get used to okra after awhile, 'specially if you got some Wild Turkey to wash it down."

Granny reached over and swatted him on the arm. "I'll give you Wild Turkey, boy!"

The phone rang inside the house and everyone jerked upright to alertness, leaning on the handles of their hoes and rake. Granny and Beau stared at Rachel, as if silently inquiring what they should do. Rachel's heart just stopped beating for a moment, and a tightness lingered in her chest even after it resumed its rapid rhythm. She couldn't speak.

Beau made a rough sound of disgust and jogged inside, saying it might be Mary Sue calling about their date that night. Mary Sue was the girl he'd met at The Swamp Shack on Saturday night.

Within seconds Beau returned to the porch and called out, "Rachel, it's those two friends of yers. Laura and Jill. They's on a conference phone to you. Are you here?"

She would have to be now since Beau had announced her presence loud enough for them to hear.

"You were supposed to say she was indisposed." Granny shook her head and made *tsk*-ing sounds at Beau.

"Huh?" Beau said.

Rachel took the call in Granny's sitting room. "Hey, guys!"

"Well, hello, stranger," Laura greeted her.

"What's new, pussycat?" Jill inquired.

"Not much. I was just outside helping my grandmother and my cousin Beau do some gardening."

"Gardening? You?" Jill laughed.

"Yep. And I'm thinking of shipping a bushel of okra to each of you."

"Yeech!" they both said at the same time.

"We miss you," Jill declared dolefully.

"Does Hank want his truck back sooner?" Rachel asked.

"No. He doesn't even know it's missing, hardly," Jill answered. "He has a new hobby. Motorcycles."

"Uh-oh! All that vibrating machinery and stuff. Bet your love life is interesting these days." Rachel smiled to herself.

"Interesting!" Laura interjected. "You won't believe what Jill told me they did after a biker's meeting over the weekend. They call it Hog Sex, and—"

"That'll be enough, Laura. Let's leave some secrets to lure Rachel back home. Are you coming home soon, sweetie?"

"In October, same as before. I really need this time with

my grandmother. If it weren't for her, believe me, I would be coming back today."

"Rachel, what's wrong?" Jill's voice rose with alarm.

"Nothing. What do you mean?"

"You can't hide anything from us," Laura said. "We've been friends for ever. We can tell when something's wrong. You sound as if you're about to cry, and you hardly ever cry."

"Oh, man!" Rachel took a deep breath to stifle a sob, then sank down to Granny's upholstered rocker. "I'm in a bad way."

"It's a man, isn't it?" Jill hooted, as if she'd just guessed the answer to some big puzzle.

"What's his name?" Laura wanted to know.

"Remy LeDeux."

"Oh, my God! I'm wetting my pants just hearing such a sexy name," Jill said.

"Jill, you wet your pants at the wink of your husband's eye," Laura commented.

"Do not!" Jill countered. "But, Rachel, do tell. Why are you so glum if you've got this Cajun hunk, Remy what's-his-name?"

"I don't have him," Rachel replied, trying to brace herself for the crying jag she felt coming on. She was unable to keep the tears from her voice, though, when she added, "It's over."

"It's over?" Laura shrieked. "How could it be over when you didn't even tell us, your best friends, that it had begun?"

Rachel would never tell anyone here in Louisiana what Remy had confided to her, but somehow it didn't feel like a betrayal to tell these friends who lived so far away and would never meet him. "He can't have children," Rachel blurted out.

"I beg your pardon," Laura said. "Since when is having children so important to you?"

"Do you love him?" Leave it to Jill to cut right to the chase.

"I did. I don't know how I feel now." She paused, then admitted, "Yeah, I love the jerk, but I'll get over it."

"Start over and tell us everything," Laura urged.

And Rachel did.

When she finished, and was weeping audibly, Laura said, "This is amazing. You've only known the man for two weeks. How could you fall in love so fast?"

"I know exactly how," Jill interjected before Rachel could answer. "One date with Hank, and I was a goner. We were married three months later. Some things happen that way, Laura."

"He sounds yummy," Laura conceded, "even with the face disfigurement that you mentioned. A pilot. A Cajun. A good dancer, for heaven's sake. Where you gonna find that?"

"And a good lover, if I'm reading between the lines," Jill remarked with a little chuckle.

"Do you want us to come down there?" Laura offered.

"Definitely not," Rachel said. "I'm a little raw because this just happened last night, but I'll be all right." *I hope.*

"Well, I can see why you were so devastated," Laura went on. "Coming right on top of David's lack of disclosure, this must feel like a double whammy of betrayal."

"Yes, it does."

"But, in his defense," Jill began, "though Lord knows the man doesn't need my defense, think about how he must feel. Men are so proud, especially when their precious you-know-what's involved. He probably considers his sterility a mark against his masculinity. He feels like less of a man. I know Hank would, no matter how illogical that would be."

"I can't believe you're defending the bum," Laura said.

"I'm not defending him. Just trying to explain why he would have acted the way he did. I'm betting that Rachel is the only person he's ever told about this."

"None of that matters. He didn't tell me, and now it's over," Rachel said firmly.

"Well, it's something to think about," Jill persisted.

"I'm not going to think about any such thing," Rachel said adamantly.

But she could swear she heard a voice in her head insist, *Think about it.*

Heartbreak Hotel, or rather, heartbreak houseboat

Remy was so lonesome he could cry.

It's over.

How could things go so wrong in such a short time? It was Tuesday morning, thirty-six hours since Rachel had stomped away from him at the party on Sunday night. And he hadn't talked to her since, except for that cold-as-a-dead-fish message she'd left on his answering machine yesterday.

It's over.

He'd love to go on an all-out bender. Lock himself in the houseboat. Hide the car keys from himself. And drink himself to unconsciousness. But he had obligations to the DEA

this week, too many jobs to do which required total concentration. He had to train the government pilots for two
days, starting tomorrow. Strategy meetings galore. And
D-Day was only a few days off.

Still, he kept thinking, *It's over.*

Things couldn't go on this way.

As with other of the injustices in his life, Remy decided
that, first, he'd allow himself to hurt. Then, he would get
angry. Finally, he would let his determination kick in. He
was about at the third stage now.

Over the years, Remy had learned to guard his defenses.
He almost never showed anyone his naked body because at
heart he believed that everyone rejected him on some level.
On occasion, he did reveal himself, when the sexual need
became too overpowering, like it had with Rachel.

But he had never, ever told anyone about his sterility.
Not even his family. Rachel was the only one, and look
what it had gotten him—a kick in the nuts.

How dare she give him the ol' heave-ho just because he
couldn't give her a bunch of mini-me's? Oh, he knew what
she'd said about the betrayal business. Hogwash! She
hadn't fooled him. Her ticking baby clock had collided with
his sterility roadblock. Deep down, she had to be repulsed
by his inability to shoot out the proper sperm. She might not
have vomited when she looked at his mangled body the first
time, but in a way that's what she'd virtually done over his
inability to reproduce. *Dieu*, what a fool he'd been! Well,
never again. *C'est la vie.*

Remy had tried all yesterday morning to reach Rachel,
to apologize, for chrissake. But not anymore. Even if
Rachel begged him to come back, which she wouldn't, he
could never trust her again. He'd laid his heart on the line,

his most intimate secret, and she'd dumped him. Then, she'd refused to take his calls the next day. No second chances. Nothing.

Well, adios, señorita. This cowboy is heading off into the sunset.

His resolution was tested quicker than he'd imagined. There was a knock at the door. His heart skipped a beat, but not because he thought it might be Rachel. He knew it wouldn't be. But he *was* surprised, nonetheless.

Rachel's grandmother, Gizelle Fortier, stood out on his deck, looking witchier than usual today with her straggly hair and unkempt clothing. Was that burlap she wore all the time? Or just swamp chic?

"To what do I owe this pleasure?" he said through the screen door.

"Cut the crap, buster. Me, I'm not here to please you."

"You gonna put a voodoo curse on me, old lady?"

"Doan think I cain't? But thass not why I'm here."

"No? What, then? I'm dying to know." Belatedly, he realized how rude he appeared, not even inviting her in. "Do you want to come in and have a drink, or something?"

She just laughed, or rather cackled. Really, the woman gave him the creeps. Good thing that he and Rachel hadn't worked things out. Hard to imagine being related to this old biddy.

"All right, Gizelle, what is it you want?"

"Ms. Fortier to you."

"Ms. Fortier then." He leaned against the door frame and waited for her to disclose the reason for her stepping onto hated LeDeux property.

"I know what you been doin' with my granddaughter."

"You do?"

She nodded. "Fornicatin' like a billy goat, you cock of the roost, but no more. I'm fixin' to make sure of that. Time to put that wee-wee of yours out of commission."

"Really? What're you gonna do, old lady? Cut off my *wee-wee*? I wouldn't put it past you. Or put a voodoo curse on other body parts?"

"Now, there's a thought."

"Does Rachel know you're here?"

"Hell, no, she's over at Charmaine's pickin' colors or sumpin." She narrowed her eyes shrewdly at him. "Or mebbe she and Charmaine are out pickin' up men—better men than you."

He had to laugh at Gizelle's transparent ploy to make him jealous.

"Enough foolery! You still wanna buy a piece of my property, yes?"

He nodded slowly, suddenly alert. He named a very generous sum that he would be willing to pay.

She waved a hand as if the amount were unimportant. "I'll sell you the land on one condition."

I knew there would be a catch. "And that is?"

"You agree to stop seeing my granddaughter."

Remy inhaled sharply, as if he'd been kicked in the gut. He hadn't been expecting this. Two days ago—hell, a day ago—he would have laughed in her face. No piece of land was worth his integrity. If he wanted a woman, he wouldn't have let money or land or anything else stand in his way.

But, in light of his recent musings—his firm conviction that things were over with Rachel—he gave Gizelle's proposal consideration. It was over with Rachel anyway. Perhaps Gizelle didn't realize that. He'd never forgive Rachel for the look on her face when he told her of his shameful secret. *Never.*

"It's a deal," he said. "I'll see you in Luc's office on Thursday to make it legal."

She cackled like a chicken as she walked away.

Remy should have been jubilant. The land would finally be his. But, instead, his body felt leaden and heavy.

And that dreaded voice in his head said, *What a fool!*

Chapter 14

Can't get no

By Thursday, Remy was horny as hell.

He'd been busy training pilots, engaged in meetings, studying maps, going over and over the plan of action for D-Day, taking cold showers. He should've had no time to think of sex, or Rachel, which were the same thing in his vivid imagination.

Besides that, the farther away from Sunday night's blow-up that he got, the more he convinced himself that she was the guilty party, not him. The only thing he'd done wrong was get shot down by an Iraqi bomb which mangled his body and screwed up his baby factory. Okay, he hadn't told her right away. *Big deal! So sue me!* Did she expect him to shout his manly imperfections to the world?

So why did he keep thinking about her? How sexy she looked, clothed and unclothed. The way she smelled, before and after sex. The soft moan she made when she came—and came again. How she'd looked when she said, "I love you." The curve of her ass, seen from behind, preferably naked, which was beyond beautiful, no matter what she thought.

He didn't care about her anymore, much less love her, but he sure-God wanted to jump her bones again. Lust, pure and simple, that's all. At least, that's what he told himself.

He'd thought about going down to Swampy's and picking up some chick for a bout of mutual satisfaction. Wham-bam-thank-you-*chère* was just the thing on occasion. But that held no appeal. He knew a few women he could call and make a date for dinner and whatever, but that held no appeal, either. Or he could hook up again with Claudia Casale, a P.I. and former Dallas police detective, with whom he'd had a brief affair a few years back and somehow managed to emerge as friends. That held no appeal, either. Why ruin a good friendship for the sake of temporary lust lunacy? He'd even thought of hitting Bourbon Street for its peculiar kind of action. Talk about no appeal!

It was just going to take time.

So, Remy rolled up the maps on his desk and opted for the best antidote to horniness he could think of. Better than an ice-cold shower any day.

He was going to visit Tante Lulu, bless his horny soul!

Who said big girls don't cry?

Every time Rachel thought she'd finished crying, she would start all over again. The least little thing set her off.

The memory of Remy's disfigured body and his self-consciousness about it. The way his skin smelled. The way he smiled, slow and sexy. The way he talked with a Southern drawl. The way he looked, all serious and focused, when he was inside her. The way he said, "I love you," putting emphasis on each separate word.

It was going to take time, she finally concluded. And keeping herself busy was the answer.

Work had begun on Charmaine's redecoration, and Rachel was pleased with the progress thus far. This morning, she'd gone over to Remy's houseboat. The skylight had been installed yesterday, and it looked wonderful. Amazing what a difference it made, not only in brightening up the interior, but making it appear much larger. The carpenter was still working on the built-ins, and he would be sanding and refinishing the floors and walls today. The seamstress wouldn't install the draperies or bring the new bedspread and cushions until next week. Ditto for the plumber and tile man.

Rachel had added an ironic touch to the decorating of Remy's home. She'd placed David's antique Roseville vase on a small gateleg hall table near the door; the table had been purchased for a song at a yard sale she'd passed yesterday on the way back from Charmaine's. Remarkably, the beautiful pottery, in the rare Della Robbia pattern, seemed almost made for this setting. Its vivid colors and floral motif provided a great contrast to the dark colors of the paneling and floor.

Besides, David would be so pissed that she would just give the piece away. Irritating David gave her great satisfaction.

Two weeks had passed since she'd seen David last, and she'd only spoken to him on the phone that one time. She marveled that no pain remained over their breakup, just sadness and a little need for vindictiveness, as evidenced over her glee regarding the Roseville vase.

Thank Goodness, Remy had been absent while she worked at his houseboat, as she'd demanded. But a little part of her mourned his absence. Perhaps she had hoped in some fanciful part of her soul that he would have shown up, begged her forgiveness, and somehow they would have worked things out.

All girls believed in Prince Charming to some extent, she supposed. Even big girls. But unfortunately modern women had to accept that most often the prince was just a royal pain.

She'd also gone jogging today, for the first time in weeks, part of her "keep-busy" plan, not to mention her "work-off-Granny's-food" plan. Glancing down at her dust-covered running bra and nylon shorts, she winced. Jogging on a dirt road didn't quite match city jogging, for sure.

Anyhow, Rachel had other problems today. Her missing purse, the one she had lost in the bayou jungle when she and Tante Lulu had run for their lives, was proving to be a bigger pain than the other big pain. Since theft was not an issue, just loss, she had mistakenly thought it would be an easy matter to cancel the credit cards and get a new driver's license. Not so. Being away from home and all her stored documents, she was having trouble conducting the transactions over the phone. It wouldn't be impossible, she was told over and over, just extremely difficult. "Can't you try to find your missing purse?" more than one person had asked her.

Finally, that's just what Rachel decided to do. Hopping into her red pickup truck with the REDHOT vanity plate, probably red in the face from aggravation, she drove over to Tante Lulu's house. She didn't even bother to change her clothes for fear she might back down. How silly! After all, she was a grown woman. She needed her purse. What could be so hard about going in a boat with the old lady again?

That strange little voice that she'd been hearing in her head lately said, *Uh-oh!*

You want to do WHAT?

Remy was sitting with Tante Lulu at her kitchen table with a large map rolled out before them, trying to pinpoint exactly where she'd seen the submerged "coffin." Explanations like "just past the crooked loblolly, turn left, or was it right, no left, then sharp right, 'til you see the half-sunk log that looks like a man's too-too, then the Queen cypress with all her ladies in waiting, then right again . . ." just didn't help much.

He hadn't called ahead, but Tante Lulu greeted him warmly, as always, and insisted on whipping up a meal for him of catfish chowder with fresh-made beaten biscuits dripping with butter, a side of *couche-couche*—fried corn meal mush topped with sugar and cream—and several cups of thick, black coffee. All this, despite the fact that he'd caught her in the middle of frosting her hair, which was magically coal black today, a change from yesterday's gray with purple streaks. The process amounted to her having little pigtails wrapped with tin foil and slathered with white goop all over her black curly head. Her flowered muu-muu and flat house slippers completed the ludicrous picture.

You had to love a woman who had so much self-confidence she could walk around looking like a goofball and not even blanche with embarrassment.

"So, what's the deal with you and Rachel? I been workin' on the bride quilt," she pointed to the frame set up in one corner of the living room, "but Charmaine tol' me it's all off with you two. Kaput!"

"Charmaine talks too much."

"You allus was a prideful man. Doan be lettin' yer pride get in the way of true love, boy."

"Who said anything about true love?"

"Is this a pride thing?"

"Yeah," he admitted, "but that doesn't mean it's unimportant. There are some things a man needs to be a man, and women just don't understand."

"Huh? That was clear as bayou mud."

"Forget about it."

"Ah, Remy, what happened? I see in yer eyes that you still care. Cain't it be fixed, sweetie?"

"You don't see anything in my eye, auntie, and, no, it can't be fixed. So, just forget about it. A bulldozer and a thousand prayers to St. Jude won't change things now."

The voice in his head said, *Wanna bet?*

A voice outside yelled, "Yoo-hoo! Anybody home?"

"That'll teach you to put down St. Jude," Tante Lulu said, slapping him on the arm.

Remy put his face in his hands for a second before standing and looking out the window. It was Rachel in her bright red pickup trucking flashing the hooker plate reading RED-HOT. She probably didn't realize he was here since he'd driven his small boat down the bayou, instead of his Harley.

"Come on in," Tante Lulu invited Rachel cheerily through the screen door. To Remy, she added, "Behave yerself, and mebbe, jist mebbe, you'll be having make-up sex by nightfall."

Make-up sex? Where does she get this nonsense? She

better not mention it to Rachel. "Don't you dare do or say anything. It's over with me and Rachel. Period."

His aunt just ignored him, as usual.

Rachel walked through the door, and all he could say then was, "Holy crap!" Her hair was wild and frizzy today from the humidity, so she'd pulled it up into a high thingamabob atop her head with loose tendrils trailing out. She didn't appear to be wearing any make-up, but one never knew; women had a way of fooling men with invisible make-up tricks. In any case, she looked fresh-scrubbed and scrumptious, if that was a word that could be used by a man to describe a woman. *Yes*, he decided, *scrumptious is a perfectly good word for her.*

She wore a stretchy bra type thing and swishy exercise shorts which led down miles of shapely legs to white athletic shoes with half socks peeking out. There was lots of exposed creamy skin between the bra thing and the shorts. He wondered with testosterone-induced irrelevance if she still smelled of coconuts. If his aunt weren't here, he might be tempted to toss Rachel over his shoulder and carry her down the hall to his boyhood room where they'd have wild sex with Richard Petty and Heather Locklear looking on. Hell, even with his aunt here, he was tempted.

So, what did he say, brilliant guy that he was? "What are you doing here?" His voice, which apparently had a mind of its own, reeked with surliness.

"Remy! For shame!" his aunt reprimanded him.

"I didn't know you were here," Rachel told him, a bit too defensively for his taste.

"Obviously. But now that you know I am, scram!" *Dieu, who is putting these words in my mouth.*

"Remy!" his aunt repeated.

"I came to see your aunt, not you. So, why don't *you* scram?" She raised her pretty nose so high in the air it was a wonder she didn't get a nosebleed.

"Is this a lovers' quarrel?" his aunt wanted to know.

"No!" they both answered at the same time.

"Why did you come to see my aunt?"

"That's none of your business."

"I think I'll go pour us some sweet tea, and wash this crap out of my hair." His aunt waddled off toward the kitchen, leaving them alone.

Rachel stood with her hands on her hips, staring at him belligerently.

"I was rude. I'm sorry," he said. *You look like sex on the hoof, babe.*

"So was I." But she didn't say she was sorry. And she looked at him as if he was something on the hoof, all right, and it wasn't sex.

"I brought maps in hopes that Tante Lulu could pinpoint exactly where you two saw those men on Sunday," he explained grudgingly. "Then I can give that information to the authorities." He didn't say which authorities, which wasn't really a lie.

She nodded. "That's why I came, too, in a way."

He raised his eyebrows at her in silent question.

"I lost my purse that day, with my license and credit cards. I want your aunt to take me back there to find it."

"You want to do WHAT?" he practically shouted. He heard his obviously eavesdropping aunt drop some ice cubes on the floor in the kitchen. Rachel jumped with surprise, too.

"Look, I don't relish the idea of getting in a boat with

your aunt again, but those men are long gone, I'm sure, and I really need my purse."

"No!"

"No? You're telling me no? You are presuming that you have the right to dictate *anything* about my life?"

He took a deep breath for patience. "It's dangerous. I can't allow it."

"Ooooh, you are pushing me, LeDeux. *Allow* is a word I would have never accepted from you when we were . . . when we were . . ."

"Screwing each other's brains out?"

She gave him a look that would curdle milk. "When we were *together*," she corrected him, "but it is definitely off the radar now. You won't *allow*? Well, allow this, mister!" Rachel gave him the finger then.

He was shocked. He really was. Oh, he knew some girls and women flipped the bird today, but not females he knew. Not Rachel.

Tears rose in her eyes, which she swiped away immediately.

He felt lower than the spots on a snake's belly for making her cry.

"See! See what you made me do," she snapped. "I have never made such an obscene gesture in all my life. You bring out the worst in me."

Remy's spirits rose, learning it was a first-time thing, and he took perverse pride in the fact that he could rile her that much. "I also bring out the best in you sometimes, too, darlin'," he said in a voice little more than a whisper.

"Oh, right. Remind me of that now." She spun on her heels, about to go out the door.

"Where are you going?" Now that she was leaving, he

felt desperate to make her stay. How could he hate being in her presence, and hate her absence as well? *The woman is driving me up the wall!*

She turned slowly to face him. Anger flushed her pretty face. "I'm going to go get Beau and his pirogue. Then we're going to row up and down this damn bayou 'til I find the spot where I lost my purse. Do you have any objections?"

"Yeah, I do," he said with a sigh of resignation, putting his hands up to bar her from speaking again. "I'll take you and Tante Lulu. God help me!"

He will, St. Jude said.

Somethin' fishy in the bayou, and it ain't trout

All Rachel wanted was to get her purse back. Was that so difficult? She never expected a "posse" to come to her rescue.

"What is going on here, Remy?" she demanded to know, not for the first time since she'd entered a boat with him.

He just grunted, same as before. The jerk!

Yeah, Remy had agreed to take her and Tante Lulu to look for her purse. What he'd neglected to tell her was that he had to make a phone call first to "clear the trip," whatever the heck that meant. Nor did he inform her that four other men would be coming with them: two in the first boat with Tante Lulu, and two in the boat behind her and Remy, including Larry Ellis, the man she'd met at The Swamp Tavern. All of them wore bulletproof vests and carried weapons—rifles, pistols in shoulder holsters and big things that were probably uzis. Even Rachel and Tante Lulu had been forced to don protective gear. Tante Lulu's was worn over her muu-muu, and on her head was a clear plastic rain cap that tied under her chin because she claimed it was going to rain, despite the bright sun and clear blue skies with swirling clouds.

"I've lived in D.C. too long not to recognize Feds when I see them," she told the silent Remy. "I'd bet my Feng-Shui manual that these straight-backed, no-smile guys work for some government agency—if not the CIA or FBI, then some other enforcement division. They are not local police, for sure."

Remy just laughed.

"This is not funny to me, Remy."

"Yeah, it is," he said grumpily. "Do you have any underwear on under that outfit?"

"Of course I'm wearing underwear." Not that it was any of his business anymore. "Why?"

"Just enjoying the view, babe."

She turned her head to look back at him without moving the rest of her body, mainly because her hands were gripping the sides of the low-riding boat he called a "Go-Devil" which skimmed over the surface of the water. She gasped when she saw him staring at her behind in the flimsy nylon shorts—her *big* behind which perched on the little wood seat, probably hanging half off. "Don't you dare look at me *there*!"

"Where would you rather I look? At your nipples that are clearly visible in that little scrap of Victoria's Secret?"

"Victoria's Secret? More like Extreme Sport Exercisewear." She looked down at her very demure sport top and saw nothing sticking out, certainly not her nipples. "You can't see anything."

"I can imagine . . . from memory."

Rachel very carefully turned herself on the bench seat so that she faced Remy. He wore pleated khaki slacks, loafers and a white golf shirt, open at the collar. In the bright sunlight, his eyes pierced her with their darkness. How could one man, with his scars, look so drop-dead gorgeous? She had a good reason to be upset with him, but instead she melted just looking at him. Was Jill right? Was she being too hard on Remy? Should she give him a chance to explain, if there was an explanation, if he wanted to explain? "Why are you being so mean to me?" she finally asked.

"Admiring your ass-ets is being mean?"

"You know what I mean. You've been nothing but obnoxious since I arrived at your aunt's. I've done nothing to you to warrant this kind of treatment."

"Is that what you think? That you can dump me just because I can't have kids, then say 'Howdy' next time I see you? Well, sorry, sugar, but I've got a little more pride than that. And turn around if you don't want me to stare at your tits."

She gasped. She couldn't help herself. Remy wanted to hurt her, and he was doing a darn good job of accomplishing his goal. "You don't even know how to do vulgar well, Remy, do you know that? You're all embarrassed over being crude, and don't you dare deny it. More important, I did not dump you because you can't have kids. How many times do I have to tell you that?"

"Forget about it. It's water over the dam."

Rachel's heart was breaking over Remy's stubbornness. It appeared he didn't want to explain—or to make up. Maybe their argument had given him an excuse to break up their relationship before it went too far. Better to change the subject, she decided, before she burst into tears, or begged him to come back to her, regardless of his transgressions. "Remy, what do you do for a living?"

"Huh?"

"I thought you ran a helicopter service for tourists and land surveyors and stuff like that, but the company you keep . . . well, I'm beginning to wonder."

"It's none of your business, Rachel. What do you care what I do with my time, business or otherwise."

She just stared at him, stricken, at the finality of his words.

"You and me," he shrugged, "it's over."

He couldn't make it any clearer than that. "Yeah, it's over," she agreed.

On the other hand, she saw the way he looked at her, with sadness and longing, even as he spit out the hateful words, and she wondered.

Is it really over?
Do I want it to be?
Does he?

Raining cats and dogs—and Feds

Once they arrived at the designated spot, all the boats stopped and dropped anchors.

With perfect timing, the skies opened up with a maddening cloudburst of hard rain. Thunder roared in the distance. Lightning cracked. A miserable, typical afternoon in Louisiana. A ground soaker that would no doubt be over in minutes. But not before drenching everyone and everything in the process.

His aunt pulled out her umbrella and sat beaming with

self-satisfaction in her boat while the DEA agents jumped onto the muddy bank up to their ankles, cursing under their breath.

"God musta been thinkin' of hell when he created Louisiana," Larry Ellis grumbled, to which Tante Lulu countered, "How'd you like an umbrella broken over yer thick head?"

Frank Porter added, "Did you see those friggin' alligators back there? For chrissake, we have mondo snakes in Alabama where I grew up, but I prefer them to these big ol' sonsabitches."

"Watch yer mouth, mister. There's ladies present," Tante Lulu warned.

"Everybody stay here 'til we secure the area," Shelton Peters shouted over the clamor of hard pellets hitting the water and vegetation. "Remy, can you stand guard?"

He nodded, pulling his pistol out of its shoulder holster. The other men spread out in four directions.

"Why don't I just go look for my purse while they're gone?" Rachel said as she stood, rocking the boat. She was drenched to the skin. Her hair had come loose from its elastic atop her head and lay straggly about her face. Her bra and her shorts were plastered to her body, making her appear almost nude to Remy. No matter if he'd lied before, her nipples definitely stood out now from the cold rain, like freakin' berries.

Meanwhile, a very important part of Remy's waterlogged body came immediately to life. He'd like nothing better than to take her against that tree over there in a knee-trembler to beat all knee-tremblers, giving vertical sex way new meaning. Or down on all fours in the mud—talk about dirty sex! Maybe they could even rock the boat, literally.

That's what he thought in his fantasy-sodden brain. What he said was, "Why don't you just sit your pretty ass down?" No way in this world was he going to stand and push her back down to her seat—not with his embarrassing erection. *I am pitiful, pitiful, pitiful. Getting excited by a woman who hates my guts.*

Rachel was about to snarl something back at him, something which would be undoubtedly nasty, when she glanced down at his crotch. Why she had any inclination to peruse that area of his body at a time like this—at any time, actually—defied explanation, but her eyes went wide when she did. Then she surprised the hell out of him. She smiled.

"All clear," Pete said, coming up to the boats. "Doesn't appear to be anyone about. You want to show us where you saw that coffin, Ms. Renaud?"

Tante Lulu stood carefully and was folding her umbrella since the rain had already stopped. She used it like a cane as she emerged onto the bank in her floppy house slippers.

Meanwhile, Remy noticed that all four agents were staring goggle-eyed at Rachel and her nipples.

He made a low growling sound which caused the four men to turn guiltily away and Rachel to smile some more.

She is going to pay for that smile, he promised himself.

After a mere fifteen minutes, several facts became evident. The drug container was gone, as evidenced by the cut strap dangling from a streamside tree and by one of the agents taking off his clothes down to his boxers and diving underwater to discover nothing. Most important, to Remy at least, Rachel's purse was gone.

How could it have disappeared? Remy wondered.

You want me to play hide-and-seek with WHOM?

Rachel just couldn't believe that her purse had disappeared into thin air. "Could some animal have run off with it?" she asked Pete.

"Could be, I suppose," he said dubiously. "What address was on your license? Is anyone living there now?"

Rachel looked at Remy, then back to Pete. "Yes, my former fiancé, David Lloyd."

She saw Remy flinch at her mentioning David. Why he would be upset over her old lover, she had no idea. Well, yes, she did. Even though their brief affair was over, she would probably be jealous if the name of one of his old lovers came up.

Pete handed her his cell phone and demanded, "Call him."

Huh! For two weeks I've been avoiding any contact with David. I am definitely not initiating a call to him now. "No."

Several men rolled their eyes at what they must consider her irrational behavior. One of the agents had handed Rachel his shirt a short time ago because she'd been shivering. Thank goodness, because she'd been very uncomfortable with them all staring at her revealing garments. Except for Remy. She'd been glad to see that she could still turn him on.

"Miss, I'm gonna have to insist that you make that call, and ask Mr. Lloyd if anyone unusual has been by, asking for you."

"On whose authority do you insist?"

Pete exhaled loudly with exasperation, then pulled out a leather wallet and flashed her his credentials.

"DEA?" she exclaimed. "Why is the DEA here?"

"What's a DEA?" Tante Lulu wanted to know.

"Drug Enforcement Agency, ma'am," Pete explained.

Tante Lulu was gathering some plant stems and putting them in the pockets of her muu-muu, figuring it wouldn't be a wasted trip if she gathered some herbs while here. She opened her mouth to ask more questions.

"Never mind," Remy said to his aunt. "I'll explain later."

Well, she wished he'd explain *to her.* "Are you a DEA agent?" she asked Remy.

He blinked with surprise. "Hell, no."

"Then what are you doing with them?" *And isn't it kind of dangerous? What a stupid question! Of course, it's dangerous. Why does that bother me so much? I don't care what happens to him. Well, I care if he gets killed or injured or something. I just don't care the other way. Aaarrgh!*

"Ma'am?" Pete said, still extending his phone to her.

"He probably won't be home in the middle of the day anyhow," Rachel muttered. She punched in the numbers, waited a few seconds while it rang, then practically jumped when David answered. "David? What are you doing home during office hours?"

She held the phone away from her ear as he yelled so loud that others in the clearing probably heard him, too. "Rachel? Have you lost your effin mind? Some of your friends stopped by to beat the shit out of me. That's why I'm home—after being in the emergency room all night."

"What? What friends? Are you okay?"

"No, I'm not okay. I have a black eye, a chipped tooth,

bruised ribs, possible internal injuries, and two pieces of broken Roseville."

"Who did it?"

"You tell me. All I know is that two thugs showed up here yesterday looking for you. When I told them I had no idea where you were, they apparently didn't believe me, so they tried pounding the information out of me."

"Oh, David, I'm sorry to have gotten you involved in this. It's all because of my missing purse. A mistake."

"A mistake?" he shouted. "A parking ticket is a mistake. A forgotten appointment is a mistake. A botched liposuction is a mistake. Criminals on my doorstep are not a mistake."

"Here, let me talk to him," Pete said and took the phone from her. He spoke for several moments, trying to explain in a cursory way what had happened and promising that two government agents would be at his place within the hour to take his statement and give him protection. When he clicked off the phone, Pete looked at her somberly and said, "That settles it. We need to relocate you to a safe haven till this operation is completed, Miss Fortier."

"Huh? What operation? You can't make me go into hiding. Can you?"

Pete turned to Remy. "You understand that they may be able to trace her here—that her life might be in danger."

Remy nodded grimly, his face ashen.

"Can you handle this?" Pete asked Remy. "I don't have any agents free at the moment. It would really help—"

"Handle what?" Rachel wanted to know.

"Protecting you," Pete explained. "Just 'til early next week. Six days at most."

"Remy? You want Remy to go into hiding with me?" Rachel flinched at the shrillness of her voice.

Pete nodded.

"No!" she and Remy said at the same time.

Pete raised his eyebrows, not amused by their vehement refusals. "You know how important this mission is, Remy."

"No!" Remy insisted, and "NO!" Rachel insisted even louder.

"Is there some life-or-death reason why you can't help us provide a temporary safe haven for Miss Fortier?" Pete asked Remy.

Rachel saw the tight muscle in Remy's jaw twitch. She saw his eyes flash angrily. She saw him clench and unclench his fists. She saw how very much he did not want to go anywhere with her, let alone some hidden spot where they would be alone.

She felt the same way, but dammit, she had the right to those emotions. He didn't.

Tante Lulu spoke up. "I know jist the place where they can go into hiding." Everyone jerked up in surprise, not realizing she had been following the conversation. "Luc's old cabin. It's so secluded, even Luc has trouble findin' it sometimes."

Remy groaned.

Rachel groaned.

And Pete said, "Perfect."

Chapter 15

Biting the bullet

Okay, how hard could it be to call up Gizelle Fortier and say, "Hey, Gizelle, baby, looks like I won't be able to make the meeting this afternoon"?

Remy was thirty-three years old. Gizelle was at least seventy, he would guess. Or ninety. Why did he drag his feet over calling the woman?

Because she was a witch, that's why. And she would probably put a voodoo curse on him and some essential body parts.

He did not, did not, did not want to go into a remote safe haven with Rachel.

But he had to, had to, had to, if he expected to maintain any credibility with the DEA for this, or future, contracts.

Talk about a Catch-22! Damned if he did, damned if he didn't. How could he ever put Rachel behind him if they plopped her butt in front of him for five friggin' days?

Finally, he bit the bullet and dialed the number. "Hello. Ms. Fortier? This is Remy LeDeux."

"Well, pickle my tush and call me a cucumber. Should I be dancin' with joy or what?"

Remy gritted his teeth and counted to five.

"Rachel ain't here. Not that she would wanna talk to you anyhows, you slimy varmint. Made her cry, you did."

Remy didn't want to think about having made Rachel cry now. And, of course, he knew Rachel wasn't there. She was throwing a hissy fit back at Tante Lulu's where two DEA agents guarded her. At the last minute, she would phone her grandmother and say she got called out of town for an emergency, but that she would return in a week or so. The Feds didn't want to let Rachel go back to Gizelle's house today and raise any suspicions, just in case the drug perps showed up at her doorstep. Better that she knows nothing.

Gizelle would be suspicious that Rachel didn't even pack a bag, or that Remy might be with her, but Rachel had her instructions. Make sure her grandmother accepted the story of abrupt departure.

"I didn't call to speak to Rachel. I want to talk to you."

"Joy, Joy!" the old witch said.

Her sarcasm really grated on his nerves. "I need to cancel our meeting for today."

There was silence at the other end.

"Perhaps we could reschedule for one day next week."

"Are you backin' out, boy?"

He hesitated for only the briefest second. "No."

"You know, this deal ain't final 'til the papers are signed. Iffen yer gonna diddle around, mebbe I'll be the one to cancel."

"You have every right," he assured her. "Just know that I wouldn't be cancelling today if it weren't imperative."

"Imperative, huh? Mus' be real important fer a greedy LeDeux to give up a sucker deal."

Dieu, the woman was beyond bearable. She was intolerable. If she were a man, and she stood in front of him, he would knock her lights out for that insult. Not that his father didn't take advantage of every opportunity to make a quick buck, but he was not his father, and dammit, she had no right to paint them all with one flick of her condemning brush.

He inhaled deeply for patience and said, "How about a week from tomorrow—next Friday? Would you like to meet then in Luc's office, say three o'clock?"

There was a brief pause, then, "Mebbe." With that, she hung up.

Staring at the dead phone, Remy asked no one in particular, "Am I doing the right thing?"

The dreaded voice said, *Mebbe*.

Depends on your definition of what "it" is

"Granny, an emergency has come up and I need to go away for a few days," Rachel said into the telephone while Remy, Tante Lulu and the Feds looked on. Rachel had been backed into a corner on this going-into-hiding business, but she was not happy about it. Not one bit. And forget about them "offering" her a "safe haven" rather than them forcing her to go into hiding. That's how she viewed the situation. No choice.

"Right away?"

"Yes."

"Is someone hurt?"

"Actually, David was beaten up pretty badly. He even had to go to the emergency room." She hadn't actually said that she was going to Washington to see David, but she knew that Granny must think that.

"See. Thass what it's like livin' in the city. Muggers and mobsters and such all over the place."

"Uh-huh," Rachel said noncommittally.

"David? Is that the skunk what had the wires to his man-engine shorted out?"

Rachel burst out laughing, which caused everyone in Tante Lulu's kitchen to raise their eyebrows, except for Pete who was listening in on her call. "You could say that."

"You ain't gettin' back with him, are you? Menfolks has a way of playin' on a woman's affections when they's hurt."

"No way will David and I be mending any fences. I'm just concerned about him, that's all."

"Will you be comin' back?" Granny asked with a slight tremble in her voice.

"Of course. Hopefully, by Tuesday."

"Well, can I help you with packin' 'n such?"

"No. I've got to go right away. My flight leaves in less than an hour." Which wasn't really a lie since a hydroplane sat outside in Tante Lulu's bayou which Remy would fly to God-only-knew-where to keep her in hiding. She couldn't think that far ahead or she'd dig in her heels and hide under Tante Lulu's bed.

"Are you sure this isn't about that Remy LeDunce? Yer not plannin' on goin' off somewhere to do *it* with him, are you?"

Pete put his hand over his mouth to stifle a laugh.

"Absolutely not. There will be no *it* going on, that I can promise you." She glared at Remy who leaned back against the kitchen sink, arms folded over his chest, ankles crossed, looking sexier than any man had a right to look. He glared right back at her, probably figuring out what they talked about from her end of the conversation. To give him credit, Remy was no happier about the situation they'd been placed in than she was.

"Take care, honey."

"I will."

"When you get back, I have sumpin important to tell you about Remy that'll put him on yer manure list forever, iffen he ain't already there."

Rachel looked over at Remy and said, "Oh, he is already on my manure list, guar-an-teed."

Up, up and away in my beautiful hydroplane

Remy looked over at Rachel, sitting next to him in the small Piper aircraft, stiff as a virgin before the sacrifice.

This whole impossible situation was her fault, dammit. If she hadn't gone into the swamps with his aunt, they wouldn't be here now, dammit. If she hadn't chosen to take a purse with her—*Good God! Did she expect to find a mall in the middle of a bayou jungle?*—he wouldn't be taking her to a safe house now, dammit. If she hadn't dumped him over his "problem," this little trip could be heaven, instead of hell, dammit. Yep, she had only herself to blame, dammit.

Still, he could see that she sat rigid as a board beside him. As a pilot, as a man, he couldn't ignore that. He and Luc and René had once referred to themselves as The Cajun Knights because of this innate tendency toward chivalry that they all had, no doubt due to their attempts to be the opposite of their very unchivalrous father. So, best to tamp down his anger, and be a knight.

"Are you afraid?"

"Of flying?"

"Of course, flying. What else?"

"My life, maybe. No, I'm not afraid of flying." She resumed her no-talk zombie routine, which had been going on since they'd entered the plane about a half-hour ago.

So much for chivalry! "Rachel, it's going to be a long five days if you won't talk to me. Can't we call a truce here, at least 'til Tuesday?"

"And what? Hop in the sack, to while away the time?"

There's a thought. Knights deserve some token for their good deeds. "I'm just making small talk. Try to be pleasant."

"Are you insinuating that I'm unpleasant?"

Bingo! "Who, me?" *You are not behaving like Guinevere, m'lady love. Best you shape up or Lancelot is out of here. Not that you're my love, anymore—lady or otherwise. And, truth to tell, I'm not much of a Lancelot.*

"What do you do for a living, Remy? I thought you flew tourists over the bayou, or charter flights for commercial real estate developers. Stuff like that."

"I did. Still do, sometimes." *Great! Now we're going to chitchat. How's the weather? What do you think of the elections? Think the Saints will beat the Buccaneers? Hohum.*

"Why would you expose yourself to this kind of danger?"

"Because it's the right thing to do. Because I hate drug dealers, especially ones who deal to kids. Because it finally gives a little meaning to my freakin' empty life. Because the money is good. Because I was bored. Pick one." *Knighthood sucks.*

"I don't appreciate your sarcasm. I'm not the bad guy here."

"And I am?"

The fact that she didn't answer gave him her answer.

"What am I going to do for clothes?"

At least she'd moved on to another subject. "Tante Lulu threw some of Charmaine's old stuff into my duffel bag for you." The last time Charmaine had stayed at Tante Lulu's was probably when she was fourteen and had run away from home, but Rachel didn't need to know that.

"Oh, great. I'll be wearing a Hooters shirt and crotchless underwear."

Remy smiled. *Could be. Charmaine was wild, even then.*

Without looking at him, she said, "Stop smiling."

"Why are you so mad at me? I'm not the one who suggested that you go into a safe haven with me." Remy gave himself a mental thwap on the head. Rachel had changed the subject. Now he changed it back. *Dumb, dumb, dumb.*

"You could have refused."

"It's my job, Rachel."

"You're taking your job too far. If you had refused, one of the DEA agents probably would have gone into hiding with me."

"Hah! You're nuts if you think I'd allow one of those horn dogs to be alone with you for five days. If anyone was going to be required to stay with you, it damn well better be me. Did you see the way those guys gawked at your nipples?" He realized as soon as the words were out of his mouth how bad they sounded.

She turned sideways and sliced him with a dirty look.

"Are you going to give me the finger again?"

"No, but I might slap you upside the head."

Don't bother. I've already done it to myself mentally.

Rachel wore the same jogging outfit she'd had on this morning, except that it had dried. *Darn it!* No make-up. Her hair was going in about fifty different directions; she looked as if she'd stood in a wind tunnel, backwards. Not one of her finer moments. But to show how far gone he was, she looked pretty damn good to him.

Does she appreciate my appreciation of her, though?

No.

"It's just as hard for me to be around you, as it is for you to be around me," he pointed out with pure male idiocy. "You might take that into consideration when you're playing your aggrieved party game."

"Game? Game? You think I'm playing a game?" Her voice trembled with indignation.

"We're almost there," he told her cheerily, not waiting for her to continue her Remy-Is-A-Jerk tirade. "Hold onto your seat, darlin'. It's gonna be a rough landing."

"*There*? We're *there*? Are you crazy? This is nowhere," she shrieked, gazing out her side window at what must appear to her as a thick bayou jungle. Which it was.

"Here comes the moat, baby," he warned with a laugh.

"Moat? What moat? I don't see any moat."

"Just joking." Really, Remy was an expert when it came to flying, and he knew exactly where he was and what he was doing. *I am a Flying Knight, as well as a Cajun Knight*, he told himself. *I am also an Idiot Knight.* She didn't have to know that, though. So, he rocked the plane from side to side, up, then down, finally landing it in a narrow stream with a huge splash. About a hundred herons and other water birds took flight in a cloudy wave. Native trout, Bluegill and a lone gator swam for cover. Even the mosquitoes said, "Holy shit!" and flew away. Good thing Rachel didn't know he'd done it deliberately as a form of pathetic revenge for all the heartaches and headaches, not to mention inconvenience, she caused him. Besides, this should teach her to appreciate a good knight.

At first, silence prevailed. Then, Rachel, white-faced by now, unbuckled her seat belt and picked up a small, mesh bag of okras off the floor which Tante Lulu had insisted they bring from her garden. Without warning, she hit him over the head.

Apparently, she knew just how pathetic he was, after all.

Club Med it was not

The first thing she saw when she entered the cabin was the snake. They probably heard her scream all the way to Big Mamou.

Remy rushed in past her, lifted the coiled snake with a broom handle and proceeded to carry it toward the outside. "Don't worry. It's just a black snake. Not poisonous. Calm down." He also muttered something about being a good knight and protecting "m'lady," but she could be wrong about that, her brain being so numb with fear.

"Calm down?" she shrieked. "There's a snake in the safe house where I'm supposed to feel safe. And you better not be dumping that thing in the front yard, either. I don't want that slimy critter slithering back in."

"I promise, I'll take the *slimy critter* downstream. For

chrissake, Rachel, stop screaming. You're scaring the snake."

"And don't kill the snake, either," she shouted after him. "Killing a snake is bad *chi*."

He gave her a look that pretty much put her in the same category as brainless broads, then turned and left the house. "I'm really worried about a snake's negative energy," he called back to her from the porch, without turning around.

"You don't have to be sarcastic."

He said a really foul word then.

Geesh, I was just trying to help.

While he was outside, she heard a motor turn over, followed by the sound of the refrigerator in the kitchen beginning to hum. She assumed he'd turned on a gas-powered generator somewhere.

When he came back in and tried to take her shaking body into his arms, she shoved him away. "Don't."

He lifted his chin proudly. "I was only trying to help. I wasn't trying to nail you."

Nail me? "The longer I know you, the cruder you get."

"You bring out the best in me, babe."

"And don't call me babe, either."

"Stop giving me orders, *babe*."

Remy visibly inhaled and exhaled several times, combing his fingers through his hair with frustration. "Look, this is an impossible situation. Unless you and I find a way to live together peacefully, it's going to become even more impossible."

"You're right," she finally conceded. "Maybe if we set some ground rules, we can declare a truce—a temporary truce."

He narrowed his eyes at her suspiciously. "Like?"

"Like, no sex."

"Define sex."

"Nothing involving hands, tongues, lips, or intimate body parts. In fact, no hot looks or sexy talk, either."

"I'm not sure I can control my hot looks," he said.

Rachel wasn't sure if he teased her or not, but she didn't care. All he had to do was look at her in a certain way, and her bones melted. She wasn't taking any chances.

"Okay, no hot looks," he agreed. "But I have conditions, too."

Uh-oh! "Like?"

"Like, you are not bringing up my sterility in any way whatsoever."

"But—"

He put up a halting hand. "I mean it, Rachel. You're not going to ask me when the last time was that I was examined by a doctor. You won't ask exactly what the doctor said. You won't ask if I couldn't have more operations. You won't ask if I've considered adopting kids. And you sure as hell won't ask how I feel about not ever having kids of my own. Bottom line, I've accepted my physical limitations. You are not going to pity me or psychoanalyze me. It's no longer any of your business. That's my condition. Take it or leave it."

Well, he had certainly put her in her place with those rules. And, yes, she probably would have wanted to discuss every one of those things . . . still did.

"Furthermore, I never should have told you at all because, frankly, I shouldn't have let myself care so much. So, if you're still looking for blood in the way of apologies, forget about it. The only thing I'm sorry for is that we got so involved in the first place. Live and learn."

Remy's words cut her to the quick. At first, she could not speak for the constriction in her chest. In the end, all she could think of to say was, "You are a pig."

"Yep." He raised his chin defiantly. "So, is it a deal? No sex in return for silence about my . . . uh, condition."

She agreed. What else could she do?

The expression on Remy's face turned so bleak then that she wondered if she was wrong not to probe deeper. But he had drawn the line. Besides, she felt pretty bleak, too.

"How about if I clean up this place a bit, and you check for snakes thoroughly?" she offered as a way of changing the subject.

He nodded.

"Plus, you better bring in all those bags of supplies that your aunt sent."

He groaned.

Tante Lulu had gone a bit overboard in packing up food supplies for them—everything from staples like rice to perishables like butter. Enough to last a month, instead of five days.

It was a charming little raised cabin in the Cajun style with one large room downstairs, combining living room, alcove bed, kitchen and bathroom, with stairs leading up to a loft bedroom, but the place must not have been used for years because a thick layer of dust covered everything.

"Chances are it was alone. Snakes don't usually come indoors."

"I am not sleeping in this place tonight until I know it is snake-free. Good heavens, if that was the papa snake, there's probably a whole herd of other snakes hiding out— the mama snake, the baby snakes, the cousin snakes, aunt and uncle snakes." She shivered dramatically.

"A *herd* of snakes, huh? I guess I could lasso a few before nightfall."

"Are you making fun of me?"

"Just a little."

"Well, I'm going to the bathroom. After that miracle landing of yours, it's a wonder I didn't pee my pants. My bladder is about to explode."

He grinned sheepishly but didn't acknowledge what she already knew: he had deliberately pulled that kamikaze move in the airplane. "I'll start bringing in the supplies," he offered.

She was about to enter the bathroom when he added, "Let the water run for a while before you drink it. We have a cistern here that collects rainwater, but it's been sitting for a long time. It'll probably be brackish at first."

She nodded, not even looking back at him.

"And Rachel . . ."

She did turn then.

"I'll do everything I can the next few days to make you safe."

"I never doubted that."

"And I won't bother you, I promise."

That was exactly what she wanted to hear.

So why did she feel like crying?

A *temporary truce*

Nightfall already seeped into their bayou hideaway by the time Remy had completed his snake hunt. No more snakes, surprise, surprise.

Meanwhile Rachel had dusted and swept the small

cabin, laid out the handwoven carpet of brilliant blue and white on the floor, which had been rolled up in tobacco leaves to protect against mildew and moths. And she'd put fresh linens and mosquito netting on the beds and clean towels in the bathroom.

Now, the two of them were preparing dinner, *together.* Rachel cooked the way she made love: with concentration, relish and good humor. Remy decided that his goose was about to be cooked if he continued thinking along those lines.

They reheated some jambalaya which Tante Lulu had sent frozen in a Tupperware container, but Remy made "dirty rice" and a fresh salad of mustard greens and scallions, both of which he'd picked outside near where there had once been a small garden years ago. He topped the salad with a hot bacon dressing which he'd learned from his aunt as a youngster. Rachel had transformed Tante Lulu's homemade French bread into a warm stuffed garlic loaf oozing with olives, tomatoes and provolone cheese. For a beverage, they had homemade dandelion wine which Remy had discovered in one of the cupboards.

So far, they hadn't argued once.

But the night was still young.

Replete from all the good food and seeming peace, he tipped his chair back against the wall, sipped at his remaining wine, and asked, "Tell me about yourself."

"Is that a hokey line or what?" Rachel laughed merrily, and his heart lurched. Probably a little heartburn, or something.

He shrugged. "You know everything about me, and I know almost nothing about you, except you were engaged until recently and that you are a Feng Shui decorator.

Where did you grow up? Were you a feisty little girl in red pigtails? A tomboy or a girly-girl? Did you go to college or decorating school? That kind of stuff." *In other words, safe conversation territory. No sex. No sterility.*

Her face went suddenly serious. "Feisty? Hardly. I was always a good girl, always on my best behavior. My mother abandoned me when I was four years old. I lived in a dozen foster homes over the next decade, the hope always being that someone would adopt me. I was always tall for my age. Even when I was four, I looked older. And people want to adopt little kids—babies preferably, but if not babies, then toddlers or pretty little children. I was never that. It wasn't my fault, but believe me, at the time, it felt like failure. I tried constantly to be a good girl, an excellent student, pretty, thin, all the things I thought would make me adoptable."

"Rachel!" Remy was shocked at the misery of her childhood, and horrified that he'd brought up such a painful subject.

"Now see," she said, "I don't like pity any more than you do. So, cut it out."

She spoke so fiercely that Remy had to smile and hold up his hands in surrender.

"Lest you think I was misguided at the time, let me tell you about the parties and picnics that child services used to hold. They never called them adoption screenings, but that's what they were. Cattle calls for little and big kids to be paraded before interested couples. I got lots of advice when I struck out so many times. Maybe I could slim down a bit. Can you imagine telling an eight-year-old girl she was fat? And I wasn't . . . I know that now. Then, I was dressed as a much younger child. And once, a counselor suggested

I might have my hair dyed because red was not a popular adoption color."

Rémy didn't care what Rachel said about not wanting pity, he reached across the table, took both her hands in his, and squeezed. She didn't pull away—not right away, anyhow.

"Anyhow, I was adopted when I was fourteen by a lovely older childless couple, college anthropology professors. They probably considered me an experiment of sorts. But they were nice and loving to me—too late, of course, my dreams being gone by then, and too old and big to be cuddled anymore. True to my bad luck pattern, they died in an earthquake in Brazil when I was twenty, leaving me with no family once again."

"You had it tough, babe—in its own way, as bad as Luc and René and I had it with my Dad after our mother died. We were pretty young, too. But we had each other, Thank God!"

Rachel looked wistful for a moment. "Oh, you have no idea how I wished I had brothers and sisters, even one. In fact, I used to fantasize that I had one of each—siblings that my mother had given away, just like me, and one day they would show up at my doorstep and welcome me into their loving families."

Remy's heart sank. Rachel might not realize it, but having a family of her own was extremely important to her. If he didn't know it before, he knew now: they had absolutely no future together. "So, how did you connect with your grandmother, after all these years?"

"Don't ask me why it took me so long, but last year I finally went onto one of those Internet websites where they locate birth parents. Within weeks, I had my mother's name, address and phone number. She was living in Biloxi."

"And?" he urged when it appeared she would say no more.

"And she was a total disappointment. If I had been expecting a joyful reunion, boy, was I in for a rude awakening. In her defense, my mother was dying of cancer by then, and all she cared about was *her* needs and *her* dashed dreams and all that stuff. Not one word of regret. I don't think she would have been any different if I'd met her pre-cancer. Anyhow, it's all over. She died without telling me that I had any living family, by the way. To her, they were long dead, I suppose. Or maybe she was just selfish to the end. In any case, her obituary was put in both the Biloxi and Houma and New Orleans newspapers—my idea, since she wasn't around to say me nay—and I was listed as her only survivor. That's when my grandmother contacted me."

"Well, the bad times are over, and you're happy now, right?" *That was stupid, asking her if she's happy now. We're both miserable, that's obvious.* "I mean, you have a good life in D.C., don't you?"

"I put impossible dreams behind me long ago, but my present reality is pretty darn nice, in my opinion. A grandmother and a cousin I never knew I had and am growing to care for day by day. That's not bad."

It was a sketchy story Rachel had told him. Missing were all the details and emotions that must have filled those years from four to thirty-something.

"You're thinking that you and I have a lot in common, aren't you?" she asked with a hint of amusement in her voice and twinkling eyes.

"Yeah, I am," he confessed, giving her hands a final

squeeze and releasing them. "But it's made us both stronger, hasn't it?"

She considered his words for a moment, then nodded. "I'm glad we can still be friends, Remy," she said. "Aren't you?"

"Oh, yeah." *But friends and lovers would be even better. Talk about impossible dreams.*

Chapter **16**

When you're hot, you're hot

Rachel awakened late the next morning to the sound of whistling. She became aware of the extremely high humidity and the smell of roses.

She stretched out the kinks from her marvelous sleep—at least ten hours—and walked over to the small window in the bedroom loft. Outside she saw Remy trimming back the pink and white climbing roses, which had overgrown two sides of the cottage and the roof, and placing the branches in a burn barrel in the side yard. He whistled while he worked. *Whistling?*

If she hadn't been wide awake already, she would be now at the sight she beheld. *Remy.* Mercy! What a picture this hot Cajun rogue was, wearing short, low-riding, black nylon shorts, athletic shoes sans socks, a Tulane baseball cap, and work gloves. And nothing else. Sweat rolled in glistening rivulets over his bare skin. And, Lordy, Lordy, there was a lot of skin exposed. Smooth skin, sexy skin, mangled skin, tanned skin, muscled skin, sexy skin, masculine skin, sexy skin. Every couple minutes, he swiped a forearm over his forehead to stem the tide, a useless exercise in this heat, made even worse by the fire he was feeding.

Truth to tell, the wretch fed a fire in her, as well. She was hot, hot, hot for the man. The question was how to bank the embers before she imploded, or did something rash, like offer to wipe him down.

Well, Rachel had always been a list maker. Once she finished with her shower and breakfast, she decided to find a pen and tablet and begin making some lists. A checklist of jobs to be completed for Remy's houseboat and Charmaine's spa. Things she wanted to do with her grandmother before returning to Washington next month. Pros and cons of her career: Should she stay with Daphne's firm in D.C., or go off on her own? A shopping list of gifts to buy for Granny, Beau and her friends back home. Finally, and most important in the short term, a new and revised list of conditions for living with Remy during their enforced stay. In particular, no more revealing, or non-existent clothing, which could lead to her seduction.

In all honesty, the problem lay with her, not Remy. She had to regain her self-control, not put the onus on him to stem his effect on her. Still, he could at least cover himself more; she added that to her Remy List.

There was only one snag with this whole list-making enterprise when it came to Remy. What trade-off would he ask of her in return?

Oh, well, one day down. Only four more to go.

We're havin' a heat wave

Remy executed a shallow dive into the four-foot-deep stream and swam three circular laps underwater for a good minute and a half.

It was hotter than hell today. No day to be doing hard physical yard work, but necessary for him in order to douse the fire within—a fire that had absolutely nothing to do with air temperature or humidity.

He came up out of the water with a splashy whoosh, tossing his hair back off his face. Standing waist-deep in the cool stream near the bank, he glanced toward the cabin. Then he glanced again.

There she sat, the bane of his existence, on an ancient rocking chair. Her bare feet were propped on the porch rail—bare feet which led up about a mile of bare leg to a pair of Charmaine's old cheerleading shorts. Her legs were bent at the knees, with her thighs serving as a desk for the tablet on which she wrote rapidly. On top, she wore a stretch T-shirt with the logo, GIRLS JUST WANNA HAVE FUN, bracketed by two smiley faces in two whoo-boy strategic places. That brought a smile to his lips. This outrageous bit of cotton was what he and his brothers had always called sex-bait shirts as teenagers.

She had no right to tempt him so. Surely, she could have found something less suggestive in the bag Tante Lulu had packed for her, like one of his aunt's muu-muu's.

Still deep in concentration, Rachel put the end of her pencil in her mouth and sucked on it. That innocent action on her part shot the lead slam-dunk into his own pencil. *Just call me LeDeux #2.*

With a muttered expletive, Remy dove back into the water. And swam, and swam, and swam.

Oh, well, one day down. Only four more to go.

Remy wondered if he would survive.

Nope, the voice in his head said.

This time when he completed his laps and started walking toward shore, finger-combing his wet hair off his face, he noticed that Rachel no longer scribbled. In fact, she stared at him, lips parted with astonishment, or something.

Well, hell! He glanced down to his sopping shorts to make sure he was decent. A-okay there. No "pencils" sticking out, as far as he could tell, although the package was clearly outlined. Nothing she hadn't seen before. Tilting his head to the side, he looked back at Rachel. Yep, she stared at him as if he was a cold popsicle on a summer day and she'd like to lick him up one side and down the other.

He smiled.

Quickly, she masked over the hungry expression on her face, replacing it with one of bland disinterest. But she couldn't fool him. He'd already seen. Hot damn, he had seen.

Rachel wanted him.

Bad.

The question was: *What do I do with that information?*

Dumber than dirt, good ol' Jude proclaimed.

Didn't we almost have it all?

Rachel snapped her jaw shut, but couldn't help staring at Remy as he walked toward the porch.

He wore only a pair of wet shorts which clung to his hips

and belly and genitals. He may as well have been naked. His stride was slow and confident, but Rachel saw beneath the surface. He didn't relish anyone, especially her, staring at his disfigured body. Oh, if he only knew how she saw him! True, the skin on one side was pinkish in places, scarred in others, even downright mangled, but his appearance surpassed everything in her imagination that she had ever considered manly, or handsome, or sexy. In essence, he was beautiful to her. All he had to do was look at her, and she went breathless. And it wasn't just sexual chemistry, either, though there was plenty of that. He touched her soul in a way no other man had.

But it was over. He'd made that clear. Heck, she'd made that clear. And it *was* over. He'd betrayed her with his deliberate omission about his sterility. He hadn't been all that honest about his work either. In neither case did he lie, precisely. Bottom line, she could never trust a man with all those secrets. Who knew how many more there were!

Still, she kept coming back to the same old thing. Wasn't there some way they could work things out? They'd almost had it all—the perfect love, or so it had seemed. But he couldn't be trusted, and she was too vulnerable after her experience with David. If he promised to be totally honest with her in the future, would she be able to trust him? Not at this point. His male pride, his job loyalty, his family, his honor—any number of things would stand in the way. She knew at heart that they would. Even now, he refused to discuss the sterility issue, a taboo subject, a secret of sorts with him.

On the plus side, he was a supremely good man. He would be a faithful lover or husband. Family would always matter to him. He would protect her with his life. He would love her deeply.

But she would always be waiting for the other shoe to drop.

With a sigh of resignation, she reflected, *Didn't we almost have it all.*

Unfortunately, that was not enough.

Do ya think I'm sexy?

"Keep looking at me like that, cupcake, and our pact is ashes."

"Pact?" she stammered out, flustered because he'd caught her in the act of ogling him. She knew what pact he referred to, all right. She damn well knew.

"Yeah. No sex, no questions. Remember?" *God, it's fun making her face turn red.* Immediately, he amended that with, *Man, am I pathetic, getting my jollies by embarrassing a woman!*

"Well, how about *you* stop sabotaging our pact, buster."

"Sabotaging? Me? How?" He had trouble following her thinking, but then he wasn't thinking so clearly himself.

"By prancing around half-naked, in those skimpy, sexy shorts that practically shout, 'Here I am. Take me, baby.' "

"These are fifteen-year-old, ratty shorts from my boot-camp days, which are in no way skimpy. And I never pranced a day in my life," he declared indignantly, hands on hips. Then he thought a second about what she'd said, and a big ol' grin crept over his mouth—the slow, lazy kind that he sensed she loved/hated. "You think I'm sexy?"

"Get a life." Her face turned even redder.

"You think I'm sexy," he accused, coming up onto the porch to stand in front of her. In fact, he put a hand on each of the arms of the rocking chair and leaned over her. Water droplets still stood out all over his skin, and dripped down on her, but he threw off heat like a furnace—a carnal furnace.

She put her tablet aside, ducked under his arms, and stood before him. Real close. "Don't get any ideas."

Oh, I have ideas, all right, sweetheart. Hard not to with that sex-bait "fun" T-shirt flashing in front of my face like a neon sign, saying "Catch me if you can." Not that I would tell her that. Wouldn't want her to hide all that fun.

"You're laughing at me."

I can't help myself. You think I'm sexy. "Am not."

"Stop being so immature."

You wanna talk about immature? Imagine the situation from my perspective. Trying to carry on a sensible conversation with a grown woman standing knee-knocking close to me in a teenage sex-bait shirt. "Honey, we have a pact," he said with exaggerated patience. "What makes you think I'd do anything to jeopardize that pact?" *See, I can be all sweetness and innocence, too.*

"You already are."

"By wearing shorts?" *Man, what would she think if I shucked these pants and showed her real jeopardy?*

"And nothing else."

This is incredible. We had an agreement. No sex in return for her not asking about my sterility. And she thinks I'm jeopardizing the whole thing. Does she think I'm deliberately trying to tempt her? That's just what she thinks. Does that mean she's temptable? Hmmm. "You think I'm sexy."

"Here," she said, tearing one of the sheets off her tablet and shoving it at him.

"Remy's Rules," he read aloud. *Was she crazy? Sittin' here making lists of rules for me? While my brain, and other body parts, are about to implode with testosterone overload?* He had no idea what the other lists still attached to her tablet detailed, but he sure as hell wasn't amused by her making a list for him, as if he was a little kid.

"Rule One. No sex, including hands, tongues, lips, intimate body parts, hot looks or sexy talk. Trade-off, no discussion about Remy's sterility." He winced at her verbal mention of his condition. It looked so black-and-white and insignificant on paper, when he knew it was monumentally significant. "Rule Two, no deliberate tempting from either side, including lack of clothing, sexy talk, hot looks, touching, etc." He looked at Rachel, who waited expectantly until he was done reading, and asked her, "Are you for real?"

"What? You disagree with my rules?"

"Yeah, I disagree. Bigtime. You've got this agreement formatted all wrong, and not just because you failed to put a trade-off item next to your latest rule." He took her pencil and tablet from her, flicked through to a blank page and began to write. Then he tore out his sheet and handed it and the tablet back to her.

She read aloud:

"Rule One. No sexual intercourse. Trade-off, no sterility discussion.

"Rule Two. No kissing. Trade-off, to be decided.

"Rule Three. No deliberate touching. Trade-off, to be decided.

"Rule Four. No sexy talk. Trade-off, to be decided.

"Rule Five. No deliberate flaunting of bare skin, or showing of buttocks or nipples. Trade-off, to be decided." He looked at Rachel and asked, "So, what do you think?"

She looked as if she'd like to wallop him over the head with the tablet. "I have never deliberately flaunted those things you mentioned."

"You mean nipples and buttocks?" he asked innocently.

"Yes, those." She took a deep breath which caused two of those body parts to come to his attention. "Look, we already agreed to the one trade-off. What makes you think you get four more, when all I added was one more rule?"

"Your first rule was too all-encompassing. The best rules are flexible—made to be revised when necessary. Your rules are in need of a major revamping."

She narrowed her eyes at him. "So what kind of trade-offs were you thinking of?"

"Hmmm. I hadn't really thought that far." *Mon Dieu, it's all I can think about.* "Okay, in return for no deliberate flaunting of bare skin, unless a person gives warning in advance, like, 'Hey, Rachel, I'm about to go swimming now. You might want to close your eyes.' Or, 'I'm in the shower and forgot a towel, could you hand me one . . . and no fair peeking.' That kind of thing. Well, in return for that—"

"You are not taking this seriously at all."

I am very serious when it comes to bare skin. Especially yours, babe. "Yes, I am. Anyhow, the trade-off for the bare skin thing could be one dance."

"Huh? What kind of dance? Where? How?"

"There's an old tape player inside with René's cassettes. Assuming it works, one song of my choice. One dance."

"Can I assume this would be a slow dance?"

"Darn tootin'." *Reeaaal slow.*

"You're impossible," she laughed, but then added, "Agreed."

Man, this is easier than taking candy from a baby. "On to the rule about no deliberate touching—other than the dance, of course—how about you agree to let me give you a massage? I do good massage, honey. Learned during my physical therapy days in the hospital."

"You already gave me a massage at Charmaine's spa. Remember?"

Are you kidding? I will never forget. "This is another type of massage. This is normal, therapeutic massage." *Man, I am on a roll.*

"Fully clothed?"

"Sure." *Here, baby. Here, baby. Here, baby.* "On to no sexy talk. Hmmm. That one shouldn't be too hard. I usually don't talk sexy unless intercourse is involved, or right around the corner. How about you?"

She appeared speechless for the moment.

Speechless is good. Real good. "Anyhow, I'll give you that one for a freebie. See how easy I am to get along with?"

She remained stiff as a board and suspicious as hell. She should be. He was going for the kill now.

"As to the no kissing rule, well, my trade-off calls for one kiss to seal the deal. Just one kiss." *Believe that and I've got a bridge to sell you.* "Don't go puckering your mouth up like you swallowed a lemon. I'm not trying to trick you." *Much.* "Honest. Just one kiss. After all, I deserve that for the freebie I just gave you." He stopped when he realized he was overselling this last trade-off.

"I agree. Just so we can get along and survive these next four days. But I have to say I'm surprised at you. You've made it clear, just as I have, that things are over between us, that we have no future. Why would you ask any of those things of me, those trade-offs, when you know they are pure temptation?"

He could have given her a flip answer, but he didn't. Instead, he went for honesty. "I don't want you for a wife . . . just as you don't want me for a husband." He quickly added the latter when he saw hurt flash across her face. "But I sure-God want to have mind-blowing sex with you. I have a powerful, *very powerful*, need for you that I can't argue away logically. So, I figure that it's like tossing a piece of candy to a sugar addict. Maybe it will appease the hunger for awhile."

"Oh, Remy." Tears misted her eyes, and he understood her silent message. She shared the hunger.

"If it were up to me, we would screw each other's brains out over the next four days, get it out of our system, then go our separate ways after that. Sex, but no commitment, no strings, just sex."

"Men view sex differently than women do, Remy. We can't separate the sex from emotion. Getting laid is a man thing. Making love is a woman thing."

"I know. That's why I agreed to your silly rules."

They both stared at each other, aware of the hopelessness of their situation.

Then he smiled at her. A weak smile, but a smile nonetheless. "Speaking of hunger," he said, trying to lighten both their moods, "how do you feel about worms?"

"Eating them?" she asked with horror. "You Cajuns are crazy, I swear. The things you eat. Okra is bad enough. I refuse to eat worms."

"No, not eating worms," he replied with a laugh, chucking her under the chin. "You said Feng Shui-ers think it's bad luck to kill a snake. How about worms? Is it okay to kill worms?"

"I suppose so," she answered tentatively, unsure where he was going with this conversation. "I've never seen worms mentioned in a Feng-Shui manual."

"Good, because there's something I would like to do with you. It can get wet, and slippery, and downright dirty at times, and on a day like today, hot as hell, but it can also be very satisfying and lots of fun."

"Reeemy," she cautioned.

"*Tsk-tsk,* Rachel. Get your mind out of the gutter. What I want you to do with me is . . ." He paused for a *ta-da* ending.

"What?"

"Fish."

Gone fishin'

"I got one, I got one!" Rachel shrieked with delight, almost knocking the Vanderbilt baseball cap off her head. Vanderbilt was the Catholic high school in Houma.

"And probably scared every other fish away with your screams," Remy grumbled, but with a smile on his face.

At her insistence, he'd donned the same T-shirt, Tulane cap and athletic shoes he'd worn before, to comply with the new and revised rules, but he was still tempting as all get-out. That was beside the point. Rachel had a fish to catch, and Remy just stood there at the edge of the water, net in hand, waiting for her to haul it in.

"What do I do now?" she asked. "Holy cow! Look at

how taut the line is. Look at the way the rod is bending. I'm gonna catch a fish. Yippee!"

"What you're gonna do is lose a fish if you don't stop squealing and start working, babe," Remy told her, shaking his head at her enthusiasm.

"Tell me what to do, Mr. Sarcastic."

"Set the hook."

"Huh?"

"Pull back hard. Harder than that. C'mon, I know how strong you are, Rachel. I've got bruises on my head from your okra thwap to prove that."

She shot him a glare, then jerked her rod back as hard as she could.

"Keep the pressure on now, sweetie. Nice and easy. You want to keep the line taut at the same time you're reeling him in. Just like a woman, tease a little, tug a little, tease a little, tug a—"

"I got the message," she snapped.

He grinned at her, slow and sexy. The wretch. He'd been teasing her.

"Remember, no hot looks," she reminded him.

"That was not a hot look. You would know if I gave you a hot look, believe me. That was only lukewarm."

"Whatever." She started to panic then. "The line is going out farther, even though I'm reeling it in."

"That's the drag. A good thing. Relax. This sucker will play itself out in good time."

"My arms are starting to hurt. Maybe you should pull it in."

"*Pull* it in?" he said with a laugh. Then, "Uh-uh, sugar, this is your fish. You do the work."

"I see it, I see it," she yelled.

Remy put his hands over his ears, pretending that her screams were piercing his eardrums. Meanwhile, he stepped into the water. Just when she thought the fish would get away, he swooped down with his net and captured a big fish.

"What is it?"

"A red fish. About five pounds. Not really big for a red fish, but then they usually aren't found this far inland. You did good, baby," he said, and appeared as if he was about to give her a hug, then thought better of it, probably because of the rules she'd insisted upon. Darn it. No, not really darn it. Well, sort of darn it. *Aaarrgh!*

Rachel loved watching Remy fish, and she loved the gentle patience he'd exhibited in teaching her how to bait a hook and hold a rod. She loved his teasing sense of humor when she fumbled and made dumb mistakes. He was a dark man with a lighter side long buried and fighting to come out. He would make a wonderful father. But, no, Rachel had promised Remy not to bring up that subject, and, frankly, it hurt too much for her to even think about all that he would never have. It was a crying shame that this gentle man would never have children of his own. And it was a crying shame that she would never have children, or anything else with him.

Rachel shook her head briskly to rid it of these morose thoughts. She refused to allow negative energy to spoil this nice day.

After that, Remy caught a speckled trout, a Bream, and a Black Drum, all of which he deemed too small and threw back in. An egret perched on a nearby limb swooped down and caught the Bluegill before it even hit the water and took off for its nest, she supposed, where he and the egret-wife and birdlets would share a tasty dinner. Remy caught a couple of Sac-a-lait, a fish known as "sack of milk" because of its fine-textured meat. These were a local version of crappies, he told her, and, although smaller than the other fish he'd rejected, he kept all three of them.

"I don't think I want to eat something with crap in its name," Rachel said.

"You'll love 'em," Remy promised, "fried in butter and garlic. Yum."

She was doubtful, but deferred to his better judgment on the matter. Next, Rachel caught what had to be the ugliest fish in the world.

"It's a catfish, Rachel. They're not supposed to be pretty," Remy chided her.

"It has whiskers. Yeech!"

"There is nothing better for breakfast than a slice of hot fried catfish on a piece of crusty bread," Remy told her. "Luc and René and I ate it all the time when we were growing up. We'd have a nice wood fire going down by the stream, and cook the fish right after we caught them."

He didn't say it, but Rachel suspected that it was all they'd eaten sometimes. She imagined the three little boys having had to fend for themselves when their father went off on a binge or a beating rampage, running off to hide by some bayou stream, camping out, feeding off of what nature offered.

"Did you and your brothers come here, to this cabin, when you were growing up?"

"Not much. It was too far out when we were younger, a good two hours by boat, but we did come occasionally when we were teenagers and older. It's Luc's cabin, him being the oldest, passed down through my mother's family, but he's always shared it with us. I don't think he's been here in the last few years, though, judging by the overgrown bushes and dusty interior."

"I know I've said it before, but you are so lucky to have your family."

He nodded, giving her an odd look, almost bleak. "Family is important to you, isn't it?" It wasn't the first time he had asked her that question.

"Isn't it to everyone?"

He shrugged.

Rachel suspected that there was more to his question than met the eye, but had no time to ask him because there was another tug on her line now. What she pulled up about caused her to have a heart attack. At her first view of her latest catch, she screamed, threw her rod on the ground, and jumped back about three yards.

"Oh, my God! I caught a snake, a big, fat, slimy snake! You didn't tell me I might catch a snake. Why didn't you warn me? Oh, my God! Is it poisonous? What kind is it? Betcha it's a water moccasin. Oh, my God!"

Remy picked up her rod and began to reel the snake in. "It's not a snake, Rachel. It's an eel."

"Hah! If it looks like a snake, and slithers like a snake, it must be a snake."

"It's an eel."

"Whatever it is, let it go."

"Why? You've never eaten eel? It's a real delicacy." Remy laughed at her.

She flashed him her fiercest glower.

"Are you going to give me the finger again?"

"No."

"What? Eel catching isn't finger-worthy?"

"Remy," she cautioned through gritted teeth. "Let it go."

He did, more slowly than necessary, if his continuing laughter was any indication.

Despite the eel, Rachel really enjoyed her day with Remy. Even without sex, or the prospect of sex, it soon became clear that she enjoyed his company. In different circumstances, they might have even become good friends. No, that wasn't true. Too much sizzle existed between them to ever become just friends. Still, it had been a nice afternoon, which reminded Rachel of something she hadn't considered before. She and Remy had jumped right into a sexual relationship without ever getting to know each other. Minus the usual dating rituals, she and Remy were strangers in many ways.

The problem was, the more she got to know Remy, the more she liked him.

Chapter 17

Crazy little thing called love—lust—whatever

Remy sat down at the table with Rachel to a meal that would have pleased the finest New Orleans restaurant palate.

Blackened redfish, which he'd cooked over a wood fire outside, not wanting to smoke up the inside of the cabin. Stirfry Crappies with improvised vegetables, including wild onions and mushrooms, canned corn and frozen green peppers from Tante Lulu's supplies, all served over plain white rice; Remy had picked up the recipe from Sylvie after many of her dinner parties. And his Cajun *tour de force*, a sinfully rich bread pudding made with their leftover, stale French bread topped with whiskey sauce using the half-cup of booze left in a bottle under the sink.

They'd both taken short showers to conserve water. The humidity remained horrendously high, but the rain hadn't come yet. He worried about depleting the cistern's resources.

And now Rachel sat across from him wearing a very respectable Daisy Mae kind of puffy short-sleeved shirt with an elastic neckline, which would probably pull down real easy and become instantly unrespectable. Her hair, which was unusually frizzy in a cute kind of way due to the humidity, was pulled back off her face with a headband, but that only made her ears and the sweet curve of her neck stand out as if in invitation . . . for what, he didn't even want to venture. For God's sake, she looked like Little Orphan Annie with breasts. On her bottom, she wore something she called pedal pushers, which reminded him that he'd like to push her pedal, for damn sure. The pants went all the way down to her calves. No bare skin there, but did she have a clue how tightly they fit her backside and just what a view of every nuance of her ass he got every time she turned around?

She ooh-ed and aah-ed over his culinary prowess, when he wanted nothing more than to show his prowess of a different kind. It was crazy, this Ping-Pong game they played with each other. Lunatic Rules. Insane pretensions that they didn't want to jump each other's bones. A demented testing of the erotic currents that zigzagged between them. A mad kind of constant shifting of the line they'd drawn in the sand between them.

Am I crazy?

Is she crazy?

You're both crazy, St. Jude pronounced with decided disgust.

"Who's crazy?" Rachel said, sipping at the last of her ice water.

Remy was really going bonkers if he spoke his thoughts aloud. "Nothing. It's just the heat getting to me, I guess."

"It is horribly humid. Do you think it'll rain soon?"

He shrugged and downed the last of his own ice water. He needed an icing-down all right, and not just in his mouth. "Hopefully, we'll get a real soaker sometime during the night, but there are times when it takes a day or two to let loose."

"Thanks for the meal, Remy. Everything was delicious. Tomorrow it's my turn to cook."

Soft Cajun ballads played in the background on René's tape player, which did indeed work just fine. Two mismatched candles on the table provided soft lighting, although it wasn't quite dark yet. The ambience was perfect. Too perfect.

Remy shifted in his seat and tried to think of normal, everyday conversation, something to take his mind off that *other* thing. "Think you can make a meal out of the oddball things my aunt sent and what's been left in the cupboard here?" *Like I care!*

"Sure. If you can do it, so can I. I'm no great shakes in the kitchen, but I have a few specialties." She smiled at him tentatively, as if daring him to contradict her self-assessment.

He would never do that. Hell, he already knew about some of her specialties and she sure-God excelled at them. "Okay, Martha, tomorrow night my kitchen is yours." *My bed could be yours, too, if you'd only ask. No, no, no! I don't want that. Well, yes, I do, but it would not be a good idea. It would be a bad idea. The best bad idea I ever had. God, I feel as if I've got a fire in my groin that only she can put out.*

"Why don't you go out and douse that fire, while I do the dishes?"

"What?" he choked out. *Was I thinking aloud again? Geesh, this is getting embarrassing.*

"The wood fire. Shouldn't you put the embers out?" She

cocked her head in question and looked at him as if he had a few screws loose.

He did. And they were all rattling about right where his thighs met his, um, screwdriver. "Oh, yeah. Sure." He pushed back the chair and was about to do just that when she asked shyly, "Are we going to dance tonight?"

His screwdriver about went ballistic. *Are you crazy?* "Uh, not tonight. I'm a little tired and I need to work up to it."

"You need to work up to dancing?"

"Oh, yeah."

"By practicing dance steps?"

"That and a few other things."

"Like?"

"Self-control."

She smiled then, finally understanding.

"But tomorrow night, dancing, for sure," he promised.

I'm losin' my friggin' mind.

The lull before the storm

The next day, day three out of five of their enforced stay, it still hadn't rained. Humidity hung at about ninety-nine percent.

Remy handled the excess heat by busying himself with yard work and repairs about the cabin, alternating with lengthy conversations on his cell phone, presumably to DEA contacts, and frequent, cooling dips in the stream. This was Saturday. Supposedly some big deal with the DEA and the drug lords was supposed to go down on Monday. Then, she and Remy could go home on Tuesday. That was the plan, anyhow.

She'd spent the early morning working on her lists. Actually, she'd been surprisingly productive, coming up with some new ideas.

"What would you think of an aquarium window for Charmaine's spa?" she asked Remy when he came in for a late breakfast of fried catfish sandwich, which proved to be just as delicious as he'd promised.

"What's an aquarium window?"

"The whole window is actually a narrow aquarium, let's say ten feet by ten feet, and about one foot in width. It creates an interesting dimensional aspect and obviously draws lots of attention. We could put fresh- or saltwater fish in the tank. Either would be beautiful."

"Sounds great. Not sure what it has to do with a beauty spa, but it would get my attention."

"Hey, even mermaids have to get prettified sometime."

To which he'd smiled, and her heart did flipflops.

After he left, she started an even more complete cleaning of the cabin. Remy came in to get a hammer and nails to fix one of the shutters when he saw her on her hands and knees trying to get a dust mop under the couch. He said something like, "Lord have mercy!" while staring at her behind, but when she'd asked him what he said, he replied, "What are you doing down there?"

"Cleaning."

"You don't have to clean this place, not that well anyway. Hell—I mean, heck—I don't think anyone's been under that couch in ten years."

"I know I don't have to. I want to. I need to keep busy,

or I'll go nuts in this heat. I used to hate cleaning with a passion, but now I kind of like it."

He raised an eyebrow in question at her.

"One of the foster homes I stayed in when I was about ten years old insisted on obsessive cleaning. Toilets, tiles, and faucets had to be cleaned weekly with a toothbrush and Lysol. Dustballs under a bed were considered anathema. My bed had to be made dime perfect. The kitchen floor had to be swept with a broom, then a vacuum, then wet-scrubbed by hand twice. Three times a week!"

"What happened if you didn't do it all just right?"

"A spanking," she answered matter-of-factly.

"Oh, Rachel."

"Don't go getting maudlin on me. That was a long time ago, and I'm not anal about cleaning now."

"Maude who?" he teased. His words said humor, but sadness for her remained in his eyes.

"Go play carpenter and leave me alone," she advised, touched.

She noticed that he waited 'til she was back on her hands and knees and he got another gander at her butt before leaving. This time she was certain that he muttered something about "mercy."

After that, Rachel started on her gift list. For Jill, who loved to cook, she was going to buy several Cajun cookbooks and a set of the spices they sold in gift shops throughout Louisiana. For Laura, it was a no-brainer: a Cajun quilt. Hank deserved something for lending her his truck; so, he would get a bottle of one hundred–proof bourbon with directions for making Oyster Shooters. For Beau, she would buy a video of that movie *Joe Dirt*, in which the comedian David Spade paid homage to the merits of the mullet hairdo. Finally, she thought and thought but could come up with nothing that her grandmother needed or would want. Then, she decided that a makeover at Charmaine's spa would be just the thing—a new hairstyle, manicure and pedicure, a facial, and most definitely a mustache waxing.

By early afternoon, she decided to go looking for wild blueberries and strawberries, to make a cobbler for desert. She donned jeans, socks, sneakers and a tank top. She was taking no chances with snakes biting her bare skin, assuming they couldn't leap up and bite her arms or neck. Before she went out with her bucket in hand, she mixed a pitcher of dry milk with water and put it in the fridge so that it would be cold by dinnertime.

Remy was talking on the phone again, an argument by the sound of his raised voice, and didn't notice her leaving. To the far side of the house she noticed the cistern and generator, and had to smile at what stood between them: a weathered old plastic statue of St. Jude, which was a good five feet tall. She guessed that Tante Lulu must have placed it here years ago. God bless the old lady who felt the need to have the patron saint of hopeless causes looking after her nephews even out here in this remote bayou.

There was also a rope hammock strung between two tupelo gum trees out front, which she planned to try out one of these days. She envisioned herself taking a nap out there. Snakes didn't crawl up hammocks, did they?

After a half-hour in the woods, she had half a bucket which she considered sufficient for the two of them. She'd been lucky to encounter no snakes or fierce animals, but she was so hot that perspiration poured off her. When she came back to the clearing before the house, she saw that Remy was still on the phone. He hadn't even noticed her absence.

Well, enough was enough. She put down her bucket of berries and stomped toward the stream. Snakes and eels and sharp-toothed fish be damned! She was going for a swim, or die of heat stroke.

"Rachel! What are you doing?" she heard Remy call out, but she ignored him and walked fully clothed into the stream, shoes and all. A deliberate choice. Heck, she was hot but not insane. She wasn't about to step on an eel-snake in her bare feet. She walked all the way to the middle, which was waist-deep, then sat down 'til she was fully submerged. The water was blessedly cool, almost orgasmic in the relief it provided her hot skin.

When she came up, unable to hold her breath too long, Remy stood in the water next to her, also fully clothed, including his Tulane cap. "Rachel, are you okay?" He brushed some wet strands of hair off her face.

The concern in his voice was endearing. He probably thought she was having a breakdown of sorts. She was, sort of. "I'm fine. Just hot beyond belief. Am I going to get bitten by a snake or something, even with these clothes on?"

"Honey, you scared every snake or *something* away with all the splashing you did going in. They were probably afraid you were going to bite them."

"Very funny. Stop looking at my breasts."

He smiled.

And butterflies the size of baseballs revved up their wings in her stomach, and lower. "Don't smile, either," she ordered irrationally.

He continued to smile, of course.

"Go ahead and swim for awhile. I'll watch for snakes

and ferocious *somethings* while you cool down," he offered. "You can even take off your shoes and jeans and I won't count it against 'The Rules.' In fact, you can take off *all* your clothes and skinny dip, and I won't even look." The mischievous twinkle in his eye was priceless.

"Hah! I'm in more danger from you than snakes, I think. Go away." She gave him a shove in the chest to start him moving.

He slipped and grabbed for her. They both went under and came up laughing. His cap was floating downstream; he swam after it and tossed it on the bank. Since they were both wet, and reasonably well-covered as per "The Rules," they continued to swim together, floating on their backs and treading water, splashing, laughing. If she hadn't thought it before, she did now. *I like this man.*

Finally, both stood and headed toward the bank. Without thinking, Remy draped an arm over her shoulder and tugged her close. He jumped out of the water first, then held a hand to pull her up. When he did, he pulled extra hard so that she landed against him. With her standing on tippy-toes, they were chest to breast, stomach to stomach, genitals to genitals. And it didn't matter a bit that they were soaked to the bone, she felt his heat . . . and threw off plenty of her own.

She looked up at his dark eyes with their water-spiked lashes which gazed down at her, as if conveying some hidden message. For several long moments, they simply stood, not speaking.

Finally, he asked, "If I were to kiss you now, would I be violating 'The Rules'?"

Reluctantly, she nodded.

"If I were to kiss you now, would I be making a big mistake?"

Reluctantly, she nodded.

"Then go, before I do something we'll both regret."

She went, but she was regretful anyway.

Make her an offer she can't refuse

That night, the rain still hadn't come, and the tension in the air was so thick it could be sliced with a knife. Of course, some of that tension could be attributed to the coil springs of sexual yearning he and Rachel contributed to by the hour.

If that wasn't bad enough, all hell was breaking loose back in Houma. He'd been on the phone most of the day with Pete and Larry. It appeared that the drug operation was bigger than they'd expected and more sites needed to be surveyed and manned in preparation for Monday's shakedown. And here he sat, twiddling his thumbs with makework yard projects, babysitting the sexiest woman alive.

Which was a ridiculous assessment regarding Rachel, considering the fact that she wore a big Houma High School football jersey, Number 33, and a pair of black-and-white polka-dot boxer shorts which had been popular outer attire back when Charmaine was a teenager. She was barefooted. *Dieu, I love her feet. How pathetic is that?* Speaking of teenagers, he didn't want to think about how Charmaine had gotten Jake Doucet's Number 33 football jersey back then when Jake, known as Lucky Jake for obvious reasons, had been four years older than her at fourteen.

With a sigh of surrender, he sat down to the dinner Rachel had prepared from the potluck ingredients they had laying around. What he should have done is hit the sack early and pray for a three-day sleep 'til they left this place on Tuesday. Instead, he asked brightly, "So, what have we got here, Ms. Crocker?"

Not that she resembled Betty Crocker by a Loo-zee-anna mile. Who knew a loose football jersey and non-revealing boxers could be so damn tempting? Who knew a center-piece arrangement of pink and white roses in a Mason jar could turn an everyday meal into a romantic event?

"Hamburger Surprise, vinegar and oil endive salad, fried green tomatoes, beaten biscuits, and mixed fruit cobbler."

"Hamburger Surprise? That's not like Hamburger Helper, is it? With all that sawdust filler kind of stuff?"

"No. It's ground beef. At least, I hope that's what was in the white freezer paper Tante Lulu sent. It better not be ground-up alligator or ground woodchuck, or worse, ground snake! Anyhow, ground beef, fried onions, elbow macaroni and canned tomato sauce, topped with melted Swiss cheese. It's good. Really. I learned to make it in college when cheap dishes were the *haute cuisine*." She smiled at him expectantly, waiting for him to take a first bite.

It was good, really good. But he wasn't surprised by that. Everything Rachel did was good, from her Feng Shui decorating to her cooking, to, well, everything.

"And the beaten biscuits. That's a Cajun *thang*, honey. Bet you didn't learn how to make those in college."

"No, my grandmother taught me last week. Hers were light as air. Mine are probably like lead sinkers."

He took a bite, slathered with butter. It wasn't bad. He told her, "Great.

"Did good ol' Gizelle teach you how to make fried green tomatoes, too? It hardly seems proper for a Yankee to be making such a Southern dish."

"No, my grandmother didn't teach me that." She gave him a playful whack on the forearm with a spatula. "There are some things Southern I learned myself."

She smiled then, and his stomach did this odd little churning thing, like butterflies were doing the rhumba inside.

As they did the dishes together—he washed, she dried—thunder rumbled in the distance. Rain, finally. "Pete told me this afternoon that a big storm is heading in off the gulf, probably tonight. I better batten down the plane, just in case."

"You go now. I'll finish up here."

It took him more than an hour to secure the aircraft, which floated downstream a bit from the cabin, using an extra heavy anchor, bungee cords, and industrial-strength ropes. He tied the cords and ropes around trees on both banks. Now, if only the trees weren't uprooted, he'd be okay.

As the thunder increased in volume and seemed to be coming closer, Remy punched in Luc's cell phone number, figuring it wouldn't hurt to get a more up-to-date weather forecast. All he got was static. Apparently, the weather was screwing up the airwaves, which could happen in a small storm, too. Even so, he decided to lock the shutters closed and tie down the loose items in the cellar on the first floor. Just a precaution, he kept telling himself.

When he stepped back outside the cellar, the hair stood out on the back of his neck, and he understood why his bayou intuition had kicked in without warning. An eerie silence pervaded. No birdsong. No frogs. No breeze. The skies were gray with a glaring underlight. Leaves on the trees were turned up. All signs of a pending storm.

"Remy, what's wrong?" Rachel asked. She'd come out on the porch. "Why is it so quiet?"

"Storm's comin'."

"Why do you look so funny?"

He shrugged and smiled at her as he came up the steps. "Guess I'm just a funny guy."

"Don't patronize me. I'm not a little kid."

He patted her on the shoulder.

She shoved his hand aside. "Tell me."

"I told you, a storm is coming." He paused, then added, "A big storm."

"How big?"

"How the hell should I know?" Almost immediately, he regretted taking out his concern on her. "I'm sorry. It could be a hurricane. Hopefully, just a tropical storm, but hurricanes are a fact of life here. Gotta be prepared."

A great blue heron flew overhead, as if in a rush to get home and hide. They both watched until it was out of sight.

"Can't you call someone, your aunt or your brother, and find out for sure?"

"Phone's dead."

"What should we do?"

He looked at her, all nervous and scared, and said something really stupid. "How 'bout that dance you promised me?"

Someone once said dancing is just a form of foreplay. Yep!

Once the dishes were done and the tables pushed to the side, Rachel asked Remy, "Should I put shoes on?"

"Nah, I won't step on your feet," he answered with absolute confidence. He was flicking through some cassettes next to the tape player. "By the way, what's with the no nail polish look?"

"Huh?" She looked down at her bare feet.

"You always wear nail polish on your toes. Pink, peach, you know. Not your fingernails, just your feet."

"You noticed my toenail polish?"

He looked up at her and winked. "Oh, yeah!"

Unbelievable! We haven't even begun to dance and already he's turned me on with talk of toes, and a wink!

Thunder roared in the distance and a flash of heat lightning brightened the clearing where the cabin stood for a few seconds. The humidity was close to one hundred percent. Outside, she could hear the wind start, just a slight, refreshing breeze. Nothing to be frightened of, yet.

Remy continued to examine the cassettes, searching for just the right song for their dance. Little did he know that she could care less about the music. She just wanted to feel his hands on her and the rhythm of his body.

"What exactly are you looking for?" she asked, still standing on the other side of the room, suddenly shy.

"You wouldn't believe these tapes. They belong to René from about a decade ago. He used to bring his girlfriends up here for little weekend flings. These are his idea of mood music."

Rachel barely registered his words. She was more interested in looking at Remy, while she had the chance and he didn't notice her scrutiny. He wore an ancient pair of acid-washed jeans with holes in the knees and a black T-shirt with the logo, TALK DIRTY TO ME on front and POISON on the back. She'd been a fan of that music group in the late eighties, too, but the song's title seemed oddly appropriate, or inappropriate, in this setting. The clothes had been left in one of the drawers here since he was a teenager.

Remy was barefooted, too, and his narrow, high-arched feet were oddly appealing to Rachel. Perhaps she had a foot fetish just like Remy did. Well, not a fetish, but an appreciation. Yeah, a foot appreciation. That wasn't so bad, was it?

"Why are you smiling?" Remy asked, coming up on his feet in one fluid motion.

"I was thinking about perversions," she said.

"Really?" The grin on his face showed decided interest. "Care to share?"

"No."

The slow, ultra-husky sound of Barry White came out of the tape player, a slow, sexy love song. Remy held his arms open and did a slow dance of invitation toward her which involved rolling his hips from side to side as he walked.

"Lordy, Lordy!"

"What did you say?" Remy asked as he pulled her into his arms, hands linked loosely behind her waist.

She put her hands on his shoulders and answered honestly, "I said that I am in big trouble here."

He smiled. "I sure-God hope so."

He pulled her closer then so that she could feel just how big the trouble was. She put her hands behind his neck and laid her head on his shoulder. Following his lead, she let the music and Remy's sweet rhythm seep inside. There was no need for talk. Their bodies did their talking for them.

Times like this were special. Memory builders. When something extraordinary happened to a person, the kind of things remembered forever after, it didn't have to be a life-changing event like a graduation or marriage or birth of a child. It more often was the small things. The sheer joy of summer sunlight on a fragrant flower. The giggle of a toddler. The brush of a lover's fingertips. And the person marks the moment with the flashing insight, *This is special. I should remember this.* There had been only a few such events in Rachel's memory, but she recognized with tears misting her eyes that this image of her slow dancing in Remy's arms on a warm September evening would be forever imprinted in her mind.

They swayed, they turned, they even dipped, always to a slow, slow beat. Remy was an excellent dancer. No extravagant moves. But a good sense of rhythm. He danced like he made love, with quiet expertise.

One song led to another and another, and Rachel didn't have the heart, or inclination, to protest. Not even when Remy put his hands on her buttocks and tugged her up on tiptoes so that her core more perfectly aligned with his. Now, she rode the ridge of his erection as they danced.

He moaned softly and murmured, "Sweet, sweet, sweet!"

She kept her own moan to herself. In truth, she probably couldn't speak for the incredible white heat pooling in her with a pulse that defied description. An erotic pulse, for heaven's sake.

"Time for another trade-off, *chère*," he said in a voice as rough as Barry's. "The kiss." Without waiting for her assent, he half-danced, half-carried her across the room 'til her back was against the wall, her toes dangling just above the floor. Grinding his pelvis against her belly in emulation of the sex act, he began what could only be described as an assault on her mouth—an assault of the most delicious, agonizing kind.

"Open," she said against his lips which had been pressing back and forth, adjusting and shaping her. "Open for me, Remy." He did, and it was Rachel who assaulted him then with soft bites, deep thrusts of her tongue which were met by Remy's sucking, and wet, devouring slides of her lips across his. At one point, it became unclear who kissed whom. Rachel's heart raced and that pulse between her legs became a full-fledged, continuous series of spasms.

Suddenly, Remy jerked away and sank to his knees. He sat down on the floor and put his face between his knees, panting for breath.

She sank down to the floor beside him, alternately humiliated that he was the one to end their kiss, and concerned that something might be wrong. In the end, his welfare mattered more than her ego, she decided. Putting a hand on his heaving shoulders, she asked, "Remy? What's wrong?"

"What's wrong? I'll tell you what's wrong. Just one kiss from you and I was about to come in my pants, like a teenager with his first lay."

She thought about what he'd said, including the crudity of the way he'd expressed himself, and decided to forgive him. "So what? I came. Why shouldn't you?"

His shoulders still heaved, but within seconds, Rachel realized that he was laughing now. *At her.* The wretch.

She tried to scramble to her feet, but he grabbed for her,

wrestling her back to the floor. After a little pushing and shoving, she ended up pinned to the floor by his body.

"You were laughing at me," she accused.

"No, I wasn't. I was laughing at myself. I am so pitiful that I can't even control myself in a kiss with you."

"I couldn't control myself, either. Am I pitiful?"

"Never, sweetheart, but it's different for a man."

"What a ridiculous, sexist thing to say," she declared, shoving his chest hard.

He didn't budge an inch.

Any further discussion on the subject was cut short by a rip of lightning, which struck real close outside, followed immediately by a loud clap of thunder. All the lights in the cabin went out and the fridge and overhead fan turned off.

"Uh-oh!" Remy said, lifting himself off her. "Looks like we're in for a big one." He helped Rachel to her feet.

When the next rumble of thunder actually shook the house, Rachel teased, "I've heard about some men making their lover's world move, but this is a stretch. Isn't it?"

"Ah, not when the man is a Cajun, *chère*," he boasted, swatting her a good one on the behind. He had good aim, even in the dark.

Just then lightning struck, close to the house again, the wind picked up, and rain began to come down with driving force.

Remy said the oddest thing then. "All right, already, Jude. I get the message."

Chapter 18

The best laid plans of . . .

Remy stood at the screen door, staring out at the turbulent bayou stream. The wind had died down totally after its first gusting, but only for fifteen minutes or so. This new wind was stronger, causing narrow limbs to break and moss to fall from the trees and fly about like spooky ghosts.

He saw all this through the beam of his flashlight. Power remained out, and probably would until tomorrow, or whenever the storm ended, when he could go out and check the generator. Even with lights, visibility ranged no more than a few feet due to the pelting rain.

Hurricane winds could be brutal, up to two hundred miles per hour, but they usually never hit land at all. Instead, they usually blew themselves out to sea, or they could alter their course several times in one day. Furthermore, most hurricanes hit in the low-lying coastal areas, not this far inland. But then, the official hurricane season in Louisiana was June through September, which was its peak month, and since this was mid-September, a real possibility. Even so, this storm was nothing by Louisiana standards, so far. Barely a tropical storm. He hoped it stayed that way.

He'd urged Rachel to go upstairs and try to sleep. Maybe by morning, when she awakened, it would all be over. Assuming she could sleep, that is, with this roaring wind. He hadn't told her, but there was nothing they could do at this point, except wait out the storm. There was no hurricane cellar or protected shelter. Most important, this cabin had withstood more than a hundred and fifty years of bayou storms and still stood pretty much the same as when it was built before the Civil War by Rivard family trappers. In fact, it had even been used as a stopping place for escaped slaves going North at one point. Ironic that it was a "safe house" once again, though for an entirely different purpose.

When lightning flashed across the sky, briefly illuminating the clearing before the cabin, he saw something gold standing on the other side of the stream. A cougar. Rare to the point of being almost extinct in the bayous these days. Remy felt privileged to have seen it, even if only for a moment.

Like magic, the rain suddenly stopped. He looked out and saw that the cougar had fled. No wonder. An eerie calm now pervaded. The bayou was soundless as a vacuum. It was the eye of the storm.

He closed and locked the door. Using his flashlight, he walked lightly across the room and up the steps. He turned the flashlight off and tiptoed to the edge of the bed, wanting to know that Rachel was all right, but not wanting to wake her if she already slept.

"I'm awake," she said.

"Just checking."

"How is everything?"

"A tropical storm at this point."

"At this point?"

"I won't lie, Rachel. It could get bad. Or it could avoid us altogether."

"Is it a hurricane?"

"Not here. Not yet. Maybe not at all."

"You're a lot of help," she said with a shaky laugh. "Shouldn't we move to the basement or something?"

He shook his head. "If it reaches a certain level, we'll hunker down in the bathroom. Not the cellar. It would be flooded."

"Oh, geez!" Her voice quivered with distress.

Remy had lived through lots of storms in Louisiana, from little puddlemakers to full-fledged hurricanes. While he was never blasé about their devastating potential, they didn't terrify him the way they obviously did Rachel. He had to do something to divert her attention. No, he wasn't thinking about sex, but something equally mind-diverting. *Aah! Maybe . . .*

"Hey, babe, I think it's time for our final trade-off," he announced suddenly.

"And that would be?"

"A massage." *God, I hope I'm not making a mistake.*

That infuriating inner voice in his head was laughing.

"Now? Are you crazy?"

"Yeah, but that's beside the point." Honestly, he hoped to help her relax and take her mind off what might come next. It was worth a try, wasn't it? The winds were already picking up again, almost deafening in their ferocity. She was going to have the living daylights scared out of her in a few minutes if she just lay here listening to the storm.

"Turn over on your tummy, sweetheart. You're in for a treat."

"Don't you need light?"

"I have a flashlight if I need it, but, no, massage is all about touch and instinct and learned skills. Relax. And enjoy."

"I don't think I can relax."

"You'll relax, Rachel. Believe me," he said with utter confidence. *Not sure about me, but I'll have you boneless in no time, guar-an-teed.*

Hey, you angels over there—Michael, Rafael—got any popcorn? This is going to be a great show. Sometimes, Jude had a warped joke mentality.

"I'm not taking my clothes off. I'll tell you that right now."

He laughed. "I don't want you to take your clothes off." *I'm not that much of a glutton for punishment.* Besides, she wore the football jersey and underpants. That's all. Plenty enough punishment for him. "I'm fully clothed, too; so, not to worry."

"Hah!" Despite her skepticism, Rachel rolled over onto her front, with her head on the pillow and arms raised above her head.

"And another thing, I'm only giving you a back massage," he said while he knelt on the bed, then straddled her body near the hips. He placed both his thumbs on the hollow at the base of her skull, pressing, with his middle fingers rotating.

"Oh, my God! That feels wonderful already." As an afterthought, she asked, "Why only a back massage?"

"Because I would enjoy a frontal massage too much."

Hell, I practically blew my wad in my drawers already with just a kiss. I am not taking any more chances like that.

"Oh," was all she said, apparently understanding perfectly. But then, he thought he saw her smile. Her face was turned to the side on the pillow, and it was dark; he might have been wrong about that.

To her neck and shoulders, he gave particular attention because it was here that most body tension got lodged.

"Do you use some particular method of massage?" she asked lazily.

"Um, more like a combination of several techniques. I learned them by their letters. WHPK, which is wringing, hammering, pressing and kneading. Then, the three C's, as well, which are caressing, circling and corkscrewing." *What a crock! I've never given a real massage before in all my life. Had plenty in physical therapy myself, though. How hard could it be?*

"That feels so good," she said as he continued to work her neck and shoulder muscles. "I didn't realize how tense I was. Well, to be honest, I was tense before this storm ever hit."

He didn't ask what she meant by that. He knew. Sexual tension was as potent as any other stress to the body.

Working on the hands next, he took special care to be gentle on the palms, an especially sensitive spot. Then he kneaded each of the fingers in turn, between the fingers, the knuckles, the wrists, the back of the hand.

Bypassing her body from shoulders to legs, he moved down to her feet. He had her bend her knee so her foot was raised.

"Oh, I don't know about this, Remy. My feet are really ticklish and—oh, Good Lord, what are you doing?"

"I'm just kneading your instep, babe."

"It felt like you licked it."

Who? Me? "A good massage therapist has to have fingers like a feather on occasion." *I am good. Man, I am good!*

"Really? I never heard that before."

Neither have I.

When he finished kneading and massaging her ankles, Achilles tendons, toes and foot pads, he worked his way up her legs. He loved her legs and he showed his admiration by alternately hammering and caressing her until she was practically boneless and moaning with pleasure. Her football jersey had worked its way up to her waist so that her white panties were exposed.

Should I tell her?

Nah.

He did plenty of looking then, every time lightning illuminated the room. Hey, it was part of being a masseur, he supposed. Narrow waist. The curve of her hips. The sweet swell of two globes. So engrossed was he in the tantalizing sight that at first he didn't realize that the walls of the cabin were shaking.

"Did you just shake the bed?" she asked, then gasped. "Oh, no! It's the storm, isn't it?"

He did the only thing he could think of then to stem her fears. He aimed his fingers right for the gluteal fold where the buttocks met her thighs, and at the cleavage of her buttocks. Her body immediately stiffened. He knew too well how women hated to be handled there, except in the fever pitch of hot sex, but at least he'd shocked the fright right out of her. Before she had a chance to react, he worked his knees between her legs and spread her thighs. Immediately, he began kneading her behind and the fold with his thumbs firmly placed between her legs.

"You . . . you said there would be no sex," she accused him.

"This isn't sex."

"It feels like sex."

At her words, the half-erection in his pants went full-tilt boogie. He let his thumbs stray a bit along the crotch of her panties and discovered a wetness there. All the bells and whistles on his pinball machine went haywire then. For a minute, even in the darkness, he saw stars in vivid reds, and whites, and blues. Finally, when he could catch his breath, he asked, "Do you want me to stop . . . the massage?"

"No." There wasn't a bit of hesitation in her voice.

Rachel went silent then as he pressed and kneaded the deep muscles of her upper and lower back. He drew light circles with his forefinger. He outlined the shoulder bones. He hammered her with the edges of both hands, then soothed the same spots with deep-finger presses. Meanwhile the wind buffeted the cabin.

Suddenly, she flipped over on her back and stared up at him. "All right, that's it."

"Huh?" He sat back on his heels, still straddling her body.

"If I'm going to die, I want to have sex with you one more time."

"I beg your pardon." *Talk about back-handed invitations!*

She shimmied herself up to a sitting position, legs straight out, with him now straddling her in the knee area. "This is silly, Remy. Forget about the storm. What will be will be. But you and I are mature adults who are behaving in an absurd manner. I hate your secrets. You hate my reaction to your one secret in particular. But none of that changes the fact that you and I want each other—sexually, at least."

"Rachel, we've had this conversation before," he pointed out with strained patience. "What's your point?"

"Point is, I want to make love with you. Probably more than once . . . until we leave this place."

"I thought we already established that you're a sex-*with*-commitment kind of gal, and nothing less will do."

She shrugged. "I'm going to get hurt, either way, Remy. That's a fact."

He started to disagree, then stopped himself. She was right. They were both going to be hurt, regardless. "Rachel, honey, I don't have much self-control where you're concerned. Don't tempt me like this. I'm trying to be chivalrous."

"This lady is not looking for a knight in shining armor. I gave up on that a long time ago."

He raised his eyebrows at her. "A knight in tarnished armor, then?" He laughed, trying to joke her out of this ridiculous but tantalizing idea. "Really, Luc and René and I used to call ourselves The Cajun Knights or sometimes Knights of the Bayou, fashioned ourselves sort of noble fellows, exactly the opposite of our Dad. There's probably some psychological reason for all that, but . . ." Remy realized he was rambling and couldn't seem to stop himself.

A brief moment of silence followed. Then Rachel said, in a low, loving voice, "Remy, the moat outside is dangerous. You've already crossed the drawbridge. Are you coming in to my castle or not?"

With a soft groan of surrender, Remy replied, "Yes, m'lady."

Making it through, with the long, hard knight

The storm continued to pound wildly outside, but Rachel wasn't afraid of dying or catastrophe. Not really. As long as Remy was with her, she could face anything. Perhaps she'd become a fatalist, willing to let destiny rule her course. As long as Remy was with her.

Remy stood to remove his clothing in the darkness. She knew that he thought her sudden decision to make love with him was based on the storm and her fear of death. Lots of books had been written about the principle of enemies becoming friends under fire, that people behave recklessly in the face of danger. Not so in her case. Sometime between their kiss downstairs and Remy coming up to check on her, she'd subconsciously surrendered to the pull of her heart. Nothing had changed. In reality, she still didn't trust him; in reality, he was still angry with her. But there would be no reality checks here. Just for tonight they would set their differences aside. No strings. No recriminations. No promises. Just for these few days they had left, she would give herself to him. A gift of love.

She wiggled out of her panties and drew the football jersey over her head, then waited for Remy.

He slid onto the mattress beside her.

Both remained silent as they contemplated what they were about to do. Unsure of themselves, in the oddest way.

Rachel had the most compelling urge to have Remy inside her. *Now.* No preliminaries. Just joined with her. Before she could voice that need, Remy said, "I want you so much, Rachel. I'm afraid I'll hurt you."

"I feel the same way."

He laughed. "You can't hurt me."

"Oh?" She pushed him to his back, and before he could ask what she was up to, Rachel swung a leg over his hips, took his very hard erection in hand, and guided him into her.

"Oh, sweet Jesus!" he gritted out. Then, with a self-deprecating chuckle, he added, "I was wrong. You *can* hurt me."

Rachel sat perfectly still with her knees on either side of his hips, her butt on his upper thighs, and his penis imbedded in her to the hilt. "*Am* I hurting you?" she asked with alarm, prepared to disengage.

He put his hands on her waist to hold her in place. "In the best possible way, sweetheart. Delicious agony."

"I needed you in me, right now," she confessed. "Is that slutty of me?"

"Very slutty."

"I mean, it's usually men who want to forego foreplay, not women. This time I didn't need all that. In fact, I had to have you this way. Does that make sense?" She still sat on him, unmoving, and it was the most wonderful feeling of fullness. Two vital parts connected.

"I need something, too. Can you give me what I need?"

"I don't know. Is this another perversion?"

He laughed or tried to, but it came out strained, as if it might hurt to laugh when he had a rock-hard penis planted in a willing vagina.

"Just sit still and don't move, no matter what," he ordered. Putting his hands on her knees, he spread them wider, which caused her outer folds to open and her inner folds to grasp him tighter. He gasped. Then, he did the most outrageous thing. He put the three middle fingers of one hand into her mouth and used the wetness to moisten her, as if she weren't already wet enough. "Remember, don't move." He still had one hand on her waist.

"Remy, I have to move."

"No! No, you don't. I want to see how it feels to have you come around me, on me, without moving. Besides, I really am afraid I'll hurt you if I thrust right now. Come on, you can do it. Put your hands back, and hold onto my knees. That's the way, honey. Just like that."

He began to strum her slickness then with a middle finger: a constant, fast-paced flick that barely skimmed the surface. Almost immediately, her inner muscles began to convulse around his shaft. Not just once or twice. A continuous grasp-release, grasp-release that matched the tempo he set. She could swear that his already huge erection grew more huge. A wail began deep in her throat and emerged as a long continuous, "Ohhhhhhhhhhhh!" She tried to move, to undulate her hips on him, but he had both hands on her hips now, fingers digging into her skin.

"Ride it out, chère. Relax and let it come. You feel so good. So good. Like a million squeezing fingers tempting me."

Rachel threw her head back and keened into an incredible orgasm. Finally, her body went limp.

Remy was anything but limp.

She was so sated, she wanted to curl up in his arms and fall asleep.

Remy had other plans.

"Now, darlin', a special treat," he announced breathlessly. "You know that I used to be a cowboy?"

"Uh-huh," she answered tentatively.

"Well, I'm gonna teach you to ride."

"A horse?"

"No, silly. A Cajun."

And, boy, did he ever!

Do it to me one more time, or two, or three

Remy was pounding into her body, relentlessly.

The storm outside had died down to a steady rain. No more thunder or lightning or high winds. The worst was over.

But the storm inside Remy still raged. Sweat poured off of him. Cords of tensed muscle stood out on his arms and neck. His knees would have linen burns, for sure. Hell, his cock would be raw meat before he was done. And poor Rachel! She would be black and blue if he kept this up—down below, for sure, but also on her breasts, her thighs, her butt, everywhere.

But he couldn't seem to get enough of her and, much as he wanted to, he could not end the exquisite torment in his center. Even when she'd ridden him to her own orgasm a half hour ago, he could not come. It was as if subconsciously he knew this tenuous bond between them would last one or two days at the most, and then she would be gone. Some deranged part of his psyche was dictating that if he did not come, he could forestall the end.

Someone moaned. He guessed it was him.

Rachel cradled his jaws in her hands and said, "Remy, did you hear me?"

"Huh?" he asked through the daze of his arousal.

"I said slow down."

He did, immediately.

"I love you."

He moaned again.

"Don't try so hard. No matter what happens, I love you."

Oh, God! She understands. She knows how friggin' pitiful I am. Oh, God! In this unusual darkness, where visibility was almost nil, Remy had felt whole. He could pretend that his body was undamaged, not a beast. But her words had called him back to the present and the fact that even a blackout couldn't hide his flaws.

His strokes were long and exquisitely slow now, accompanied by her soothing hands running from his shoulders down to his buttocks, then back again. Over and over. With each stroke, she whispered, "I love you."

He said the words, too, but only to himself, because words were beyond his powers right now.

When she arched her hips off the bed—a mighty feat of strength—and undulated in counterpoint to his slow rhythm, he lost it. Finally! Bless the saints! With a guttural roar, he slammed into her one more time and spilled himself in hot spurts into her welcoming womb. With his senses heightened to the point of almost-pain, he wondered if anything in the world could compare to this mind-blowing orgasm. It reached beyond his cock and rushing blood and racing heart deep into his soul, shaking him, then releasing him in blissful, decreasingly less powerful ripples of satisfying shocks. In the end, he lay atop Rachel with his face between her breasts, her hands caressing his shoulders, and fell asleep—or maybe he passed out.

Moments later, he awakened to Rachel's continued soothing caresses. He raised himself on straightened arms and looked down at her, seeing nothing in the dark, but sensing the smile on her face. He knew for sure that she smiled with her next words.

"Was that good for you?" she asked.

He laughed then, and laughed, and laughed.

Life was good . . . for now.

Just surprise me

"This bed smells of sweat and sex," Rachel said a short time later.

"Aaah! The male aphrodisiac. Eau de SweatySex."

Rachel punched him in the vicinity of his belly and he said, "Ouch!" though she probably hadn't hurt him.

Then, the precious man did the most precious thing. He felt his way in the dark to the downstairs bathroom where he got towels and some kind of rose-scented antiseptic cream—something concocted by Tante Lulu, no doubt. When he came back and proceeded to lay the towels over the damp bed, he kept apologizing, "I am so sorry, Rachel." Over and over. Then, he forced her to lay back down and rubbed the cream onto her neck and breasts and belly and her buttocks and most especially—*Holy Moly!*—between her legs. You'd think she had war wounds.

"Stop saying you're sorry. For what, for heaven's sake?"

"I hurt you. I know I did."

"If you hurt me, it's a good kind of hurt." *What was the name of that song? "Hurt So Good," or something like that.*

"Really?" She could hear the smile in his voice. The cad!

"And, frankly, I'd bet that I hurt you, too."

"Oh, yeah," he agreed. "Black 'n Blue 'R Us."

"Come to bed," she said with a wide yawn, holding her arms open for him.

"Not now, honey. I've got to go down and check on the storm damage. Go to sleep. I'll be right back." He leaned over, gave her a quick kiss, then picked up the flashlight and left. By the time he returned an hour later, she was fast asleep, on her back, with her arms and legs splayed, probably drooling.

"Wake up, Rachel, I have a surprise for you."

"Reeeemy. I've had enough of your surprises for one night." She turned over on her side, away from him, and pretended to still be asleep.

"Not that kind of surprise," he said with mock indignation. She could feel the mattress on his side shift as he sat down. "Hamburger Surprise. Aren't you hungry?"

She rolled over and sniffed. Yep, he'd brought the leftover casserole dish from supper. "And what else?"

"Bread and a jug of water."

"Drink," she pleaded. "I'm dying of thirst."

He put the lip of the bottle to her mouth and she drank greedily. Then, with the two of them propped on pillows in the dark, they used two spoons to eat Hamburger Surprise in bed. The sheets were already a mess; now the towels would probably be a mess, too. Oh, well.

"Is everything all right outside?" she asked when he set the dish and bottle aside on the floor.

Remy slid back into bed beside her, still naked, fluffed the pillows and pulled a single sheet over them before answering. "Hard to tell by flashlight and with it still raining. At the least, there will be a lot of broken branches, but my biggest concern—the snakes—proved to be no problem." He suddenly went silent as if regretting his last disclosure.

Rachel went stiff. "What snakes?"

"Now, don't go getting upset, but sometimes in a storm the bayou streams flood the banks which causes snakes to seek higher ground. There were no snakes on the porch that I could see."

"I could kill you for planting that idea in my head."

"I told you, it's not a problem."

"But it could have been a problem, and you didn't tell me."

"Are we having an argument?"

"What do you think?"

"I think you might be giving me the finger."

"Would you forget about that finger business?" Rachel began to sniff again. "What is that smell in your hair? Pine? Oh, you rat! You took a shower while you were downstairs, didn't you?"

"Just a little one."

"Oh, that is so unfair. Now I stink, and you don't."

"I like your stink, darlin'," he said, laughing as he forced her into a spoon-embrace where he held her close and pretended to be sniffing her shoulder. Then he softly kissed the side of her neck. "Relax, babe, and sleep some more. I have something I want to show you tomorrow."

"Oh, goody, I can't wait. Is it long and hard and purple?"

"Purple!"

"My night vision isn't so good."

"Purple!"

As they both shifted and shuffled their bodies into a more comfortable position, still spoon-style with Remy's arms locked about her waist, Rachel said softly, "Remy?"

"Hmmm?"

"I love you."

He hesitated for only a second, long enough for Rachel to think he might have fallen asleep. But then, he said, "I love you, too."

Chapter 19

In days of old when knights were clueless

"So, have you taken a vow of celibacy?"

Remy practically fell out of the hammock at her question, whether from shock or being abruptly awakened from sleep, she couldn't say. "Wha . . . what?"

"You heard me. You haven't made love to me since the middle of last night. It's now three in the afternoon."

"A whole ten hours?" he teased.

"I know your appetite for sex. You've either gone celibate or your wazoo fell off. What's the deal?"

"My *wazoo*?" he sputtered, still trying to steady the hammock. When he did, he folded his arms beneath his neck, crossed one ankle over the other, and grinned at her. He was wearing a pair of ancient jeans that had faded to almost white, and that's all. His hair was still damp from a recent shower, after having spent the morning and part of this afternoon fixing the generator, clearing up all the debris left by the storm, searching for hidden snakes (at Rachel's insistence), and talking ad nauseam on his now-operating cell phone, to Luc, to Tante Lulu, and to every muckety-muck in the DEA. But did he have time for her? No way, José. He was avoiding her like the bloody plague. And she knew why. One night of loving, and he already crawled back into his Remy shell, shutting her out. Or else, he was pulling the Cajun Knight act, protecting her, from himself or herself, she wasn't sure.

Enough was enough! She'd donned her armor: a full-fledged teenage Charmaine outfit. Criminey, Charmaine must have been hell on wheels at fourteen if she sported stuff like this. On top, Rachel wore a form-fitting bustier-type blouse that laced up the front with a built-in push-up bra. Down below, she wore denim shorts so tight she'd had to lay on the floor to zip them up, and when she stood, they rose so high the bottom edge of her butt cheeks peeked out.

And what did Remy do as his eyes made a quick survey of her teenage hooker get-up? He grinned even wider. "Going somewhere?" he asked. "Like a biker bar?"

"I would, if there was one nearby. And I'd pick me up a randy biker guy, too . . . someone who was more interested in me than you apparently are." She blinked hard and turned away, not wanting him to see the tears welling in her eyes. How could Remy have been so hot for her last night, and now so cool? How could he have told her that he loved her then, and not once since then? And how dare he flash that slow, sexy grin at her?

"Rachel, I was really rough with you last night," he said, the grin gone. "I'm trying to be considerate of you, to let your body heal, before I attack you again."

Well, she hadn't thought of that reason for his avoiding her. "Are *you* hurt?" she asked, looking down at his crotch. "Is it broken?"

"No!" he said with what started out as a laugh and turned into a bout of choking.

She didn't feel sorry for him. "I'm thirty-three years old, perfectly capable of taking care of myself. So, cut the chivalry crap, LeDeux," she ordered him in blunt terms. "This lady isn't appreciating it one bit."

"Crudeness, Rachel? *Tsk-tsk!* What's got m'lady in a royal snit?"

Oh, that did it. The grin and now a patronizing attitude. She did what any self-respecting lady would do then. No, she didn't give him the finger again; that would give him too much pleasure. She raised her chin high, spun on her heels and stomped away.

She heard him shuffle off the hammock and swear, probably having been dumped to his knees by said hammock. Soon, he was closing in on her. "Where you going, Rachel?"

"I'm walking back to Houma."

"In your bare feet?"

She didn't answer, but he brought up a good point. There might be snakes or other slithery things. Yeech.

"Besides, you're going the wrong way."

Without losing a beat, she took a sharp right.

"Stop smiling." She couldn't see him, but she knew he was probably getting a kick out of her antics.

"Hot damn!"

She refused to look back and see what had brought that response. Even if it was a snake, she was not going to look.

"Darlin', do you have any idea how short your shorts are?"

Uh-oh! She did a quick peek over her shoulder and sure enough Remy was ogling her big behind in the short shorts. She stopped abruptly and he almost ran into her, so hard was he concentrating on her bootie.

"I'm sorry," he said.

"For what? Ogling my butt?"

His lips twitched as he stifled yet another grin. "I'd never be sorry for that. No, I'm sorry about hurting you last night, and I'm sorry if I hurt your feelings today."

"And I'm sorry you feel so sorry. No, I'm not. I'm sick to death of your sorrys. Get over it."

She had a whole lot more to say to the lout, but she never got to say it. Remy picked her up and started carrying her back to the cabin. At first, she was too surprised to protest, but then she began kicking and squealing. "I'm not making love with you now after I had to practically force you into it. Forget about sex, big boy. You lost your chance." She was kicking and thrashing but he wouldn't let go. In fact, he was laughing.

"Now, Rachel, calm down. I have a surprise for you."

"I've had Hamburger Surprise up to my eyeballs. Don't think you can tempt me with food."

"It's another kind of surprise," he told her with his lips pressed against her ear. "But it involves eating."

Here comes the terrible trouble

The rest of the day was absolutely perfect.

Remy had been almost afraid to breathe for fear something would go wrong, but it hadn't . . . not for this day, anyway. The love between him and Rachel was ironclad. But the bond that kept them together was tenuous as tissue paper and could go up in flames in an instant of misspoken word, careless act, or remembered grievances in their past.

As a result, they both treaded with extreme care, mentally knocking on wood.

All day, he and Rachel had made gentle love, they'd fished, they'd eaten their catches, they'd made gentle love, he'd shown her a beautiful bayou spectacle—two blue herons having sex in a way that involved among other things the male and female twining their necks around each other for long periods of time—after which they'd made gentle love again . . . he and Rachel, that is. Not the herons. Well, actually, the herons, too.

Now, they lay in the downstairs alcove bed watching the bayou sunset, all orange and brilliant blue. His arm cradled her shoulder. Her face pressed against his chest, her fingertips tracing the outline of hair surrounding one nipple. There was nothing sensual in her actions or their posture in bed. It was a quiet time, a moment of peace in the world and their relationship. He found himself praying suddenly, something he hadn't done seriously in a long time. *Please, God, help me find a way to make this work.*

Remy hadn't told Rachel yet, but he had to leave for Houma early tomorrow morning, at dawn, without her. It was only a temporary situation, an emergency with the DEA operation that required his presence and flying skills for the D-Day operation. He was going, but no way would he risk her life by bringing her with him. Nope. Luc and Tee-John would arrive here to take over his "babysitting" duties for Rachel until his return. Not that he would ever use the "babysitting" term around Rachel.

"Rachel," he started.

"Remy," she said at the same time.

"I have something to discuss with you."

"Me, too."

"You go first," he offered, wanting to avoid as long as possible the argument they were sure to have.

"Remember when I told you about all the years I spent in foster care," she said tentatively.

"Uh-uh."

"Well, I've experienced firsthand just how many children there are out there in need of mothers . . . and fathers."

He stiffened, suddenly suspicious. *She wouldn't. She promised. Surely, she wouldn't.*

"Children of all ages . . . even babies. I don't need to give birth to feel like a mother, and you don't need to fertilize an egg with your sperm to be a father."

He disengaged himself from their embrace and shot off the bed. "How dare you! We had a pact."

"Screw that ridiculous pact. You and I are adults. We need to talk about this if we're ever going to have a future. Please listen to me."

"No, you listen to me. I will not talk about my sterility to you or anyone else. It is a dead subject. Just because we made love doesn't give you that right."

"Not just because we made love, but because we love each other. That gives me the right." Rachel had climbed off the bed and stood before him now, unwavering.

"Let's get this straight once and for all. I'm never going to be a father—not to my own kid and not to some unwanted freak in a foster home." *Oh, my God!* Immediately, he regretted his words. But it was too late. Rachel stepped back from him as if *he* was the freak. He was. What kind of man would say such a thing, even in the heat of outrage? "Rachel, I am truly sorry. I didn't mean that."

She waved a hand in front of her as if his apology didn't matter. Tears pooled in her eyes and were beginning to seep out, despite her blinking. "This freak doesn't want or need your apologies. Sometimes people say what they really think when they're angry, and maybe that's really how you feel. Lots of people do."

"I don't. Dammit, I don't. God, how did this get so turned around? I just don't want to talk about my sterility." He could feel tears burning his eyes, too. Tears, for chrissake! He hadn't cried since the accident.

She noticed his tears and, offended as she was, her expression softened toward him. He did not want her pity. "Forgive me for my stupid remark, Rachel, but forget me. Children are obviously important to you, or you wouldn't have brought it up, against my wishes. Accept it. There will not be any children with me."

"But—"

"No buts." He turned away from her. Maybe a walk would clear his head. He saw no way out of this disaster, though, clear head or not.

"Oh, Remy, it's just that Jill suggested that I rethink my resentment over your not telling me about your sterility. She said you might be overly proud—that male pride is a powerful thing. She said you might be thinking that it made you less of a man, which is ludicrous, of course. So, that's why I brought it up. I had to try. Can't you see that?"

Remy went board stiff. Blood rushed to his head and he reached for a chair to support his suddenly dizzy body. When he turned around, he was still rigid, but with fury now. "You told someone about my sterility?"

"Just Jill and Laura, my two friends back home."

"Two people! You discussed my secret with two friggin' strangers?"

"Not strangers. My best friends. You're probably never going to meet them. Why should you care?"

"I care."

She was wringing her hands with distress now. Tears ran down her face. She was really, really upset.

But Remy didn't care. She wasn't half as upset as he was. Talk about betrayal! "Who's next, Rachel? Your grandmother? My aunt? Charmaine? Your ex? Why not broadcast it on the local radio station? 'Remy LeDeux isn't the man you think he is. Talk about!' "

"I would never tell anyone else," she said indignantly.

"Yes, you would. You're a woman. You're stubborn as a mule. You think you know what's best for me. If you thought in your own deluded mind that discussing my sterility with them would help me, you would do it in a minute."

The hand which she raised, then lowered in defeat, told him he'd made an accurate assessment. "I love you, Remy," she said hopelessly.

"Too bad love isn't enough." With that, he left the cabin, steeling himself against the sound of her sobbing. The screen door slammed with a clatter after him. Once he was outside, he looked skyward and asked with utter despair, "What do I do now?"

Try prayer.

Oh, Brother!

Luc was in a helicopter flying toward his bayou cabin with Tee-John, wondering why in God's name he'd ever allowed his brother to accompany him. Even the pilot, Remy's friend, John Pitre, couldn't stop smiling. As always, Tee-John's questions were outrageous and intimate, intended to tease and shock.

"How did it feel when you got snipped?"

"Just peachy."

"Did it hurt?"

"No."

"Can you still get it up, same as before?"

"Tee-John!"

"How am I going to know these things if no one tells me?"

"Read a book."

"Do they have books on vasectomies?"

"I'm sure they do."

"*Dieu*, what do you think Ms. Arsenault, the librarian, will think when I ask her about books on vasectomies? Oh. I can always tell her it's so I can learn about *your* operation. You went to school with Ms. Arsenault, didn't you?"

"Don't you dare!"

There was a moment of blessed silence as they contemplated the sun coming up over the horizon, always a spectacular sight in the bayou. It never came up slowly. Always an explosion of light, the sun and clouds looking like yellow fireworks chased by billowy white smoke.

"Do you need me to come back for you?" John asked.

"Nah," Luc answered. "Remy will leave in his hydro-plane once we get there, and he'll come back for Rachel, and us, tomorrow. Hopefully." Luc was worried about Remy and his involvement in this DEA project, but it was his brother's business. All he could do was offer to help. Still, his role as big brother never stopped, and he wished he could do more to protect Remy. Sometimes he even felt responsible for not having been there to protect him from the Desert Storm crash, which was ridiculous, of course. At least, that's what Sylvie told him all the time.

"I have another question," Tee-John said.

Luc groaned, and John grinned.

"Did you ever try one of those penile rings?"

"WHAT?" he and John both exclaimed at the same time. John immediately started laughing under his breath.

"A penile ring. You know, one of those things you put on the base of your limp dick which gets tighter and tighter when dickie gets thicker, if you know what I mean."

Dickie? Dickie, for chrissake! "You are impossible!" Luc was laughing himself. "Where did you ever hear of such a thing?"

"Saw one in a sex shop on Bourbon Street."

"And what were you doing in a sex shop on Bourbon Street? Wait, don't tell me. I don't want to know."

"Does that mean you've never tried a penile ring?"

"You could say that."

"Do you think Remy is shacking up with this Rachel person?"

"I think that's none of your business."

"Do you think he's ever tried a penile ring?"

"I think you ought to ask him. There he is now."

Looking out the side windows of the 'copter, through the still dim dawn light, they saw Remy standing on the bank near the hydroplane. Just then, Luc's cell phone went off. It was Remy.

"Hey, Luc, I've got to get out of here right away. Rachel's still asleep. I'm going to take off. Then John can pull the 'copter in close to my spot and drop a rope ladder for you and Tee-John to disembark."

"Be careful, Remy."

"Will do. And thanks, Luc. I owe you one."

"No prob."

They circled about, watching as Remy waded into the stream, then jumped into his plane, which was already running. Within minutes, Remy was in the air and they were on the ground, watching John fly away, too.

"Think the fish are bitin'?" Luc asked Tee-John.

"Hah! There'll be catfish for breakfast."

Trouble always comes in twos

The sound of a running motor awakened Rachel just after dawn. Trying to ignore the noise, she pulled the sheet over her head. The noise continued, followed by a different-sounding motor, a whirring sound.

At first, she forgot where she was and imagined that a car took off from her townhouse parking lot back in the D.C. suburbs. But the whirring sound didn't fit with that picture. Soon reality began to seep into her consciousness. She remembered her horrible argument with Remy and how she'd tried all night, until two A.M., to get him to talk with her. He'd refused, not just to discuss their disagreement, but to speak with her at all. Every time she'd approached him, he walked away. Finally, about three A.M., she'd drifted to sleep.

So, that couldn't be cars she heard. It must be the airplane. Then she heard voices.

Oh, my God! Could the drug dealers have found us? No, that couldn't be it. The conversation isn't heated. And, be-

sides, the two voices have a Cajun accent. Wait, I know who that is. It's Remy's brother, Luc.

She didn't want to be caught wearing Charmaine's baby-doll pajamas; so, she quickly jumped off the bed, then reeled back at the force of the cry-headache that assailed her. More gingerly, she got up then and dressed in a pair of shorts and a T-shirt, then hurried downstairs.

It was Luc, all right, and a young boy of about fourteen who resembled Luc.

"Luc," she said, coming into the living room, where they stood with duffel bags.

"Rachel," he said in return, then introduced the boy. "This is my brother, Tee-John. Tee-John, this is Rachel."

They nodded at each other.

"Where's Remy?" she asked, noticing his absence.

Luc and Tee-John looked at each other in surprise, then glanced back at her guiltily.

"Didn't he tell you?" Luc shifted nervously from foot to foot.

"Tell me what?"

"That he had to go back to Houma this morning. An emergency."

She cocked her head to the side, not fully understanding yet. "Remy left, without telling me?"

"He said you were asleep," Tee-John explained. "He probably didn't want to disturb you."

She gave him a look that clearly said that wasn't reason enough.

"Uh-oh," Tee-John said. "Someone's in big trouble, and for once it ain't me."

"Keep quiet," Luc told his brother.

"He'll be back tonight, or tomorrow at the latest," Luc explained, sensing her distress.

"Did he tell you that?"

"Yes. Yes, he did."

It didn't matter if he came back or not. Rachel felt as if a knife had been stuck in her back. *He left, he left, he left.* Now she would never have a chance to rectify their differences. She just knew it.

"When did Remy make arrangements with you to come here?" she asked as a niggling suspicion hit her.

"Yesterday morning," Luc answered.

She inhaled sharply at the pain of Remy's betrayal. Before they'd ever had the argument, he had intended to leave and not tell her. That's how little he trusted her, even before she'd broken their pact.

"So, you're the one, huh?" Tee-John asked then, smiling from ear to ear. Good heavens, were all the LeDeux males this good looking? Apparently. This one must have the pick of all the local Cajun teenage girls.

"Don't ask," Luc warned her.

Too late. "The one what?"

"The one that Remy is crazy in love with."

"Not anymore," she stated flatly.

You win some, you lose some

For eleven straight hours, Remy didn't think about Rachel or the disaster that had become his life. He hadn't had a moment to himself until now, six P.M.

In the end, he returned to his houseboat. His shoulder ached from the gunshot wound he'd sustained this afternoon, which had been treated and bandaged at the local hospital. Other than that, he was all right.

Well, no, he wasn't all right. The pain in his shoulder was nothing compared to the pain in his heart. He hurt so bad, and there was *nothing* he could do to make it better. All day he'd been able to push thoughts of Rachel aside, but now he had to face the facts. It was absolutely, and totally, over. He'd put the final punctuation mark on that with his remark about foster kids being freaks; she'd put the final punctuation mark on it by discussing his sterility with other people. That didn't mean that he didn't still care. Of course, he loved her, but like he'd told her, love was not enough.

For twelve years, Remy had had to live with the outward marks of being half man, half beast. People saw his mangled flesh and pitied him; they couldn't help themselves. But he couldn't bear to have people know that he was half man inside, too. The kind of pity that would engender would be unbearable.

Enough! He couldn't keep going over this in his mind. And he couldn't keep avoiding the call he had to make. He flicked open the cover on his cell phone and called Luc.

Luc picked up instantly. "Where the hell have you been?"

"Sorry I haven't called sooner, Luc. I had to make a little trip to the emergency room."

"The hospital! Are you hurt?"

Like you wouldn't believe! "I'm fine. Just a shoulder wound."

"How'd the DEA operation go?"

"Successful. Six arrests, one of whom is critically injured, and two dead. Larry Ellis has a pretty bad concussion, and is in intensive care. On our side, there were two other minor injuries. About six million in drugs confiscated."

"Holy shit! So, it's over?"

"For now. We didn't get the bigwigs in the cartel, but maybe some of the arrestees will spill their guts."

"You're going to continue to work for the DEA, aren't you?" Luc asked with a huge sigh.

"I hope to."

"Rachel isn't going to be happy about that."

His silence spoke volumes. But then, he had to gulp several times before he could speak. "How is she?"

"Alternately, so devastated she can barely stand, and then so angry, she swears a blue streak."

"Rachel? Swearing?"

"Oh, yeah! I think Tee-John's been taking notes."

He had to smile at that, but only barely.

"She's outside with Tee-John right now, taking a walk. Tee-John's been grilling her on *Sex and the City* type stuff."

"You're kidding."

"Nope."

"Did you know that she made a bonfire out of her ex-fiancé's exercise equipment, and that he took twenty-seven different kinds of vitamins and muscle enhancers? Tee-John's been eating up everything she says. She won't tell us what you did to her, though."

Thank God for that.

"Did you ever have a penile ring, by the way?"

"WHAT?"

"Don't be surprised if Tee-John asks you about it. Anyhow, I see Rachel out front now. You want me to go get her?"

"No," he said quickly. "Just tell her . . . just tell her that a helicopter will be there in the morning to pick you all up."

"Can I assume that you won't be the pilot?"

"Right."

"Oh, Remy, don't do this. If you want my opinion—"

"I don't give a rat's ass about your opinion. Not on this subject." He inhaled and exhaled to calm himself down. It wasn't Luc's fault that his life was falling apart. "Anyhow, can you give Rachel a message for me?"

Luc hesitated. Finally, he said, "Okay. Shoot."

"Tell her I'm sorry."

"You are one dumb schmuck."

Ditto, the voice in his head said.

Surprise, Surprise

Rachel arrived back at the small airport in Houma the next morning.

She hadn't really expected to find Remy waiting for her there. If he hadn't felt the need to tell her that he was leaving, if he hadn't felt the need to call her and let her know he was wounded but all right, if he hadn't felt the need to come for her himself . . . well, she would have been surprised to see him there. She would be less than honest, though, if she didn't admit to being hurt at his absence.

She felt like the walking wounded herself as she emerged from the helicopter and started to walk across the tarmac. She wanted nothing more than to get back to Granny's home before she broke down. She looked up, then did a wide-eyed double take at the person she saw emerging from the waiting room of the terminal. It wasn't Remy, of course. Not even Beau, or Granny, or Charmaine.

It was David.

She had no idea how he'd found her, or why he was here. Right now, it didn't matter. He represented a familiar face in a world that was collapsing around her. Without thinking, she ran into his open arms.

What you see isn't always what it appears

Remy came around the side of the building and halted in his tracks. Rachel. In the arms of another man! A stranger. He knew—he just knew, without ever having met him or even seeing a picture—it was the infamous ex-fiancé.

If his heart had been aching before, it felt as if it was being ripped right out of his chest now. Rachel—his Rachel—letting another man hold her. How could she?

Did she call the jerk?

Is she going back to the jerk?

What happened to the love she professed for me?

Almost immediately, Remy reversed himself.

I should have told her I was leaving.

I should have called her.

I should have gone to pick her up.

I should have come sooner.

Remy was so mixed up he didn't know what to think. Maybe he should just wait and think this through before approaching her; be certain what he wanted, or more accurately, was willing to surrender in order to keep her.

You snooze, you lose, the voice in his head advised.

"Shut up!"

"Hey, we didn't even say anything," Luc said, walking up to him, with Tee-John at his side.

"Hello to you, too," Remy said grumpily.

"Go after her," Luc said, nodding his head toward where Rachel was walking into the terminal with the guy's arm over her shoulder. He wanted to yank the guy's arm out of its socket for taking such liberties, but he had no right. He shook his head.

"You want to. Do it, for chrissake."

"No!"

"She's really nice," Tee-John interjected. "You made her cry a lot. She tried to hide it from us, but we could tell."

Remy couldn't take much more of this. "Thanks for helping me out," he said to both of them and turned toward the parking lot. He wished Luc and Tee-John would just go home and leave him alone. He needed to be alone, preferably with a bottle of booze. A two-day bender appeared in order. But, no, the two thorns in his butt fell in beside him.

"Did you know that you can have sex with a girl when she's on the rag?" Tee-John announced out of the blue.

He and Luc turned as one to gape at their brother.

"What? It's true. Rachel said so."

"I can't imagine any conversation in the world in which that subject might have come up." Luc was shaking his head hopelessly at Tee-John, who just grinned.

"I asked her. What's wrong with that? No one else tells me anything."

"You are incredible," was the only thing Remy could think of to say.

Then Tee-John began, "Remy, have you ever had—"

"Don't ask. Don't ask," Luc advised, breaking out with laughter.

Remy hadn't taken Luc's other advice. Why should he start now? "Have I ever had what?"

"A penile ring?"

Remy burst out with hysterical laughter then. And he didn't stop 'til tears filled his eyes and rolled down his cheeks.

Luc understood, though, as always. He looped an arm around his shoulder and squeezed. "You can fix this, Remy. Tomorrow."

Unfortunately, Remy knew that for some guys tomorrow never came.

Chapter 20

Sometimes the frog turns into a prince, and sometimes . . .

"Why did you come here, David?"

Rachel leaned back against the headrest, inhaling the rich aroma of the butter-soft, platinum-colored leather in David's BMW as they headed back toward Houma. The car drove so smoothly, they never felt a bump in the road, or heard a sound of traffic from outside.

After weeks of living practically out of doors with all the sounds and smells of nature assailing her at every turn, the luxury of David's car struck her in the oddest way. She soon realized what it was. She felt as if she was in a coffin.

"I came because I love you," he said matter-of-factly.

Now that surprised Rachel. She sat up straighter and looked at him with interest. Truth to tell, she had been waiting for him to ask about his precious Roseville vase.

"I never doubted that you loved me, David."

"Yeah, well, I behaved like an ass. I realized that soon after you left. I'm hoping you'll forgive me and come back."

Surprise, surprise!

David wore a Ralph Lauren golf shirt and Boss slacks with a perfectly ironed crease and designer loafers—casual wear for him. His hair was perfectly groomed. His after-shave was subtle and expensive. He was a good-looking man. Physically fit. Intelligent. A doctor, for heaven's sake.

But Rachel felt nothing when she looked at him, and that made her feel good.

"You're smiling," he said. "I take that as a good sign."

"David—" she started to say. There must have been something in her voice that alerted him to potential bad news.

"Don't say anything now." He put a hand over hers on the seat, and kept it there. "You've been through an ordeal, sweetheart. You need to rest and recover. Let's see how things go while I'm here. We'll go out to dinner. See some sights. Then, we can talk. Okay?"

"You're staying here, in Louisiana?" For the life of her, she couldn't picture David down on the bayou. "For how long?"

"Three days, max."

Max meant that he expected her to capitulate before then. Rachel didn't have the heart to argue with him about it right now. She had too many other things on her mind. And she had been through an ordeal, for sure.

"Turn here," she said, then gave him directions to her grandmother's house. "How did you find me, by the way?"

He winked at her.

How was it that one wink from Remy and her bones melted, and David's wink didn't do a thing for her? How was it that David was a near-perfect physical specimen, except for the receding hairline, whereas Remy was half-mangled skin, and yet there wasn't any doubt in her mind which was the more appealing man?

"Actually, I did a nose job on the wife of a DEA official last week. I gave him a break on the price, and he gave me a little inside information. Don't look at me like that. It's the Beltway Barter Club, baby. That's the way things are done in the capital."

"Well, the whole drug mess is over now. It's unbelievable how I got involved to begin with. A pure case of being in the wrong place at the wrong time."

He nodded. "You can give me the details later. Tell me about your grandmother. Are you enjoying your visit? What's she like?"

"You'll find out soon enough. That's the road right there. Go left, then a sharp right into the driveway." Hank's red truck was still parked there beside the house.

David's mouth dropped open. "It's a cabin—a freakin' cabin—right out of a Dogpatch cartoon!" He didn't realize how offensive his words were.

"So?" she said, bristling.

He must have realized his mistake because he quickly added, "How quaint!"

Her grandmother was already coming down the steps, and Beau stood on the porch.

She heard the electric lock on the doors click suddenly. "Be careful, Rachel. That old hag looks dangerous, and that trailer park dude with the rifle looks no better."

"David! That's my grandmother and my cousin."

His jaw dropped down practically to his Polo crest. "No way!" Then, "Oh, Rach! You poor thing! You have been through an ordeal in more ways than one."

She pressed the button to lower her window and yelled

out, "Granny! I'm home." She wasn't about to let David spoil her homecoming.

Her grandmother smiled widely as she hobbled quickly toward her. As she crossed the yard, she spit a stream of tobacco juice into the grass.

David groaned and put his face against the steering wheel.

Rachel smiled at David's discomfort. She could only imagine how appalled he must be. In his defense, she remembered being a bit appalled herself, at first.

"Unlock the door, David."

He did, after raising his head and staring at her dolefully.

She felt sorry for him, but only for a second. Because then, just before she exited his vehicle, he said the one thing that cinched things for her.

"Just out of curiosity, where's my Roseville vase?"

And if that wasn't enough, as she began to exit the car, he remarked with alarm, "Honey, have you gained weight?" He was staring at her butt.

Only the lonely

Two weeks later, Remy was so miserable he could barely function. He'd tried drinking, reading, working, even bowling—*if that wasn't pathetic, what was?*—but nothing could take his mind off Rachel.

He'd heard that the doctor dude had left town, but he wasn't sure if that was significant or not, because he'd also heard that Rachel was making plans to leave herself. In fact, Charmaine had taken great pains to go out of her way and inform him that she and Rachel had gone shopping together for goodbye gifts. The whole time Charmaine relayed this information, she glowered at him and muttered, "Dumb men! Talk about!"

"What the hell are you doing?" Luc said as he stepped inside his houseboat and slipped on one of the dozens of Ping-Pong balls that littered the floor.

Great! That's what I need in the mood I'm in. Company. "Playing Ping-Pong hoops. Isn't that obvious?" Remy was leaning back in a chair on the other side of the room tossing the little plastic balls into the pottery vase sitting on the table next to the doorway. He was getting quite good at it, too. Some of them he dunked in big arcing shots from across the room. Some he dunked by bouncing them off the wall first. It was a sign of his extreme boredom, or depression, that he got his jollies this way. "What are you doing here, on a workday yet?"

"Tante Lulu and Sylvie made me come."

He arched an eyebrow at that news.

"They're worried about you. I am, too."

"Stop worrying. I'm a big boy."

"Sometimes you don't act like one." Luc walked over to the fridge and took out a long neck.

"*Mon Dieu*, you came to give me the big brother lecture, didn't you?"

"Damn straight!" Luc took a long swig of beer, then looked around the room, as if noticing it for the first time. "Hey, the houseboat looks great, other than the Ping-Pong balls. Rachel Feng Shuied you up real good."

He walked around the room examining the skylight, the plush cushions on the window seats, the drapes, the kitchen galley booth. Then he ducked his head in the bedroom and grinned back at him. "Verrry nice. I especially like the shrine with all those heart thingees, and that big ol' plant that looks like badass red tongues sticking out at you."

"That last was probably a symbolic gesture from Rachel."

"For sure." Coming back into the main area Luc peeked into the bathroom and said, "Sonofagun! I want one of those." He was referring to the high-tech shower, of course. "Not much room to piss or brush your teeth but who the hell cares with that water-massage mecca."

"Rachel did a good job," Remy admitted.

Luc pulled a chair over to sit next to him and tried a few Ping-Pong shots himself, most of which bounced off the vase. "Hope that thing isn't expensive."

Remy shrugged. "I'm sure it isn't or Rachel would have billed me for it."

"Have you talked to her?"

Remy shook his head.

"Have you called her?"

"I called yesterday . . . five times. She refused to talk to me."

"How many times did you call her before that?"

Remy declined to answer.

"How many times did you go over there?"

Remy still declined to answer.

"Oh, please, don't tell me you waited two friggin' weeks and then you did something so impersonal as calling her on the phone? *Tsk-tsk!* Haven't I taught you anything about women?"

"Apparently not. Besides, her boyfriend was here, at first."

"Give me a break, bro. You've never been afraid of competition a day in your life. There has to be some other reason. You had an argument. Big deal! What could be so important that you tucked tail and ran?"

Luc was really beginning to annoy him. "You don't even know me. So, don't try to psychoanalyze me."

Stunned, Luc turned in his seat to look at him directly. "I don't know you? Are you insane? I know you inside and out."

"No, you don't."

"Tell me, Remy. For God's sake, I can see that it's eating you alive. What's wrong?"

"I can't have kids." Immediately, he closed his eyes and pinched the bridge of his nose. How could he have blurted out his secret after all these years?

"Can't or won't?"

"Can't."

"Ever?"

"Not ever."

Silence reigned for a minute that seemed like a year. When he opened his eyes, Luc was standing before him with tears in his eyes. Tears, for the love of God! Before he had a chance to shove him aside, his brother pulled him up and into his arms, giving him a tight hug. "Jesus H. Christ, Remy! Why didn't you ever tell me?"

"Because I knew you'd behave like this," Remy said, putting his brother aside, gently. "What I do not need any more of in my life is pity."

"I don't pity you, you dumb shit. I feel your pain the same way you would for me. But, dammit, it's not the end of the world."

"Easy for you to say with three kids and a vasectomy."

Luc sucked in his breath at the insult. He probably

would have socked him if they weren't brothers. "So, Rachel dumped you 'cause you can't have kids, huh?"

"Hell, no."

"Then what? It's obvious you love her, and vice versa."

"At first, she was furious because I didn't tell her. Then I got mad at her because she went and discussed my sterility with two of her friends—a major breach of confidence. Then she got hurt by me because I made a dumbass remark about not ever wanting to adopt unwanted freak kids from foster care."

"Let me guess. Rachel was in foster care at one time?"

"Bingo."

Luc shook his head at his hopelessness. "And then you left without telling her, didn't call to tell her you were all right, and didn't go back to pick her up yourself. Does that about sum it up?"

"Yep."

"I would say the slate of affronts is about even, but you missed the mark bigtime, when you didn't contact her for two asinine weeks. Why didn't you go over there?"

"Gizelle would probably have met me with a gun."

"Speaking of Gizelle . . . ?"

"Last week's meeting is rescheduled for tomorrow in your office, as you would know if you'd consult your secretary's calendar."

"Oh, Remy, what am I going to do with you? Is having children that important to you?"

"Yeah, I think it is."

"You and Rachel alone . . . that wouldn't be enough?"

"It would be for me. I'm not sure about her. Family is super high in her list of priorities. She envies our family, if you can believe it."

"What's wrong with adoption?"

"That's what she said. But, Luc, if I adopted kids, people would know about another one of my flaws."

"You are bigtime screwed up if that bothers you so much."

"What's that supposed to mean?"

"Do you love Rachel?"

"Yes."

"Are you miserable without her?"

Remy looked pointedly at the Ping-Pong balls surrounding them.

"Then, why would you give a pig's tail what anyone else thinks if adopting a kid makes you both happy? And, besides, this whole disaster isn't about kids, and you know it. If you and Rachel loved each other, the rest could be worked out some way . . . with or without kids."

"It's probably too late."

"How would you know if you don't *really* try?"

Hello Goodbye

Rachel was planning to leave next week for Washington.

She would probably return to Louisiana again someday for another visit, but not for a long, long time. She'd invited her grandmother and Beau to come visit her at Christmas—she would be settled in her own place by then—and, although Granny had demurred at first, she hadn't actually said no.

David had finally returned to the city after his "three days max." It had taken her all that time to convince him that their relationship was truly and finally over. She had no intention of seeing him again. Maybe he really did love her. Then again, his last words to her, once he accepted her decision, were questions about his missing vase and a not-so-subtle suggestion that she invest in a new Butt Buster machine. Besides that, she was pretty sure David's love couldn't withstand a grandma-in-law who might spit tobacco juice on his designer leather shoes.

She'd already called Daphne and told her when she'd return to work. She'd already given her grandmother and Beau their parting gifts. She'd already completed her work at Charmaine's spa and Remy's houseboat. She had, of course, supervised the final work on the houseboat, but always when Remy was away. She had no idea how Remy felt about the renovations because she'd just sent him a bill. Charmaine, on the other hand, was ecstatic over the job, but most especially the window aquarium which had been installed two days ago. The local newspaper even did a story about it, which should further enhance spa business.

Throughout it all, Rachel operated like a zombie. Numb was the only way to describe her feelings. She wouldn't allow herself to think about Remy at all or she would break down. There were so many things he'd done which she could not forgive, but the most significant was the things he had not done. He had not told her about his sterility until after they were involved. He had not informed her that he worked with the DEA. He had not told her he was leaving the cabin. He had not called to tell her he was wounded but safe. He had not come to pick her up. And, most hurtful of all, he had not tried to contact her for two whole weeks. The jerk! As if she would talk to him after all this time!

"Rachel, honey, I'm going into town. Beau's driving me," Granny said. Rachel was sitting at the rug loom on the front porch, performing some rudimentary exercises which her grandmother had taught her. With her clumsy fingers, it would probably be no more than a potholder. "Is there anything you want me to pick up?"

She glanced up to see her grandmother more dressed up than usual. She wore a long black skirt and matching belted tunic blouse, both edged with fine, multi-colored embroidery. On her feet were black sneakers that matched her outfit. Her gray hair was pulled back into a sort of bun at her neck. And there was no tobacco bulge in her cheeks. Geesh, she almost looked like a real grandmother.

"No, I'm fine. This rug is going nowhere for me, though. Guess I'll go inside and copy some more recipes. I'm going to try jambalaya tonight." Rachel had been copying the Fortier family recipes from an old journal which had been passed down in the family to Granny. Some of Granny's— or her predecessor's—comments in the journal were politically incorrect to say the least. For example, Rachel had learned that every Cajun dish started with a *roux*, the best *roux* being made with lard and cooked to just the right color. In the journal, it stated that the roux should be "brown as an Indian's butt." Rachel had been experimenting with the actual cooking, too, mostly with good results.

Granny nodded, but hesitated, even though Beau was already waiting for her in his rusted-out sedan. "Honey, I don't want you heartaching any more over that Remy LeDeux. You'll get over him in time. I'm gonna make sure of that today."

Rachel turned around on her stool to get a better look at her grandmother. "What do you mean?"

"I'm gonna sell the skunk those ten acres of land he craves so much. Got a meetin' at his shyster brother's office in an hour to sign the papers. Doan you be worryin' none, though, I don't need that bit of swamp anyhows. I still got forty acres left."

"Why? I don't understand. How would selling him your land make me get over him?"

"Well, you see, honey, I agreed to sell him the land on one condition. That he would never see you again."

Can my heart break any more? Oh, my God! "And he agreed?"

"Oh, yeah."

"When? When did he agree to this?"

"'Bout two weeks ago, before you went away on that emergency, but we kept havin' to postpone the settlement."

Rachel's head suddenly drained of blood, and tremors shook her body. She had to hold onto the porch rail to prevent herself from falling. *Remy made this agreement before we went to the cabin. He made love to me there, knowing he was going to sign this agreement when we came back. When will I ever learn not to trust a man?*

"Now, honey, dontcha be upset. Mebbe I shouldn't have tol' you this, but I thought you had a right to know."

"No, Granny, you were right." *About everything, including the skunk.*

Well, this had to be the final nail in the coffin of their relationship. The corpse had been dead for weeks, she just hadn't been willing to admit the fact. The casket was sealed and the whole mess buried, once and for all.

That's what Rachel told herself.

You've got some nerve, buster

Remy had a plan.

Beware of men with plans.

"Shut up, Jude. This is going to work." *Please, God, let it work.*

God is busy right now with a celestial choir recital . . . or was it an Angels Against Wild Flyers meeting? In any case, He sent me in His place.

"I'm doomed."

Ha, ha, ha.

"Your sarcasm is not welcome. A litte encouragement would be helpful, though."

Go get her, big boy!

"Is that the best you can do?"

I'm praying, I'm praying.

Good ol' Gizelle and Mullet Man Beau were back in Luc's Houma office getting the news that Remy had changed his mind about the land deal. Remy figured he had one hour tops to get Rachel alone and plead his case before those two came galloping back here to her rescue. He hoped he and Rachel would be riding off into the sunset by then, or at least to his houseboat.

He knocked lightly on Gizelle's screen door which was open to the combined kitchen/living room area. Rachel stood at the sink, slicing vegetables or something. Good heavens! Could that be okra she was about to cook? She hated okra.

Rachel turned her head, and her mouth dropped open. With shock at his nerve, or consternation at his nerve, or amazement at his good looks, he wasn't sure. But before she could say a word, he stepped inside.

"Rachel . . . honey?"

"Get lost."

"I need to talk to you."

"I'd say you lost that golden opportunity about two weeks ago, give or take a day or two." She continued to slice the okra pods, ignoring his presence behind her, on the other side of the table.

"Your ex-fiancé was here. I wanted to give you a chance to make up with him, if that's what you wanted."

"Bull!"

Stepping up beside her, he took the paring knife and okra out of her hands and set them in the sink. "Look at me, please."

"Remy, there's nothing more to say." She did look at him then, but there was such hurt and anger in her eyes. "By the way, why aren't you in Houma signing the legal documents to get your precious land?"

He sucked in his breath. *So, she knows. I hoped to tell her myself.* "I'm not signing the papers."

"Oh? Sudden burst of guilt?"

She is not going to make this easy. "I don't think I ever intended to sign them, not if it meant agreeing to never see you again."

"Well, too bad for you, because I'm leaving, and we're not seeing each other again. So, you might as well get the land. If you hurry, you might still get there before Granny leaves."

He shook his head. "I don't want her land. Not even if I can't have you. It would always represent something to me that was, well, less than honorable."

"First of all, there is no longer any question of 'if I can't have you.' You can't. Second, I'm sick to death of your honorable decisions because, frankly, I'm always the butt of that stupid male ethic of yours."

"What's that supposed to mean?" He bristled at the implied insult.

"It means that you couldn't tell me you were involved with the DEA because you were ethically bound to secrecy. It means that no one in the bloody world can know that you have a sperm shortage because, God forbid, it would be less than honorable to be unable to clone yourself. It means that you thought it was honorable to step aside for David, without giving me a choice in the matter. Those are just a few examples. Given the time, I could probably come up with a dozen more. Bottom line: your male pride is monumental, and you're too blind to see that it's affecting your whole sad life."

Well, when you look at it like that . . . "I love you, Rachel."

"Well, as a not-so-wise man—*you*—once said, 'Too bad love is not enough.'"

"I can change."

"Bluebirds can polka."

"Are you saying I can't change?"

"I'm saying it's not in you. For example, would you mind if I discussed our problems with Tante Lulu—including your sterility?"

"Oh, no!"

"See, you are not ready to change."

"Do I have to take flying leaps all at once? How about a few baby steps at first?"

"Remy, baby steps aren't going to do it at this point."

"Speaking of babies," he said, and gulped a few times

over the sudden lump in his throat, "I would be willing to adopt babies . . . or big kids . . . if that's what you wanted."

That got her attention. She turned around and leaned back against the sink, arms folded over her chest. "You'd be a father to freaks?"

"Rachel! You know I didn't mean that."

She gave him a considering look. "I know you didn't," she conceded, "but I also know it wouldn't be a first choice with you. How about artificial insemination? Would you do that?"

"You mean, come in a bottle and have them insert it in you?" He cringed at the prospect, but bravely offered, "Yeah, I probably would."

"I'd like to see that," she said with a laugh.

"You'd like to see me come in a bottle? Hey, whatever yanks your chain, baby."

"You are a piece of work, LeDeux." She was more serious now. Apparently, humor wasn't working.

"Give me a chance to make it up to you, Rachel?" He reached for her, but she backed up and moved to the other side of the table. Was it a good or bad sign that she needed that much space between them?

"Remy, I am extremely fragile right now, and I can't take much more. I realize now that I was a walking glass heart when I arrived here. I never should have gotten involved with another man so soon. It was crazy."

"Crazy isn't always a bad thing, *chère*."

She shook her head sadly at him. "I've been hurt a lot the last few months . . . mostly by you. I don't even know for sure if I want to have children. I just don't trust you anymore. I never did, actually. It's over. It really is."

"No! I won't accept that."

"You'll have to. I'm leaving on Monday."

This was Tuesday. That meant he had only six days at most to win her back. Could he do it? With a little help, maybe. Oh, no! Was he really going to . . . ask his family for help?

She walked up to him and gave him a soft kiss on the lips. "Goodbye, Remy."

No way was he going to accept that. He yanked her back, gave her a real kiss on the lips, one which left her breathless and gaping at him. Glass hearts be damned! Then, he flashed her the slow, lazy grin that she loved/hated.

"See you later, sugar. Best you batten down the drawbridge, m'lady, because this knight is getting ready for battle."

Chapter 21

A *family affair*

"Tante Lulu, sit down for a minute. There's something I need to discuss with you." It was the day after his meeting with Rachel, and Remy hadn't made much progress so far.

His aunt looked up from the pot of jambalaya she was stirring on the stove. Seeing the serious expression on his face, she immediately set aside her wooden spoon and sat down at the table with him.

Outside, Luc and Tee-John were setting up tables for the picnic supper. Charmaine was spreading out tablecloths. Sylvie was chasing the three little ones down by the stream. René, who was home for the week, was sprawled out on a self-supporting hammock, sunning himself.

"I can't have children," he told her without any preamble. Somehow, in the past twenty-four hours, he'd convinced himself that he needed to bring his secret out in the open, with his family at least. It was liberating, really.

"So?"

"*So?* What do you mean 'so'?" Remy was shocked that his aunt wasn't shocked.

"I already knew that."

"Huh?"

"I cornered your doctor way back after your tenth operation—or was it the eleventh?—and asked him if those burns near your privates were gonna keep you from having babies."

"Tante Lulu! You've known for more than ten years and never said anything?"

She shrugged. "What was there to say?" She patted his hand gently. "Thass not the worst thing in the world, honey. Marry a nice Cajun girl what has chillen. Or adopt some little ones. Or doan have none at all. Yer alive. You gots all yer limbs. Yer healthy. Praise the Lord!"

He sighed deeply.

"Okay, why are you so unhappy, boy? Betcha it involves that Yankee gal. Oh, well! Tell me all of it."

He did. He told her. All of it, including his many mistakes with Rachel.

"*Tsk-tsk-tsk-tsk!* Never thought I raised such a dumb one. Well, there's nothing to do but get her back."

Don't I wish! "But how?"

"We'll all put our heads together."

"No, no, no! Don't blow this up into a huge family affair."

"Sweetie, it's already a family affair. What happens to one of us happens to all of us."

Sometimes his aunt cut right to the heart of the matter. Family. Even so, he didn't need his family fighting on his behalf. "I don't think—"

"Shhhh. Don't you be worryin' anymore. Help me carry this pot outside. Food's ready. We gots to fill our stomachs. Never make plans on an empty belly, thass what I allus say."

Plans? Ooooh, boy!

After the meal was over and they all sat about the tables outside, and the kids were inside taking a nap, and they'd discussed in way too much detail Remy's pitiful actions with regard to Rachel, Charmaine stood up and said, "I have an idea."

They all looked at her suspiciously. Charmaine's ideas usually ranged from outrageous to bizarre.

"Have you all seen the movie, *An Officer and a Gentleman*?"

Everyone nodded hesitantly, except Tante Lulu who asked, "Is that the one with that Richard Gere fellow? They even showed his bare tushie in that movie. Whoo-boy, he was hot!"

"Tante Lulu!" Tee-John said, as if shocked, though he grinned.

"What's your point, Charmaine?"

"You still have your Air Force dress uniform, don't you?"

"Yeah," Remy answered slowly.

"Oh, Charmaine! I know where you're going with this," Sylvie said. "I think it's a wonderful idea."

"How about explaining it to us dumb menfolks," Luc grumbled.

"Well, remember that final scene where Richard Gere comes to the factory for Debra Winger. He's wearing his Air Force uniform, and—"

"That was a Navy uniform," Remy pointed out.

Charmaine waved her hand in the air dismissively. "Navy, Air Force, what's the difference. Women go apeshit over men in uniforms." Charmaine always did have a way with words.

Luc and Tee-John and René smirked at him.

Like there's any way in this world I'm pulling that uniform out of moth balls. Forget about it!

"Anyhow, Richard Gere is walking through this factory to go get his gal, and that song, 'Up Where We Belong' is blasting in the background . . . you know, 'Love lifts us up where we belong . . . ' lyrics. Well, he scoops her up in his arms and carries her out while everyone is chanting, 'Way to go, Paula.' What do you think?"

"You have got to be kidding," Remy said, his mouth agape.

"Hmmmm," Tante Lulu said.

"It has possibilities," Sylvie said.

"I can't wait to see this. Can I be one of the chanters?" Tee-John said.

"Apeshit, huh, Charmaine? Maybe I should buy me a uniform," Luc said, winking at his wife.

"You're plenty sexy enough without a uniform," Sylvie told Luc.

"Good answer," Luc responded with a quick kiss to his wife's lips.

"I think you're all nuts," René said.

"Thank God, someone here agrees with me." Remy slapped his arm around René's shoulder and squeezed.

"Nope, what we need here is a revival of The Cajun Men. Remember that time, Luc, when we did a Cajun version of The Village People so that you could win Sylvie back? We called ourselves The Village People of Southern Louisiana."

"I remember," Luc said with a groan.

"I remember, too," Sylvie said wistfully.

"No!" Remy said forcefully.

No one even looked at him.

"Can I be in the act?" Tee-John asked. "I wanna be the carpenter guy. The one that wears a tool belt." He waggled his eyebrows as lasciviously as a fourteen-year-old kid could pull off.

"No!" Remy repeated.

"Maybe I could wear my accordion and nothing else," René said. He glanced over at Tante Lulu, then added, "Maybe not."

"Do I get to do a striptease in my lawyer suit again?" Luc inquired, with another sly wink at his wife. "Sylvie loves it when I do a striptease for her!"

Sylvie jabbed him in the ribs, but she blushed prettily.

Man, oh, man, I have a wacko family. Then he remembered to say "No!" again. He thought of something that might change their minds. "You do know that The Village People were gay, don't you?"

That gave his three brothers pause. But only for a second.

Luc beamed at him. "We'll be the non-gay Village People."

"Sylvie and I could be the mistresses of ceremony," Charmaine interjected. "I still have my slinky minidress from that last time. Did you save yours, Sylvie?"

It appeared that Sylvie did, which seemed to surprise Luc.

"Best of all, Remy will come out wearing his Air Force uniform," Charmaine announced in a *ta-da* manner.

Everyone clapped. The dumb twerps, all of them, including Tante Lulu.

"No!" Remy shouted. Even that didn't stop them.

"Where would we have this event?" René asked.

"Swampy's would be too obvious, and their stage isn't big enough."

"I know," Tante Lulu said. "Our Lady of the Bayou Church is having a picnic this Sunday. You could do it there as part of the entertainment."

"Uh, I don't think so," Luc declared. "We are way too risqué for them."

Risqué? I am not being risqué. Not even for Rachel. Well, in private I might, but not in public.

"I know, I know." Charmaine jumped up and down with glee, which was something to see with her in a braless T-shirt which proclaimed, HAIR I AM. Her hip-hugging jeans defied gravity. "The Dixie Women's Club is having a bachelor and bachelorette auction on Saturday. I'm sure they would welcome us as additional entertainment."

"Sounds good," René said.

The traitor. "There is no way in the world you are going to get Rachel to go to such a program."

"Well, actually, there is," René the traitor proclaimed. "Beau will bring her."

"And why would he do you any favors?" Luc wanted to know.

"Because I happen to know that he wants to be a professional wrestler—"

"A professional wrestler!" they all exclaimed.

"—and I happen to know an agent who represents professional wrestlers."

"Where do you meet these people?" Sylvie asked in amazement.

"Mostly in bars, I suspect," Luc told his wife.

René ignored Luc's comment and continued, "Methinks

a little bayou-style bargaining should convince Beau."
René preened as if he'd just invented crawfish.

Everyone nodded at René's brilliance, except Remy,
who put his face in his hands and groaned.

"I'm gonna say a novena to St. Jude that this plan
works," Tante Lulu added at the end as her contribution.

I'm listening, I'm listening, you-know-who said.

Macho, Macho Men

Rachel sat at a back table with Beau at The Dixie Women's
Club Bachelor and Bachelorette Auction. At least five hundred men and women crammed the hotel ballroom where
the sold-out event was being held.

She hadn't wanted to come, but Beau talked her into it.
His girlfriend, Mary Sue, was one of the bachelorettes, and
Beau said he felt uncomfortable coming to such a "high fa-
lutin" event alone. Actually, he looked rather nice in a suit
and tie with his mullet impeccably groomed for the night.

In addition, Charmaine and Sylvie were involved in the
program in some way, and she wouldn't mind seeing them
one last time before leaving. Charmaine had assured her
that Remy was out of town; so, no chance of running into
him here.

In truth, Rachel was having a nice time. The soft jazz
melodies being played up front by a local band provided
just the right ambience. Apparently, there would be a short
entertainment program, followed by the actual auction. In
the meantime, although Beau griped from time to time that
he'd rather have a beer, he sipped at a glass of white wine
just like she did in the relaxing atmosphere.

And relaxation was just what she needed. She'd been in a horrible state after she'd sent Remy away four days ago. Seeing him in person had had a devastating effect on her, but she was certain that she'd made the right decision. Difficult but right. She hadn't been lying when she described her fragile condition. Her emotions truly needed a calm period, a "No-man zone."

Tante Lulu joined them. For once, she looked normal, wearing a black knee-length dress and matching pumps and handbag. A string of pearls adorned her demure neckline. Her hair was a mass of charming gray waves.

"Rachel," she said, "how nice to see you again."

Rachel narrowed her eyes at the old lady. Tante Lulu was rarely nice to her. She didn't like her. Something was up.

"What are you doing here?" Rachel asked.

"What? I caint bid on a bachelor iffen I want to?"

Rachel arched her eyebrows in disbelief. "You're looking for a man?"

"And why not? I'm not dead yet."

Hmmmm.

"About Remy . . ." Tante Lulu began.

Uh-oh. "Please don't discuss Remy."

"It's not his fault, and you shouldn't be blaming him fer that."

"For what?"

"You know." She rolled her eyes meaningfully.

"You know about *that*?"

"'Course I know about *that*. I've known for a long time."

"Too bad he never knew that you knew." Geesh, this was an inane conversation.

"He does now."

She wanted to ask what Remy's reaction had been to that disclosure. That's probably why he was out of town—off somewhere licking his wounds. But that was none of her business now. *Even so, he has to be making progress if he discussed it with his aunt. Too bad I won't be around to see his further progress. Well, no, it isn't too bad. It's good. Aaarrgh!*

"Waiter," Tante Lulu called out to the man with a tray passing by them. "Give this lady another drink." Rachel thought she added under her breath, "She's gonna need it," but she just smiled brightly at her and walked away.

"That was really odd," Beau commented.

"Wasn't it?"

Then Charmaine and Sylvie came up, each of them giving Rachel a warm hug. Rachel's eyes about popped out at their attire, and Beau's jaw was about pressing his tie clip. They wore really short spandex dresses with rounded necklines that cut all the way to their rears in the back. Sylvie's was flame red, and Charmaine's was shocking pink. They wore black stockings and stiletto heels.

"Great outfits," Rachel said with dry humor.

"Aren't they?" both women answered, which surprised Rachel. Not from Charmaine. Hooker clothes were her norm. But Sylvie usually dressed much more subtly.

"The outfits are part of our costume," Sylvie explained.

Oh, well, that explained it.

"Uh, Rachel, I've wanted to call you, but didn't know quite how to say this," Sylvie began. "You really should give Remy another chance. The, uh, problem he has . . ." She looked pointedly at Beau, as if measuring her words, ". . . well, it's understandable why he would be so sensitive about it."

"Yeah, Remy is a dumb bozo lots of times. All men are, but *that* shouldn't be a reason for a breakup." Charmaine flirted with a guy at the next table while she talked.

"You two know about it, too?" Rachel truly was shocked. "Has Remy suddenly decided to blab his secret to the world?"

"Nah! Just his family," Sylvie said.

"Hey, waiter, can you bring this lady another wine?" Charmaine waved down another passing waiter, just as Tante Lulu had done.

Are people trying to get me drunk?

She had no time to ponder that because the band suddenly stopped playing and the event chairwoman stepped to the stage. That must be the cue for Charmaine and Sylvie to get ready, too, because they hustled off, promising to talk to her later.

Even as she watched a new band set up, probably a rock band by the looks of them, even as the chairwoman called for quiet in the room so she could speak, Rachel pondered the news she'd heard. Remy was finally discussing his sterility with family members. Was he doing so at her prodding? Was he taking the giant steps she'd mentioned? Was he trying to show her that he could, indeed, change? Did he think it would change her mind? Would it change her mind? She had no idea. It was all so unexpected.

"Ladies and gentlemen, welcome to the third annual Dixie Club's Bachelor/Bachelorette Auction. We have fifteen lovely ladies and fifteen gorgeous men who've offered to participate in this year's event. Let's all have fun and bid high!"

Everyone cheered.

"We've got variety here today, folks, if nothing else.

Everything from a lingerie model—and he's a man—to a real-estate broker . . . and she's a woman. We've got a car mechanic, a pilot, a teacher, a limo driver, a baseball star, a ballet dancer, a musician, a doctor, a nurse, a stripper . . . well, you name it, we've got it."

People laughed and hooted their opinions.

"Everyone got bidding cards when they entered today. Keep them handy to facilitate the auction once we get going. Runners will be stationed around the room. Remember, too, that this is all for a good cause, the Breast Cancer Awareness Project. As you can see, we have a runway stretching out from the stage through the audience. So, if everyone remains seated, you should all be able to see."

Rachel noticed for the first time what the chairwoman had pointed out. A fashion show–style runway cut through the center of the room, perpendicular to the stage.

"But first, we've got a little last-minute entertainment to offer you before the auction begins. The act defies description. Let me introduce to you to their hostesses, our own Houma ladies, Charmaine LeDeux and Sylvie LeDeux."

The audience clapped as Charmaine and Sylvie came onto the stage together. Sylvie started first. "Just let me say that The Cajun Men, or rather The Village People of Southern Louisiana, did a program four years ago at an event benefiting the Southern Louisiana Shrimpers Association. They were wildly successful." She rolled her eyes meaningfully at the audience which catcalled their appreciation.

"They've agreed to revive their act a second time, just for us," Charmaine added. "They swear it will be the last time."

People in the room who apparently recalled the previous

performance laughed hysterically. Rachel heard a woman at the next table say, "You aren't going to believe this!"

"Without further ado," Charmaine said, and she and Sylvie both shouted into the microphone, "The Cajun Men!"

The lights dimmed slightly in the audience and the spotlights brightened on the stage where the band was already playing that old song, "Macho Man," except that the band members had changed the lyrics to "Cajun Man." And then, Rachel couldn't believe her eyes.

Out danced René, wearing a vest with no shirt, tight jeans and his accordion. *Talk about rhythm!* Following him was Tee-John in a hard hat, no shirt, tight jeans and a tool belt. *Who knew young boys could shimmy like that!* Luc wore a business suit with loosened tie and suspenders, all of which Rachel suspected were going to come off at some point. *I see nothing businesslike in that twinkle in Luc's eyes.* Charmaine's ex-husband, Rusty Lanier, came out in a cowboy outfit. He didn't dance at all. In fact, he whacked Charmaine on the behind as he passed her by and practically glared at the audience. Rachel imagined that René must have conned him into participating, and he wasn't very happy about it. But, *Good Lord, Charmaine! Are you nuts? This guy is gorgeous.* There was also a fireman in rubber pants and jacket and hat who kept flicking his suspenders as he danced and sang. A cop did outrageous things with his baton as he winked at the women in the front row. A football player from the New Orleans Saints looked as if he had no underwear on under his uniform—not that anyone complained, especially when he turned his back on them and shook his bootie. A motorcycle guy in black leather rattled his chains for them in a very interesting manner. A Native American wearing traditional Louisiana Indian garb twirled his tomahawk in a way that made some women want to be his captive. And a pilot—the same one who had flown them back to Houma from the cabin—wore an aviator jacket and sunglasses and looked arrogant and hot enough to make a few women in the audience fly. To the music of "Macho Man," they all danced and shimmied and in Luc's case and some others, removed a few items of clothing, the whole time belting out, "Ca-jun, Ca-jun Man. I want to be a Ca-jun man." They danced and sang on the stage, went up and down the runway, even took a few bills tucked into their belts, for charity.

They were wonderful. Rachel couldn't believe that these men, mostly LeDeuxs or their friends, were so self-confident in their masculinity that they could laugh at themselves like this and let others laugh at them, too. Missing, of course, was Remy. In fact, it was a glaring omission. Obviously, his insecurities couldn't bear this kind of scrutiny. How sad!

The dance number ended and Rachel thought the performance was over, and the auction would begin, but, no, The Cajun Men stepped off to the side, five on each side of a sort of path. Then Charmaine and Sylvie stepped back to the microphone.

"Since this auction today is all about romance or the potential for romance, we thought we'd give it an additional boost," Sylvie said.

"You know, Sylv, women understand love and romance, but guys just don't get it," Charmaine contributed.

"They refer to romantic movies as chick flicks," Sylvie said. Women in the audience agreed with a resounding "Yeah!"

"They think they can learn about romance from a *Playboy* magazine." Charmaine put a hand on one hitched hip as she relayed that opinion.

A lot of men in the audience groaned, and one guy yelled out, "What's wrong with that?"

"Ask any woman if she can name the ten most romantic movies—the ones that make her melt and sigh—she'd have no trouble at all," Sylvie explained.

"Ask a guy and he'll say 'Duh' or *Die Hard.*" More male groans erupted at Charmaine's remark.

"For example," Sylvie said, "Take the movie, *An Officer and a Gentleman* . . ." Immediately, the band started playing the soundtrack softly in the background. It was that memorable song, "Up Where We Belong."

Rachel loved that movie.

"Is there a woman alive who's seen that movie that hasn't shed a tear and sighed at the final scene where Richard Gere in his military uniform comes to carry Debra Winger off in his arms, and the whole time the music is blaring as if from loudspeakers?" The audience went silent and Rachel could swear she heard a collective sigh.

Suddenly, the spotlight dimmed on Charmaine and Sylvie and shone instead on a man at the back of the stage in a dress blue uniform complete with hat. The band which had been playing softly picked up tempo and blared out the music. Charmaine and Sylvie began to sing, and the audience joined in, "Love lifts us up where we belong . . ."

The officer was gorgeous. Tall, dark, and obviously Cajun. He was Remy, of course.

Rachel had been set up.

But she couldn't think about that now. Remy was walking determinedly across the stage, toward the runway, just like that blinkin' Richard Gere had. This wasn't a factory, but an upscale ballroom. No difference! Rachel suddenly realized what this was all about. *Me, for God's sake!* She started to stand, intending to run for her life. Beau put a hand on her shoulder and shoved her back down. "Sit down," he ordered. Rachel would have protested his surprising action, but there was no time.

This was unbelievable. She didn't know what to think. Yes, she did. Remy had put aside his reticence to show his face in public like this *for her.* He took his cap off when he reached the end of the runway and jumped off. Everyone had to see the mangled skin with the spotlight on him. He didn't even cringe. His concentration was centered not on himself, but on her.

How could she not be flattered?

He did love her. He was willing to change. He'd already taken a first step by talking with his family. Now he was saying in a very public way that he didn't care what anyone else thought of his deformities. He only cared about her.

Rachel blinked back tears and watched as he halted next to her table. For a second, he just stared questioningly at her.

She nodded. Of course, she nodded.

He grinned—that slow, sexy grin that she loved so much—and scooped her up in his arms, carrying her out of the room. While the crowd cheered "Way to go, Rachel" at Charmaine's instigation, and Remy put his cap on her head and whispered, "They made me do it," Rachel began to believe that perhaps there was hope for them after all.

Over her shoulder, she saw Luc and René and Tee-John and Sylvie and Charmaine, all smiling happily for them. And she saw Tante Lulu with her hands folded, probably in prayers of thanksgiving to St. Jude. Family. That's what Remy offered her here . . . not just love, which was overwhelming in its unselfishness, but family.

Suddenly, Rachel realized something important. She wasn't going home to Washington. She was already home.

Sometimes dumb men do smart things

Remy took Rachel in the atrium of the hotel gardens. Literally.

He'd carried her out of the ballroom, down the corridor and into the hotel gardens in a daze, still shocked with delight that Rachel wasn't struggling against his embrace, but, instead, nuzzled her face into his neck. When he put her down on her feet behind a huge magnolia tree, he immediately began kissing her with all the pent-up hunger of the past two weeks. And she kissed him back, just as hungrily.

"I love you, Rachel. I honest-to-God do."

"I love you, too, Remy. I never stopped."

"Forgive me, please. I behaved badly."

She put her fingers to his lips. "I overreacted and behaved badly, too."

They kissed some more, a lot more. He lowered his head and took her breast through the silk of her dress, sucking wetly. She moaned and ran a hand over the ridge of his erection. He moaned then and began to shimmy her short dress up her hips. She moaned and undid his belt.

This was going way too fast in way too public a place. Although they were screened from the rest of the garden by the magnolia leaves, it was still public.

He pulled back with superhuman discipline and said,

"Rachel, let's get a room and go upstairs. Let me get out of this uniform and make love to you on a bed."

"Not on your life, mister!" She laughed. "You're not taking this uniform off for a long time."

He laughed then, too. Apparently, Charmaine had been right. Women did go apeshit over uniforms. He made a promise to himself to never put the uniform back into mothballs. He would take it out on special occasions, lots of special occasions.

But, whoa, when had Rachel unzipped his pants and inserted her palms into the back of his boxers, cupping his buttocks. *Holy mackerel! Whooo!*

He had a lot of work to do to keep up. He lifted her dress the rest of the way, past her waist, and slid her panties off. She shoved his pants and boxers down to his hips before he could say, "Way to go, Rachel!" And just like that he was inside her hot sheath, with her back to the wall and his knees trembling like crazy. A real wall banger, for sure.

At first, he could not move, too shocked and excited at the position he found himself in. If Luc were here—*what a thought!*—he would tell him to praise God and move the ammunition. Which he did.

"Rachel, honey," he said near the end when he could feel her climax and his approaching. "Will you marry me?"

"Oh, sure," she gasped out, "wait 'til I'm weak before asking that question."

"Are you weak, honey?"

"Bone-melting, heart-stopping, I'll-love-you-'til-I-die weak."

"Good," he said and put his hands under her butt, lifting her higher so that he could plunge into her one last time. They both saw stars then, the best kind of erotic stars.

Moments later, they sank to the floor and adjusted their clothing. She sat next to him with her head on his shoulders. The only sounds came from the gurgling fountain and their heavy breathing. Off in the distance, they could hear an auctioneer raffling off the bachelors and bachelorettes.

"I have been so miserable without you the last two weeks," she said. "What have you been doing?"

"Playing Ping-Pong basketball with that stupid flower vase you put in my houseboat."

"What?" she practically shrieked, turning to look at him. "Remy, that Roseville vase is an antique, worth close to ten thousand dollars. I stole—uh, got it from David."

That surprised him. Not that it was an antique, but that she'd gotten it from her ex-fiancé, then put it in his home. There was probably some kind of macabre female revenge logic involved. "Hey, maybe I'll play golfball basketball with it when I go home."

"No, you won't," she asserted. "We're going to give it to David for a wedding gift."

"Is David getting married?"

"No, we are."

And they did.

A Cajun kind of love

The wedding of Rachel Fortier and Remy LeDeux was a Cajun kind of *thang*.

Father Philippe performed the traditional ceremony at Our Lady of the Bayou Church, complete with tuxes and formal gowns; nothing else would satisfy Tante Lulu. Luc served as best man, with René, Beau and Tee-John backing him up as ushers. More than a few ladies sighed as these Cajun rogues walked down the aisle. Charmaine preened happily as maid of honor with Jill, Laura and Daphne trailing behind her as bridesmaids. Blanche, Camille and Jeanette led the bridal parade into church as flower girls, except that shy little Jeanette bailed out at the last minute and had to be carried down the aisle by her daddy.

The church service might have been refined and conservative. The reception was just the opposite. The after-church party was a casual, low-down Cajun affair held under tents on Remy's Bayou Black property. Folding tables groaned with customary Cajun foods served with lots of beer, Oyster Shooters and lemonade. Even Useless wore a red ribbon around his scaly neck in honor of the event; it only took Beau Fortier five hours of gator wrestling to accomplish that feat. Beau was to start his professional wrestling tour next week as The Swamp Monster, thanks to René's influence, and he claimed gator wrestling would be added to his act. To which most people responded, "Talk about!"

Grandma Fortier stole the day, having submitted herself to a make-over at Charmaine's spa. She wore a gray silk pantsuit, pearl earrings, and low-heeled, black, patent-leather dress pumps. Her long straggly hair had been cut short and permed in a stylish bob. The mustache had been removed, and best of all, no tobacco plug—at least none that anyone could see. A reluctant participant in the festivities, Gizelle was heard warning the groom, "Hurt my granddaughter and I put a *gris* on yer man part. Is that understood? I gots the doll made up already . . . with a teeny-tiny weinie."

Remy's response was to throw his head back and laugh,

then dance his grandma-in-law around the lawn to the tune of "Louisiana Saturday Night" till she finally laughed, too. A LeDeux getting a smile out of a Fortier was considered by all to be a remarkable thing.

Tante Lulu behaved herself at the church, but she came to the reception dressed as what some described as a Bourbon Street hooker outfit, probably borrowed from Charmaine. "Now that Remy is settled, I gots to find myself a man," she explained to a blushing Luc and René. She had her eye on James Boudreaux, who was at least eighty-five, but still had that Cajun twinkle in his eye. She was probably just teasing them. They hoped.

And Tante Lulu morphed into her usual matchmaker mode when she saw René dance five times in a row with Rachel's friend Laura from Washington. Laura appeared rather stunned by the attention from the handsome rascal with obvious wicked intentions, especially when he slow-danced her off to the side and stole a kiss. "Mebbe I need to get someone a hope chest," Tante Lulu murmured to no one in particular.

Valcour and Jolie LeDeux had been invited but did not show up. Everyone breathed a sigh of relief over that.

The bride and groom remained in their wedding clothes, except that Remy shrugged off his coat and tie and cummerbund. "Is there anything sexier than a well-built man in suspenders?" his bride asked, pretending to swoon. Rachel removed her veil and detachable train and shoulder cover so that she was left in a cream-colored, knee-high, strapless dress. Her groom's response to this transformation was a slow, sexy grin.

As the evening wore on and the party wound down,

Remy and Rachel walked down to the bayou to be alone for a bit.

"I will love you forever, Rachel."

And Rachel responded in the only way a Cajun girl could. "Prove it."

Somewhere in the celestial sphere

"We did it!" St. Jude told God, giving him a high-five.

"Remy was a hard one, but he finally came around. The good ones always do," God said. "Who's next?"

"Well, that Charmaine has been due for a good shake-up for some time now. And René . . . that boy needs an anchor in his life. Whoever you want."

God sighed. "A God's work is never done."

Epilogue

Five years and six children later

Remy and Rachel were lying on a blanket on the lawn outside their Bayou Black home, a rambling two-story, eight-bedroom log house. The houseboat was still docked down the hill, but it was used only for guests now. His grandmother-in-law Gizelle had sold him not ten but twenty acres so he could build the home and the landing pad.

They watched their six children play and fish and feed gingersnaps to Useless. Yes, *six* children. They'd gone a bit overboard in the adoption business, but how could they resist all the needy youngsters they'd discovered, lost in the foster care system?

There was eleven-year-old Rashid, a black orphan from Baton Rouge with a learning disability but musical talent that placed him in the prodigy category; ten-year-old Maggie, a Down Syndrome child from Chicago, who was always smiling; Andrew, a nine-year-old Romanian refugee, who could throw a football like a budding quarterback, even though he'd come to them malnourished and half the normal size; the twins, Evan and Stephan, who they referred to as Even-Steven, rogues to the bone already, at age thirteen;

and Suzanne, their two-year-old Cajun darling. All of them had been deemed "difficult to place" children, like Rachel had been.

Their life was chaos, but Remy had never been happier in his whole life. This was his destiny—Rachel and these children.

"Are you feeling all right, *chère*?" he asked. With his head propped on his braced elbow as he lay on his side facing her, Remy put a hand on her huge mound of a stomach.

She nodded happily.

Their son would be born in one more month, thanks to the miracle of modern medicine. But sometimes, in the middle of the night, he wondered if St. Jude might have played a part.

For sure!

About the Author

Humor (and sizzle) are the trademarks of Sandra Hill novels, all fifty or so of them, whether they be about Cajuns, Vikings, Navy SEALs, or treasure hunters, or a combination of these. Readers especially love her notorious Tante Lulu, the bayou matchmaker/folk healer, and often write to say they have a family member just like her, or wish they did.

Growing up in a small town in Pennsylvania, Sandra says she was quiet and shy, no funny bone at all, but she was forced to develop a sense of humor as a survival skill later in her all-male household: a husband, four sons, and a male German shepherd the size of a horse. Add to that mix now a male black lab and two grandsons—a rock musician and an extreme athlete—and a stunning granddaughter, who is both gifted and a gift, and you can see why Sandra wishes all her fans smiles in their reading.

Don't miss the hilarious next installment of Sandra Hill's Cajun series, featuring Charmaine and Raoul!

Please see the next page for an excerpt from

THE CAJUN COWBOY.

Chapter 1

Give me a buzz, baby . . .

"I'm a born-again virgin."

Charmaine LeDeux made that pronouncement with a faint feminine belch after downing three of the six oyster shooters sitting on the table before her at The Swamp Tavern. She was halfway to meeting her goal of getting knee-walking buzzed.

The jukebox played a soft Jimmy Newman rendition of "Louisiana, The Key to My Soul." The jambalaya cooking in the kitchen filled the air with pungent spices. Gater, the bald-headed, longtime bartender, washed glasses behind the bar.

Louise Rivard—better known as Tante Lulu—sat on the opposite side of the booth from Charmaine. She arched a brow at the potent drinks in front of Charmaine compared to her single glass of plain RC cola and looked pointedly at Charmaine's stretchy red T-shirt with its hairdresser logo I CAN BLOW YOU AWAY. Only then did the old lady declare, "And I'm Salome about to lose a few veils." In fact, Tante Lulu, who had to be close to eighty, *was* wearing a harem-style outfit because of a belly dance class she planned to attend on the other side of Houma that afternoon. In the basement of Our Lady of the Bayou Church, no less! But first, she'd agreed to be Charmaine's designated driver.

"I'm sher . . . I mean, serious." Charmaine felt a little woozy already. "My life is a disaster. Twenty-nine years old, and I've been married and divorced four times. Haven't had a date in six months. And I've got a loan shark on my tail."

"A fish? Whass a fish have to do with anything?" Tante Lulu sputtered.

Sometimes Charmaine suspected that Tante Lulu was deliberately dense. But she was precious to Charmaine, who teared up just thinking about all the times the old lady's cottage had been a refuge to her whenever she'd run away from unbearable home conditions. Being the illegitimate daughter of a stripper and the notorious womanizer Valcour LeDeux had made for a rocky childhood, with Tante Lulu being a little girl's only anchor. She wasn't even Charmaine's blood relative; she was blood aunt only to Charmaine's half brothers, Luc, René, and Remy.

So, it was with loving patience that Charmaine explained, "Not just any fish. A shark. Bobby Doucet wants fifty thousand dollars by next Friday or he's gonna put a Mafia hit on me; I didn't even know they had a Mafia in southern Loo-zee-anna. Or maybe they'll just break my knees. Jeesh! Yep, I'd say it's time for some new beginnings. I'm gonna be a born-again virgin."

"What? You doan think the Sopranos kill virgins?" Tante Lulu remarked drolly. "And, yeah, there's a Mafia in Louisiana. Ain't you never heard of the Dixie Mafia?"

"The born-again-virgin thingee is a personal change. The loan-shark thingee would require a different kind of change . . . like fifty thousand dollars, and it's going up a thousand dollars a day in interest. I gotta get out of Dodge fast."

Tante Lulu did a few quick calculations in her head. "Charmaine! Thass 10 percent per day. What were you thinkin'?" Tante Lulu might talk a little dumb sometimes, but she was no dummy.

Charmaine shrugged. "I thought I'd be able to pay it off in a few days. It started out at twenty thousand, by the way."

"Tsk-tsk-tsk!"

"I don't suppose you could lend me the money?"

"Me, I ain't got that kind of money. I thought yer bizness was goin' good. What happened?"

"The business is great." Charmaine owned two beauty shops, one in Lafayette and the other a spa here in Houma. Both of them prospered, even in a slow economy, or at least broke even. Apparently, women didn't consider personal appearance a luxury. Nope, her spas were not the problem. "I made a lot of money in the stock market a few years back. That's when I bought my second shop. But I got careless this year and bought some technology stocks on margin. I lost more money than I put in. It was a temporary problem, which spiraled out of control when I borrowed money from Bucks 'r Us. Who knew it was a loan-shark operation?"

"Well, it sure as shootin' doan sound like a bank. Have you gone to the police?"

"Hell's bells, no! I'd be deader'n a Dorchat duck within the hour if I did that."

"How 'bout Luc?" Lucien LeDeux was Charmaine's half brother and a well-known local lawyer.

She nodded. "He's working on it. In the meantime, he suggested, maybe facetiously, that I hire a bodyguard."

Tante Lulu brightened. "I could be yer bodyguard. Me, I got a rifle in the trunk of my T-bird outside. You want I should off Bobby Doucet? Bam-bam! I could do it. I think."

Off? Where does she get this stuff? Charmaine groaned. *That's all I need . . . a senior-citizen, one-woman posse.* "Uh, no thanks." With those words, Charmaine tossed back another shot glass filled with a raw oyster drowning in Tabasco sauce, better known with good reason as Cajun Lightning, then followed it immediately with a chaser of pure one-hundred-proof bourbon. "Whoo-ee!" she said, accompanied by a full-body shiver.

"Back to that other thing," Tante Lulu said. "Charmaine, honey, you caint jist decide to be a virgin again. It's like tryin' to put the egg back together once the shell's been cracked. Like Humpty Dumpty."

Hump me, dump me. That oughta be my slogan. Oughta have it branded on my forehead.

A more upbeat song, "Cajun Born," came on the jukebox, and Charmaine jerked upright. Shaking her fifty-pound head slowly from side to side, she licked her lips, which were starting to get numb. "Can so," she argued irrationally. Or was that rationally? Whatever. "Be a virgin again, I mean. It's a big trend. Some lady even wrote a book about it. There's Web sites all over the Internet where girls promise to be celibate till their wedding day. Born-again virgins."

"Hmpfh!" was Tante Lulu's only response as she sipped on her straw.

"Besides, I might even have my hymen surgically replaced."

Tante Lulu was a noted *traiteur*, or healer, all along the bayou, and she was outrageous beyond belief in her antics and attire. For once, Charmaine had managed to shock her. "Is hey-man what I think it is?"

"It's hi-man, and yes, it is what you think."

"Hey, hi . . . big difference! You are goin' off the deep end, girlie, iffen yer thinkin' of havin' some quack sew you up *there*."

Deep end is right. "I didn't say I was going to do it, for sure. Just considering it. But born-again virgin, that I am gonna do, for sure."

"Hmmm. I really do doubt that, sweetie," Tante Lulu said, peering off toward the front of the tavern, which was mostly empty in the middle of the afternoon on a weekday.

Frankly, I shouldn't be here, either, Charmaine thought. She should be at one of her shops, but she was afraid Mafia thugs would catch up with her in advance of the deadline.

"Seems to me that all yer resolutions are 'bout to melt," Tante Lulu chortled.

Charmaine turned to see what Tante Lulu was gawking at with that strange little smirk on her face. Then Charmaine did a double take.

It was Raoul Lanier, her first ex-husband. Some people called him Rusty, a nickname he'd gained as an adolescent when his changing voice had sounded like a creaking, rusty door. She'd preferred his real name in the past. He always said he liked the way it sounded on her tongue, slow and sexy, especially when . . .

She'd been a nineteen-year-old student at LSU and former Miss Louisiana when she'd married Rusty. He'd been twenty-one and a hotshot football player and premed student at the same school. As good as he'd been at football, which earned him a scholarship, his dream had always been to be a veterinarian. His last words to her before they'd parted had been, "Once a bimbo, always a bimbo." She would never forgive or forget those words. Never.

Charmaine had been avoiding Rusty for weeks, ever since he got released from prison. And, yes, she was bound and determined to think of him as Rusty now. She thought about ducking under the table, but he'd already seen her. And he had a look in his dark Cajun eyes, unusually grim today, that said, "Here I come, baby. Batten down the hatches."

Man-oh-man, her hatches had always been weak where Rusty was concerned. All he had to do was wink at her, and she melted. He wore faded Wrangler jeans with battered, low-heeled boots, a long-sleeved denim shirt, and a cowboy hat. He was six-foot-three of gorgeous, dark-skinned, dark-haired Cajun testosterone. Temptation on the hoof.

Good thing she was a born-again virgin.

Women are the root of all trouble, guar-an-teed!

Finally, after a month of off-and-on bird-dogging Charmaine, Raoul had finally caught up with her. She wasn't going to escape.

"Ladies." He took off his hat and nodded a greeting, first at Charmaine, then at Tante Lulu, who together made an odd couple, with Charmaine being so tall at five feet nine and the old lady such an itty-bitty thing at barely five feet. And Tante Lulu was wearing the most outlandish outfit. Looked like a belly dancer suit or something. But then, Charmaine wasn't any better. She wore her usual suggestive attire designed to tease, which didn't bear close scrutiny in his present mood. Not that he wasn't teasable, especially after two years in the state pen.

But, no, he couldn't blame his reaction to Charmaine on his two years of forced celibacy. She'd always had that hair-trigger arousal effect on him. When she'd dumped him ten years ago, he'd about died. Quit school for a semester. Lost his football scholarship. A nightmare. Every time he'd heard about her remarrying, he'd relived the pain. He couldn't go through that again, especially not with all the current problems in his life.

Steel yourself, buddy. She's only a woman, the logical side of his brain said.

Hah! the perverse side said.

He pulled up a chair and sat down, propping his long legs, and crossing them at the ankles on the edge of Charmaine's side of the booth, barring any hasty departure on her part. He was no fool. He recognized the panic in her wide whiskey eyes.

After taking a swallow from the long neck he'd purchased at the bar, he set the bottle down, noticing for the first time the line of oyster shooters in front of Charmaine. Holy shit! Had she really drunk four of them already? In the middle of the afternoon?

"What are we celebrating, *chère*?" he asked.

"*We* aren't celebrating anything," Charmaine answered churlishly.

Hey, I'm the one who should be churlish here, Ms. Snotty.

"We're celebrating Charmaine's virginity," Tante Lulu announced.

"Is that a fact?" Raoul said with a grin.

Charmaine groaned at Tante Lulu's announcement and downed another oyster shooter, first the oyster, then the bourbon. Gulp-gulp! He watched with fascination the shiver that rippled over her body from her throat, across her mighty-fine breasts, her belly, and all her extremities, including her legs encased in skintight black jeans. Then his eyes moved back to her breasts, and her nipples bloomed under her sizzling red hooker T-shirt. Charmaine watched him watching her and groaned again.

Was it possible he still affected her the way she affected him? *Don't go there, Raoul*, he advised himself.

Tante Lulu chuckled. "Yep, Charmaine's a born-again virgin. She's joinin' a club and everything. Might even have her doo-hickey sewed back up."

Raoul wasn't about to ask Tante Lulu what doo-hickey she referred to. Instead, he commented to Charmaine, "Hot damn, you always manage to surprise me, darlin'."

He immediately regretted his words when Charmaine batted her eyelashes at him and drawled, "That's my goal in life, *darlin'*."

He gritted his teeth. He was so damn mad at her, not because she was being sarcastic now, but because she'd made his life miserable the past few weeks . . . in fact, the past ten years.

Tante Lulu giggled. He glanced toward the old lady, not wanting to rehash old—or new—business in front of her. "Charmaine and I shouldn't be squabbling in front of you."

Tante Lulu just waved a hand in front of her face, and said, "Doan you nevermind me, boy. Squabble all you want. Jist pretend I'm not here."

Right. Like everything we say isn't going to be broad-cast on the bayou grapevine by nightfall.

"Was you framed?" Tante Lulu asked him all of a sudden.

He hesitated. Getting sent to Angola for drug dealing was a sore subject with him and not one he was ready to discuss. "Yes," was all he disclosed in the end.

"I knew it!" Tante Lulu whooped, slapping her knee with a hand, which set her bells to jingling. "This is yer lucky day, boy, 'cause I been thinkin' 'bout becomin' a dick."

That pronouncement boggled his mind till he realized that the old lady meant private eye and that she was offering to help clear his name.

He heard Charmaine giggle at his discomfort.

"Uh, thanks for the offer, but no thanks."

"Are you still an animal doctor?"

Raoul's heart wrenched with pain, and he couldn't breathe for a second. This was definitely a subject he did not want to discuss. Finally, after unclenching his fists, he said tersely, "I lost my veterinary license when I went to prison."

"Oh, Raoul." That was Charmaine speaking. Her eyes were filled with sympathy.

Yep, that's what I want from you, babe. Pity. And now you call me Raoul. Talk about bad timing!

"Being a vet was always the most important thing in the world to you."

Not the most important thing. "I'll get it back."

"I hope so," she replied softly.

Before Tante Lulu had a chance to voice her opinion, he steered the conversation in another direction. "What's the reason for the binge, Charmaine?"

"None of your business." She licked her flame red lips, which were probably desensitized from all the booze.

He'd like a shot at sensitizing them up.

No, no, no! I would not. That would be a bad idea. I am not going to fall for Charmaine again. No way!

Still, if she doesn't stop licking those kiss-me-quick lips, I might just leap over the table and do it for her.

Back at the beginning of time—probably post-Garden of Eden since Adam was a dunce, for sure, when it came to Eve—men had learned an important lesson that even today hadn't sunk in with women. The female of the species should never lick anything in front of the male. Licking gave men ideas. Raoul would bet his boots good ol' Eve had licked that apple first before offering it to Adam. *So, keep on lickin', Charmaine, and you might just see what's tickin'.*

"The Mafia is after her," Tante Lulu said. "And her life's in the outhouse."

"The toilet," Charmaine corrected her aunt, with another lick.

"Huh?" Raoul had lost his train of thought somewhere between Charmaine's new virginity and her licking exercise.

"You asked why Charmaine's on a binge. And I said the Mafia is after her," Tante Lulu explained. "You thick or sumpin', boy?"

Raoul should have been insulted, but it was hard to get angry with the old lady, who didn't really mean any offense. Tante Lulu just smiled at him. Every time she moved, the bells on her belly dancer outfit chimed.

"Great outfit, by the way," he remarked. It was always smart to stay on Tante Lulu's good side.

"It's a *bedleh*," she informed him.

He said, "How interesting!" Then he addressed Charmaine. "What's this about the Mafia, darlin'?"

"Don't call me darlin'. I am not your darlin'." How like Charmaine to home in on the most irrelevant thing he'd said.

"They's gonna kill her, or break her knees," Tante Lulu interjected.

"How about her doo-hickey?" he teased.

But Tante Lulu took him seriously. "They doan know 'bout that yet."

"Tante Lulu! I can speak for myself," Charmaine said. She turned to him, slowly, as if aware she might topple over—which seemed a real possibility. "I just have a little money problem to settle with Bucks 'r Us."

Her words were slurred a bit, but he got the message. "A loan shark? You borrowed money from a loan shark?"

"Doan s'pose you have fifty thousand dollars to spare?" Tante Lulu inquired of him.

"Fifty thou?" he mouthed to Charmaine, who just nodded. "No, I can't say that I do."

Charmaine probably hadn't expected him to help her, and the question hadn't even come from her. Still, her shoulders drooped with disappointment.

In that moment, despite everything the flaky Charmaine had ever done to him, he wished he could help.

"So, you can see why Charmaine's a bit depressed," Tante Lulu said. "That, on top of her pushin' thirty, not havin' a date fer six months, and being married and divorced four times. Who wouldn't be depressed by that?" Tante Lulu stood then, her bells ting-a-linging, and said, "I'm outta here. Gotta go to belly dance class. Will you take Charmaine home, Rusty?"

"No!" Charmaine said.

"Yes," he said.

After the old lady left, he moved beside Charmaine in the booth, which required a little forceful pushing of his hips against hers. He put one arm over the back of the booth, just above her shoulders, and relished just for a brief moment the memory of how good Charmaine felt against him. Same perfume. Same big "Texas" hair as her beauty pageant days. Same sleek brunette color. Same soft-as-sin curves. "So, you haven't had a date in six months, huh? Poor baby!"

She lifted her chin with that stubborn pride of hers. "It's not because I haven't been asked."

"I don't doubt that for a minute, *chère*. And, hey, I haven't had a date in two years, so we're sort of even."

"Go away, Rusty. I want to get plastered in private."

He didn't mind people calling him Rusty, except for Charmaine. He wanted her to call him Raoul, in that slow, breathy way she had of saying Raaa-oool. No, it was better that she called him Rusty. Besides, it was an apt description of his equipment these days—out of use and rusty as hell.

"I have a bit of good news for you, baby." He could tell she didn't like his calling her baby by the way her body stiffened up like a steer on branding day. That was probably why he added, "Real good news, *baby*."

Her upper lip curled with disgust. She probably would have belted him one if she weren't half-drunk. "There isn't any news you could impart that I would be interested in hearing."

Wanna bet? "You know how Tante Lulu said you were depressed over being married and divorced four times?"

"Yeah?" she said hesitantly.

"Well, no need to be depressed over that anymore. Guess what? You're not."

She blinked several times with confusion. "Not what?"

"Divorced four times." He took a long swallow of his beer and waited.

It didn't take Charmaine long to figure it out, even in her fuzzy state. Her big brown eyes went wider, and her flushed face got redder. "You mean . . . ?"

He nodded. "You're not even a one-time divorcée, darlin'. You've never been divorced." *How do you like them apples, Mrs. Lanier?*

She sat up straighter, turned slowly in her seat to look at him directly, and asked with unflattering horror, "Rusty, are you saying that you and I are still married?"

"Yep, and you can start callin' me Raoul again anytime you want." *Dumb, dumb, dumb.*

That was when Charmaine leaned against his chest and swooned. Okay, she passed out, but he was taking it as a good sign.

Charmaine Lanier was still his wife, and it was gonna be payback time at the Triple L Ranch. Guar-an-teed!

Chapter 2

Waking from the dead . . .

Charmaine awakened slowly.

She felt as if her body were cemented to the mattress, and her head pounded mercilessly, but she was in the bedroom of her own little house out on Bayou Black. Good news, that.

But then she glanced downward and saw that she was wearing the same red T-shirt over black thong panties. And that was all.

Uh-oh! She turned her head slowly on the pillow, noticing the bright explosion of orange, yellow, and blue outside her window—the light show of a bayou dawn—meaning she must have slept a full twelve hours since the previous afternoon when she'd started out at Swampy's. She moaned then in remembrance. It all came back to her, even before the current bane of her existence walked in carrying a tray of strong-smelling Cajun coffee and whistling. Whistling when her head was about to explode!

"Hi, wifey," he said with way too much cheeriness. "Did you know you snore?"

I do not snore. Do I? Well, maybe when I'm sleeping

off a drunk, but I can't remember the last time I did that.
"Go away," she groaned, pulling the sheet over her head.
Under the linens, she swiped a hand across her mouth,
just to make sure she hadn't been drooling.

"Not till we talk," he insisted, "and you sign some
papers."

That sounded reasonable. He must want her to sign the
divorce papers, though she had done just that ten years
ago when his father, the late Charlie Lanier, had brought
them to her. She'd assumed that the divorce was formal-
ized after that. She could swear she'd received documents to that effect, but maybe not. She had not been in
a logical frame of mind, more like brain-splintering
devastated.

She sat up straighter and let the sheet fall to her waist.
Taking the mug of black coffee from him, she sipped
slowly, eyeing him warily as he walked about the bedroom checking out photographs and knick-knacks,
including a few St. Jude statues that Tante Lulu had gifted
her. St. Jude was the patron saint of hopeless causes, and
if ever there was a hopeless cause, she was it, apparently.
At the foot of her bed rested the "Good Luck" quilt Tante
Lulu had given her after her marriage to Rusty. Lot of
good it had done her. She saw the look Rusty gave the
hand-crafted heirloom; he probably recognized it since it
had been in their apartment. He must also recognize it as
a mark of her failure—well, *their* failure—and of hopes
dashed.

There were no pictures of Rusty in her room, if that
was what he was searching for. Too painful a reminder
of a short, blissful period in her life. They'd been married for only six months . . . or so she'd thought till
yesterday.

Are we really still married?

How awful! the logical side of her brain exclaimed.

How interesting! another part of her brain countered.

Charmaine was honest, if nothing else, and she had to admit to being a tiny bit thrilled at the prospect of Rusty Lanier still being her husband. Not that she was going to hop in the sack with him. *Uh-uh!*

Still . . .

And there was definitely exhilaration in knowing that she was no longer a four-time divorcée. Maybe she wasn't so inadequate, after all.

Rusty seemed to fill the room as he prowled about, poking in her stuff, but not just because of his six-foot-three height and her low ceilings. There had always been something compelling about him. People's heads turned when he walked down the street. Men, as well as women. No wonder she'd been sucked in before. Well, never again!

Still . . .

"I have to go to the bathroom," she said, once her head stopped spinning and her stomach settled down and she'd pulled her ogling eyes off Rusty's tantalizing figure. Cowboy charisma, that's all it was. There was something about women and cowboys, sort of like women and men in military uniforms. *That's all it is*, she told herself.

"So, go," he replied, settling his tight butt—which she was not noticing—into a low rocking chair. Rock, rock, rock, he went, just watching her in a most infuriating way.

"I'm not dressed and I'm not parading my bare behind in front of you."

He grinned. "Who do you think undressed you, *chère*?

Besides, there ain't nothin' you've got that I haven't seen a hundred times . . . maybe a thousand."

She bared her teeth at him. The schmuck! Flipping the sheet aside, she stood and walked past him, pretending not to care that she presented a full-monty posterior. No doubt he was comparing her twenty-nine-year-old butt to her nineteen-year-old one and finding her lacking or, worse, exceeding what she'd had before. She wasn't about to look and see his reaction, but she thought she heard him mutter, "Mercy!"

Once she was done in the bathroom, she brushed her teeth and hair, skinning the whole mess back into a high ponytail. She scrubbed her face clean, and considered putting makeup on—she never went out in public without makeup—but Rusty would probably think she did it for him; so she put that aside. Then, after pulling on a pair of capri pants, she went into the kitchen and turned on the radio. BeauSoleil was singing *"C'est un Péché de Dire un Menterie,"* their own rendition of that 1930s Fats Waller song "It's a Sin to Tell a Lie."

Rusty soon followed after her, leaning against the doorframe with a casualness belied by the grim expression on his face. He wore the same boots and jeans as yesterday, but somewhere he'd come up with a black T-shirt. And he'd shaved . . . probably with her razor and, yep—she sniffed the air—with her lilac shaving gel. He looked good enough to eat, and Charmaine was hungry.

"You look about nineteen and innocent as a kitten," he remarked, taking in her hairdo, scrubbed face, capri pants . . . in fact, all of her.

Rusty is hungry, too, she realized. But any pathetic notions Charmaine entertained in the feed-the-Cajun category, and she didn't mean food, soon evaporated with his next words.

"Charmaine, exactly how close were you to my father over the years?"

Her head shot up with surprise. There were some things about his father he didn't know . . . that his father hadn't wanted him to know. She hadn't lied to him during the time they'd been together or since, not exactly, but it had been a sin of omission. Like the song. "I visited your father occasionally, and I went to his funeral last year. I liked Charlie. I never got a chance to offer my sympathies to you on your father's death, but I *am* sorry."

He nodded his acceptance of her condolences.

"Charlie was saddened over our divorce, you know?"

"Our nondivorce," he reminded her. "And, no, I didn't know that he was saddened, or gladdened, by anything involving me. He never once came to see me in prison. At my insistence. My old man did not need to see me in that hellhole." He shook his head to clear it of unpleasant images. "But then, you didn't, either."

"Me?" *Why would he have expected me to visit him? Would he have even approved me for his visitor list? Does he still care? Does he think I do?* All that was beside the point. Charlie and his son had never been close. Although his parents had never married, paternity had never been an issue. Despite that, through no fault of Charlie's, the only time the father and son had been permitted to see each other were occasional weekends and summer visits. In Charmaine's opinion, his mother had been a world-class bitch, using her illegitimate son to get back at his father, just because he was an uneducated rancher. "Why did you ask about my relationship with your father?"

"Because he left you half the ranch."

Stunned, Charmaine just gaped at Rusty.

The hostility he leveled at her was palpable in the air. "Why do you suppose he did that, Charmaine?" Hard to believe that these same eyes, which were hard as black ice now, could ever have danced with mischief or gone smoky with passion.

"I . . . I don't know." But in the back of Charmaine's mind, hope bloomed. *I own half of a freakin' ranch? Maybe I'll be able to pay off my loan, after all.* "How could this have happened? I mean, Charlie's been dead for a year. Why am I just now finding out I was in his will?"

Rusty shrugged. "Dad's lawyer told me at the time of his death that I was in the will, but details weren't to be disclosed till after my release. I didn't know you were in the will, too, until I walked out of Angola several weeks ago. That was also at Dad's instructions. Thank God, there was a foreman in place when he died. Clarence has been a lifesaver. But, like I said . . . a mess!"

"Unbelievable!"

He slammed some papers and a pen on the table.

"What are they?"

"Just sign them, dammit."

"What are they?" she repeated. He might think she was a ditzy bimbo, but Charmaine was an astute businesswoman, despite her recent loan fiasco. She did not sign legal papers without reading them first. Besides, these would have to be notarized, wouldn't they?

Briefly scanning the papers, she noted that the first set was a petition for divorce. Okay, there was a tiny pang in the region of her heart. *Only one day after finding out I'm still married, and the brute is this eager to get rid of me.*

The other papers were even more ominous. "You want me to sign over my half of the Triple L Ranch for a token one dollar. Do you think I'm stupid? No, don't answer that."

"Charmaine, you have no use for a ranch. Sign the papers, and I'll be out of here."

"I deserve fair compensation."

"Really?" He gave her an insulting once-over, as if she'd asked about her personal worth, not that of the ranch. "How much?"

"Fifty thousand dollars."

He laughed. "Darlin', you haven't been to the ranch lately if you think that. The property is run-down, the fences are broken in so many places I can't count, and the cattle are emaciated and hardly worth keeping. If you must know, you own half of a helluva lot of debt."

Something peculiar is going on here. She tilted her head in confusion. "How did that happen?"

"I don't know. You tell me since you and dear ol' Dad were so chummy."

Chummy? I swear, you are going to pay for that insult. If I were a man, you'd be flattened by now. "That's not fair."

He shrugged. "Life's not fair."

"Well, I'm not *giving* you my half of the ranch."

"Then I'm not *giving* you a divorce."

She went wide-eyed at that announcement. "Is that a punishment? Of course it is. Torture by marriage. Hey, I'm kinda liking not being a divorcée. Maybe I won't *give* you a divorce. So there."

Clearly not amused by her rebellion, he came up way

too close to her, backing her into the sink. She felt his breath on her mouth. He deliberately invaded her space, trying to intimidate her.

She wasn't scared of him. She was more scared of herself and the effect he still had on her. And he knew it, too. Dammit.

"Be reasonable," she said, trying to move away.

He put an arm on either side of her on the sink, bracketing her in. "Reasonable? I'll give you reasonable. If you want to be half owner of the Triple L, you are going to do half the work. And that means shoveling cow manure, castrating bull calves and all the other necessary jobs that might interfere with your perfect manicure. You are not sitting your pretty little ass out on the veranda while I do all the work."

This is just great! You couldn't turn me into a cowgirl if you tried. And broken nails are a killin' offense, honey. Ha, ha, ha. "Stop being a jerk."

"I've heard you like jerks. Four of them, to be specific."

She made a conscious effort to restrain herself from belting him. *He is just baiting me. He wants me to lose my temper. But, really, he's been through a lot. Going to prison. Losing his vet license. Losing his dad.* Still, Charmaine thought about slapping the louse. Or shaking him silly. Or giving him a talking-to in the blue language she excelled at. But, instead, she did something better. She took him by the ears, pulled on him hard, then kissed him with all the pent-up stress of the past weeks and the hunger of ten long years. She bit his lip, she thrust her tongue inside his mouth, she ground herself against him. They were both moaning. She undulated her hips against him; he pressed his erection against her belly. She'd meant to teach the weasel a lesson, but somehow she was the one learning something.

He finally raised his head and stared at her, dazed for a moment. Then he gave her a little salute and said, "This is war, Charmaine."